ANITA NAIR

Anita Nair lives in Bangalore and Mundakotukurussi, Kerala. Her books have been translated into over twenty-five languages around the world. Visit her at www.anitanair.net.

MISTRESS

 A Novel

ANITA NAIR

St. Martin's Griffin
New York

Extracts from *Letters to His Son Lucien* by Camille Pissarro, carried on p. 77, are from the edition published by Kegan Paul, Trench, Trubner & Co Ltd, 1943; "The Shadow Times" by Dom Moraes, carried on p. 214, is taken from *Typed with One Finger*, published by Yeti Books, 2002; "Final Act" by Rainer Maria Rilke, carried on p. 336, is translated by Bruce Gatenby.

www.stmartins.com

Library of Congress Cataloging-in-Publication Data

Nair, Anita.
    Mistress : a novel / Anita Nair.—1st St. Martin's Griffin ed.
      p. cm.
  ISBN-13: 978-0-312-34947-9
  ISBN-10: 0-312-34947-5
  1. Travel writers—Fiction. 2. Dancers—Fiction. 3. Triangles (Interpersonal relations)—Fiction. 4. Kerala (India)—Fiction. I. Title.

PR9499.3.N255M57 2006
823'.92—dc22

                                            2006040024

First published in India by the Penguin Books India

First St. Martin's Griffin Edition: August 2006

10 9 8 7 6 5 4 3 2 1

For a family of uncles—
Mani in Mundakotukurussi in Kerala and Mani in New York.
And in memory of Sethumadhavan, Rajan, Sreedharan
and V. Ramachandran

CONTENTS

Acknowledgements

Help and support were extended to me by many as I wrote this book:
The Kerala Kalamandalam, which allowed me to enrol as a short-term student.

K. Gopalakrishnan, Assistant Professor, Kathakali, at the Kerala Kalamandalam, who led me through the alleys and hallways of kathakali to make me understand the many dimensions of this art form. Apart from the academic point of view, what Aashaan also gave so generously of was the weight of his experience, his understanding and reminiscences and, most importantly, an insight into what it is to be a kathakali artist. I am deeply grateful to him for instilling in me the courage to attempt writing about kathakali. Without him, this book would have remained a mere idea.

Nalini Suryawanshi, who took me on a tour of the deep south of Tamil Nadu and kindled my imagination to move into realms I wouldn't have reached otherwise; her father, the late Dr Thomas Gyanamuthu, who shared with me his experiences as a doctor in Thoothukudi in the 1930s.

Dr P.K. Sunil, who patiently researched all that I asked him to, and gave me pointers to work on.

Patrick Wilson and Enrique Murillo, who delved into their memories of London in the late sixties and early seventies and made them available for me to unabashedly draw from.

Babu Nainan, who gifted me a copy of the Bible; Ashish Khokar and Dominic Vitalyos, who sent me the right kathakali books at the right time, making a veritable difference.

Kalamandalam Vasu Pisharody and Kaladharan, who made the time to answer every query with patience and, sometimes, barely concealed amusement.

Acknowledgements

Laura Susijn, literary agent, for her active encouragement and sustained support.

Karthika V.K., for being the kind of editor one dreams of: she saw all that I did and helped make it better.

Jayanth Kodkani, Rebecca Carter and Enrique Murillo, first readers who thrust aside my doubts and propelled the book forward.

Dimpy and Suresh Menon, whose love and friendship have been a mainstay, for drawing me into their inner circle and propping up my spirits each time they flagged.

Waseem Khan with his camera and Gita Krishnankutty with her insightful translations, for pitching in so readily and with such enthusiasm.

In countless ways, there were:

Anand, Sumentha and Franklin Bell, Francesca Diano, Amy Eshoo, Achuthan Kudallur, Carmen Lavin, Prasanna, Rajeswari Amma, Rajini, Bala Sethi, Jayapriya Vasudevan, and Vishwas.

My parents Soumini and Bhaskaran, who have always supported all that I have done and do.

Unni, who with great patience accepts that art is a jealous mistress.

Sugar—shadow, foot warmer and love guru.

And Maitreya—companion and writer's best friend, for putting everything into perspective.

In art, don't you see, there is no first person
—Oscar Wilde

Prologue

SO WHERE DO I BEGIN?

The face. Yes, let's begin with the face that determines the heart's passage. It is with the face we decode thoughts into a language without sounds. Does that perplex you? How can there be a language without sounds, you ask. Don't deny it. I see the question in your eyes.

I realize that you know very little of this world I am going to take you into. I understand your concern that it may be beyond your grasp. But I want you to know that I would be failing in my intentions if I did not transmit at least some of my love for my art to you. When I finish, I believe that you will feel as I do. Or almost as I do.

Trust me. That is all I ask of you. Trust me and listen. And trust your intelligence. Don't let someone else decide for you what is within your reach or what is beyond you. You are capable of absorbing this much and more, I assure you.

Look at me. Look at my face. The naked face, devoid of colour and make-up, glitter and adornments. What do we have here? The forehead, the eyebrows, the nostrils, the mouth, the chin, and thirty-two facial muscles. These are our tools and with these we shall fashion the language without words. The navarasas: love, contempt, sorrow, fury, courage, fear, disgust, wonder, peace.

In dance as in life, we do not need more than nine ways to express ourselves. You may call these the nine faces of the heart.

In time, each one of them would remember it differently. But for as long as they lived, it wouldn't ever fade: the memory of that moment of grace. Of light that tripped down the aluminium staircase, casting as its shadow a white radiance, of a breeze that had cooled itself over the pools speckling the river bed. Of Chris waiting, an isle of stillness on that busy railway platform.

He stood, oblivious to the curious glances, the urchins who stood around him with hungry eyes and open palms, the vendors who beseeched him to try their wares. He stood unaware that his baggage blocked the way to the staircase, making people mutter and grumble as they stumbled over his bags.

Chris looked around, whorls of light captured in his hair, the weight of what seemed to be a giant violin case listing his body to one side. As if to compensate, his mouth was drawn into a thoughtful, lopsided line.

They stood there for a moment, looking at him. Then he raised his eyes and saw them as they paused at the top of the staircase. Old man, young woman and not-so-young man. Hesitant, unsure, eclipsing the path of light and stilling the flow of feet.

The line mellowed into a curve, a gesture so transparent with gladness and so untainted by all that was to come later that they felt, each one of them, as if a moth's wing, soft and ethereal, had brushed their souls. It was a caress so brief and so enchanting that they ached for it the instant it was over.

Such was the grace of that moment.

Then, as if to stake the first claim, the young woman stepped forward. 'Hello, you must be Christopher Stewart,' she said. 'I am Radha. Welcome.'

Her hand stretched towards him even as Chris folded his hands in a namaste as his guidebook had suggested he do when greeting women in India.

She dropped her hand as if reproached. He reached for her hand as if to apologize. With that fumble of gestures, manners and awkward beginnings, Chris planted himself in a new land.

'Hi, I'm Chris. Pleased to meet you, Ra-dha.' He spoke her name softly, lingering over the syllables, committing them to memory, savouring each cluster of sounds.

Radha shivered. Ra-dha was a feathery trail at the base of her spine. To break the spell, she turned to the not-so-young man. 'This is Shyam,' she said.

The not-so-young man beamed and stretched out his hand.

'Sham,' Chris almost yelped, feeling as though he had slipped his fingers into a mangle. What sort of name was that? For that matter, what nature of beast was this, he wondered, as he extricated his fingers from the handshake. Behind his back, he clenched and unclenched his nearly numb fingers slowly.

Oblivious to Chris's discomfort, the not-so-young man protested, 'Sham, I am no sham. It's S-h-y-a-m.'

But Chris had already moved towards the old man. 'And you, sir,' he said slowly. The old man knew some English, he'd been told. 'You must be Mr Koman.'

The old man nodded. Chris smiled, uncertain. In the few days he'd been in India, he had already encountered the nod and was still unable to decipher if it meant a yes or a no.

Radha moved closer to the old man. 'Uncle,' she said. 'This is Christopher Stewart.'

Chris said slowly, unsure how much the old man would understand, 'Your friend Philip Read has told me a great deal about you. I am honoured that you agreed to meet me.'

The old man took both his hands in his and smiled. The warmth of his gaze ate into him. Chris let his eyes slide over the old man's face, examining each feature surreptitiously for some familiar line or curve. He saw crow's feet crinkling the eyes beneath bushy eyebrows. He saw how the high cheekbones stretched the old man's skin, giving it an almost youthful countenance and then he saw the dimple in the chin and he felt a flaring within. He let his eyes settle on the clasp of their hands.

Hello, he mouthed. Hello, old man from across the seas. Hello, maybe father. Hello, hello, hello...

BOOK 1

Kandaalethrayum kowthukamundithine, pandu
Kandilla jnan evam vidham kettumilla

How beautiful it is to look at, never
have I seen or heard of anything like it

—Nalacharitam [First Day]
Unnayi Warrier

Sringaaram

Love. Let us begin with sringaaram.

Do we know other words for it?

Or do we know it by the widening of the eye, the arching of eyebrows, the softness of the mouth that curves, by that swelling of breath from each nerve-end wanting to cup a contour?

We have words for this flooding that can sweep away all other thoughts. Pleasure, longing, lust…we call it by so many names. It is human to do so. To give a name to everything and everybody, to classify and segregate. For only then can we measure the extent of this need to know, to conquer, to hold this wondrous being, this creature that suffuses every moment with a strange and inexplicable yearning.

Look around you and tell me, what else is love?

Could it be this month?

August.

There are flowers everywhere. Balsam and hibiscus. Yellow trumpet-shaped flowers and the tiny, delicate ari-poo in the hedges. Marigolds, chrysanthemums, countless hues that shape our needs. The undergrowth is dense. Snakes slither through unkempt land. This is an untamed month, wild and wilful. Rain pours, so does sunshine.

The harvested fields stare at the skies with a forlorn vacantness: the past and the future. The present is the harvest that lies in homes, in wood-walled manjas, golden and plump. Love lives in the present. All else is memory and hope.

There are no fruits. Neither cashew apple nor jackfruit, mangoes nor palm fruit. Perhaps in some untended part of the garden, a pineapple rests, nestling among ash-green swords. The fruit of the month is paddy. Kernels filled with the sweet fullness of plenty. This is how sringaaram feels.

The skies are lit up with the moon. A night orchestra plays: crickets with malaccas strung on their wings, the frog with the rattle in its throat, the hooting owl, the rustle of palm leaves, the wind among trees.

During the day, high up in the skies, the crested lark sings. The vanampaadi. From heaven's doors, a trail of the unknown, caressing the soul, stoking desire, propelling needs into words...

Love for the unknown. That, too, is the face of sringaaram.

Radha

We walk up the staircase, two to a row. Chris and his cello; Uncle and I; Shyam and the red-shirted railway-porter laden with bags.

Chris pauses at the top of the staircase and then walks towards the railing.

Beyond the railway lines is the riverbank. Or what is left of it. Most of the sand has been carted away to build homes. The river, when it is swollen with the monsoon rain, creeps into the houses that line the riverbank. Mostly, though, the Nila is a phantom river, existing only in the memories of those who have seen it when in full spate, swift and brown and sweeping into its waters all that dared stem its flow.

Chris stands there and takes a deep breath. I try to see the view as he is seeing it: the gleaming line of water, the many pools that dot the river bed, the herons fishing, the treetops and the tall grass that grows alongside the river, ruffled by a breeze, the distant hills and the clear blue skies, and I know fear. Already, in these few minutes of being with him, the familiar is endowed with a new edge.

I look at him. With every moment, the thought hinges itself deeper into my mind: What an attractive man.

It isn't that his hair is the colour of rosewood—deep brown with hints of red—or that his eyes are as green as the enclosed pond at the resort. It isn't the pale gold of his skin, either. It is the way he's combed his hair back from his forehead: a sweep of order that gives up midway and tumbles into disorderly curls. It is the strength of his body and the length of his fingers, that belies what seems to be a natural indolence. It is the crinkling of his eyes and his unhurried smile that throws his face into asymmetrical lines. It is the softness of his mouth framed by a brutish two-day stubble. It is how he appears to let order and chaos exist together without trying to separate one from the other. He looks as if he doesn't give a damn what anyone thinks of him.

I see Chris turn to speak to Uncle. 'Philip told me about this view. He said I should stand here at the fourth pillar on the bridge and what I saw would make me want to never leave.'

Uncle goes to stand alongside Chris.

When they had clasped hands at the foot of the staircase, there had been a peculiar silence, resonant with secret words they spoke to each other in a language that neither I nor anyone else had ever heard before. But Shyam, Sham as Chris calls him, broke that moment of grace with a carelessness that is so typical of him.

'What is this?' he asked, pointing to the instrument that Chris carried on his back. 'A violin's grandfather?'

'I don't think it's a violin.' I tried to interrupt Shyam before he made an ass of himself. 'I've seen it in films and a few times at musical performances. I can't remember what it's called, though,' I hastened to add. Was it a cello or a double bass? I wasn't sure.

Chris drew his hands from Uncle's and stepped into the conversation with the ease of one walking into a familiar room. 'This is a cello,' he laughed.

'A what?' Shyam asked. 'Did you call it a cello?' He turned to include me in the sweep of his joke. 'When you get to the resort, I'll show you our cellos,' he said with a broad wink.

Chris looked puzzled. He searched my face for an explanation. How could I tell him that Shyam was referring to the hot cases that kept the food warm in the buffet at the resort? It trivialized the magnificence of the instrument. I turned away in embarrassment. He wasn't just a sham, he was an uncouth boor, this husband of mine.

Now, he walks to where Uncle and Chris stand drinking in the view, and says, 'It's a pity that you can't see the resort from here.

Haven't you seen enough of this? The view from the resort, I promise you, is even better. But first, I have something to show you. Come along.'

The two men prise themselves away and, with a look that I read as resignation on Chris's face and as long-suffering on Uncle's, follow Shyam. He leads them to a yellow board slung on the side of the staircase. 'Now this is what I can't tire of looking at,' he says, flicking a dried leaf off its frame.

'Near-the-Nila,' he reads. 'A river retreat with everything you wished for and more. A/c and Non A/c cottages and rooms. Multi-cuisine and Kerala Speciality Restaurants. Ayurvedic Massages and Cultural Extravaganzas. Business or Pleasure, Near-the-Nila knows your needs better than anyone else.' He pauses. And then, darting an earnest glance at Chris, he says, 'This is what I hope will make you want to never leave. In fact…'

I can't stomach any more of this Near-the-Nila promotion. I nod to the porter and we begin the descent to the other side of the platform where the car is parked.

'Who is he?' the porter asks. 'Has he come to study kathakali?' Mohammed the porter is as much a fixture at the Shoranur railway station as the Non-veg Refreshment Room and the SLV newsstand. For as long as I can remember, Mohammed has carried our bags. It is part of the ritual of every journey. When I was a child, Mohammed took our bags, brought the biriyani parcels and then went with me to the newsstand to buy a comic. Later, when I was a grown-up and travelling to Bangalore where my college was, he would guard my bags while I bought a magazine.

These days I hardly go anywhere and seldom come to the railway station. But Mohammed had spotted me as I walked in and had rushed to my side, to fetch and carry as always.

'No, no,' I say, suppressing a smile at the thought of Chris studying kathakali. 'He's a writer. He's come to meet Uncle. And he will be staying at the hotel.'

Retreat and resort are words that have no room in Mohammed's vocabulary.

'What's that thing on his back?' he asks, gesturing towards the cello.

'That's a musical instrument,' I say.

'How does he play it? Do you know? Does he keep it on a table or does he prop it against a wall?'

The cello is going to be part of many a discussion, I realize.

I smile and unable to resist mischief, I say, 'I think he holds it between his legs.'

Mohammed flushes and looks away.

'Here, Mohammed,' I say, pressing a few notes into his palm. 'Some tea money.'

Mohammed pockets it carefully. He clears his throat and looks into the middle distance. Both of us know what the money is for.

'Ah, here they are,' Shyam says, opening the car door. 'Porter, put the bags in,' he orders.

'So how much will that be?' he asks, drawing out his wallet.

Mohammed lets the lungi he had hitched up when carrying the bags fall to its proper length. Then he crosses his legs as a measure of humility, and scratches his head to suggest ignorance.

'In which case, this should suffice,' Shyam says, drawing out two ten-rupee notes.

For a fleeting second, Mohammed's eyes meet mine. The twenty I had given him earlier was part payment, paid in advance.

Mohammed's mouth twists into a half smile. I can see contempt in the curl of his lips and I cringe. He rubs the notes between his fingers and I worry that he will say something caustic. But he holds his tongue and, as if they were five-hundred-rupee notes, he folds the money with great care, thrusts it into the pocket of his shirt and walks back to the station.

Chris looks at the car and asks, 'How do we all fit in?'

Shyam pats the bonnet of the car. 'This, my friend,' he says, 'is an Ambassador, the first car to be manufactured in India.'

I steel myself to show no emotion. When Shyam set up Near-the-Nila, all the staff who worked there and even I, mistress of the property, though only in name, were given a sheet with all that we were supposed to know. Everything a foreign tourist would ask about: Ayurveda, kathakali, kalarippayatu, Kerala cuisine, the Thrissur pooram, Mangalore tiles and, although the car is manufactured in West Bengal, the Ambassador.

Shyam pauses. He wants me to describe the car's features. I pretend not to understand. He sighs and begins, 'The Ambassador, like I was telling you, was the first car to be manufactured in India. It's fuelled by diesel, which makes for unparalleled economy in running costs. Petrol in India costs a great deal. This car has a fuel tank that can hold forty-two litres. It costs about US $42 to fill her up full tank. Not much by your standards, but that's monthly wages for a labourer here. The Ambassador has an easy cold start and $9^{1}/_{8}''$ diameter brake drums for effective braking.' Shyam mimics with his hand the motion of the brake.

Three more lines and he will be finished. Hurry up, I want to tell Shyam. Can't you see Chris doesn't care whether it has a five-speed gearbox or independent front suspension?

'The suspension is what makes an Amby, as we call it, perfect for Indian roads. Now, I could get a Japanese or a Korean car or even a Ford, but in ten years, while my Amby will still run, these new cars will be scrap.'

Chris wipes his forehead and asks, 'But how do we all fit in?'

Uncle, who hasn't uttered a word for a while now, beckons to the driver of an autorickshaw. Chris says, 'I'll go with him. Problem solved, right?'

He opens the rear door of the car and lays his cello carefully on the seat.

Shyam doesn't say anything. I know he isn't pleased. There was so much more he had planned on telling Chris.

Uncle turns to me and says, 'We'll be at the resort before you. Where do I take him?'

'Cottage No. 12,' I say. 'But first, do take him to the restaurant for breakfast. We'll meet you there.'

I know that Shyam wants Chris to have the best cottage, the one closest to the river and farthest away from the main building. Chris, Shyam hopes, will include a glowing account of Near-the-Nila in the travel book he is writing.

So we drive to the resort, Shyam and I wedged in the front seat with the driver.

In the back lies the cello, a proxy passenger, foreign and aloof and stirring in me much of what I have steeled myself to never feel again.

I turn to glance at Shyam's face. Shyam is handsome. His skin is light and smooth; though he shaves every morning, by late noon, a bluish shadow appears, hinting at facial hair that he keeps ruthlessly under control. His features are even and chiselled; his body straight and supple; his hair jet black, abundant and neatly combed. He looks like a popular Malayalam film star. An action hero. Shyam knows that other women look at him. That he incites interest and perhaps even lust. I, however, feel nothing for him except perhaps a habitual annoyance.

I see that Shyam is upset with how the morning has progressed and suddenly I feel a pang of pity for him.

The car ride back to the resort is usually one of the highlights for him. Down the main road, and then Shyam would point to a stack of chimney towers by the river and say, 'That used to belong to Radha's family. The oldest tile factory in the region.'

'This,' he would say, pointing to a modern three-storey building, 'used to be a cinema house. Murugan Talkies. It belonged to Radha's grandfather. Some years ago, it burned down and this came up instead.'

And so the list would continue. A shopping complex. A rice mill. A row of houses. A rubber plantation. A mango orchard. A line of coconut trees...all of which my family own or once owned.

Then it would be his turn. This was the moment he waited for, when he could point out his trail of acquisitions, leading up to Near-the-Nila. And sometimes, me. He has been cheated of this, I think now.

Everyone in Shoranur knows everything about us. It is only with strangers that Shyam knows the measure of his triumph.

I pat his arm and say, 'Don't be upset. There will be more opportunities.'

Shyam's eyes bore into mine. 'What are you saying? What makes you think I am upset? I'm just annoyed. Who does he think we are? His porters? To follow with his bags and his silly buffalo of an instrument...'

'Ssh...' I try to calm him down.

Shyam has an exaggerated sense of self-worth. Or perhaps it isn't as exaggerated as it is reduced. He sees slights where none are intended. And for this, too, 'Radha's family' is to blame.

Suddenly I know what it is I feel for Shyam. Neither pity nor even affection. Just responsible.

'I know, I know,' I say.

Shyam slides his fingers through his hair, which parts and falls back. Once, I used to run my fingers through it. Now, when I look at it, all I feel is a certain detached interest.

'You need a haircut,' I say, trying to change Shyam's mood.

'Do you think so?' he asks, tugging at a lock to check its length. It doesn't matter if he thinks otherwise. Shyam will cut his hair because I've asked him to.

Shyam would bring me the moon if I asked him to.

The car sinks into a pothole and lurches out, on to the road. The cello in the back moves precariously. 'Stop,' I tell the driver and we pull to the side of the road.

I get out and try to move the instrument case into a safer position. I think of what's within. The burnish of the wood, the satiny feel. I let my fingers slide along its length in a swift furtive caress. How is it that I have begun to care about something I haven't even seen before? How is it that I know that within this case is perhaps the most beautiful thing I would ever see in my life? I feel dread swamp me again.

When I sit beside Shyam, he smiles approvingly. 'The last thing we need is that instrument damaged. We don't want him going back and giving our resort, or our roads, caustic notices. Though I wish he had brought something easier to transport. Like a flute, maybe?' He sniggers.

The driver's mouth stretches into a smile. 'Do you think he's a flute man?' he asks, impishness flaring in his eyes.

Shyam darts me a quick look and grins. 'You never know with these arty types! I suggest you keep your distance, anyway.'

They smile at each other, pleased with their gutter humour. With being able to be ribald in my presence, secure in the knowledge that I wouldn't understand.

Playing the flute. Cocksucker. Wimp. Low-life...They don't really mean it, I tell myself.

I keep my face expressionless. Shyam has forgotten what I know. Shyam has forgotten that I have lived outside this protected world he likes to keep me in.

In that hot car, I feel cold and shivery. I feel alone. I lay my hand on my thigh, palm up. I wish Shyam would take it. If he does, all will be well, I think.

My hand lies there, open and untouched. And then it occurs to me why I would never ask Shyam for the moon.

I hate having to ask.

Shyam

Why is Radha wearing her 'the woes of the world are on me' face? Sometimes she tires me with her unhappiness. What is she unhappy about?

I am the one who has a rightful claim to unhappiness, but I have put it all behind me. And so should she. Besides, we now have Near-the-Nila, apart from everything else.

I knew that taking Uncle with us to the railway station was a bad idea. I had told Radha so. But she was adamant. 'Christopher is coming here to meet Uncle. And Uncle's very keen to go with us.'

'I know,' I tried to persuade her. 'But we don't want him to focus only on Uncle.'

'Shyam,' she said, in that tone that makes me want to slap her. As if I were a little child who had to be made to see sense. 'As far as Christopher Stewart is concerned, Near-the-Nila is just another resort. If we shove it into his face, he'll either be dismissive about it or ignore it totally. He's staying with us, isn't he? We have all the time to woo him and impress him with everything you want to impress him with. But right now, we mustn't forget that Uncle is his top priority.'

I said nothing. I could see what she was getting at, but I didn't want to admit it. Uncle, I knew, would put in a good word for us. Put in many good words for Near-the-Nila.

He is very fond of me. He is Radha's uncle, but he has much affection for me. I know that. I think it is because the two of us, he and I, have only a precarious hold on the bloodline. We are outsiders, after all. Though, when I said this to Uncle, he glowered at me as if I were a fly in his paal kanji and snapped, 'I really don't understand what you are talking about. They are my family. Sometimes, Shyam, you talk a lot of nonsense!'

I said nothing. I didn't mind Uncle snapping at me. I know the truth, as he does. As much as Uncle might claim kinship, he is only Radha's father's half-brother. And nothing is going to change that. He is as much an outsider as I am. So it is natural that we watch out for each other.

Which is why, when Christopher wrote to Uncle asking if he could find him a house to rent for the three months he intended to be here, I emailed him back offering him Cottage No. 12 at the resort, at a very reasonable rate.

Radha had smiled and patted my arm. 'That's very generous of you, Shyam. Uncle is happy that you are doing this and that, too, for a stranger!'

The light in her eyes made me want to sing. Usually Radha's eyes are like the bulbs in the evening. Just barely alive. So how could I tell her that when Uncle showed me the letter, I had copied Christopher Stewart's name on a piece of paper and done a random search on him on the Net? Or that I had discovered that he wrote a column for a travel magazine and regularly contributed travel features to several publications all over the western world? I knew that this was perhaps one way of getting into the international tour circuit without paying a hefty commission to tour operators. Christopher promptly mailed me back saying he was delighted and that he had visited our website and though he seldom did such pieces, he thought, given what he had read about Near-the-Nila, it might be possible to write a small piece about the resort.

I was puzzled by the foreigner's interest in Uncle. It isn't as if he is a world famous performer. Uncle is not so well known, even in India. There is no point in discussing this with Radha, however. She springs to Uncle's defence if I make even a casual remark about his lack of success. 'Not everybody is like you, Shyam. Money isn't everything,' she said once. 'People make choices, you know. This is Uncle's. He is happy with his art and that is enough for him. A successful artist isn't always a good artist or even a happy one.'

I didn't say anything then. Sometimes she talks utter nonsense and there is no use trying to make her see things any other way.

I looked at Radha's face again. 'I am happy that Uncle's true worth is finally being recognized and I am glad that I can be part of that…facilitate his recognition in some way,' I finished lamely, wondering if I was overdoing it. But the truth is that as I spoke those words, I knew that I really did feel that way. I am fond of Uncle, very fond of him, though I don't think I will ever understand him. Or why he does what he does.

Such as going away in the autorickshaw and taking Christopher Stewart with him before I could even tell him what to expect at the resort. It isn't that I particularly wanted to be with the foreigner. Now that I've met him, I don't think I like him all that much. He's much too young, for one. I expected an older man and he can't be more than thirty-two or thirty-three years old. Maybe it's also because Uncle couldn't seem to take his eyes off him. As for Radha, it wasn't that her eyes were as bright as emergency lamps, but they seemed to shimmer.

What the attraction is, I can't understand. He's pleasant looking enough, but then so is my driver Shashi. As for that music case…he's here only for a few months. Why did he have to bring it along? How did he bring it with him on the aircraft? I must remember to ask him.

I must admit that the first glimpse of Chris standing there on the platform did clutch at my throat. It was like a photograph. One of those old photographs with curling edges, of a perfect stranger. You look at it and without knowing why, you feel a strange connection with the person in it, so much so you think you can't rest till you have it framed and hanging on your wall. That was how I felt in that first moment. The next moment, I saw that two more days of unshaven chin and he would look like a backpacking budget tourist. The kind I certainly don't want staying at my resort, lest they drive the big spenders away. I will have to find a way to tell him that I can't allow that…what is the word, the grunge look. Maybe I can couch it as a joke. I will also have to teach him the right way to pronounce my name. Is it so difficult to say Shyam?

I could have done all this if he'd been with us. Instead, he ran off with Uncle and left us to bring his bags. Bastard!

Each time I look at Near-the-Nila, I feel a great frisson of excitement shoot through me. This is mine, I tell myself, all of it, from the concept to the last tile. If it wasn't for me, Shoranur would have remained a dying railway town. Now there is a trickle of life, which I have breathed into it. I, Shyam, twice removed poor nephew and outsider. It is I who have done this, not the heaving bulwark of Radha's family.

Outside the gates we stop and I look at the two lions seated on the gateposts, on either side of the black metal gate topped with gold-coloured spikes.

I had the lions painted gold to match the spikes. They glitter in the sunlight, my twin lions, and I feel that swell of pride again.

Radha hates my lions. 'I told you gold was the wrong colour. They look so garish. I wish you had left them as they were. White. Or, if you wanted colour, why not terracotta?'

'I hate terracotta,' I say.

'In which case, why don't you paint the roof tiles gold as well?' she says in that other voice she reserves for me, tinged with scorn and frilled with contempt.

I ignore her. I don't want us to quarrel. So I do what I usually do when I want to avert a squabble. 'Shashi,' I ask, 'is your wife back?'

Shashi's wife works in a tailoring shop and supplements her income by sewing bedcovers and pillowcases for the resort. I am all for promoting local industry.

Radha mutters, 'Fuck!'

I pretend not to hear her. I don't think the driver has heard her, either. I don't think he knows the word. His English doesn't extend to fuck, I think.

'Fuck,' she says again. 'Fuck the tiles. Fuck the lions. Fuck you.'

'Shashi!' I raise my voice to smother hers. 'I'd like Ammu to start work on the pillowcases right away. We need six sets urgently.'

That settles Radha as I knew it would.

We drive into the resort and when the car pulls into the portico, I time the doorman. He has an allotted time of two minutes to welcome the guest and open the car door before the guest does.

Sebastian, the new recruit, takes four minutes. He is an impressive looking man, six feet tall, with broad shoulders and a great handlebar moustache. While I did hire him for his looks, I expect some efficiency. He's been told this. I will have to call a meeting later this evening, I think. Radha could do so much here, but she chooses to flit in and flit out. That reminds me—I wonder if the gardener's assistant has remembered to spray Flit around Cottage No. 12. Can't have mosquitoes sucking Christopher Stewart's blood and virility away. I want him alive and well and willing to write paeans about Near-the-Nila.

'What is this?' Radha asks.

I hear the surprise in her voice. I turn and walk to where she is. There are several trees along the driveway and there amidst the trees stands Padmanabhan, tearing the fronds off a palm leaf and stuffing them into his mouth.

'Oh, is Padmanabhan here already?' I ask.

'What is this elephant doing here?' Radha demands.

'Nothing in particular.' I try to inject breeziness into my voice.

'Then why is it here?'

I shrug. 'This is Kerala. How can it be Kerala unless we have an elephant?'

'But we don't have an elephant, Shyam.' She stares at me. 'Have you bought this creature?'

'Don't be silly. Much as I would like to own an elephant, I can't afford to. I fixed this deal with the elephant's owner. We have the palms that elephants like to feed on and a few leaves from the trees aren't going to cost me anything. I also pay the mahout a small wage. So you see, everyone is happy. The elephant, the elephant's owner and the mahout. In return, the elephant has to be brought to the resort twice a day, except when he has to attend a temple pooram or garland some visiting MP. Don't you think it's a good idea? My guests will get to see an elephant really close, perhaps even feed him a hand of bananas. It all adds to the atmosphere.'

'But it's such a damn cliché. Kerala and elephants…it makes us look foolish.' The scorn in her words eat away my smile.

'Clichés are clichés because they are true. Besides, I'm not wrong in saying my guests expect it. Look, you go to Rajasthan and you expect to see camels. You come to Kerala and you expect to see elephants. Tourists like these things. It makes travel exciting for them. Seeing things they don't see at home, doing things they don't do at home.'

'If you ask me, I think it's in poor taste!'

I give up. Radha, I have learnt, very often dissents for the sake of dissent. So I smile and say, 'Never mind.' And then, something perverse in me makes me add, 'Can you truthfully say that you don't pass an elephant on the road almost every day?'

Radha sighs. 'It could be the same elephant. For heaven's sake!'

'How do you know?' I ask slyly.

'Grow up, Shyam!' She stomps away.

I stand there admiring Padmanabhan for a while. His tusks gleam in the light. I walk towards him. The mahout smiles. 'Don't you want to be introduced?' he asks.

I nod.

The elephant moves. The chains around his feet jingle.

'Is it safe to go near him?' I ask. He seems enormous.

'He's as gentle as a baby,' the mahout grins.

I stroke the baby's trunk and feel something warm gather within me. One day you will be mine, I think.

I walk to the reception. 'Are they here?' I ask.

Unni, the reception clerk, smiles. Unni is a prince; a descendant of a branch of the royal family that lived in this region. He has a university degree and little else. When I decided to start the resort, I offered him a job. He's smart and efficient, and in the course of a conversation with my guests, I let it drop that he is a prince. They like the thought, too. Of having a prince call them a taxi and arrange shopping expeditions and sell them postcards. Some of them go to the other extreme and almost apologize for having to ask him for their room key. Unni doesn't mind either way. After a few days of working for me, he said, 'I just wish I was a full-fledged raja. It would please them better to be able to say "Maharaja, two postcards please."'

Unni shuts the register he is writing in and says, 'Uncle and the Sahiv have arrived. They are in the restaurant. The Sahiv said to leave his instrument in the car and that he alone would take it out and no one else should.'

I turn around. Sebastian, to make up for the delay in opening my car door and hoping to please me, has already pulled out the instrument case from the car. Damn! 'Put that back,' I say quickly. 'The Sahiv will take that out himself. You can take the luggage to

Cottage No. 12. And if you see the gardener, ask him to spray some Flit around the cottage. Not inside. Only outside. The Sahiv will run a mile if he smells it!' I smile to take the bite from my voice.

'Where's the Sahiv from?' Sebastian asks.

'America,' I say. America will impress him more, I think.

Sahiv and Madaama. No matter how often I teach them to refer to foreigners as tourists, they continue to call them Sahiv and Madaama. I go to the restaurant, where Radha is seated with Chris and Uncle. The steward rushes to my side when he sees me. 'Sahiv asked for a boiled egg and toast and coffee,' he murmurs in Malayalam.

Chris darts me an amused look. 'What's a Sahiv? I heard that on the railway platform as well.'

Radha smiles. 'A corruption of the word Sahib, which is Hindi for master. Sahiv and Madaama, from the days the white men reigned rather than visited.'

I listen to her. She can be charming if she wants to be. How pretty she looks today. Her waist-length hair falls straight and silky as rainwater down her back. She's wearing a pale pink cotton sari that casts a rosy flush on her cheeks. Her eyes shine with merriment and her lips are stretched in a smile. If she was this charming more often, I could concentrate on the administrative details of running the resort.

Chris grins and says, 'Touché!'

'We've left the instrument in the car,' I say, feeling a little left out.

'Don't you trust us with it?' Uncle teases.

I stare at him. I have never heard Uncle speak English. I didn't know he spoke it so well. Why then does he insist on making his students speak Malayalam and wrap their tongues around syllables that are like blocks of wood?

'Zha,' he makes them parrot. 'Zha as in mazha, pazham, vazhi...'

Mazha—rain; pazham—fruit; vazhi—way: he would gesture the words with his hands, with mudras they could decipher, while their tongues flipped, flopped and tried to slide through the sound of zha.

'No, it isn't that,' Chris tries to explain. 'It's just that the cello is very valuable. I had always dreamt of being able to afford a cello like this one and now that I have it, I am extra cautious with my dream.'

'Tread softly because you're treading on my dreams.' Radha's voice is soft.

What does she mean, I wonder. Uncle has a strange expression in his eyes. Only Chris seems amused. 'Yeats, isn't it?'

I repress my sigh. One of her poets. I thought she was past all that.

'Is this all you are eating?' I ask as the steward comes in with a tray. 'Why don't you try some of the Kerala dishes?'

Chris slices the top of his egg deftly and says, 'Oh, I will. Thank you very much. I am not very hungry now.'

The restaurant is half full. It is only eight in the morning. In a little while, most of the guests will arrive for breakfast.

We are not full up. In fact, only six of the twelve rooms and three of the eight cottages are occupied. Later in the day, a group of Germans is expected. Tomorrow, when Christopher wakes up, the resort will bustle with life and the ja ja ja of Germans. That will show him how popular we are.

I get up and go into the kitchen. 'You forgot…' I tell Baby George, the cook. He looks at me blankly.

One evening, Varghese, who owns a machine-tools unit in the small-scale industries complex at Kolapulli, and I were coming back from Alappuzha. Varghese's sister and her husband own a small island in the backwaters. They converted the family home into a resort and are now booked through the year. Varghese offered to take me there so I could see how everything was organized. On our second day there, he took me to a toddy shop. Unlike most toddy shops that have only a number, this one had a name: Chakkara Pandal.

I don't like toddy. Never have, except when it's freshly tapped. Then it tastes like coconut water and bears little resemblance to the foul-smelling, sour toddy. But Varghese said that the food at Chakkara Pandal was worth a visit.

'What kind of food is it?' I asked, thinking that a place called Chakkara Pandal probably served only sweet things.

'The usual—matthi-poola, meen pappas, erachi olarthiyathe— toddy-shop food,' Varghese said as we rowed up the canal—or rowed down; I don't know. All I could think of was, I hope the fish didn't come from these filthy waters.

'The owner likes old songs. He named it after one—*Chakkara pandalil, then mazha pozhiyum…*' Varghese hummed the song.

Chakkara Pandal, when we got there, was nothing like the sugar bower the name suggested. It was dark and dank, and smelt of stale sweat and fermented coconut sap. But there was Baby George, dishing up the finest food. All I needed was one mouthful of beef olarthiyathe to know that this was the man for Near-the-Nila.

'You are wasting your talent here; come to my restaurant and you'll be appreciated,' I said, offering him three times his pay, with full benefits.

Baby George agreed instantly. All was set, I thought. The only thing I had to watch out for was that Baby George didn't get too friendly with Chef Mathew.

Chef Mathew had been to catering college; he knew how to make soufflés and puddings, soups and steaks—everything a guest might want, but seldom asked for. Mostly they preferred to dine on Baby George's creations. And yet, I paid Chef Mathew twelve times more than what I paid Baby George. If Baby George ever found out...I shudder at the thought of his leaving.

At first, I wanted to call the restaurant Baby George's Kitchen. Then it occurred to me that Chef Mathew might be offended. Besides, Baby George after a few days might stake a claim to the ownership of the restaurant. This is Kerala after all, where even squatters have rights. So I decided to take a cue from the toddy shop where I found Baby George and called my restaurant Mulla Pandal.

I trained jasmine to creep along a trellis and scent the air. On every table, we placed a little card that explained the legend of the mulla pandal—the jasmine bower.

'Baby George, you forgot the coconut oil,' I say again.

Baby George grins. 'Sir, you scared me,' he says and takes a special can of coconut oil reserved for this purpose. 'I didn't forget. I thought I'd wait for the guests to come in. No point in wasting oil.'

He drizzles coconut oil into a saucepan. The oil heats and slowly an aroma spreads, filling the kitchen and percolating into the restaurant.

Just a faint whiff. Too much, and it would turn their stomachs. Just a faint whiff to conjure images of wood fires and bronze cooking pots, rustic life and discovery. Usually the guests would let it trickle up their noses and instead of settling for a frugal breakfast would ask for a full Kerala spread.

It isn't easy managing a resort. I have to think ahead of my guests all the time.

I let the aroma trickle up my nose. My stomach rumbles. 'Baby George, I'll eat here this morning,' I tell him and am rewarded with a beam.

Would Radha want to join me? It's been so long since we ate a meal together at the resort.

The table overlooking the river, my favourite table, is unoccupied. The others have gone, leaving as their signature bread crumbs, shards of eggshell and three used coffee cups. I wonder where they are: Uncle, Radha and the Sahiv.

In my mind, I have begun to think of Christopher as the Sahiv. Where has he spirited my family to?

The steward pads to my side. I look up. It's Pradeep.

I run a small, tight ship. Fifteen employees in all, and each one of them handpicked by me. Anyone who shows the slightest inclination to laziness or an unwillingness to do more than the scope of his job has to go. I can't afford it otherwise.

'Look at Unni,' I tell them. 'He is a prince, but he doesn't mind being reception clerk, postcard vendor and travel agent. He even carries the baggage to the room or the car if the doorman is busy with another guest's bags! I know this is not how other resorts run, but you must understand that there is nothing to this town. And the guests are not as many as we might like. I can't hire too many people and have them sitting around twiddling their thumbs. I'd have to close this place down. This way, you can be sure of a regular salary. It's up to you, of course.'

Pradeep helps in the kitchen and during meal times dons a uniform and transforms into steward. 'Sir,' he says. 'Madam said they'll wait at the reception.'

Then he looks around and says softly, 'The Sahiv at table four was complaining of the smell of coconut oil.'

'What did he say?'

'He said it was much too strong for his taste!'

Pradeep is one of my best employees. Apart from being able to speak English, his loyalty to me is complete.

I sniff the air. The smell is a little excessive. 'Tell Baby George to use less oil next time,' I say.

Pradeep nods his head and pads away. The boy walks like a cat, on the balls of his feet.

I pick up the card on the table.

≈

Once upon a time, a young maiden fell in love with the moon. Every night she stood under the night skies and appealed to the moon to make her his. The moon bathed her loveliness with his light but remained far away. One night he could resist her beauty no longer and kissed her on her lips. She felt herself flower and so great was her joy that she became a jasmine. A flower that blossoms at night only when the moon touches it.

The Jasmine Bower is a celebration of earthly appetites. Let the Jasmine Bower rule your senses and we assure you it will be a truly memorable experience.

≈

I had written the text myself. Radha had giggled as she read it. She said, 'You do this very well. I never thought you could write stories or that your imagination was so, so…'

'I am a businessman, not a storyteller,' I interrupted, though I was delighted by her praise. 'Here is the English translation. I did it myself. Will you read it for me, please? I didn't go to a fancy school like you did; mine is basic SSLC English! So there might be errors.'

Uncle had put his glasses on and read the Malayalam text.

'Do you think I should add something?' I asked.

Uncle looked up. 'No, it's very good. I didn't think you had it in you…this artistic streak!'

I said nothing. What did they know of me? I used to write poetry. Until Radha's father found my book of poems when I was fourteen and said, 'All this is very nice, but poetry is not going to put food in your belly. For that you need money. Put aside this nonsense and do something worthwhile, chekka.'

Chekka. He always called me that. As though by referring to me as boy, he could rob me of even the dignity of a name. Since he kept my family fed and clothed, I didn't protest, though I hated the word.

'I am not a boy; I'm almost a man,' I told my mother angrily. He had referred to me as chekkan in the presence of a group of relatives. She hushed me as she always did. 'Don't let him hear you, or he'll start his rant about ingrates and how it's better to bathe a stone in milk than help relatives…do you want to hear that all over again?'

Yet, when he needed to sort out the mess Radha had caused, he had come knocking at my mother's door and then the word chekkan magically disappeared. For the first time, he called me Shyam. I was Shyam, the man whose eyes he couldn't meet.

'Your breakfast is getting cold,' Pradeep says in my ear.

'Why do you creep up on me?' I snap, dragged from my thoughts.

I see the hurt in his eyes. I pride myself on never losing my temper. To make up for the spurt of anger, I try to joke. 'You must have been a cat in your last birth.' I pause and peer at him. 'Has the cat been sipping some foreign milk when no one was looking?'

'Not this cat.' His mouth wobbles with suppressed laughter. 'This cat is afraid of hot water and AIDS.'

Ribaldry is a great leveller.

I tear off a small piece of appam and dip it into the egg masala. In my mouth, the soft fluffy appam melds with the spice of the gravy. It is delicious. I eat slowly, savouring each mouthful. Let them wait, I decide.

Uncle

I do not understand this. Even in that first moment, I felt I knew him. It can't be. How can it be? He has never been to India. 'This is my first visit to India,' he told me in the autorickshaw.

Was he in the audience when I performed in Houston a couple of years ago? He did say that he has been living in America for some years now. But all I can remember is a line of faces uniformly Indian:

the women in mundu-veshti and laden with jewellery, and men in silk jubbahs and mundu. I can't remember a white face, no, not even in the periphery of my vision. So why do I feel as though I know him?

When I took his hands in mine, what was it about him that tugged at me, somewhere in the pit of my stomach? A sweeping tenderness that made me want to clasp him in an embrace. In my heart syllables tripped: *Ajitha Jayahare Madhava*…Krishna meeting his childhood companion Sudama after many years. Krishna the king who can read the woes of Sudama the pauper. Krishna, who forgets that his life is blessed with abundance while Sudama's is cursed with emptiness. There is sanctity in the moment. All I can think of is, he's here. I am Krishna. Or is he? Who is the blessed one? I do not know.

For the past two years, Philip has mentioned him in his letters. His name is as familiar to me as the names of Thomas and Linda, Philip's children. Is it just that? A bonding born of knowledge? That Chris prefers beer to wine; that he douses his food in hot sauce; that he tore a ligament last year playing tennis; that he is working on a travel book in which I am to feature. No, it isn't that, either. I try to put it out of my mind. In my old age, I have discovered that the imagined and the real tend to cross over.

But now, as he gently draws his cello out from the back of the car, it seems a gesture I ought to recognize. The squaring of shoulders, the tensing of his back, the tilt of his head. I think of a scene from Kalyanasougandhikam. Is this the unease Bheema felt, I wonder, when he found an old monkey blocking his way to the garden of divine flowers? Obstructing his path wilfully, as if to thwart his beloved wife's desire to adorn her hair with the fragrance of the divine blossoms. Is this the feeling that crept up Bheema's spine? That this is someone I ought to recognize. That we are more than we know.

When Christopher shuts the car door with a backward heft of his hip, I am certain: I know him.

Radha walks down the steps to where I am. Her gait is measured and languid. My niece bears on her face marks of dissatisfaction. It makes me sad.

Some days ago, as I sat on my veranda chatting with her, I said, 'Radha, do you know the significance of the katthivesham in kathakali?'

She smiled as if to suggest that my question was a silly one. 'Of course I do,' she tossed back at me. 'The villains of Indian mythology; the destroyers of all things good and noble. Isn't that it?'

'I don't think you do,' I said. 'Ravana, Narakasura, Hiranyakashipu…you know why these demon kings are classified as katthivesham? They are men born with noble blood in them. They could have been heroes. Instead, they let their dissatisfaction with their destinies curdle their minds, and so they turned out arrogant, evil, demonic. Like you said, destroyers of all things good and noble.'

'Why are you telling me this?' Radha asked. Her eyes blazed into mine. Her voice was quiet and low but I could read the rage in them.

I reached forward and touched her forehead with my index finger. Then I touched the skin around her nostrils.

'The lines here speak of dissatisfaction. They could just as well be the white bulbs a katthivesham wears on his forehead and the tip of his nose,' I said, trying to smooth the lines away.

Radha brushed my finger away and got up. 'Sometimes, Uncle,' she said, 'you let your imagination see things that don't really exist. These lines, marks of dissatisfaction as you call them, are an indication that I am growing old. I should buy an anti-ageing cream. That's what I need. Dissatisfaction! Why on earth would I be dissatisfied?'

I did not want us to quarrel, so I let it rest. You cannot make someone see the truth unless they want to.

Radha, my darling niece, my surrogate child, is not afraid of the truth. She has always stared it in the eye. This time, though, she pretended it wasn't there.

Since then, when she's with me, Radha tries not to let her unhappiness show. Her creams do their work; they repair and heal the skin and add lustre, as if someone has dusted her face with a handful of abharam.

But mica dust is like fool's gold: a false glitter that doesn't endure. And so, when she thinks I am not watching her, the marks emerge. A clenching of muscle, a tightening of skin, a whitening of hue, a stillness in the eyes. Dissatisfaction perches on her face again.

Now Radha's gaze follows mine. I see that, like me, she cannot keep her eyes away from him.

She walks forward. 'Do you need any help?'

There is a lilt in her voice. Where has the discontent seeped away to? There is no need for abharam. Her face is radiant. Her eyes throw him a sidelong glance.

Chris turns to her. His smile gathers her in his arms.

I think of Nala and Damayanti. Of lovers in kathakali who embrace without actually doing so. Only an experienced veshakaaran, an actor with more than mere technique, can perform that embrace. With arms that do not touch the woman, and with only his eyes, he lets her know that he desires her.

Chris, I see, desires Radha. And she, him.

Who is he, I wonder again. This young man from across the seas, with a cello and a smile on display. And knowledge he hides in his heart.

I have no time to think any more. For Shyam is here. Striding down the stairs two at a time, swaying on the balls of his feet, a sheaf of papers tucked under his armpit, making a thwack as he slams a fist into an open palm, an approximation of energy and entrepreneurial spirit. 'So, shall we get going?'

Radha cringes. Chris drops his eyes and breaks their embrace. And I look away. After all these years, I still do not know how I feel about Shyam.

How shall I describe him?

I have played him. I have been Keechakan, the able commander-in-chief of the kingdom of Vidarbha. Keechakan, who with his might and battle strategies kept the kingdom inviolable. But his longing for Sairandhari, his sister's handmaiden, blinded him. He couldn't see that she detested him. He thought it was pride. He thought he could break that pride.

Or is he Bheema, I wonder. Bheema, the hasty one. Bheema, who jumps into battles and life without any introspection. Bheema, who doesn't realize that when his wife sent him away on a quest to find the divine flowers, all she was doing was buying time away from his bumbling, his uncouthness, his lack of finesse. She did that by appealing to his strength, his ego. She sent him away and he thought it was love.

Sometimes I think Shyam is Bheema. A great, big, good-hearted creature whose goodness Radha makes use of. Whose gaucherie she flees from. And sometimes I think that perhaps he is Keechakan. All he wants to do is possess her. He hides his conniving behind a mask of besotted love, and when he has her on her knees, he'll kick her. Then I think Radha is wise to keep him on a leash of unreciprocated longing.

'What are you thinking about, Uncle?' Shyam's voice creeps on to the stage where I am trying to place him.

'You,' I say absently. 'You,' I repeat, unable to relinquish the soul and skin of the characters my mind has sought.

'Me?' The syllable jerks with fear that he modulates into surprise. 'What is there to think about me?'

I hear the tremor in his voice. What does he think I know?

Suddenly I know who he is. Like everybody else seeking parallels, I sought him among heroes and villains. I should have looked, instead, into the shadowed zones of the stage, at the minor characters whose doings let men live or die. Shyam is the aashaari.

The carpenter with his betel-nut, leaf and tobacco pouch, his chisel, hammer and yardstick. The comic who makes people laugh. And yet, there is underlying his buffoonery a knowledge that is both sound and crafty.

Not everybody can play the aashaari. I know; I have played him. It requires an understanding that is beyond the comprehension of a novice. The carpenter is both fool and master craftsman. It is he who brings warning of impending death, whispering in the ears of the Pandavas that the wax palace will turn into a funeral pyre that night. It is he who digs their escape route and camouflages it. He devises their escape with a flourish of gestures and exaggerated movements. He makes a mess of the steps, skids, falls, rolls his eyes, looks this way and that, and does it all with perfect timing. Only an actor with an impeccable sense of rhythm and versatility of expression can handle the aashaari. And Shyam is that aashaari, wearing the guise of a fool and never missing a step.

'Uncle?' Radha is concerned.

'Is he all right?' Chris asks.

'He hasn't been feeling very well,' Radha tries to explain this habit of mine of slipping away; she calls it my trance.

Shyam snaps a finger. 'Bring a chair.'

I sink into the chair. Shyam fans me with the sheaf of papers in his hand. The breeze cools my brow. I feel the tension in my muscles loosen. Just like a child's, Shyam's features are taut with the effort he's putting into the fanning. I like him for now. I close my eyes. 'Water...'

Someone brings me a glass of water. Radha holds it to my lips. I sip slowly.

Radha murmurs, 'We should let him rest.'

Shyam looks down at me and says, 'I think he's done too much this morning. I told you we shouldn't have brought him with us.'

I feel my liking turn inside out. I dislike this way he has of talking about me as if I am not there. I stand up. Blackness threatens to swamp, then settles.

'Don't talk about me as if I am not present,' I say. 'I forgot to take my betel-nut box. If I have a chew, I will be all right.'

'It's just the heat that is making me ill,' I try and explain to Chris, who looks concerned.

I wish they would stop fussing. I am not a doddering old fool. Strangely enough, it is Shyam who bails me out.

'Have you seen my elephant?' Shyam asks. I look to where he is pointing. An elephant is parked there.

'Whose...' I begin, but Shyam cuts me off.

'Would you like to go closer and see him?' he asks Chris.

Chris smiles. 'He is enormous,' he says and there is something akin to wonder in his voice.

I see Shyam glance at Radha. There is triumph in his eyes.

'He is enormous all right. An enormous baby,' Shyam says. 'A very nice elephant to know, in fact!'

I shake my head. What new scheme is this? Only Shyam would think of something like this.

'Shall we go to your cottage?' I say to Chris, getting up from the chair.

Radha and Chris look at each other. Then they move to either side of me. Chris turns to Shyam. 'Would you ask someone to carry my cello? Carefully, please.'

So we walk, Radha and Chris flanking me on either side. Shyam follows with the cello and its bearer.

I tell myself that I did not see the vile look Shyam threw Chris. It is the heat, I think. Or perhaps my imagination.

When we reach the cottage, Shyam flings open the doors with a flourish. 'Your home away from home,' he says.

Inside, the cottage smells faintly of many things: furniture polish, room freshener, mosquito coil and Flit. The smells tussle with each other for supremacy, but the breeze from the river enters and subdues everything. The curtains at the windows billow as Shyam opens them one by one. 'The cottage has an air conditioner but I suggest that you don't bother with it.'

I catch Radha's eye. She is embarrassed. I know what she's thinking. That having offered the cottage for so little, Shyam is trying to economize. Then Shyam says, 'If you are worried about mosquitoes, I could have a mosquito net pegged around your bed. But you should leave the windows open. The night breeze is cool and brings with it the fragrance of all the flowers in the garden and the neighbourhood. You can hear the night birds. And on a moonlit night, if you lie in bed, here,' he pats the head of the bed, 'and look out of the window, you can see the moon and then if you sit up, you can see the river shimmering in its light. It's very beautiful.'

I feel the breath catch in my throat. Who would have thought the boorish Shyam capable of such sensitivity? I try to catch Radha's eye, but she is looking elsewhere.

Chris smiles and says, 'But this is wonderful, Sham!'

Shyam stares back at him unsmilingly. 'S-h-y-a-m. It's Shyam.'

He appeals to Radha, 'Isn't there a name in English that is like Shyam?'

Radha shrugs. Shyam deflects the slight with an animated wave of his arms. 'So, do you think you will be happy here?' he asks Chris.

Chris shrugs. A long-drawn, yes shrug. His eyes are shining when he says, 'Great! I love this place. Oh yes, I'll settle for the mosquito net, and if it gets very hot, I'll consider the air conditioning.'

'Thanks.'

'Mr Koman.' He turns to me.

'Call me Aashaan,' I say. 'Everyone here calls me Aashaan.'

'Aashaan is teacher, master,' Shyam explains. 'In fact, once you learn to say Aashaan, you'll be able to say Shyam properly.' There is a teasing note in his voice.

I smile. There is a side to Shyam, I am discovering, that both Radha and I choose not to see. Learning to like Shyam requires an effort that neither she nor I seem to want to make. Perhaps it's his own fault. He makes it so much easier for us to dislike him. Though, there are others who think differently. His employees love him and he is much admired in town, I hear. What do they see in him that we don't?

Shyam looks at his watch. 'I have a meeting with the municipal chairman at a quarter to twelve. I should be leaving soon. I suggest you shower and rest. Uncle needs to rest, too. You can call for room service, or lunch at the restaurant. It's up to you. And do feel free to call me any time.'

Shyam draws out a card from his wallet. 'This has my mobile number. By the way, would you like a mobile connection while you are here?'

Chris stretches and yawns lazily. 'No, I don't think so. But thank you for asking.'

Radha takes the card from Shyam and writes her mobile number on it. 'And this is mine,' she says. 'Just in case you get lost or want any help or anything, you can reach me on this.'

'I live in a tiny house nearby,' I tell Chris. 'It is alongside the resort. Come by later, in the afternoon.'

'I'll bring him over,' Radha offers.

Shyam frowns but doesn't say anything.

I stand up. Shyam rushes to my side. I take his arm.

'I am tired,' I tell him. 'Could you ask the driver to drop me at my house?'

'Yes, of course,' Shyam says. 'You mustn't exert yourself like you've done this morning.'

'I know,' I concede. 'Sometimes I forget I am not young any more.'

Again we walk the path. Shyam and Radha flank me on either side. I feel Chris's eyes on us. Who is he looking at? Radha? Or me? Or the picture the three of us make?

I lie in bed and stare at the ceiling. My window overlooks a low wall beyond which are steps leading to the river. When the Nila is full, the water rises to the top step and licks at the low wall. But now it is almost dry and there is just a green pool that ribbons into a brown stream further down.

There are a few water birds in the deep-green pool. Paddling, bathing, fishing…making do with what they have. I can hear the bird noises.

The room is dark and spare. I like it this way. Too many things in a room make me feel as if I am in a crowded market. I raise my hand and feel the wooden bars of the window, worn with age. Like the wooden ceiling and the bed I lie on. And Malini, my parakeet. She is asleep with her head tucked under her wing. A feather flies. A pale-green feather. She is moulting with age, just as I am.

I drift in and out of sleep. I am unable to still my mind.

I think of the morning. Of the young man. Of Radha and Shyam. Of all three of us and Chris.

I am too tired to think. I close my eyes and let the bird sounds lull me into calm.

I wait for them. The evening is warm and still. Then I see them. How perfectly they complement each other, I think. I feel a great sadness. There is grief in this, I can already see it happen.

The two of them, Chris and Radha, oblivious to the mischief destiny can wreak, smile happily at each other, at the evening, at me.

'You are looking refreshed.' Radha's voice swells to include me in her circle of joy.

Her face wears the radiance of a minukkuvesham: the lovely damsels of kathakali who have chanced upon an inner grace. As for Chris, he is the hero. Nala to her Damayanti. Arjuna to her Subhadra. Krishna to her Radha.

'Chris has so much to ask you,' she says.

He smiles almost shyly. 'I really don't want to tire you, but I do have a few, actually several, questions.'

I nod. This is what he is here for. 'What would you like to know?'

Chris draws out a file. 'Philip helped me put this together.' He turns the plastic sheets. 'It has a bio with dates of performances, facts and details that are very impressive, but I do need to know more.'

Radha comes out of the kitchen with three glasses of tea. 'You'll have to drink from a glass. Uncle doesn't have any cups in his kitchen.'

Chris holds the glass carefully. It is hot and the tea will scald his mouth. I can taste tea only if it burns my tongue. Tobacco has numbed my taste buds and now only the heat can make them bloom.

'Would you like me to cool the tea for you?' Radha asks.

Chris puts his glass down. 'Oh, I'll wait for it to cool,' he says. I realize then that he doesn't like the intrusion.

Chris touches the file to take up the thread of our conversation.

'I'd like to know everything about you,' he says.

I hold up my hand. I am not ready for this. 'You are not writing my biography. Or is this for a novel, maybe?'

His eyes drop and then rise to meet mine. 'I don't know what I intend to use this material for, or how. All I know is that to understand you as an artist I need to know the man. I know so many artists—writers, painters, musicians, dancers—and they all talk about their art as if it's a living creature. Something that possesses them to the exclusion of everything else.'

'Yes,' I say. 'Art can be a very demanding mistress…'

Chris taps his pencil against the table impatiently. 'I think I will understand what art means to you only when I know how much you have let your art rule you. Your dreams, your hopes, your compromises, your sacrifices—everything that your art has demanded of you.'

Radha sucks in her breath. She knows how reticent I am and how much I hate to talk about myself. 'I don't know if Uncle will…' she says, rushing in to protect me as she always does.

I throw her a smile. It's all right, I tell her with that smile. The honesty of his reply draws me. The man and the artist. I have never thought of myself as split into dual parts. Is it possible?

'Before I begin, I must tell you something that is intrinsic to kathakali. This dance form requires the performer to interpret. It demands that the veshakaaran imagine beyond the poet's—what is that word you use, libretto…In my story, what I think is real could perhaps be the imagined, and vice versa. Do you understand?

'I have to imagine and interpret not just my own life, but the lives of all the others who have been part of my life. My facts could be wrong, the details could be missing, but I shall hide nothing. That much I can assure you. When you've heard it all, you can tell me if the man and the artist are one or dual creatures. You can tell me who rules, the man or the mistress.'

Chris peels the flap of a pocket on his trousers. He brings out a small tape recorder. 'May I?' he asks.

I nod. It is better this way. For me to imagine my life, and for the words to capture the flow as I speak.

I open my betel-nut box. I have had this box for god knows how long. I choose two tender, green betel leaves, smear a little paste of lime and wedge the whole into my mouth. Then I pare a few shavings of areca nut with a pocket knife. The fresh areca nut floods my mouth with a juice that settles the sting of the betel leaves. I add a small piece of tobacco.

I push the betel-nut box towards Chris and gesture for him to help himself. He doesn't.

The betel leaves and areca nut wrap me in a fug of comfort.

I am ready to talk now, I think. I rinse my mouth and drink some water.

Chris presses a button on the tape recorder. Radha leans back in her chair. Somewhere the flapping wings of a pond heron slash the air.

'In the beginning was an ocean,' I say.

Chris raises his eyebrows. 'An ocean?'

I smile. I know what he is thinking. That perhaps I am referring to Noah's Ark, or maybe Vasco da Gama. But he is too polite to say more, or maybe he is scared that if he offends me I'll clam up. So he swallows his trepidation.

'Yes,' I say. 'An ocean.'

1937
The Prayer of Humble Access

This wasn't how he was meant to die: the water swirling above his head, cascading into his ears and nose, filling his mouth and rushing to his lungs, stilling forever his flailing arms and legs. Salt in his eyes, salt lining the back of his throat, salt poisoning his blood. He rose to the surface one more time and knew that if he were to allow it, he would be pickled in brine.

Then, from the recesses of his childhood years, from those countless hours spent thrashing his arms and legs in the river, from the humiliation of knowing that he alone hadn't learnt to master the water while everyone else had, he sought one memory that would allow him to live, to escape the sea and its salt.

It came then, swimming into his being with the frantic swish of a tadpole's tail. That one lesson that was to be his mantra for life: Don't fight it. Close your mouth. Hold your breath. Let your body be.

Slowly he felt his body lighten. The waters loosened their hold and he knew as his hands tightened on a piece of wood that floated into his grasp that it wasn't his time yet.

When he opened his eyes, the face that hovered above his head beamed. 'Praise be the lord!'

Sethu wondered where he was, but his tongue wouldn't form the words to ask. The nurse, a kindly creature with scraped back hair, glasses and a complexion that resembled the bottom of his mother's cooking pots held his wrist, noting his pulse. Providing that first human contact that rushed tears to his eyes.

'I'm Sister Hope. We've been waiting for you to wake up. The fishermen thought you were dead when they saw the gash on your head. Then one of them wasn't so sure. So they thought of Doctor.'

He heard the note of awe in her voice for the doctor. But mostly it was her accent that made him want to hug her. What was this place where Tamil had the ring of Malayalam? The roundness, the gathering and pouting of vowels, the heaping of consonants as if they were dried teak leaves...He couldn't be too far from home.

The nurse tucked the sheet around him. 'The fishermen told Doctor that if anyone could help, it was him...and they were right. Now you lie here quietly and I'll fetch Him.'

Him. Doctor Aiyah. God incarnate to the villagers. Miracle worker of Nazareth. Father figure. Sethu was to discover that Dr Samuel Sagayaraj would be all this for him as well. But first, Dr Samuel was to play priest at his christening.

'How are you?' the doctor asked.

Sethu looked at the man by his bedside. So this was his saviour. This man with a square head and even features. His skin was smooth and moustache trimmed. His eyebrows were the only unruly vagrants in the otherwise well-groomed face—furry, thick caterpillars locking horns at the bridge of his nose. The hands that held Sethu's wrist were strong and capable. The doctor wore horn-rimmed glasses. He radiated a presence that made Sethu want to turn himself over to him and say: Look after me. I need your protection.

'Can you tell me which year we are in?' the doctor asked in Tamil, his accent more neutral than the woman's.

'1937. It is 1937, isn't it?'

The doctor nodded. He allowed his mouth to soften into a smile and asked, 'Do you remember what happened?'

Sethu licked his lips. They felt dry and crusty; salty, too.

'No,' Sethu said. 'No, I don't remember.'

Sethu wasn't lying. He didn't want to remember.

'And what is your name?'

'My name,' Sethu hesitated, groping for a name that was familiar and yet wouldn't give him away, and he thought of what the American missionary in Colombo had called him, 'is Seth.'

'Yes,' Sethu said in English. This would tell the doctor that he was an educated man. A man of means. 'My name is Seth. I used to work with the health department in Ceylon.'

Seth. It was an unusual name for an Indian. But it was a common Christian name and one that Dr Samuel recognized. And so Dr Samuel's eyes widened. Was this the miracle he had been waiting for? A Christian health worker!

'Pleased to meet you, Seth. Is there an address you'd like to give me? Your family must be worried. We must inform them about your whereabouts. What about your employers?'

Seth closed his eyes. Home? 'No,' he said. 'I am an orphan. And I quit my job some months ago. There is no one waiting for me…'

'Don't say that, Seth,' Dr Samuel said quietly, patting Sethu's arm. 'For those who have none, there is God. Whither thou goest, I will go; and where thou lodgest, I will lodge: thy people shall be my people, and thy God my God. Ruth 1.16.'

Nurse Hope nodded approvingly.

'Give him the Bible, Sister. Let God be with you as you recover,

Seth. Don't forsake the good book and it won't forsake you. God's word will guide you where your heart doesn't. It will be as is said in 1 Kings 9.7: A proverb and a byword.'

Sethu swallowed. How long could he keep up this pretence?

As he lay there, he wondered what it was about him that drew these types. These men who wished to take him by the hand and lead him down what they considered the chosen path. First Maash, then Balu, and now Dr Samuel. Why did he allow it to happen? He felt a great weariness settle over him and it seemed so much easier to sleep rather than think.

When Sethu woke, the Bible was at his bedside and two beaming Nurses Hope. Sethu blinked.

'This is my sister, Charity,' Nurse Hope said. 'She is training to be a nurse. I have one more sister. Faith. She's a nurse, too.'

She straightened Sethu's bedclothes, rearranged the medicines and then stuck a thermometer into the mouth of a man in the next bed.

'Two days and you'll be out of here,' Nurse Hope said suddenly.

'I've brought you the Bible,' Nurse Charity said shyly. He shifted and turned his head away. Her gaze unnerved him. Why does she look at me like she's never seen a man before, Sethu thought, feeling the weight of the Bible in his hands. On the flyleaf, printed in copperplate, was her name: Charity Vimala Jeyaraj. 'You shouldn't have,' Sethu said.

'Oh, I can share Akka's Bible. Anyway, this is the only English Bible apart from Dr Samuel's.'

Sethu thought of what the man in the next bed had said earlier. 'I wish the kondai sisters would pay me some attention. All three of them were here while you were asleep, hovering around you all the time, while I lay wide awake groaning for a bedpan.'

'Who?' Sethu had asked.

'The kondai sisters...who else?'

Sethu smiled. The 'bun sisters'. 'Is that what they are called?'

'The whole town refers to them as the kondai sisters. Periya kondai, chinna kondai and jadai kondai. Their hair buns are the only way to tell them apart.'

Sethu felt a chuckle gather within him. It was true. Big bun, little bun and plaited bun...but where was the plaited bun?

Sethu felt his chuckle grow into a fit of giggles and so hastily, he began reading the Bible even as they stood there. Perhaps they would leave him alone then.

Why had he chosen to give himself a new name? It wasn't as if he was a Known Defaulter. Or was he one now? KD. Synonym for rowdy, hooligan, criminal, anti-social element. How could you, Sethu, Uncle would ask. How could a member of my family become a KD?

Sethu was fourteen years and three days old when he ran away from home. He didn't know what else to do.

He stood staring at the school noticeboard. He had failed in his exams again, for the third year in succession, and now he would be expelled. The headmaster had said as much to his uncle the previous year. 'We don't keep a student if he fails for two years in the same class. In Sethu's case, I'm willing to make an exception. You see, his marks are good enough in all the other subjects, but how can I promote him to the next form if he doesn't even scrape through in mathematics? I don't understand it. He has an amazing memory. All he has to do is look at a page just once and he can tell you everything there is on it. Yet, in mathematics, he is worse than the worst dunce in his class. I don't think he is applying himself. What else can it be?' He turned to Sethu and said in a voice that was meant to scare him, 'This is your last chance. If you don't work hard enough, I'll have no option but to expel you. Do you understand?'

Sethu nodded. He always did when he had nothing to offer by way of explanation or comment. Even then he knew that mathematics would crush him.

On their way home, his uncle didn't speak a word. Later, when they sat down to lunch, he said, 'You heard what the headmaster said, didn't you? If you want to make something of yourself in life, you need an education. Or, if you'd rather be a farmer like me, you can quit school tomorrow. It is your decision.'

This was his uncle's way. Other men would have torn a young branch off a tamarind tree, stripped it of leaves and then stripped the skin off their wards' back. Not Sethu's uncle. He stripped the skin off Sethu's soul with his quiet reproach. Sethu said nothing, feeling the heaviness within rise to his eyes and clamp his throat.

Sethu didn't understand what it was about numbers or water that defeated him so. It wasn't as if he didn't try hard enough. He did. He worked, he wheedled, he did everything he could to make them heed his bidding. But neither the numbers nor the waters of the river succumbed to his advances. They mostly ignored him, or merely let him down. Like now. Sethu knew he must flee his uncle's reproachful eyes and the waters of the river that questioned his adequacy day after day.

He walked along the riverbank. Sometimes, he felt a great surge of restlessness and he would walk along the river not knowing where he was going or what he would do if he got there. It was just enough that he was walking. Then his legs would tire and he would turn back, glad to go home.

Now he walked towards the railway station. He would take the train to Madras. That's where everyone ran away to. In Madras, he would make a life that didn't require him to master numbers or water. Or ever encounter the disappointment in his uncle's eyes. Perhaps he might even meet his father, who had gone away to Madras five years ago and never returned. His mother had a new husband now, and Sethu hoped his father would take him in.

He patted the pocket of his shorts. He had some money. His fees and book money for the next year, and some money his mother had given him to buy a pair of sandals and a few groceries in town. It wasn't much, but there was enough to buy a train ticket to Madras and a meal or two till he found a job.

He didn't have to wait long for the train to arrive. He got into a carriage and found a seat. Opposite him sat a man and a woman. The woman smiled at him. He smiled back and let his eyes drop. The train began to move and Sethu turned to look out of the window. 'Where are you going?' the woman asked.

Sethu dragged his eyes away from the window, where the landscape seemed to have acquired a certain beauty he hadn't noticed when he lived there. 'Madras,' he said absently.

The woman looked at the man. He leaned forward and said, 'But this train doesn't go to Madras.'

Sethu felt as if someone had kicked him in his gut. 'But this is the train to Madras,' he said, willing it to be so. 'I checked the timetable.'

'No, this isn't the train to Madras,' the man repeated in a gentle voice. His eyes were sympathetic. 'The train to Madras is an hour late. All trains on this line are. Didn't you hear the announcement? This train goes elsewhere and the compartment we are in will be attached to another train in Coimbatore. This is the Rameswaram compartment.'

'What do I do now? I have very little money left.' Sethu's voice crumpled.

How could you, Sethu, a voice muttered. His uncle's voice, full of reproof and sorrow. How could you? How could you be so silly as to not read the train's name? Or ask where it was going? Speaking of which, how could you run away and abandon your mother, your family and me? How could you?

It was the thought of encountering the voice and those eyes that caused tears to emerge in the eyes of fourteen-years-and-three-days-old Sethu.

'Don't cry,' the man said, rising from his seat. He patted Sethu's shoulder and sat by him. 'What is the need to cry? Will crying help? Tell me, is anyone expecting you in Madras? An uncle, an older brother, someone?'

Sethu shook his head. 'No.'

'Do you want to go back home?'

Sethu shook his head again. 'No, no.'

'In which case, come with us to Rameswaram.'

'But what will I do there?'

'Do you have a job waiting for you in Madras?'

Sethu shook his head again.

'We are going to Ceylon. To Colomb,' the woman said. 'Come with us.'

Sethu stared at them. All his life, he had shuddered every time someone mentioned Colombo. It was as if the very word resonated with the boom of the ocean. Wave upon wave piling on to the shores of a tiny island. Wave after wave conspiring to suck in boats and lives that rode on it. Colombo. But how easily she said it. Colomb. As if, by swallowing the 'o' at the end of the word, the waters that surrounded the island disappeared down her throat. Freeing the journey of his worst fear. Water.

'Yes,' the man said. 'We'll take you to Ceylon and I'll find you a job there.'

Sethu swallowed his fear of crossing the ocean with the countless questions that danced at the tip of his tongue. But all he would ask for now was why. His uncle's voice wouldn't let it rest: How could you trust a total stranger so?

So Sethu cleared his throat and asked in his most polite voice, 'Why are you doing this? Why are you helping me?'

The man smiled. He looked down at his fingers and said, 'I don't know. I am not an impulsive man. But something about you makes me want to be impulsive. To help you find a place where you can stand on your feet. I am not questioning my impulse; perhaps, neither should you.'

So Sethu rode the train and crossed the waters, buoyed by an impulse. And there in Colomb—for he too swallowed the 'o' to erase the thought of the swirling waters—he found it was possible to make a life. Despite the unruly numbers. Despite the unforgiving waters.

Later in his life, when and if Sethu ever referred to those years, he would say cryptically, 'Maash was a good man.'

He called the man in the train Maash. Master. Mentor. 'Maash and his wife looked after me very well. I never needed for anything in their home,' he would say if anyone probed further. 'Maash found me a place in the health department. I had to do a health inspector's course, then a year of training, and by the time I was eighteen, I was actually earning.'

How could Sethu tell anyone of everything else that those years had been made of? Like the 'o' in Colombo, they existed even if he never spoke of them...Until Saadiya, that is. Saadiya. Saadiya Meherunnisa. Good Girl. Peerless among women. Light of the skies. Saadiya, who lit a beacon and demanded that he trail it through his past. But that was to be many years later.

First, Sethu had to cling to the new name that was his lifeline and be born again. Sethu knew that for a while, at least, he would have to be Seth and let the good book lead him to light and a place in Dr Samuel's kingdom.

A high wall ran around Dr Samuel's house. Instead of a gate, there was a door painted green. A door with a padlock and chain. Within those walls Sethu felt safe.

When Sethu was well enough to leave the hospital, Dr Samuel

offered him a job. 'I need someone like you' was all he said.

Sethu looked at the doctor's face, trying to read the meaning of his words. 'But I am not trained to do this sort of work,' he said, suddenly afraid.

Dr Samuel merely smiled. 'You'll learn as you go along. As thy days, so shall thy strength be. Deuteronomy 33.25. Think about it.'

Sethu sat outside the doctor's room. He sat with the patients who were waiting to see the doctor. He looked around him. This was a small town, significant for the fact that a missionary organization had chosen to build a hospital here. The town saw many strangers: people who came in from the surrounding villages and the nearby districts. Births. Deaths. The town saw people come and go, and no one asked questions. Sethu stared at the floor. He thought of a line that he had chanced upon in the Bible: I have been a stranger in a strange land.

Perhaps it contained a message for him. He would be a stranger in a strange land. Once again, life was throwing him a line. Don't fight it. Let it be, he told himself. He would go with the tide.

Dr Samuel gave him a room off the enclosed veranda that ran along the front of his house. It was a huge house with many rooms and much furniture. Dr Samuel barely used a couple. 'There is enough space for the two of us here.' The doctor laughed almost apologetically.

Sethu wondered if the doctor was lonely. And what about a wife and children? Sethu bit back the words. He would ask the doctor no questions and hopefully the doctor would ask him none. He looked around him and said, 'Thanks.'

He thought he saw gratitude in the doctor's eyes. The doctor was lonely, he decided.

So Sethu found a home to house his new life. There, in the garden filled with mango and tamarind, papaya and coconut trees, he discovered a cork tree and saw that it thrived, a foreigner amidst the natives. He took comfort in the lesson. That behind the high wall with the door, there was a place for him, as there was for Hope, Charity and Faith, Dr Samuel's acolytes. Sethu belonged, just as they did.

As the days merged with the weeks, Sethu worried less and less that he would be discovered. Dr Samuel found him things to do. He was part secretary, part compounder of medicines, part dispenser of prescriptions, part odd-job man, part record keeper, part errand boy; his day had so many parts that he didn't know where it sped. There, in Nazareth, enfolded in the all embracing arms of St Paul's Hospital, Sethu knew content.

When the days grew hotter and drinking water became scarce, Dr Samuel gave Sethu one more part to his day. Every morning, the women who lived in the houses around the doctor's, stood in a line by the door in the wall and Sethu would draw a pot of water for each of them. 'They will have to walk miles to get the brackish water for everything else. As long as our well has enough water, we will give them a pot each. That will suffice for drinking and cooking. But you will have to see that they get only a pot each, or it won't last very long,' Dr Samuel said.

Then the water level in the well began to recede too, and Sethu took the doctor to show him how much was left. 'We have to stop providing water now,' Sethu said.

Dr Samuel peered into the well with a worried expression. 'This might sound silly, but if the water goes below that level, we are in for trouble. I thought we would be spared this year, but if it doesn't rain soon...'

'Drought?' Sethu asked, realizing for the first time the implications of a dwindling water supply.

'Drought, and cholera. Just last year, this district suffered a cholera epidemic.'

What next, Sethu wondered. What would a cholera epidemic be like?

He soon knew.

Where did they come from, these hordes with cracked heels and dry lips, oozing from their orifices, with cramps that gripped their bellies and bodies that craved for fluids and yet were unable to hold it in? Who were these people who emerged from a countryside that in all his viewings had seemed empty of life?

They kept coming. Old men, young children, able-bodied men and matrons with a touch of grey in their hair, bound by a bacteria. Kindred spirits in suffering, they were stalked by a nameless dread: would it be their turn next?

Then Sethu had no time to ponder. Dr Samuel drove them with his manic will. 'We don't have enough of anything—people, medicines or energy. But we must cope. We must manage somehow,' he barked as he went about ministering hope and help.

The beds were full and even the corridors were lined with palm-leaf mats. Every inch of space in St Paul's was covered with disease and despair. Sethu had never seen suffering on such a scale. For the rest of his life, the odour of phenyl and palm-leaf mats would bring back to him the stench of cholera, the coming of death.

'What do we do now?' Sethu asked, coming back from the storeroom. 'We have almost entirely run out of medicines. We need a miracle now.'

Dr Samuel rose from his chair. 'Come with me,' he said. Through the deserted streets of Nazareth, Dr Samuel led him to a little church with a high steeple. Its inner walls and pillars glistened a curious white.

'You have been living in Nazareth for some months now, but you never seemed to want to come here. And I let it be because I knew that when you were ready to seek God's house, you would do so,' the doctor said.

Sethu bit his lip. You brought me here, he wanted to say. But he let the words rest, as usual.

Sethu reached out to touch the wall. 'They must have mixed at least a million egg whites into the lime for the plaster to be so smooth and pearly.' His voice reflected the awe in his eyes.

Dr Samuel warded off a fly as if to dismiss Sethu's comment. 'I agree, the walls are quite amazing, but that isn't why I brought you here.'

He paused. Once again, his hand flew in the air to brush the errant fly away.

Sethu suppressed a smile and the thought that sometimes the good doctor was a pompous prig. 'Some years ago,' the doctor began.

Sethu leaned against a wall. He knew by now the doctor's predilection for telling a story. How every moment, every emotion, every expression, even everything unsaid, would be dwelt upon.

'Some years ago,' the doctor said, seating himself in a pew. His pew. There were only four lines of pews. The rest of the congregation sat on the floor. 'Nazareth was afflicted by God's curse. Why God chose to curse Nazareth, I do not know. It has only as many sinners as any other town of this size does. Nazareth is not Sodom, and yet we had four cholera epidemics in one year and...'

The doctor stopped, overwhelmed by the horror of that memory.

'And...' Sethu prompted. For that, too, was one of the parts Sethu was expected to play: mesmerized audience and chief prompter.

'And when it seemed that nothing but divine intervention would help, the priest here, Father Howard, made an offering. He vowed that the entire parish would come to Confession every day. Spare us, we'll confess our sins and do penance for our trespasses, he prayed. He fell on his knees and I am told he stayed there for a whole week, pleading and beseeching. And the epidemics ceased to be. Now cholera comes just once a year.'

'I would have thought that God would have eradicated cholera for good, now that there are no sinners here,' Sethu mumbled, unable to help himself.

Dr Samuel frowned. 'Seth, I have been meaning to talk to you about this for some time now. I have noticed that you barely know your Bible. You show no inclination to pray. And worst of all, you tend to question God's will. In fact, you don't behave like a true Christian should. You might think it's fashionable to question the existence of God. But it isn't right, believe me. I have seen so much disease and despair, and yet I never ask God why. You see, God moves in mysterious ways.'

Sethu realized that they were treading dangerous territory, so he steered the discussion in another direction. 'Doctor, I am worried. The epidemic scares me. What are we going to do?'

Dr Samuel got up and came towards Sethu. He squared his shoulders and cleared his throat. Then he put his arm around Sethu and said, 'Stay here a while. Go on your knees and pray. Speak to God so that he may set your mind at rest. As for the epidemic, don't worry. We'll cope like we always do. Tomorrow we have to go into the peripheries. Reports have come in of entire villages that are stricken.'

'What are we to do without any medicines?' Sethu's voice rose. But Dr Samuel was already walking away. How can he be so obtuse, Sethu fumed. How can he delude himself that we can cope? He is insane.

In the early hours, Hope and Charity came to Dr Samuel's door, fear pounding their voices into thin shrills. 'Doctor, it's Faith,' they cried.

Faith lay in her bed, limp with exhaustion. 'The dysentery is severe. She hasn't begun vomiting yet,' Hope murmured.

'Didn't she have her inoculation?' Dr Samuel asked, as he fixed a makeshift IV line.

'No.' The two women shook their heads. 'She had a fever when the inoculations were being done. Besides, you know how she is. She said it would pass her by, that God would keep her safe.'

Sethu stared at them in shock. 'You should have known better. Couldn't you have persuaded her?'

Dr Samuel said nothing. Then he sighed and said, 'Perhaps God meant her to serve him a little longer. You see, I kept enough medication for the five of us. With an epidemic on, I thought it wouldn't help if one of us went down.'

Faith recovered, but it was three days before the doctor and Sethu could leave. The day before they left, a consignment of supplies and a team of five doctors arrived. 'Now do you see what I mean?' Dr Samuel told Sethu. 'God has his reasons, his own ways.'

'We'll set up camp in one of the villages and work from there,' Dr Samuel said to the three doctors who accompanied them in the ambulance to the village. Faith, Hope and Charity had been left behind to assist the two doctors in the hospital.

'I wish we could have brought one of the sisters, but they are needed at the hospital,' Dr Samuel said. 'Besides,' he said, dropping his voice, 'it would harm their reputation if they spent the nights with us in the wilderness.

'There is a woman in the village near the camp. Mary. She will help us. She is a very devout and hard-working woman. I have already sent word for her to report to the camp tomorrow morning.'

Mary didn't. That was when Sethu realized that he would be expected to fill in for her.

In the first tenement, Dr Samuel introduced him to the synonym for cholera: rice-water stools. 'See this.' He pointed very matter-of-factly to a man who lay in his faeces. Despite the extent of suffering in the hospital wards, Sethu had never seen anything like this before. 'Clear fluid with bits of mucus. No odour. No blood. Just a gushing of bodily fluids. Classic cholera dysentery!'

Sethu rushed out of the hut to retch.

Dr Samuel pushed down his glasses and rubbed the bridge of his nose. 'You'll have to get used to this,' he said. 'Now pass me the IV line. The bacteria won't kill him, but dehydration will. IV fluids with electrolytes to restore the balance and raise the blood volume, and medication to prevent further propagation of the bacteria. That's all we can do. If God wills, he'll survive.'

God willed it, and for three days Sethu trailed Dr Samuel through huts and tenements in the village. He swallowed the bile in his mouth, scrupulously washed his hands with disinfectant each time and bustled around providing Dr Samuel with hope, faith and charity. 'When I can, I'll escape,' Sethu told himself as he cleaned up a patient. 'I'd rather be a bonded labourer in my uncle's fields than clean shit and mop up vomit.'

Revulsion is elastic. It stretches, seeping into every thought, corroding the mind and splattering every waking moment with its peculiar stench and taste. Revulsion taints your mouth, fills your nose and clogs your nostrils and then one day it ceases to be. And so Sethu, too, discovered compassion where revulsion had been. Disgust was replaced by concern, and fear with the anxiety that he would be unable to do enough.

The medication was nearly finished and the IV bottles were down to a dozen. 'This isn't enough,' he told Dr Samuel, showing him their meagre stores.

Dr Samuel nodded and wouldn't say anything beyond 'If this is what God wants…'

That night Sethu couldn't sleep. How could he? In the past few days death had revealed itself to him. A new face of death that could be vanquished by fluids.

Next morning Dr Samuel took him back to the first tenement. 'Look at him,' he said, pointing to the first patient Sethu had tended to. Arasu. King. Sethu thought of him as Rice-water-stool Arasu.

The man was sitting up. In a few days he would be back at work. 'You are God in disguise,' Arasu wept, clutching the doctor's feet.

'Hush,' the doctor protested. 'God is our refuge and strength, a very present help in trouble. 21 Psalm 46.1. I am just an instrument of God.'

Sethu looked at the floor and thought that the instrument of God wouldn't accomplish much if he didn't have IV bottles. So Sethu set about doing what he knew he must. More than anyone else there, Sethu understood how precious life was. Before the disease wrapped its coils around him, he had to find a way to manage the looming crisis so they could all escape. And so Sethu added yet another part to his born-again identity.

He drove the ambulance into the horizon. He didn't have a plan, but by the time he got there he would have one, he told himself.

At the Pamban quarantine camp there were enough stores. He even knew where the storekeeper's keys were. After all, that had been his job. He knew every nook and cranny of the place, and though he had told himself that he would never go back, he had to make this one last visit.

Sethu returned to the camp thirty-six hours later. It may be too late, he thought. Or perhaps not. There were still many who lay ill in their homes. Dr Samuel looked at the stores Sethu had brought back. He wouldn't meet Sethu's eyes and instead set about dispensing medication as quickly as he could.

Later that night, he called Sethu to his tent. 'This is the day made memorable by the Lord. What immense joy for us. Psalm 118.24 Jerusalem Bible,' he began. 'When God chose to send you to me, I had my doubts. Yours was a reluctant soul, even though your flesh worked willingly enough. But now I am satisfied. God knew, even if I didn't, that you are a true Christian. I will not ask how or where you came by the stores. I will not question God's largesse. You know best. It is your secret, but if there is a sin involved, I want you to know that I will bear the burden as much as you. Shall we pray?'

Obediently, Sethu went down on his knees. He was glad that the doctor wasn't too angry with him. And hadn't sent back what he had risked his life for.

Next day, the doctor had news for him. 'The Franciscan Sisters will be here tomorrow. They will bring a team of doctors and supplies. We can go back. Once things have settled down, we need to make another visit. This time to Arabipatnam. That will be quite an experience for you. The first time I went there, I thought I had entered another land. The people, the houses, the alleys, everything is straight out of the pages of the *Arabian Nights*. Very strange! It is like a little kingdom with its own rules. For instance, all strange men are expected to leave the town by sunset. But they trust me completely and so I am allowed to spend the night there.'

Sethu smiled. It pleased him that they had moved onto another plane in their relationship. The doctor trusted him enough to take him to Arabipatnam. Sethu had heard a great deal about Arabipatnam from the kondai sisters. It was a place where no stranger was welcomed. Where the alleyways were shrouded in mystery and peopled by descendants of men who rode both horses and the seas.

Haasyam

atch carefully. This isn't what you think it is. This is glee—what is there to it, you think? Laughter is laughter. Convulsive movements of the facial muscles, a crinkling of the eyes, mouth splaying open like a whore's thighs...Stop there.

Watch me. This is what you do. Raise your eyebrows slightly, high at the bridge of your nose and low at the farther corners. Keep the eyelids slightly closed and the lips drawn down on each side. Indent the upper lip muscles. This is haasyam.

Pay attention to the mouth. It isn't merely an orifice to devour and spit and make sounds. It is the mouth that sets the seal on the intensity of the haasyam. Let your breath move from your throat to your nose. The pressure is the degree of haasyam.

Now look at this. This is mirth. You see it in the mischief that rides in with the December winds. From the plains of Tamil Nadu, they creep in through the pass at Palakkad, only to emerge on this side with a new name: thiruvadhira kaatu. Winds that come in readiness for the festival of thiruvadhira, when gigantic swings adorn the trees. Winds that come prepared to swing maidens and their dreams.

But first the wind crackles through the trees; the leaves have to them a certain brittleness, foretelling the intensity of the summer months. It strips branches, nudges the undergrowth, turns dried leaves, raises tiny puffs of dust from the front yard that is yet to be swept. Palm and coconut fronds snap; cabbage butterflies hover at knee level as though they know that if caught in the cross winds, the wind will toss them this way and that. All this is mirth, too.

Unlike the rattle of mirth is the quiet smile. Think of the peppercorns drying in the sun and tamarind pods ripening on trees, the mango blossoms that speckle the branches, the cashew blossoms weighing down the trees and the jack fruits growing quietly large.

Then there is derision. You will see this when, later in the day, the wind lifts from the hillside with renewed vigour and moves the heat. Dispersing it with a sure hand, showing a plain disregard for all and everything.

Which brings us to contempt—to look down upon. To condemn. And there is one other form of contempt. For that I suggest you seek the coconut palm fronds. Look, there it is, the olanjali. The Indian tree pie. Do you see its tail feathers? Now listen to the whickering sound it makes. Ki-ki-ki...Isn't that the sound of contempt?

It is the custom of birds to perch. Not this one. It has scant regard for custom. Instead, look at the bird's nonchalance as it skates and slides to the tip of the palm frond and dangles from it.

So you see, haasyam can be that as well. Contempt for convention.

Radha

I lie next to Shyam, unable to sleep. We have our bedtime rituals, Shyam and I. We have been married for eight years, after all, and there is no escaping the ritual of routine.

I lie on the left side of the bed and he on the right. I read in bed till my eyes begin to droop and then I turn the bedside lamp off and go to sleep. Shyam is usually asleep by then. He sleeps on his side with his arm around my middle, his chin nestling my ear. On nights that he feels amorous, he strokes my upper arm till I can no longer pretend that I do not know what he expects of me. Then I put the book down and turn to him. It is all part of this ritual and routine called marriage. Everything has its place and moment.

I can't say that I am unhappy with Shyam. If there are no highs, there are no lows, either. Some would call this content, even.

Shyam is asleep. His arm pins me to the bed. His bed. I think that for Shyam, I am a possession. A much cherished possession. That is my role in his life. He doesn't want an equal; what he wants is a mistress. Someone to indulge and someone to indulge him with feminine wiles. I think of some of the cruel acts I committed as part of biology projects in school. I think of the butterfly I caught and pinned to a board when it was still alive, its wings spread so as to display the markings, oblivious that somewhere within, a little heart beat, yearning to fly. I am that butterfly now.

One day.

It's only been one day since Chris arrived. I close my eyes and see again that image of him in the station, light trapped in his hair, a shadow of a smile on his face. I see that lopsided smile and the loose-limbed gait.

Twenty-four hours since he moved into Cottage No. 12 and into my soul.

Eighty-six thousand four hundred seconds since I realized that my life would never be the same again.

I do not understand what is happening to me, a married woman, a wife. When I married Shyam, I swore never to flout the rules of custom again. How have I become so disdainful of honour, so contemptuous of convention?

Early this evening we went to sit on the steps that lead down into the river from Uncle's house. Dusk was falling. The silhouette of a flock of birds as they flew home stood out, clear and dark, against the quiet twilight sky. From the resort grounds, the breeze drew the scent of jasmine and spread it in its wake. The silence pressed down upon us, stilling all that was merely comradely.

I stared at the sky, seeking a word, a phrase, to shatter the mute tension that was undulating between us. The western horizon was streaked a rosy red and splotched against it were masses of pewter-coloured clouds. My mother had a sari that was patterned with the same colours. I wondered if I could mention that. Something trite like, how nature inspires even sari designs. Then I saw that the colour had bled to render the rest of the sky a rosy hue.

'There will be a good catch of mackerel later tonight,' I said.

'This is called a mackerel sky,' I added, trying to fill the quiet. I sounded foolish to my own ears.

But the silence scared me. If silences were meant to create distance between two people, this one seemed to wedge it, and bridge the gap that rightfully ought to exist.

Chris turned to look at me. I couldn't see his face clearly in the dark. But I could hear the laugh in his voice when he asked, 'Do you fish?'

I pretended not to hear the teasing note.

'I am just repeating hearsay,' I said. My fingers were shredding a teak leaf to bits. 'My grandfather used to say that every time the sky turned this colour.' And then, cocking my head because try as I might it wasn't easy to resist indulging in playful banter with this man who was doing strange things to my insides, I said, 'And no, I don't think he fished.'

I bit my lip. I hadn't meant to say that. Anyway, what was I doing, sitting here in the dusk with him? What if someone saw us? Shyam wouldn't like it.

Chris rose. I froze. Was he getting ready to go? Please, no, stay awhile, I pleaded in my head. I didn't understand this fractious mood I was in. I knew I should not stay and yet I didn't want him to be the one to want to leave.

He looked into the distance for a while and then he moved to sit on the wall that shored the slope. I couldn't avoid his eyes any more.

'Is something bothering you?' he asked.

I looked at the pool of water at the bottom of the steps. You, I wanted to say. You are sneaking your way into my system. You are doing it with the casual ease of someone who knows how to. Are you a practised flirt? A seducer of women? Or is this something that neither you nor I have any control over?

I took a deep breath. Think of Shyam, your husband. Think of Shyam, who has endured much for you. How can you do this to him, I asked myself.

'No, why do you ask? I am fine,' I said.

'Then what is wrong? You have suddenly gone silent. Did I say something to offend you?'

I turned away, groping to explain the heaviness I felt. A word, a phrase, a crutch that would deflect his attention. I could see Uncle standing on his veranda. He was looking at us.

'I don't understand,' I said. 'Is there something you are not telling us? Why do you need to know all about Uncle's life? What is the relevance?'

'Radha, every writer has his own way of doing things. This is mine. I need to know everything about a person I am to profile. You wouldn't believe the lengths I go to when I am researching a subject; the kind of shit I am willing to endure. But that is how it is. I know most of the information I collect may be irrelevant but I need to know it all before I can decide what to keep and what to discard.' Chris's voice was devoid of all expression.

I felt a distance spring up between us. I wanted to tie his hand to the pallu of my sari and bind him to me. 'Oh, I didn't mean it like that,' I hastened to explain.

'I have never heard Uncle talk about himself,' I said. 'What I know of him is what all of us know in the family. But what he told you today, I haven't ever heard him talk about it.'

Chris scratched his chin thoughtfully. 'Are you sure it is about him? I am not so sure…I didn't want to interrupt his flow or offend him, so I said nothing. But honestly, what is it all about? You know, at first, when I heard him say "In the beginning was an ocean", my jaw almost dropped. What is he getting into, I thought…It's like something out of a South American novel!'

I leaned forward to interrupt him. 'That is easily explained. If you read the libretto of a kathakali play, it always begins with a shloka that puts the story of the play in context. The shloka is rather literary; what it does is give the story a setting…that is all there is to it. Really! It isn't magic realism. Just pure kathakali technique.'

I smiled. Chris was right to be puzzled. Who wouldn't be?

'Radha.' I shivered when Chris spoke my name. His voice was like a finger searching out secret places. 'Radha, who is Sethu who became Seth? What is the connection?'

Chris took the tape recorder out of his pocket and pressed the rewind button for a few seconds. Then he played the tape. Uncle's voice emerged, a little tinny, yet true: *Sethu returned to the camp thirty-six hours later. It may be too late, he thought. Or perhaps not. There were still many who lay ill in their homes. Dr Samuel looked at the stores Sethu had brought back. He wouldn't meet Sethu's eyes and instead set about dispensing medication as quickly as he could. Later that night, he called Sethu to his tent. "This is the day made memorable by the Lord. What immense joy for us."*

'Who is Seth?' Chris asked again.

'Sethu,' I corrected, 'is Uncle's father. My paternal grandfather.'

'Oh, I see.' Chris looked relieved.

'I don't think you do,' I said, leaning forward. 'Chris, do you remember what Uncle said when he agreed to tell you his story? That he would interpret not just his life, but the lives of all the others involved. It's part of the kathakali technique. The scene has to be set and explained before the character makes his appearance and the actual story unfolds. Only then will the audience understand why a character behaves in a particular way.'

I stopped and searched his face. Was he bored?

'No, no,' Chris said, pulling a notepad out of yet another pocket. There was a little stub of a pencil in his hand. 'Go on, it's fascinating.'

I leaned back against the stone steps. 'I would suggest that you take a crash course in Indian mythology, or you won't understand much of what I am saying now or what Uncle will tell you in the next few days.'

He smiled. 'My knowledge of Indian mythology is adequate. You were saying...'

'I was saying, for instance in the Ramayana—you know the Ramayana, don't you? Or, at least, about it? Well, anyway, there is this episode of Rama stepping on a stone and the stone coming to life and becoming Ahalya. The story is that Ahalya, the wife of Sage Gautama, was discovered by her husband in bed with Indra, the king of the gods, and so he cursed her to become a stone. Only when Rama stepped on her unknowingly—and Rama would come many epochs later—would she be freed of the curse. That's what the libretto of the kathakali play says. But what a good kathakali dancer will do is interpret how this episode came to be. He will show how one day, while Ahalya was plucking flowers, Lord Indra, who was cruising the skies on his white elephant, looked down and saw this woman beckoning him. The gesture that you make to pluck a flower that is overhead could very well seem like the gesture you use to call someone down from a height. Indra is attracted to the woman. Still, he asks, pointing to himself—Me? Are you talking to me?

'And Ahalya repeats what he thinks is an invitation. So he takes the form of her husband and slips into her bed when her husband is away. Perhaps he thought the disguise would dispel any doubts she might have.'

I stopped, aghast. Why had I chosen this anecdote to explain my point? Would Chris interpret it as an invitation?

I pursed my lips and finished, 'To understand my uncle as a dancer and a man, you need to know about his parents.'

Chris put the tape recorder and notebook away. 'Baggage, I suppose,' he said softly. 'None of us is free of it and yet, if we were, we wouldn't be who we are.'

I laughed. 'Considering you travelled across many continents with a cello, how can you even talk about baggage or being free of it?'

Chris reached across and tugged at a lock of my hair. I laughed again. I felt like a child who had spotted a rainbow. Then I stopped abruptly. 'I must go,' I said.

'Before you go, tell me what happened to this guy Indra. Did he get away because he was a god? Or was he cursed to become a stone?'

'Indra was cursed, too,' I said. 'In Hindu mythology no one is spared. Hinduism teaches that we cannot escape our actions. The curse of the sage is said to have caused a thousand marks on him.'

'What kind of marks?'

I flushed. 'The vagina. He had a thousand vaginas imprinted on him so that everyone who saw him knew he had been philandering.'

'The poor guy! And then?'

'And then, he was forgiven because that is the other aspect of Hinduism: redemption. So the vaginas became a thousand eyes which allowed him to see better, I guess,' I added.

Chris grinned. 'So he did get away?' He leapt off the wall and ran up the steps. I rose quietly. What could I say? He was right. Thinking about it, Indra managed to get away with little more than embarrassment. It was poor Ahalya who bore the brunt of the curse. Let that be a reminder to you, I told myself.

Chris held his hand out to help me up.

I hesitated. In his country, this was merely a polite gesture a man made to a woman, like opening a door for her. I shouldn't be reading subtexts into it, I told myself. So I laid my hand in his.

His grip tightened. I knew then that he knew what I was feeling. And that there was no escape.

I am here. But I am also elsewhere. I wonder what Chris is doing. Has he unpacked his bags? Is he playing his cello? Maybe he is writing an email to the woman he loves. Is there a woman in his life? A girlfriend? A live-in partner? A wife?

I feel jealousy corrode me. Who is she?

Then I feel Shyam's breath ruffling my hair. What am I doing, I ask myself. I lie here in my bed in my husband's arms and think of another man. What kind of woman am I? I feel contempt for myself.

I stroke Shyam's hair. Shyam, I whisper. Shyam, wake up. Shyam, wake up and love me. Shyam, you must.

Shyam opens his eyes. His pupils are sleep washed.

'Aren't you asleep yet?' he murmurs and snuggles deeper into my side.

In the morning, I wake up thinking that I will stay away from the resort.

Shyam peers at me from above his newspaper. He reads the Malayalam paper over breakfast. It feeds his lust for the bizarre and trivia. Dog bit baby—baby's mother bit dog back and its ilk. 'If you live in Kerala, you need a Malayalam newspaper to give you all the local news,' Shyam defended his choice, when I asked how he could read such nonsense.

In public, though, Shyam prefers it to be known that he reads the *Hindu*, and on Sundays the *New Indian Express* as well.

He folds the newspaper and places it neatly by his plate. Then he takes the newspaper I am reading and folds that as well. He reaches for a banana, peels and eats it slowly. He leaves the skin on his plate. It looks as if the plantain slunk out when no one was looking, the skin is so perfectly arranged. Shyam is fastidious. Newspapers have to be folded and stacked; clothes ironed and put away on their shelves; all surfaces wiped clean of dust; and glasses placed on coasters so they don't leave water marks. Candles are not allowed to drip nor are dead leaves allowed to remain on a plant. His music collection is arranged in alphabetical order and his office table looks as if he does no work on it, ever. Everything is in its place and in order.

I thrive on chaos and it vexes Shyam to see my closet and bedside table. 'How do you know what is where? How can you be so disorderly?'

It irritates me to see Shyam as he goes about regulating his universe and mine. But this morning, his need for symmetry and love of order comfort me. They contain my thoughts and pace the unruly meanderings of my mind.

'Oppol will be here this weekend,' he says.

I look down at my plate and try to hide my grimace. Rani Oppol. Shyam's sister. She is a good woman, but her insensitivity would make even a buffalo blanch. Her visits usually leave me infuriated and feeling totally worthless. But she is Shyam's sister and I know there is nothing I can say to prevent her from visiting us.

'They are on their way to Vishakapatnam, where Manoj is, and she wanted to stop over and spend some time with us,' Shyam says.

My heart sinks.

'How long will Rani stay?' I ask.

'Just a couple of days. Radha, you really mustn't call her by her name. It is so disrespectful, and you know she doesn't like it at all.'

I agree, I want to tell him. She shouldn't be called Rani. She ought to be called harpy, vixen, whinger, nag, bitch…

I can hear her voice in my head. That affected, little-girl voice that grates on my nerves. How is it, I wonder, that she knows the exact thing to say, to rob me of all self-esteem? For years now, I have been enduring it.

'But Radha, why don't you drive? All girls of your generation do.'

'I do. I used to in Bangalore,' I would protest. 'But Shyam won't let me. He says…'

'Ah, Shyam probably has a reason.'

Another time, she told me, 'The other day I met Susie, that girl who was in college with you. She is working for a multinational company. That's how girls ought to be. Smart and independent. If you sit at home, all you do is sleep in the afternoon, watch TV and get fat. It is such a pity that you are wasting your time doing nothing.'

I sucked my belly in and resolved not to nap in the afternoon.

Later, it was to Uncle that I voiced my irritation. 'She is obnoxious, she truly is. I made this chicken dish especially for her, the way she likes it. At dinner time, when we were seated at the table, my long-suffering brother-in-law said, "Rani, try some of the chicken, it's cooked the way you like it. Marinated and deep fried over a wood fire." And do you know what she did? She crinkled her nose as if I had offered her a dead rat and said, "Should I? It's only chicken, after all."

'What was I expected to provide? An elephant's egg, hardboiled?'
Uncle laughed and laughed.

I said, 'You think it's funny, do you? But I was hurt. If someone
were to criticize her cooking, she would probably have a fit. All of us
have to be careful what we say to her. My sister is so sensitive, Shyam
says. Doesn't he realize what a beastly woman she is?'

I think now, I will have to prepare myself for her arrival. I will
not let her wound me again.

'Are you coming?' Shyam asks, watching me toy with my
breakfast.

'No,' I say.

'Good. No need for you to be there every day,' he says. 'I intend
going for just an hour. I'll leave the car and driver here for you, and
take the jeep. I suppose you are going to spend the whole morning at
the beauty parlour.'

I smile. Shyam likes to think of me prettying myself for him. He
prefers a glossy, silly wife to a homely, practical one. Glossy, silly
wives are malleable.

He pauses on his way out and fondles my cheek. 'Though I really
don't know why you need to go to the beauty parlour. You are
ravishing the way you are.'

Poor Shyam. He thinks exaggerated compliments will make me
happy and ensure marital bliss. He tries so hard that at times it tires
me. This morning, though, I feel sad. For him. For us. For our
marriage. He deserves better.

Shyam complains that I don't show any real interest in his pursuits.
That I don't care enough. He speaks the truth.

Shyam is ambitious, and I find his unwillingness to hide his
ambition repulsive. Once, early in our marriage, I told him as much.

'What's wrong with wanting to make money? You don't know
what it is like to be poor. How would you anyway? You've always
had money. Your family brought you up as a princess. Everything
you wanted was made available. Not so for me. I know what it is to
want something and not be able to have it because it is "beyond us".
My mother had a whole stock of sayings to explain this "beyond us"
business. No point in crying for the moon! What is the point in a
rabbit trying to shit as much as an elephant would, etc., etc. And all
because I asked for a toy or a pen or some such trivial thing that had

caught my eye.' Shyam's face was contorted in a grimace. Then, as if he had wiped a hand over his features, it smoothened and he said in a cold but even voice, 'I am yet to understand the meaning of the word "enough". When I do, I promise I'll stop this "frantic chasing to amass wealth" as you call it.'

I didn't ever bring it up again. As the years passed, one by one, we shunted away all the topics we could converse about. We couldn't agree on anything, whether it was music or films, political parties or even the choice of plants in our garden. Now we have no conversation.

This morning, I feel the need to make an effort, to redeem myself in Shyam's eyes. Do penance for allowing this strange attraction I feel for Chris to root within me. I shall avoid the resort, I think. For there wait Chris and temptation.

Shyam owns several businesses. But none of them need me for anything. They run on their own and don't need me, the owner's wife, hovering around. When I do go, occasionally, one of the employees offers me a chair and a soft drink in a bottle with a straw and stays there while I gulp it down, so that he can see me to the car. He opens the door for me, waits for me to seat myself, slams the door shut and tells Shashi, 'Drive carefully.'

There is relief on his face; a relief that stretches his face into a smile even before the car has pulled away. I know. I have seen it.

I think of where I could go. Then I think of the match factory.

Perhaps factory is a euphemism for a shed and a batch of workers with a supervisor. But even this little place brings Shyam profits. He has a knack for making money. My grandfather would have approved of him and his methods.

Shyam manufactures four brands of matches. Two of these, Jasmine and Near-the-Nila, are made exclusively for the resort. He had picked up the idea of customized matches while on a trip abroad. The third brand changed every few months, for it relied on the flavour of the season, be it politics or films. This season we have a matchbox called Lajjavati, after a popular song. Lajjavati, the shy one, is a big hit. Then there is the 'umbrella brand', as Shyam refers to it. Shyam often uses marketing terms learnt during his days as a marketing executive with Hindustan Lever. The umbrella brand is called Foreign. 'People like going to shops and asking for Foreign matches and shopkeepers like being able to sell Foreign matches. Both parties are happy. Do you understand?' Shyam explained to me.

I had smiled then. I smile now, thinking of it. Again that sadness. Shyam, who is so sensitive to people's attitudes when it comes to buying and selling, doesn't have the faintest notion of how my mind works.

I thrust the thought away and ask Shashi to take me to the match factory.

I do not know what I will do there. But there must be something I can do beyond sitting on the proffered chair and sipping the mandatory soft drink.

There must be a way by which even if I can't exorcize the thought of Chris, I can run a stake through the heart of that thought and rein it to the ground.

Shyam

I shove the plate aside, lick my fingers one by one, pick up the glass with my soiled hand and drink the water in one gulp, then belch loudly.

The licking and belching are a rare treat, but I am alone and can indulge in it without worrying about Radha's censorious gaze. Her disapproval of such natural pleasures inhibits me and usually, even after a splendid meal, I feel incomplete. But for now I am sated.

It was almost lunchtime when I turned in at the gate. My twin lions gleamed gold-like in the midday sun. I felt a swelling of my heart. I don't think I will ever tire of gazing at them. For that matter, I don't think this sense of achievement I feel each time I drive through the gates of Near-the-Nila will ever dim.

The doorman was at the car door even as I stopped. He was keeping good time. I smiled at him. I looked to where Padmanabhan had been tethered in the morning. 'Have someone clean up that mess,'

I said. There were heaps of dung lying on the ground. 'What time did he go?' I asked.

'Just an hour ago. He will be back at four, he said.'

'Who? The elephant? Does he talk?' I teased.

Sebastian grinned. 'No, no…the mahout, I mean.'

Unni, my princely reception clerk, told me that the German group had arrived and that we had had to turn away a few guests. We were fully booked. I felt my smile grow. I peeped into the restaurant. The tables were all occupied. It was off-season, but you wouldn't know from the look of it, I thought with relief. The last few days had been quiet and I had begun to worry.

When I was finally seated in my office, Unni came in to find out if I wanted lunch. I frowned, unsure. Then I decided to eat lunch at the resort and for once not worry about my unhealthy choice of food and whether it was going to give me a heart attack before I turned forty.

I leaned back in my chair. My morning had been busy and exacting, yet all along I had felt tranquil. Radha seemed to have found herself.

Last night I had come back home to find her in a strange mood. Something was troubling her. I knew that she had spent the evening with Uncle and Chris. I had tried to cancel my evening meeting, but I couldn't. I wondered what had happened between them. I knew that Uncle had begun telling his life story. But would that affect her so?

Or had the Sahiv said something? I was not certain I liked the way Chris looked at my Radha. Or the manner in which she seemed to flower in his presence. Women are such suckers for flattery. Even a woman as self-contained as my Radha.

I poured myself a drink and sat down with a file I needed to check for the morning's meeting. She was watching TV—or that was what I thought. Then I noticed that all she was doing was flipping channels. She picked up a magazine, read a page and slapped it down; she picked up another magazine and dropped it back; she walked to the veranda as if she was going somewhere, came back and curled up in a chair; she toyed with her food and left it uneaten; and in bed she lay awake for god knows how long.

This morning, however, she was a different woman. It was as if she had exorcised whatever demons had run amok within her. She was at peace. She also showed no inclination to go to the resort, and that was when I allowed myself to breathe.

I knew I was being silly, but I worried. I saw a threat everywhere. I worried that Radha would leave me some day. That a sweet-talking, pretty boy would turn her head and she would go, lured by his flattery and charm. Then I pulled myself up. I was not bad-looking and, when I wanted to, I could sweet-talk better than anyone else.

I would have gone home for lunch, but Radha was still not home. I looked at the picture I had of her on my table. Her eyebrows, all the stray hair between them removed, arched above her large brown eyes. Her hair, the hair that I loved, framed her face. She wore it down even on the warmest of days, but in bed she wore it plaited. 'Won't you leave your hair down? It's so beautiful,' I said when I saw her plaiting it one night. I had visions of her hair snaking over me, of burying my face in that fragrant skein. But she finished plaiting her hair, threw it over her shoulder and said, 'Oh no, it will get tangled and the ends will split.'

I know I should get up and wash my hands. But I am feeling replete. Baby George doesn't skimp on oil or coconut, spice or quantities. At home, Radha insists that we eat a low-fat, low-cholesterol, high-fibre meal. Which means lots of vegetables. Meat is allowed on the table only twice a week. And the fish is always swimming in a curry. When I protest, she says, 'You are almost forty. You need to be careful about what you eat.'

I love good food and find this regime torturous. But I am delighted by her concern. So I eat my vegetable upperis, restrict myself to one egg a week and my drinking to one peg a night.

For my Radha, I am quite willing to starve myself of life's joys.

When I reach home, it is almost dusk. The thookuvilakku hanging from a wooden beam in the veranda is being lit. I stare at the lamp, surprised. I feel a warm glow within me.

The thookuvilakku was the only heirloom, apart from a bronze cauldron, that my mother had managed to hold on to. When she died, Rani Oppol took the cauldron and I brought this to the house—Radha's house and now ours. She had taken it from me and examined it. 'It's very beautiful. Such exquisite workmanship,' she said.

I caressed its bronze sides and said, 'Precious, too.'

'Does everything have to be about money?' she snapped.

Just then the phone rang and I hastened to pick it up. I meant to explain to her that I hadn't meant its value in rupees. But by the time I finished my call, the moment was lost.

At first Radha lit the lamp every evening. Then she stopped. When I asked her, a couple of days later, she said, 'I thought the lamp was an accessory to the house. I didn't realize you attached so much religious significance to it.'

'There is nothing religious about lighting a lamp,' I said, trying to keep the anger out of my voice. 'It looks nice. Adds grace to a home.'

She smiled. 'I am sorry. I won't forget. I'll instruct one of the maids to light it faithfully every evening. Happy?'

I shook my head. I didn't say anything. What was the point? She was the woman of the house. She should be the one to light the lamp and not a maid. But I didn't want to start a quarrel.

Tonight, it is Radha who is lighting the lamp.

I am a blessed man, I think. I have a beautiful home and a prosperous business. And I have Radha. My Radha.

The lamp lights up her eyes. Her hair flows down her back. She smiles at me.

In the night, when I make love to her, she responds with a passion that surprises me. Her hair is spread over the pillow; an aura of her pleasure, I think, when I look down into her eyes.

I settle her head into the crook of my arm and as I fall asleep, I think again: I am blessed.

In the morning, Radha shows no interest in accompanying me to the resort. 'I must check if the Sahiv is all right,' I toss at her.

She continues to eat. I expect her to say she will go with me. But she seems more interested in her dosa. I know relief again.

Whatever fascination Chris held for her seems to have been short-lived.

'I wonder how he is getting along with Uncle,' I pursue. 'I will ask him. Shall I bring him over for lunch?'

'Who?' Her voice is a yelp. She must have choked, for she started coughing.

'Uncle.'

'That will be nice,' she says, sipping water to clear her throat. 'But not for lunch. Dinner will be better. I have things to do this morning.'

I smile. 'What now? A visit to the tailor, is it?'

She smiles back. 'Mmmm…this and that!'

'I'll leave the car for you,' I say on my way out.

After all this time, we seem to be finally getting it right.

Chris is sitting on the veranda when I get there. His hair is wet and gleaming, as if he has just showered. His chin is smooth. Thank god, he had shaved. But the absence of stubble draws attention to the cleft in his chin. He is a pretty bugger, I think. Not masculine handsome, but boyish pretty. A fair enough Lolan.

'All well?' I ask and walk towards him. He smiles and rises. I stand on the veranda for a moment and then walk past him into the cottage. The door is open, after all. He seems to have made himself at home. The instrument is sitting in a dark corner. His laptop is on the table and there are a few books lying on a window ledge. I arrange the books neatly. Chris follows me. He doesn't seem very pleased that I have walked into the cottage or that I am handling his things, but he needs to know that I own the place and while he might stay here, I have my privileges.

Chris says, 'Thank you. All is well. Is Radha here?'

I feel my eyes narrow. 'She is at home. She is busy,' I say. Then, hoping to steer him away from any more talk of Radha, I ask, 'So, you've been spending time with Uncle. What has he been telling you? How far has he got? Do tell me.'

Chris smiles. A wry smile. 'I went there yesterday. But he wasn't in the mood, he said. Instead, he told me the story of how he acquired his parrot. A very interesting story, of course, but not what I wanted to know. I intend going back this evening. I hope he will be more forthcoming then.'

I feel a smile coming to my face. I am delighted. I had thought he and Uncle were going to be inseparable. Like jaggery and a fly. Destined to be stuck together. But it obviously isn't so. I mask my glee and switch on my but-this-is-terrible expression.

'There is no telling with these artistic types,' I say. 'We have to be patient. But it is best to be prepared. I just hope your time here won't be wasted.'

I hope Uncle will clam up. I hope you will be so frustrated by his reluctance to talk that you will give up and go back, I think. The sooner you leave, the better for all of us. I must have had an evil star eclipsing my good sense when I agreed to rent you the cottage for next to nothing. But I say, 'I hope he will be more helpful.'

'Do you think Radha will come by later this evening?' he asks.

Not if I can help it, I think. What is with this man? Doesn't he realize that Radha is a married woman? My wife has other things to do, Mister, I want to tell him. 'No, I don't think so. In fact, it may be several days before she comes here again,' I say, trying to hide how rattled I am by his need to see Radha.

'Oh,' he says.

I put out my hand to shake his. 'I will take your leave then,' I say, giving his palm a good hard squeeze. I don't go to the gym any more, but my hands haven't lost their strength.

It is a quarter past twelve when I reach my office.

Unni walks in. 'Yusuf called,' he says.

I frown. What can Yusuf want?

Yusuf runs the match factory. He used to be the supervisor of a small unit that made agricultural implements at the Small Scale Industrial Estate at Kolapulli. When the unit closed down, Yusuf found himself out of a job. It was then he came to me with the suggestion that I open a match factory.

I had stared at the tall man with the strong face who seemed to have worked it all out. He looked like an aristocrat, his bearing was so noble. As for his voice, it was a rumble when a whisper, and thunderous when he conversed. 'Why do you think I need a match factory?' I asked.

'I heard that you asked the local match factory if they could make you some special matches and that you are still negotiating a price.'

'That is true, but no one buys an orchard merely to eat a dozen mangoes, do they?'

'That may be right, but I assure you that you won't lose any money.'

'What do you know about matches?'

'Very little. But my niece works in the match factory. She has been there for several years and she will bring all the other experienced workers with her. I can assure you of that. You will not lose any money and the investment isn't all that much. You have that piece of land near Kolapulli. The old tyre retreading place. So even the shed is ready.'

He seemed to know what he was talking about and that was how I set up the match factory. Yusuf kept his word. I didn't lose any money and made only profits and well-wishers. The women who worked there sent me their brothers and sons and sometimes even their husbands to work in my other businesses.

My friends who have labour trouble all the time ask me, 'Shyam, how is it you always find good, hard-working people?'

And I tell them, 'Get the woman of the family to support you and she will ensure that her menfolk do.'

Then I would feel a wrench within, for I hadn't been able to get the woman in my house to support me in anything I did.

But all that is different now, I think with a start of happiness.

I hold the phone away from my ear to prevent Yusuf's boom from bursting my eardrum. 'Yes, Yusuf, tell me.'

'You mustn't misunderstand what I am about to tell you. I don't mean any offence, but it is imperative that I speak to you about this,' Yusuf says.

'Go on, tell me, what is on your mind?' I ask.

'Well, it's about madam.'

'Yes?' I feel my abdomen go hollow. What has she done now? When I started the resort, Radha took it upon herself to tell my staff that she and I were to be called by our names: 'none of this sir and madam business'. It took me a long time to make her understand that they would never do it. While she may not respect such divisions, they were not foolish enough to transgress them.

'Yes,' I say, shaking myself out of my reverie.

'Madam was here yesterday.'

'Oh.' Why didn't she tell me?

'She stayed all morning. She sat around for some time and then she said she would read the newspapers aloud rather than let anyone else do it. In fact, she insisted and we had to agree. Then she had someone fetch her a meal from a restaurant nearby and ate lunch with the women. It seems she told them that the food they ate wasn't nutritious enough. She was very polite. Madam is never anything but polite. But some of the women were very offended. They thought it was a slur on their cooking.'

I sigh.

Yusuf echoes my sigh. 'You see, don't you? And yet, what really worries me is her wanting to read aloud to them.'

Yusuf applies shop-floor practices from other industries, but somehow he always manages to make them work. That is how we had the system of newspapers and magazines being read aloud to the workers. Yusuf said it was done in beedi factories in Kannur and it relieved the monotony and tedium of such intensive manual work. The workers took turns to read and were paid full wages for the task. So they were all pleased with the arrangement. In the afternoon, the radio was turned on; there were enough programmes to keep them amused. The system had worked until now.

'The women don't like it. They don't like being stripped of what they think is their right. They don't like the way she reads, either. You see, they are used to a particular style of reading. But most of all, they don't like literature being thrust down their ears. All along, I have got them magazines like *Mangalam* and *Nana*. Easy reading, if you know what I mean. Yesterday madam read aloud the editorial pages, ignoring all the juicy titbits they prefer. They were willing to endure it for one day. But she is here again this morning and she has brought Tolstoy's *War and Peace* with her. I can see that they are very displeased. Irate workers are no good.'

I assure him that I will ensure Radha doesn't upset their routine again. Then I put the phone down.

What am I going to do?

I close my eyes and hear again the drone of the reader. The absence of all emotion in her voice allows the listeners to interpret the words their way. And here is Radha with her convent-educated Malayalam and her *War and Peace* and diet charts, seeking to contribute but only usurping what the workers consider their privilege. How am I to convince Radha that they don't want her there, without offending or hurting her, or ruining our new found amicability?

As I think about it, I begin to get angry. What a thing to do. To go to the match factory without telling me. And then to make an arbitrary decision without consulting me. It was better when she stayed aloof from my business activities. Now I have to clean up her mess.

Does she ever consider that such silly acts have repercussions? Besides, what will my friends and their wives say if they find out? We have a place in society. A standing that Radha has always treated rather carelessly. But this is more than I am willing to suffer.

I call Radha on her mobile. I am coming home for lunch, I say. I know she will return home then.

Radha is sitting on the veranda. She is waiting for me. This is a new Radha. Someone who waits for me to arrive, eager for my presence. Words spill out of her mouth in a rush, her cheeks glow, her eyes sparkle. I see the radiance of what she thinks is a day well spent. The angry words in my mouth halt. How can I take this away from her?

After we have eaten, we move to the sitting room. It is a beautiful room. Everything here is old and stately: rosewood sofas and upright chairs, small teak tables and a tall boy. An old clock keeps time and in a curio cabinet are some beautiful pieces of glass and porcelain. Everything is as it used to be in Radha's grandfather's time. When I was a child, I was never allowed to step into this room. Often, I would sneak a look from the doorway. Now it is here I sit when I am at home. It is the room I love best. I glance through my post. Radha has the TV on. I can see she is eager to talk. I pile the letters into a heap.

'You won't believe where I was this morning and yesterday,' she begins.

I pretend surprise. 'Weren't you at the beauty parlour and the tailor's?'

'That's what you think. I was at the match factory.'

'And?'

'And I feel that I have finally found something to do. Do you know they have a nice little arrangement there? One of them reads aloud while the others work. I have said that from now on I will do it. I plan to go there everyday and introduce them to literature. Right now they listen to serialized romances and gossip about film stars. In fact, this morning I took *War and Peace*. What do you think I should start after that? Kafka would be too morbid. Márquez would be nice. Yes, he would be perfect...'

I groan. Which world does she live in?

'You can't be serious,' I say.

'Why? What's wrong?' She stares at me.

'Everything. Don't you realize that these women don't want to hear Tolstoy or Márquez or any of your intellectual writers? They want their romantic fiction and cinema gossip.' I pause and then decide to say what is really troubling me. 'There is something else. I don't like it. You are my wife and you have a place in society. When I ask you to show some interest in what I do, I mean just that. Display interest and not hobnob with my employees or share meals with them.'

I bite my tongue. I didn't mean that to slip out.

'So you knew all along and were pretending that you didn't.' Her nostrils flare.

'I heard. My employees keep me informed. How else can I run so many business establishments?'

'You disgust me.' Her voice rises. 'These are people. Human beings like you and me. But you consider yourself a superior being, don't you?'

'Don't be silly,' I snap. 'It is not about being superior or inferior. You are breaking protocol; you are erasing lines between the employer and the employee. You are negating my position and I cannot allow that.'

Radha slams the remote control down. 'You should hear yourself. Allow that! You are a snob, a bloody fucking snob! Fine. I won't go.'

She flounces off to the bedroom.

I continue to sit there. Her rage will settle in a little while, I know. I replace the remote on top of the TV, leave the newspapers by the door so that the maid can put them away and go to our bedroom. The door is latched from within.

I consider knocking, but don't. Why should I apologize? I've done nothing wrong.

There is a day bed in the veranda. We have four other bedrooms, each with its own bed made up, but if I use one of them, it will set the servants talking. They might even mention it to Rani Oppol when she gets here. So I lie on the day bed and it occurs to me that once again we have failed to get it right.

Early in the evening Radha comes to the veranda. Her face is pale but she doesn't seem angry.

'Do you want your tea served here?' she asks.

I get up and stretch. 'No, I'll come in.'

I follow her to the dining room.

We sip our tea and crunch our Marie biscuits. The arrowroot biscuits are floury in my mouth.

'I am going to see Uncle,' she says.

I nod.

'I hope that is not going to undermine your standing in society. Is there anything I can do that won't? I wanted to teach in one of the primary schools and you said it was too much work for too little money. When I wanted to start a tuition class, you said the same. Then I wanted to start a crèche and you said you didn't want the house filled with bawling babies. So I thought I would find something else to do which didn't involve making money, but even that isn't right. Don't I have a right to an opinion? I am your wife. Your wife, do you hear me? But you treat me as if I am a kept woman. A bloody mistress to fulfil your sexual needs and with no rights.

'Then your sister comes here and tells me that I am wasting my education and time. What is right? Visits to the beauty parlour and the tailor's? Washing the leaves of the house plants and dusting the curios? Stopping by at the supermarket and calling on your friends' wives? They are your friends, not mine. Don't you see that they bore me? They are small-town people and will always be that, with small minds and even smaller lives…This is not how I expected to live my life. This is not what I want from life, don't you see?'

I ignore her. I have heard all this before. Besides, once she's said it, she usually feels better. I wonder if I should have told her the whole truth. She would have been embarrassed and upset, but her ire wouldn't have been directed at me. But then, it's also true that even if the workers had welcomed her presence I wouldn't have let her continue. I don't like it, and that's that.

'I am going back to the resort,' I say. 'We'll leave in fifteen minutes.'

'I prefer to go by myself,' Radha mutters.

I plonk my mug down. I have had enough of this. 'There is no need for two vehicles to go to the same place at the same time. Your family may have left you many things, but they didn't leave you an oil well. Since I pay for the fuel, I will decide if we need one vehicle or two.'

She is quiet in the car. I feel petty for what I said, but my head is beginning to throb and I have no energy to play these childish games.

She comes into the resort with me. I wonder if she will apologize. Or perhaps that is expecting too much. Radha will pretend that all those harsh words were never spoken. I know; this isn't the first time we have quarrelled. I decide to play along.

'I have been hearing a great deal about rainwater harvesting. So I sent for information. I think we should implement it. The details are here,' I say, pulling out a file.

'For an acre-sized plot, we need to make a hundred pits, each about three metres by three metres. Which means...'

I see that Radha isn't listening. She is standing by the window, looking out. The Sahiv is walking by. Suddenly he turns and sees her. His face lights up. Hers, too.

And I feel a darkness cloud my eyes.

Uncle

Malini barks. I know that squawk-bark of hers; it usually announces someone hovering by the gate. She is as good as a watchdog. 'Who is there?' I ask her.

She barks again. I pause from tying the pumpkin vines in the vegetable patch to look at her. During the afternoon and at night, she lives within the house. I have a little perch rigged for her, on which she sits. The rest of the time, she lives in a cage. It is an enormous cage, but I have heard an occasional comment about how cruel it is to keep birds in a cage. Then I ask the person who made the comment, 'How different is it from keeping your wife and daughters at home? Isn't that a cage, too?'

And he, for it is always a man, would laugh in disbelief. 'How can you compare the two? Birds are meant to be free.'

'And women are not?'

'Women need to be looked after,' he would tell me, and his eyes would demand: What do you know about it? You don't have a wife or children to worry about.

'If you say so.' I would let it be.

But Malini, I know, is happy in her cage. I had tried setting her free, but I found her a few days later, nearly dead. She couldn't survive without me and besides, her family didn't want her any more. So now she sits in her cage, chattering to the crows.

She has a repertoire of noises, most of them rude. Barking like a dog when she sees someone by the gate, mewing at dogs instigating trouble, and screeching like a factory siren or emitting a sound like a pistol shot when she sees other parakeets spread themselves on the mango tree by the veranda. Malini, I have discovered, detest most creatures, living or otherwise. She hates even the radio, and screeches and shrieks, making a racket loud enough to drown its sound. She, despite her name, is neither sweet-tempered nor beautiful. Malini is a nasty old moulting bird, but she makes me laugh more than anyone else I know.

I walk to the end of the vegetable patch and peer over the fence. I stare at the man by the gate. He is of medium height, with a full head of hair and a beard; his jet black hair is without a trace of grey. I feel a smile grow on my face. It is AK. What on earth is he doing here?

'AK?' I call.

He smiles and opens the gate. 'I wasn't sure if this was your house, but there wasn't any further to go. Then I heard your dog bark. Does it bite?'

'That's my dog.' I point to Malini.

I know what Malini is poised to do next. When someone walks in through the gate, she shrieks, 'Kallan! Kondhan!'

It upsets most visitors to be announced as a burglar, and a moronic one at that. I pretend to be contrite, but mostly I laugh within. 'The bird is stupid,' I say half-heartedly.

Malini cocks her head, stares at them with her beady eyes and retreats into silence. Thereafter, every few minutes, she hops to the end of the perch and says softly, 'Kallan! Kondhan!'

My visitors never stay too long, and I have no complaints. Anyway, most of them come asking for a contribution for some worthy cause, as they call it.

'Listen, AK,' I say quickly. 'Just ignore her, please. She knows only two words, but they are very rude.'

AK smiles. 'She can't be ruder than some of the art critics I know.'

I smile back at him with affection. I met AK many years ago at the Music Academy in Madras. I can't remember who introduced us, but we had realized right away that we understood each other. AK is an artist. His paintings are filled with light and somewhere I had read that 'his touch was just as vibrant with sounds'. I do not understand phrases like that, but I know that he views his art as I do mine. That it demands he struggle with it. That he could be a trickster if he wished to be one—someone who fills canvases with a flourish and turns every stroke into a circus that will fetch him the price he demands—and yet, he chooses to ignore such ease of expression only so that he can retain his integrity.

Malini does her mandatory screeching and then shuts up.

'What are you doing here?' I ask, curious.

'A wedding in the family. I thought I'd come by and see you.'

He is examining the plants in my garden. He touches a leaf, bends low and sniffs a flower, caresses the bark of a tree. I smile.

We walk towards the steps to the river.

'Do you know that your house and mine are on a straight line? Oh, I do know that you can draw a straight line between any two points, but this is almost 180 degrees. Except that my house is further down the river,' he says suddenly.

Aashaan would have approved of AK. Like Aashaan, he is not given to premeditated responses or deliberate thoughts.

'Do you want to stay here, or shall I take you to the resort next door? My niece owns it. We can get something to eat...and drink,' I say, putting a cloth over Malini's cage. The evening sun would heat up the cage and Malini detests the heat.

'But wait, AK, there is something I want you to see,' I say. 'My friend Philip the Englishman sent me photocopies of a few pages of a book he was reading. I thought of you when I was reading them and actually meant to send them to you one of these days.

'These are letters by the artist Pissarro to his son. Listen to this: *for an artist should only have his ideal in mind. He lives poorly, yes, but in his misery one hope sustains him, the hope of finding someone who can understand him.*'

I think of the receptions I have attended. I think of a woman I first met at an annual dance event, a few years ago. Every year therafter, she mouthed the same words: 'Oh, Mr Koman, I have heard so much about you. I have seen all the very big names dance. Birju Maharaj, Alarmel Valli, Mallika Sarukkai, the Dhananjayans, Padma Subramaniam, Kalamandalam Gopi...the entire who's who of dance. You are the only one I haven't seen. To see you perform, that is top of my priority list. So when and where will you be performing next?'

The first time, I told her. The second time as well. Then I realized that it was a pleasantry and no more. Even as she spoke to me, her eyes were searching the little cliques in the reception hall, evaluating which one was worth cultivating.

She understood nothing of art at all. And it is her I am thinking of as I read aloud a bit I like very much.

'There is more,' I say. '*See, then, how stupid the bourgeoisie, the real bourgeoisie have become, step by step they go lower and lower, in a word they are losing all notion of beauty, they are mistaken about everything. When there is something to admire they shout it down, they disapprove! Where there are stupid sentimentalities from which you want to turn with disgust, they jump with joy or swoon.*' You might think things have changed in the last one century; that people have acquired a sensitivity, but wait till we go next door...'

As we walk past the reception, I spot Chris.

'Who is that?' AK asks. 'He is looking at you.'

I wave. 'That's Chris Stewart. He is a travel writer and is researching a book about Kerala in which I figure!' I raise my eyebrows to suggest what I think of that.

AK looks amused. 'Are you afraid he will see more than you want to reveal?'

I shrug. Having consented to talk about myself, I am not so sure now. I had sent him away yesterday, but I can't do that every day.

Chris turns and walks towards us. Then I see Radha. She is standing by the window and soon she, too, is tripping down the steps.

Chris stops for Radha. They look at each other. I see their faces glow, warmed by each other's nearness.

I saw them two nights ago, sitting on the steps, wrapped up in each other. For a moment I had wondered if I should caution Radha. Don't, I wanted to tell her. This is happening too fast. Besides, I can see you are thinking forever, and he is thinking here and now. You can't blame him for that. But it is you who will be hurt…Then I decided not to. Everybody is entitled to making their own mistakes. I couldn't rob an experience from her even if it was a mistake. Besides, whatever was destined to happen would.

I hadn't seen her look as animated as this in a long time. Something that made her so happy surely couldn't be bad. Even though she was married? So what, I asked myself. When did you start taking such a high moral stance? She was unhappy in her marriage and if she found happiness in adultery, so be it. I realized then that my love for her would let me condone any fault of hers.

'This is AK. He is an artist. He lives in Madras, but is actually from a place nearby called Kudallur,' I introduce AK to them. I suddenly feel a wave of contentment. I am surrounded by the people I love.

Love? I catch myself. Do I love Chris? I barely know him. Yet, already I feel a wave of warmth when I see or think of him. I wonder again: Who is he? What is he hiding from me?

Shyam joins us just then. 'Hello, hello,' he says. 'Who is this? There seems to be a little conference going on.'

I introduce AK to him. 'Of course I know of him,' Shyam says. 'So AK sir, how is the art world these days? I was reading the other day about the prices Husain fetched at an auction. It must be so encouraging to see modern art being truly appreciated.'

I nearly laugh out aloud. Shyam knows nothing about art.

In fact, Shyam would have said the same to just about anybody I introduced him to, substituting art for music or literature or timber or aluminium pipes or glass bangles, depending on what the person did by way of work.

AK smiles into his beard. He can spot a fake art lover as easily as I can a fake kathakali aficionado. They are everywhere, these vermin lured by what they think are an artist's achievements. They measure his art by how successful he is. Success as defined by money, awards, and how often newspapers and magazines write about him. They parrot phrases culled from what they've read and heard, and nod knowingly about techniques and forms without knowing one from the other. AK and I have seen enough of these creatures to also know that they are usually harmless. Besides, a little lionizing hurts no one…particularly not an artist who has to suffer the public's opinion of what is essentially a very private world.

'Uncle, what is wrong?' Shyam asks.

I shake myself. My eyes tend to glaze over as I retreat into these inner worlds I live in most of the time.

'I see what you mean. This is the person you were referring to, I suppose,' AK says to me.

I see the twinkle in his eyes. 'Yes, now you know…'

Shyam beams. 'Would you like to go to the restaurant?' he asks.

'Wouldn't you prefer to go to my cottage?' Chris asks.

'I think the cottage will be better,' Radha says.

'The cottage,' I say.

Shyam scowls, but goes with us.

When we are seated on the veranda of the cottage, Shyam calls for room service. 'What would you like to eat? Finger chips? Sandwiches? Or some pakoras? Tea or coffee?' Shyam is being the genial host, and he doesn't have to be; my guests are not his. Again I feel ashamed of my earlier speculations about him.

'I was coming over to see you,' Chris says. 'I was hoping you would resume…' He stops abruptly.

I sigh. I am in two minds. It seems pointless, dredging these memories, and yet when I bring them out to examine them in retrospect and light, I feel as if I am arriving at a point I have never reached before.

'Later,' I say. 'Later. Come by tomorrow.'

Then I see Radha's face. In Nalacharitam, there is a scene where Damayanti describes her misfortunes to a messenger from her father's kingdom. She begins from the time her husband decides to play a game of dice with his brother, loses his kingdom and is forced to retreat into the forest, to finally being abandoned by her husband and all the troubles she has to face thereafter. In that scene, Damayanti depicts thirty-three expressions of loss in a few moments. These emotions do not include sorrow, for sorrow is an absolute and the sense of loss fleeting. Radha's face depicts those thirty-three emotions of loss when she realizes that she doesn't have an excuse to be with Chris tomorrow. My heart bleeds for her. I decide to set aside my decision to not interfere, to neither aid nor deter, and say, 'I want you to be there, Radha.'

She gleams.

'I have to go,' Shyam says when the food has been served and the steward sent away. 'Radha, are you coming?'

'No.' She shakes her head. 'I'll come home a little later. Don't worry. I'll have one of the boys call me an autorickshaw.'

I don't understand the inflection on the word autorickshaw, but clearly Shyam does. He stares at her for a moment and says, 'I'll send the car back for you.'

'Perhaps you should have gone,' I say.

'No, for what? To watch more TV? There is nothing for me to do at home,' she says. The bitterness in her voice startles me.

Shyam's going away eases the air. It is as if a yoke has been lifted. Chris and Radha smile at each other. They haven't exchanged a word yet, but their smiles seem to encompass all the unspoken words and thoughts.

Then AK asks, 'So what has Koman been telling you about himself?'

'Would you like to listen?' Chris asks.

I frown.

'Do you mind?' Chris turns to me, realizing that I might not approve of this airing of my life.

'No, play it for him. Then I will tell you some more. It is time you heard about Saadiya and why in the beginning was a ship...'

Later at night, I can't sleep. AK left a little while ago. We had returned to my house after dinner. 'I often think of building a cottage like this on my piece of land,' he said. 'But when you are a bachelor, everyone says, come stay with us, why do you need a house of your own? It is not as if you have children who will want to live there. Sometimes I think they are waiting for me to die.'

AK was pensive. It wasn't often he was in this mood. It must be his age, I thought. In your mid-fifties, thoughts about life and death often swim to the surface of the mind.

I think of his house in Madras: the bougainvillea-festooned gate and the many-angled house with slits and crevices trapping light. Stacked canvases fill every bit of space. For himself, he has a small living area with a narrow bed, a table and a few other things…so few possessions for so rich a life. The rest of the house is devoted to the tools of his art. He has found his place. It can't have been easy, however. He works in the state department and stays resolutely out of the art establishment and its coteries. His art is his own and perhaps that's why he is so content in his skin.

I look around me. There is nothing here to suggest the presence of my art. All I have are my steel fingernails and a little box of ghee in which my chundapoo seeds wait.

I close my eyes. I think of my father. In his last years, he came here often and some days he would talk a great deal. I do not know if what he told me was to ease his burden or mine.

He saw my art as a burden. It would forever keep me down. It would forever prevent me from being me, he said.

'I have worn many faces, played many roles, but I did that to survive. So that I could preserve the I within me. I had no choice. But what you do…I don't understand it. How can you choose to be someone else all the time? Why do you always need to be in someone else's skin? Is that the only way you can be satisfied with life?'

I had tried explaining, but it was beyond him, I thought. His life was not mine. He would never understand that I had to be someone else before I could be content in my skin.

Then I think, while telling my story I will have to wear the guise of both my father and mother. Only then will I be able to explain their love. And only when their stories are told can I permit myself to even enter the story. Without them, I don't exist.

Will Chris be patient enough? Will he understand?

It doesn't matter, I think. It is enough that I tell him. But first he has to know about how Sethu my father who called himself Seth, met Saadiya my mother.

1938
The Plank of Avidity

They cycled. The two men, Dr Samuel Sagayaraj and Sethu, cycled everywhere. Others might choose a bullock cart or a covered jhutka cart with a pony, or if they could afford it, a car. Bur Dr Samuel Sagayaraj disdained all forms of transport except his bicycle. 'I am happy with mine; you will be with yours, I assure you. My cycle has served me well,' he had said, gazing at it fondly. Then he counted the money once again.

'Why do I need a bicycle when there is an ambulance?' Sethu asked. He didn't relish the thought of cycling in the fierce heat. Besides, he hated having to admit to the doctor that he didn't know how to cycle. It would begin a round of discussions which at this point Sethu decided he had neither the stomach nor the stamina for.

'Ambulance!' the doctor expostulated, more a cry of outrage than surprise. His eyebrows locked horns even more fiercely. 'The ambulance is for patients, and emergencies. Even then, I use it only reluctantly. Running an ambulance is expensive. And running it for able-bodied men is a sin,' he said, thrusting the notes into Sethu's palm.

Then the doctor turned his head and said softly, 'Go, do all that is in thine heart; for the Lord is with thee.'

Like a baby pigeon, Sethu thought, looking at the doctor's head, which was cocked in expectation. He sighed. He was weary of this game but obedient enough to respond. It had begun during the time of the Great Cholera Epidemic when the doctor had said that he thought Sethu didn't seem to be well acquainted with the Bible. Sethu had known fear then. What if the doctor saw through him? So he began reading the Holy Book diligently and discovered that he retained most of what he read effortlessly. It stayed in his mind and, without knowing how, he once placed a quote the doctor had mouthed. Thereafter, the doctor expected him to do it each time, and soon Sethu spent all his free time reading the Bible and memorizing it. 'The Second Book of Samuel, otherwise called the Second Book of Kings. Chapter 7: God's promises to David.'

'You are simply amazing. How on earth do you do it?'

The glee in the doctor's voice made him cringe. 'It's not hard when you read the good book as often as I do,' Sethu said, knowing it was expected of him. Particularly when it is the Books of Samuel you choose your quotations from, the voice in his head added.

Ever since he came to Nazareth, the voice in his head had acquired a new timbre. It had changed from his uncle's to a gruffer version of his own. A voice that mocked him so often for what he had turned into. A voice that wouldn't let him be a true acolyte.

When Sethu's black Raleigh arrived, the doctor taught him to cycle like he had taught him, during the epidemic, to load syringes and give injections. The good doctor was relentless once he had set himself a task.

'I need you to go with me to many places, and doing it on foot will take forever. Here, don't stare at the wheel. Look ahead,' he said, giving Sethu a little push as he perched on the high seat precariously. The cycle wobbled, but Dr Samuel was there to hold the handle bar and steady it.

Sethu tried to concentrate. It wasn't just Dr Samuel but Faith, Hope and Charity who nurtured a great desire to see him cycle. They chirped, cheeped and clucked words of encouragement. Sethu glared at them darkly thinking, if I ever learn to conquer this contraption, I shall ride away from their cosseting into the horizon.

A few falls, a skinned knee and a scraped palm later, Sethu got his 'balance' as Dr Samuel referred to it.

'He's got his balance,' Faith rushed to tell Hope and Charity.

'Praise be the Lord,' Hope, the most pious of the three, cried.

'Oh holy father, thank you for giving our Seth his balance.' Charity broke into prayer.

Seth flushed with embarrassment. They made it seem as if he had swum to Ceylon and back. 'Oh shut up, you fat old hens!' he wanted to scream.

But the thought of the horror on their faces made him curb his tongue and irritation.

'Yes, praise be the Lord and our Dr Samuel,' Sethu said obediently.

The women looked at each other joyfully. That was why they liked Seth so much. He was a good Christian and a loyal acolyte, just as they were.

Sethu on his bicycle knew a freedom that in the past few months had been denied him. He had had to depend on Dr Samuel for his forays into the outer world. Now he mounted his bicycle and set forth on his own, pedalling briskly.

Uphill he would rise from the seat and pedal even more furiously, feeling the muscles in his calves tense. And downhill, he would glide on the momentum of that effort, the wind rushing through his hair, making his shirt billow and whispering in his ears. Who would have thought that two wheels and a handle could provide such a sense of escape?

Sethu did not dare seek beyond the immediate peripheries of Nazareth. Here, in Nazareth, he knew a security he had never known before, not even in his own home. And yet, a certain restlessness bruised the pattern of his quiet life, making him want more. More of what, he didn't know. But there it was. He felt the need to escape, to flee, to break out and break away.

A few months after the epidemic, in November, when the monsoon had arrived and left its trail of wetness, Dr Samuel decided it was time for them to go to Arabipatnam.

'How far is it?' Sethu asked, looking at the baskets Hope, Faith and Charity were packing. Medicines, a change of clothes and packets of food.

'The doctor won't drink any water except from his well,' Hope said, while pouring water into his surukku sembu. Its copper sides gleamed.

'And won't eat any rice except the rice grown in his paddy fields near Palaiyamkotai. Every harvest, his mother sends a huge gunny bag of grain for him.'

'Fat brown rice; that's the secret of his energy and devotion to duty,' Faith added, knowing Sethu's preference for polished rice.

'It makes sense to be careful,' Dr Samuel said. The doctor had little patience for fripperies and the sisters made him seem like a fusspot, a foolish fusspot at that.

'Most water in this region is not potable. I know that with water from this well, I am safe. As for the rice, now that's my weakness.'

'He gets constipated if he eats any other rice,' Charity murmured.

Sethu grinned. Dr Samuel shooed away a fly. And the other two nudged Charity to be silent.

Dr Samuel's bicycle bore the stamp of his profession—his doctor's bag. On the handle bar was slung a little basket with his surukku sembu, its lid screwed on tightly so as to not spill even a drop of water.

Sethu stared at the two baskets slung on either side of his cycle carrier. The doctor and his mule, he thought bitterly.

Increasingly, he felt bile corrode his thinking. The total subservience demanded of him filled him with a resentment that he couldn't explain. The voice in his head mocked him more than ever: So is this what you want? To live here forever as the doctor's pack animal until one of these days, he foists one of the kondai sisters on you? Whew, aren't you lucky? To have your pick of the three buns. So which one will it be? Big bun, little bun, or the plaited bun? And for your honeymoon the doctor might set up a health camp where all five of you can go and read each other's heartbeat.

They cycled. The two men, Dr Samuel and Sethu.

'We have to cycle towards Thiruchendur,' Dr Samuel said as they set off.

Sethu tried to read the doctor's face. Had he in some way read Sethu's mind and discovered its vagrant leanings? Is that why he had proposed the trip to Arabipatnam? If so, the doctor had got it all wrong. He barely had time to glance at the countryside. The heavily loaded bicycle needed all his attention.

But slowly, he found that it didn't seem so heavy any more. If he didn't think about the medicine bottles smashing or the food packets unravelling, the bicycle didn't seem so weighed down. And soon, he could look his fill at the landscape they were cycling through.

It was, he realized, no different from Nazareth. Flat scrublands were broken by an occasional pocket of acacia trees. Suddenly there would be a glimpse of green fields in which paddy grew and a line of palm trees, a few of them with their tops spliced by lightning. Sethu felt hot and dirty. The brownness of the landscape made his throat hurt.

At home, one never saw brown. It was always green. A million shades of green. But here, everything was the colour of mud, dried mud. Mud-coloured rocks. Mud-coated leaves. Mud-coloured rainwater puddles. Vast tracks of deserted brownness.

Suddenly, in the middle of the road, Dr Samuel braked.

'Look to your left, Seth,' he said, pointing to a little hillock of mud and stones.

'Some years ago when the public works department began cutting a road through here, the workers found an urn. When they opened it, they discovered a skeleton and many precious things.

'The workers refused to work after that. Then an archaeologist, an Englishman, organized a dig. They unearthed several such urns. And when they finished, a Hindu priest and a Christian padre came to exorcize the land. Only after that did the workers agree to return.'

Sethu looked around him with interest. 'Did they ever find out whose skeletons they were? I mean, did they belong to some ancient race or a nomadic tribe?'

'Seth, burial urns are not all that rare. What made these extraordinary was that each one of the urns contained a female skeleton. Not one was male. Not even a baby's. It makes you think, doesn't it? What kind of people were they? History would have us believe that once upon a time, perhaps a thousand years ago, a certain primitive tribe lived here. But I think this was the burial ground for the women who once lived in Arabipatnam. Wives and daughters of the original settlers. But I am not a historian, so who is going to accept my conclusion!'

Dr Samuel mounted his bicycle again, but Sethu stood rooted to the spot. Suddenly the land had acquired a sinister hue. Beneath all that placid brownness lay a darkness. Sethu shivered.

'As we go on, I'll show you more strange sights. Things that will make you wonder…'

Sethu only half-listened as he pedalled. Why did they bury their women in urns? Were these women alive or dead when they were stuffed into the urns?

Sethu felt a sense of trepidation grow within him. He darted a glance at the doctor. Suddenly he realized that the land wasn't so desolate any more. He saw a few buildings. Then more and more houses, small and with tiled roofs, each surrounded by a cluster of trees, began to dot the land. The two men turned into what seemed like the main street of a village. Houses lined the street on either side. Houses that were dressed with vermilion and white markings.

Sethu looked around him in surprise. A little Brahmin ghetto in this Christian heartland? Soon they went past a temple. He glanced at Dr Samuel's face again. No wonder he looked grim. 'What is this place called?' he asked.

'Look to it: for evil is before you,' the doctor mumbled.

Sethu stared wearily at the doctor's profile. Wouldn't he ever tire of this? Even in the heat of the midday sun, he expected Sethu to place the quote, chapter and verse.

'Exodus 10; the plague of the locusts.'

'No, no,' the doctor whispered. 'The Egyptians were as innocent as baby goats, compared to these. This place is truly evil.'

Sethu chewed his lip. What did the doctor mean? He must hate this place, this ghetto of heathens where there was not even one lamb for Jesus' flock. Why else would he brand the village evil?

Sethu cleared his throat and asked again, 'What is this village called?'

Dr Samuel muttered under his breath, 'Later. Later!'

When they had left the village and its main street behind them, the doctor stopped under the shade of a tamarind tree. He drank deeply from his surukku sembu and said, 'Ugh! Every time I have to go through that village, my stomach heaves. Their hypocrisy nauseates me! And I wonder what disease lies trapped within those walls...'

Sethu said nothing. This bordered on fanaticism, he thought. How could he react so strongly to a Hindu village? Something in him rebelled.

'They have as much right to be Hindus as others have to be Christians or Muslims,' he said.

The doctor stared at him.

'What do you mean? Do you think it is their being Hindu that disgusts me?'

Sethu shrugged. He was not going to state the obvious.

'That isn't just an ordinary Hindu village, Seth,' the doctor tried to explain. It was as if he understood the younger man's uneasiness.

Sethu held up his hand to stem the doctor's rhetoric.

'No, it doesn't matter. You are entitled to your beliefs.' As I am to mine, he left unsaid.

'No, you must listen. That isn't just a village of Hindus. It's a village of brahmins, the most orthodox brahmins I've ever known. They're so strict in their "madi" that they will sprinkle the road with chaani once we have walked or cycled past. They would like to obliterate our presence with cow dung and water.

'In the past, if one of them was ill, they would ask that I attend. Because I'm not one of them, they would bring the patient to a cowshed—if the house had one. The presence of chaani perhaps cleansed the air of my presence. I would have to clench my guts not to throw up for the smell of cow shit, but they wouldn't have it any other way. If there wasn't a cow shed, they would bring the patient to the side of the road and that's where I would have to examine him or her.

'Each time I went, I swore that I would never return. Then I would think of the patient and my Hippocratic oath and I would allow my anger to die.

'But that isn't what makes me so angry. It's what they do while wrapping themselves in such rituals and customs. That the men marry their nieces and the widows are forced to shave their heads is something all of us know about. But this...this I wouldn't have known, but for a patient.'

Dr Samuel liked stories. He liked telling them even better. Sethu often suspected him of making up stories. He had discovered that most of the tales owed their origin to not-so-well-known parts of the Bible. But he kept his discovery quiet. He was quite willing to let the doctor be Aaron: 'I know that he can speak well,' etc.

Sethu leaned forward to show his interest.

'The woman was possessed, they told me: she claimed that she was the mother of snakes. That in her womb she bore baby snakes.

'She was sitting in the cowshed. I had never seen anyone as thin as her. She was a skeleton covered with clothes.

'I have to examine her, I said. The men backed out and the woman's aunt stayed.

'Her belly was distended and I could feel a few knots. If it had been anyone else, I would have instantly diagnosed it to be a tapeworm infection. But how could that be? These people were strict vegetarians. I was puzzled.

'"Why are you wasting your time?" she said. "Can't you feel it? Those are my snake eggs. I am their mother."

'When I said it wasn't possible, she grew angry. She said the next time she gave birth to her snake child, she would show me.

'The woman turned to the wall of the cowshed and wept: "I know I am barren. I can't give birth to human babies. But the gods have blessed me. I am the mother of snakes now."

'I would like to have had stool and urine samples to help me with my investigation. But how could I ask? Nevertheless, I did. I will be back tomorrow morning, I said. I would come in the ambulance, a little makeshift lab in the absence of anything else. I would take my microscope and do a chamber study. I was intrigued, you must understand.'

'And then…' Sethu asked, knowing how the doctor liked to stretch a tale. If he didn't hurry him, he would proceed to some other inconsequential minutiae.

The doctor frowned. He didn't like being hurried. He stared into the distance as if collecting his thoughts. Then he sighed and turned to face Sethu. 'The next morning, when I got there, her aunt who was perhaps the only one who cared about the woman, had the stool sample in a matchbox and the urine in a little mud pot. All very routine stuff. And then she whispered that the patient wanted to see me. She had something to show me.

'The thought of that cowshed nauseated me. It stank of cow piss. But I wouldn't let it stop me, I thought, and went.

'The cowshed seemed darker than ever. I don't know why it reminded me of a delivery room. I knew I was being fanciful, illogical even, but I couldn't help it.

'The woman was waiting for me. She thrust a cloth into my face.

'"Here's my child," she said, opening out the cloth.

'Seth, in my entire life as a doctor I have never seen a tapeworm that big. It was at least four metres long, and banded—you know what that means, don't you? Like bands of tape stuck together.

'"How?" I stuttered in shock.

'"What do you mean how?" she demanded. "I told you, didn't I? About my snake children. But no one believes me. Which is why I kept this one to show you. I usually put them on the termite hill to the south of the house. "Go, my babies," I tell them, and every day I take a coconut shell of milk and turmeric for them."

'I stood there aghast. The poor woman probably had a cyst in her brain as well. She was a walking trogle of tapeworms. If she was ejecting them through her vagina, it probably meant she had a severe recto-anal fistula as well. And that is a rarity by itself. But none of this made me wonder as much as the presence of the parasite.

'I turned to her aunt and said in my sternest voice, "Tell me the truth. Has she a lover?"

'The woman's eyes widened in shock. "She is a married woman," she said.

'"Since when did that prevent a woman from taking a lover?" I asked. "You must tell me, for I have to know who's been feeding her meat. She has taenia cestodes. That thing she's swaddled in a cloth and calls her baby is a tapeworm, which can come only from beef or pig's meat.'

'What do you think would have happened in the normal course if I made an accusation of that sort? She would have beaten her breasts and made a ruckus. Called me names and had her menfolk throw me out for mouthing such heresy. Instead, the aunt wouldn't meet my eyes.

'"No, no," she mumbled.

'"Then how do you explain it? You get this infection only if you eat meat. And you are brahmins, vegetarians," I pointed out.

'She stared at her feet and said, "We eat pork."

'"What?" I cried in shock. I don't think I had ever been so shocked by anything before. I felt my legs wouldn't hold me up any more. These brahmins ate pork! I think I must have stuttered, "I don't understand…"

'"Many years ago, when the smallpox epidemic was raging, our priest had a dream. He told us that the goddess of smallpox, Periya Amman, said that if we wished to let the pox bypass us, we must eat pork. The thick layer of fat of the pig would serve as a talisman. It would protect us. It would keep us alive and our skins would remain soft and smooth, unpitted by scars.

'"They almost killed the priest when he narrated his dream. But every night Amman came to him. He called a council of elders and said, You know that I have never swerved from the brahminical path. That I have upheld each one of our dictates. Amman has come for a whole week in my dreams. Every night, she gets angrier and angrier. Last night she was furious. She said, Is it that you do not trust me, or is it that you think you know better? I will not appear again, but if you do not do as I say, in less that a month's time your entire village will be wiped out.

'"No one dared ignore his words then. But who would do the deed of buying the pork and cooking it? The priest suggested that we draw lots. You see, no one wanted to defile themselves. But before that happened, a group of young men offered to go. They said that when the pork was brought, everyone would have to eat it. So why worry about being defiled? They went away and came back with the meat and a recipe to cook it. The women were all summoned and told what to do with the meat. We set aside separate vessels to cook the meat and bowls to eat it from. None of us cared for it; we did it because it was a dictate from heaven and no one dared disobey. Ever after, every few months, our men travel to a place where no one knows them and bring back enough meat for the village. Smallpox, cholera, plague, jaundice, none of this affects us. As you can see, it works for us. We've never been ill," she finished defiantly.

'I said nothing. Their hypocrisy nauseated me. Nauseates me to this day. They think all the rest of us are untouchables. But to save their skins, they'll eat even pig's meat.'

Sethu shivered. This was one of the doctor's finest stories.

'How do you think they cooked the pork?' Sethu asked.

'How would I know?' The doctor's sarcasm made Sethu wince. 'Not adequately, for how would they know how to cook meat?'

'What happened then? Did you cure the woman?' Sethu asked.

The doctor wiped his brow. 'I hid my repugnance for them—or so I thought. I went back the next day with enough medicines for the woman and for the entire village. I wondered what the intestines of the others were like. Were all of them invaded by T. solium?

'Perhaps, I thought, this woman was one of the poorest of the lot and had received no medical attention, while the others were treating themselves elsewhere, just as they got their meat from some distant place. That is a common enough occurrence, you know. Why, no one here in Nazareth would come to me if they showed any symptoms of leprosy. They would go elsewhere. Leprosy is endemic to this region. Did you know that? Last month…'

Sethu cut in with, 'Doctor, what happened when you went back to the village?'

'They wouldn't let me see the woman. They said they had their means of treating madness and they didn't need my services any longer. The woman's aunt must have told one of the men about her confession. They didn't want me coming there any more. And they said if I were to tell anyone about it, they would deny everything and say that I was slandering them because they had resisted my attempts to convert them.

'"I am a doctor," I said. "And a gentleman."

'"All that is fine," one of them said. "But if we hear stories about what you know, we will ensure you never talk again. We have broken one dictate already and sinned. Do you think we are afraid of sin any more?"

'That was what scared me. They are lawless creatures. Barbarians in brahminical disguise. They are afraid of nothing and that is frightening. That is the honest truth.'

'So am I the first one you have told this to?' Sethu asked, turning to look at the village. It seemed harmless. A small drab village in a tract of barren wilderness.

'I told a few of my friends in Madras. I had to. I had to tell someone. But they wouldn't believe my story. They said I should have been a writer instead of a doctor. That my imagination was better than my knowledge of anatomy...the fools!'

Sethu turned to look at the village. The doctor's stories were normally parables. They had a moral at the end, a good Christian edict. That this story was free of it made him believe the doctor. What nature of place have I been exiled to, he asked himself, feeling more trapped than ever. A place where women are stuffed in urns and brahmins eat pork. Where Faith, Hope and Charity have feet and the landscape is a flat brown?

Then Sethu saw his first salt pan and knew that if he didn't escape soon, he never would. For here, even salt was trapped by the land.

Sethu was not to know it then, but he was right when he thought that the land exercised a power that wasn't easy to understand. It trapped all that which came into its periphery.

Long ago, or perhaps it is simpler to say, in the beginning, was a ship. A ship that had a prayer deck and sailcloths to harness Allah the Almighty's blessings and the winds. A ship that charted its course

under the captaincy of the incomparable Malik, with its most precious
cargo—the Sahabakkal: Abu Backer, Omar, Ali and Usman. Acolytes
of the Prophet, ordained by the Caliph to set forth and spread the
word.

In the beginning, they sailed the seas seeking new homes for the
word. They sailed along the coast of Malabar, turned a corner and
chose to cruise along the eastern coast. They hadn't gone too far
when they discovered the city of the holy diamond—the
Pavitramanicka patnam. On one side, the sea flanked the town and
on the other side was the river Tamarabarani. Malik said to the
acolytes, 'Here you can fulfil part of your pledge to the Prophet.
Here you can wipe out all traces of the shaitan and do what the
Prophet expected you to do.'

What that was neither the incomparable Malik nor the Sahabakkal
knew. Nevertheless, they persevered.

When the acolytes began to despair of making even one convert,
Malik decided to return. He had his men mend the sails and swab
the decks and then he told the acolytes, 'Look around you. Is there
anything here that makes the infidels of this region think of God?
Any God? Theirs, or ours? Perhaps we need to find fresh soil to sow
the seeds of Islam.'

The acolytes stared at the scrubland, the heaving ocean and miles
of sand dunes and felt a great pang of homesickness. They thought:
There is beauty in our desert kingdoms. Here the desert is barren
land. But they couldn't give up. And so they preached all that they
had been taught. When they left, their legacy to the land and the
people was the body of Abu Backer, buried in a patch of land the
villagers left alone. Thus, the acolytes sowed the seeds of
Arabipatnam, the city of Arabs.

Two hundred years had to pass before the Kahirs arrived. They
were Egyptians looking to navigate the seas for ports that would fill
their ships with the fragrance of spices and their coffers with wealth.
Mohammed Khalifi was not the incomparable Malik, but he too
had his prayer deck and sailcloth and, more than that, he had a spirit
of adventure that propelled him to go on. He ventured beyond the
Pavitramanicka patnam and there he espied a natural harbour. One
that would suffice for him to drop anchor. He saw that in the land
that lay beyond the harbour his men would discover again that the

earth was flat and still under their feet. When they turned to the Kabaah to say their prayers, it would not heave and buckle under their bodies.

In the sands beyond the natural harbour, he discovered a tomb with an Arabic inscription. It was Abu Backer's tomb. Mohammed Khalifi knew a sadness like he had never known before and in that moment he set out to build a mosque.

His men were sailors, but Khalifi had them move stone and mortar, and five times a day they paused in their labours to fall to their knees and pray. The people of the region stared at the men more than the mosque. What religion was this that demanded that a man think of God as punctuation marks to space the day? They stared at the men, puzzled, and promptly named them Anjuvanthanar—they who prayed five times a day.

Arabipatnam, the dream of the acolytes, became Arabipatnam, a living breathing city. Khalifi's ship sailed back and forth and slowly more men arrived, bearing in the bellies of their ships a cargo that would fetch them the fine spices they wanted. Look at this, the traders said, touting their cargo: the finest of Arab horses. In our desert lands there is nothing more precious than these horses that stand sixteen hands high! Look at their coats, like satin. And see this mane...when you pleat it, it will rival the finest braid of silk!

The king of the region looked at the horses and the Anjuvanthanar. The lines of the horses matched the straight gaze of the men in their white robes. The king ordered a fleet of ten thousand horses and promised to fill the bellies of the ships with pepper, cardamom and ginger.

The horses arrived, and with them in the stables, the traders did a brisk business in saddles, bridles, stirrups and reins. Ten thousand Arab horses strengthened the king's army all right, the Commander-in-chief said, but his men couldn't ride. 'What are we to do with the horses?' he asked the leader of the Anjuvanthanar.

The leader sighed. He had his men, who rode the horses as well as the seas, teach the king's men to ride and groom the beasts. Then the Anjuvanthanar left, promising to return when the monsoon winds could be harnessed again.

Ten thousand Egyptian Arab horses, all descended from the

purebred Keheilan. Each one a descendant of the horses that were part of the royal stables of the Pharaoh and so beloved to him that he, Ramses II, proclaimed: Henceforth these horses shall be fed before I am. Every day.

Ten thousand Egyptian Arab horses, each bearing the imprint of the creator in the line that ran from eye to nostril, mane flowing and tail carried high. The horses enchanted the king and his men. And such was the spell they cast that the soldiers, who had mounted no creatures apart from their women, now wouldn't stay away from their saddles.

In the saddle, each soldier, no matter how puny or riddled by fear, knew a transformation. The power of horse muscles between his legs, the lordly height, the mastery over this being that was so light on its feet and yet so steady, devouring vast distances with no sign of fatigue, made him in his own mind a warrior prince. Blessed by the gods, untouched by the vagaries of destiny.

Ten thousand Egyptian Arab horses. In less than a year's time, nine thousand nine hundred and ninety-nine were dead. And the one that survived stood with its head hanging, maimed and lame.

The Anjuvanthanar couldn't believe their ears. Nine thousand nine hundred and ninety-nine horses dead! 'How could you do this?' their leader wept. 'It grieves my heart that you have killed these horses. It grieves my heart more than any evil deed you could do.'

'We did nothing wrong,' the Commander-in-chief protested. 'We fed them, groomed and rode them…and then they dropped dead. There is one horse left. Come see for yourself this wonderful specimen you saddled us with!'

The leader of the traders went to the stables. The stalls were haunted with ghostly neighing. In a stall stood a lone horse.

The leader crooned to it in Arabic. The horse limped towards him. The leader stroked its head and when the horse looked into his eyes as if to ask, why did you leave me and my kin here with these barbarians, his heart almost broke.

The leader fell to his knees to plead forgiveness of this magnificent beast and saw that the horse had just one shoe left.

He turned to the soldier who had gone with him and snapped, 'You tell me that you cared for these horses, but all I see is neglect. Have your blacksmith shoe this horse.'

'What shoe?' the soldier asked. 'Do horses wear shoes?'

'Not real shoes, you imbecile kafir,' the leader screamed in rage, in Arabic. 'This,' he said, pointing to the horse's foot.

'No one here would know how to do this,' the soldier said.

Then it dawned on the leader that nine thousand nine hundred and ninety-nine horses had been ridden to ground by these moronic men who didn't know that horses had to be shod.

He sought an audience with the king. 'Send a few of your men with us and we'll teach them how to shoe horses, our Arab horses,' he added as an afterthought.

The king stared at the ceiling and then at a point beyond the leader's ear. He scratched the side of his nose and tugged at a lock of his hair. The king didn't like being forced into decisions. Besides, he didn't like the idea of sending his men away to a distant land. God knows what new ideas they would come back with. He thought for a while and said, 'That will be impossible. It is a sin for us to cross the seas. Send us a few of your men instead and let them teach mine how to shoe horses.'

Who would want to come here, the leader wondered. Who would agree to do so? Then he thought of the Prophet's teaching: Every man must love his horse. He thought of the nine thousand nine hundred and ninety-nine dead horses and the sole maimed survivor. The spectre of a fleet of horses would haunt him forever, he thought, and agreed.

The men arrived a few months later. Their nostrils, almost as fine as the horses', flared at what they saw. Their eyes, used to the poetry of the circles that formed when the wind raised the sand, the rise and fall of the dunes as they stretched to the horizon, were distressed by this flat brown land that was pock-marked with shrivelled bushes; here and there, like hair on a fourteen-year-old's chin stood a scraggly tree. And worse were the people. Kafirs with skin as dark as coal, and emitting a bodily odour that was unlike anything they had smelt before. Even their homes bore the same reek.

'We must live apart,' they told the leader. 'In a place where we can recreate a semblance of home.'

'Yes, you must,' the leader agreed. 'I shall ask the king for some land near the Juma. You will be a kingdom within a kingdom.'

The men smiled. They liked the thought of a kingdom within a kingdom. Then one who wasn't as shy as the others voiced aloud what was on all their minds. 'It is imperative that we remain who we are. But we are men, men with male needs. What are we to do about that?'

The weary leader offered vast treasures as meher and women were found to satiate masculine needs. Brides for those who had no wives, and second wives for married men whose wives showed no inclination to share their husbands' lust for adventure.

So the ship anchored again and this time in its belly were women. Each one light-skinned and with pale, kohl-rimmed eyes, sometimes brown and sometimes grey. With henna burnishing their hair and the fragrance of roses trailing their every step, the women enchanted the men, who felt their hearts fill with a wild happiness. Soon the men discovered that the natives were just as enchanted by the women and so was laid down the first rule of Arabipatnam: No strangers allowed within these walls.

Then, because by nature they were cautious, the men told their women, 'None of you shall go out unless we are with you.'

'We are far way from our homes. We have no one but each other. How can you deny us the little pleasure and comfort we find in each other's company,' the women wailed.

The men allowed themselves to be persuaded. For a while they let their women venture out, until one man caught his mate looking at another man's wife. Thus came the second rule: 'No man may look at a woman unless she is his wife, sister, mother or daughter. If a woman comes in his path, he must turn his back on her and let her pass.'

But what male eye can impose such curbs on itself? Not to gaze at the delicate patterns of henna on a palm, or feel a certain heat when an upraised arm contours a breast? Not to raise your eyes to trail the tinkle of an anklet bell nor feel the need to caress the curve of buttocks swinging this way and that under the confines of a skirt?

The leader, on his next trip to Arabipatnam, laughed himself silly. 'You are becoming as moronic as these kafirs. In the beginning you were just blacksmiths, but now you are merchants. How do you expect to be successful traders when you are as blinkered as pack horses?'

'What do we do then?'

'Build alleyways for the women to use, connecting a side door or a kitchen door. The men will use the main entrances and the streets. The women will keep to the alleys. That way, they have their freedom and you yours. And what is this about "No strangers allowed here"? Won't you allow my sons to come here after my time? To this town that I founded?'

'Besides,' the leader continued, 'this is a growing community. We will need more and more supplies. Food, clothes, shoes. How are we going to get these if no strangers are allowed in here?'

The men looked at one another in dismay. They hadn't thought of this eventuality.

'Rules are necessary. I agree we must segregate and protect what is our own. But I suggest we amend this one to "No strangers allowed beyond the Juma during the day and none may stay the night." You can then choose who you invite into your home,' the leader said, listing the rules on a piece of parchment.

The rule was amended and the alleyways for women made. Two feet wide and paved with stone, these alleyways snaked through the town, connecting kitchen smells and bruised hearts.

It was here, hemmed in by the alleys, that Saadiya, good girl, descendant of those ancient Kahirs and daughter of the leader of Arabipatnam, waited.

Would he arrive on a stallion, like the prince in the stories Vaapa told her? Or would he sail in with a cargo of rubies, blue sapphires and emeralds, like the incomparable Malik?

He would come, that much she knew.

And so he did. On a bicycle.

Early in the evening, the water carts entered the high gates of Arabipatnam. Behind them came the two men, the doctor leading the way.

'Wait here,' he told Seth, leaning his bicycle against a wall. 'I will tell them we have arrived.'

Sethu watched Dr Samuel walk towards a small mosque. He looked around him curiously.

Shops lined the road, and in the shops and on the road were many people, all dressed in white. Even the little boys playing a game on one side of the road wore white and on their heads were skullcaps of white lace. When a jhutka went past, the pony, he saw, was adorned with white plumes. Sethu felt a smile tug at his lips. It was as if by entering the gates of Arabipatnam he had entered a storybook, where all was strange and echoed mystery. He felt a frisson of excitement and on the heels of it he realized that there wasn't a single female in sight—child, girl or woman.

Where were all the women?

Saadiya stared at the square of blue above her head. Twenty feet by thirty feet. That was the measure of her sky, the peripheries of her life. She touched the grey walls of the terrace roof. Even if she stood on her toes, she couldn't look over the wall. It stood a solid six feet and two inches high, making sure she would never see what was not meant for her eyes, ensuring that she was not visible to anyone. Saadiya felt what was by now a familiar sense of despair. Would she, like her sisters and every other woman born here, live and die hidden by these walls? Was there never to be a way out from here?

She raised her eyes to the blue skies again. In Vaapa's recounting of history, he spoke of the Marakars—the navigators who had sailed the blue seas and found their way here. 'It is their blood that runs in our veins. Do you understand that? We are of pure Arab stock...not like these local "tulkans" who are Hindu converts. We are the descendants of the Prophet himself and it is our duty to safeguard the bloodline,' he said again and again.

Saadiya wanted to cry, 'But Vaapa, don't you see, if it is their blood that runs in our veins, then it is inevitable, the way I feel. There is a singing in my head that says, there is so much to see, so much to do, so much to know. It isn't fair that you men get to go wherever you want, see and do whatever you like, and I am expected to be content with this patch of blue and this maze of alleys.'

But Saadiya would never speak her thoughts. She was too much in awe of her father, her venerable Vaapa Haji Najib Masood Ahmed, one of the six chiefs of the town and its most respected man. How could she tell him what was right and wrong?

Besides, Vaapa had been lenient enough with her. Her three elder sisters had been married off when they were thirteen. But here she was, fifteen and unmarried, and she even had a tutor who taught her Arabic. Vaapa was waiting for Akbar Shah's second son to return from Hong Kong to fix her nikaah.

Saadiya knew that the house next to theirs had already been bought and the deed made in her name. The workers had been brought in to make the repairs and when her groom arrived, she would be decked in her jewellery and wed to a man she had never seen. Her life would go on as it always had. Even the alley she used would be the same. The only change would be that she would exchange her patch of blue for a smaller one. Her new house wasn't as big as her father's.

Saadiya thought of her father, and his stories. Vaapa was a raconteur. When he told a story, you listened, and you felt yourself become part of the story. His stories were always of men who sought distant lands, of travellers and their wondrous discoveries. Saadiya had her own favourite, second only to the story of the ten thousand horses.

'There is a land far, far away, where it's mostly night and seldom day. The cold would chill the marrow in the bones and turn even your hair into razor-sharp blades. That was how cold it was. All day, a stiff breeze laden with more ice than salt blew in from the sea and the people shivered in their homes. Since the sun never shone, there was no way of growing enough crops to feed everyone through the year. The people lived off the sea mostly. The men sailed their boats and went deep into the sea and when they returned they brought home enormous catches, enough to feed the entire village for many days. But some days the catch wasn't so good, or the weather would be stormy and no one would dare sail into the sea. So what could they do then?

'The boats were made of wood, and do you know what they did? They elongated the keel. Now, when they discovered that they had a bigger catch than usual, instead of throwing the extra fish back into the sea, they added an extra plank to the side of the boat and raised its height. They could carry a larger number of fish then. They called it the Plank of Avidity.'

Saadiya loved that phrase. It represented all that she felt was true of life. Life demands of us that we have a Plank of Avidity. How can we have more if we don't raise our expectations? How can we be content with just what we have and know? Even Vaapa, who was a teller of stories, was content with sailing the seas of imagination. But that wasn't real. Reality was to be able to see, to touch, to hear, to feel, to sense, to know, to experience.

Saadiya stared at her feet. Two days ago, in her sister Nadira's home, she had seen a book. It was Nadira's husband's, acquired on his latest trip to Singapore. Saadiya couldn't read the words, but there were pictures in it. Of places, blue seas and green hills. Of roads that ran endlessly and gardens that had no walls. Saadiya couldn't stop looking at the pictures. They gave her yearning a greater edge, a sharper definition.

Now she felt a great desire to look at the pictures again. She closed the terrace door and went into her room. The doors had several latches and the windows were barred. Every night Zuleika, their servant, slept with her in this room. Before leaving the house, Saadiya locked the doors and closed the windows. In Arabipatnam, no one took chances.

She pulled her burkha on. Its black swirls hid all of her, except her eyes.

'I am going to Nadira's,' she told her grandmother and tip-toed out.

Late in the afternoon, the alley that led from her door to Nadira's was quiet. All the women were indoors. No man came this way; they were not allowed to. Saadiya looked around. There was no one. She took away the black fold of the cloth that covered her face and flung it on to her shoulder. Then she walked towards Nadira's house. The door was shut. Saadiya thought of the book behind the door and decided to wait. Nadira would be back soon, she thought. And as Saadiya stood there, she felt a rogue desire pull at her feet. If she walked down this alley and turned left, she would reach a common alley. The broader common alley in turn led to the road.

I'll go only as far as the common alley, she told herself. I'll rush back before anyone sees me. Men were allowed in the common alley and Vaapa would be furious if he knew that she had gone there all by herself.

Saadiya hurried down the alley and turned left. She peered into the common alley, which was deserted as well.

Where was everyone? What if she walked a few steps, just a few steps, peered at the road and rushed back? No one would know and she would be able to still that vagrant voice within her.

So Saadiya, whose freedom until then had encompassed just twenty feet by thirty feet, stepped into the common alley. Her heart beat fast and she felt her mouth go dry, but she couldn't turn back now. She walked on till she reached the road. Then she looked around her and gasped.

Life. Life in so many colours and shapes. Life that breathed and walked. Life that chewed and spat. Life that screamed and shouted. Life that mumbled and tumbled, hissed and crawled. Life that waited. Life that would never be hers.

Saadiya ran her tongue over her suddenly dry lips and looked skyward to feel the sea breeze on her uplifted face. The breeze caressed her cheeks, sending a clat of pleasure down her spine. Slowly she lowered her face and as she did so, her eyes encountered those of a young man's. He stood there leaning against a wall, flanked by two bicycles, staring at her with as much shock as she had felt at her first glimpse of the road.

Saadiya tugged at the cloth that covered her face. With horror she realized that her face was uncovered and visible to the world— and to the young man whose eyes lapped at the contours of its nudity. Saadiya felt shame drown her. With a muffled cry, she pulled the veil across her face and stumbled backwards.

She turned to run back to the narrow confines of the women's alley, and saw Zuleika enter the common alley. Zuleika stood there haggling with a chicken seller. When the man spotted her black-clad figure, he turned towards the wall so that she might pass.

Zuleika peered at the black-clad figure.

'Who is that?' she asked, walking towards her.

She asked again, 'Nadira, is that you? I thought Saadiya was with you?'

Saadiya stopped. There was no fleeing from Zuleika. There was no use, she knew. A glimmer of the sky, a lungful of life, a breath of escape…that was all she had dreamt of in this life. And now hope had turned its face to the wall, dangling the weight of carcasses in its hands.

A single act of trespass. Saadiya uncovering her face, Sethu looking at it. That was the extent of their trespass. No one else knew of this violation of ancient codes, and yet it was enough.

If Saadiya had veiled her face, Sethu would never have looked.

And Sethu, if he had known that it was expected of him, would have turned his face to the wall when Saadiya appeared before him, with her naked face and hungry eyes. But when Sethu saw the flush of shame colour Saadiya's features, he felt something kindle within him. A flame that lit itself from the blazing shame and warmed his insides. And Saadiya, who ought to have vested her hero with the face of Akbar Shah's second son, now had a face, a form to fill her vacant hours and fugitive dreams.

Karunam

ho amongst us does not know this emotion? Why, I don't even need to tell you what it is, when my eyebrows slant down at the ends, my eyes crinkle at the corners and my mouth droops. My breath moves from the cavity of the chest to the base of the spine. Do you see how my belly sinks and my shoulders droop?

Karunam. All of us have known sorrow some time or the other. Let me tell you a little story. A woman went to the Buddha, asking him to bring back to life her son who had just died. The Buddha said that if she could go to a house where death had not visited even once, and bring back a handful of mustard, he would bring her son back to life. So the woman set forth. She went to every home in her village. In one house, the mother had died, in another, an uncle. One family had lost a grandfather, another a baby. There wasn't a home that hadn't known death. Then the Buddha told her, we must accept death as part of our existence. There cannot be a life free of death. So it is with karunam.

It is everywhere. It is in the month of July, the month of karkitakam, when the relief of having got past the summer is over and the sky stretches a dull grey, like ashes flung over the face of the sun. The ground is wet and squelchy. The eaves drip, and so do the leaves. A relentless drip-drip. Clothes never dry, moss grows everywhere. Cupboards reek of damp and wetness prevails.

You can sense it when you shake a tender coconut and hold it to your ear. It is there in the lapping of coconut water as it slops this way and that between the curves of soft inner flesh…the fluid ways of sorrow.

You can hear it in the song of the karinkuyil as the notes soar into the skies. Why does the koel sing so sadly, you might ask. What sorrow could the sluttish, slovenly cuckoo who lays her eggs in the crow's nest and absolves herself of all responsibility have?

Capriciousness comes naturally to this creature which, even as a child, gathers the yet to be hatched eggs and crow-babies on to her back and tosses them out of the nest. Perhaps remorse is what the koel's song throbs with as it sits alone on the branch of a tree and ponders. A remorse for all that has been. For that, too, is karunam. Remorse.

Radha

Chris wears a grim look. I find him on the veranda, listening to a tape. I hear Uncle's voice. This chapter of Uncle's story has taken more than a week in its narration.

Uncle refused to meet Chris during the day. 'The light bleaches my imagination,' he said. 'I cannot think then; come when the sun is down.'

So it was in the early evening that Chris and I went to Uncle. Shyam disapproved. He showed his disapproval in many ways, but did not voice it. I wondered why. Usually he is very eloquent, especially when it comes to something he does not like. But this time he merely lets me know it. Every evening for a week now, he has been coming home before me. He calls me on the mobile and each time he has a different reason. 'So what time are you coming home? I am hungry.' 'Rani Oppol is bored.' 'Will you be coming in the next half hour? The SP and his wife have said they will drop in.' 'Isn't it over yet?' 'Rani Oppol was saying it isn't right for you to spend so much time in the Sahiv's company...'

And when I return, he's usually sitting in the living room with his mouth set and a drink at his side. He pretends not to see me and I say nothing, either. Two can play at this game. He may be daddy, but I refuse to be the trembling, penitent child.

Lately, though, I have been wondering about this game that Shyam is playing. It is as if he is waiting. But waiting for what? I try to put it out of my mind. I am learning to block Shyam and his moods from my thoughts.

Chris had asked me if I could transcribe Uncle's voice. 'I don't understand his accent too well, particularly when he uses Indian words. Would you? I could pay you by the page or hour…whatever you prefer,' he said.

'I'll do it,' I said, and smiled. 'But I am very slow. I haven't keyed in anything for a long time now. Once in a while, I help Uncle send emails and sometimes I write to a friend…and you don't have to pay me.'

Chris was unsure. 'But you can't do it for nothing.'

'I am doing it for Uncle,' I said. 'I'm sure he would like a copy of his story. I know that I would.'

That settled it. I began work, but kept it a secret.

Shyam would be furious if he knew. 'How dare he?' he would fume. 'Are you his secretary or what? If you are so keen to do secretarial work, why don't you do it for me?'

If he ever finds out, I have my answer ready. 'I don't want Uncle's words misinterpreted. Is that a crime?' I would ask. Shyam would not mind as much if he thought that I considered it an ordeal.

I discovered that I was enjoying the work. Some mornings, as I typed, I wondered if I could become a medical transcriptionist. There were courses that would teach me what I needed to know and I had heard that in some instances you were allowed to work from home…Shyam wouldn't be able to object to that. I felt the need to resume work consume me more than ever. When I had finished with these tapes, I would start inquiries in that direction, I told myself.

Every evening Uncle would talk into the tape recorder for a little while. Ever so often he would pause to chew his betel leaves. When it was almost dark, he would stop. 'This will do for now,' he would say. 'It's Malini's feeding time.'

Uncle talked about Malini as if she were a baby. But it was futile to try and force him. He would resist by clamming up. Malini would hop on her perch and whistle and shriek. She was always happy to see us leave. But she had at least stopped calling Chris names. She even let him scratch her head. 'She must like you,' Uncle said with a note of surprise. Malini usually pecked a piece of flesh out of anyone's hand if they dared try and make even the slightest overture towards her.

Shyam had had his finger quite badly injured once and as we

drove to the hospital, he had held his finger aloft and murmured, 'Like master, like bird…'

'What did you say?' I asked.

'Nothing. Just wondering why one needs a dog when you have a bird as vicious as her.'

'But I did tell you that she is very bad-tempered. Why did you have to thrust your finger into her cage?'

'I usually have a way with animals.' Shyam scowled. 'But this isn't a bird. This is a bloodthirsty ghoul.'

But Malini, like everyone else, seemed to have succumbed to Chris.

Chris looked pleased. 'She is such a feisty thing,' he said and continued to scratch Malini's head as she shut her eyes in enjoyment.

Chris and I would sit on the steps to the river for a while till night descended. We didn't talk much. It was enough to sit there soaking in the night sounds, wrapped by the darkness. It was an intimacy with a million nerve ends. And then I would go home with a want in me that threatened to take my life over.

'How long is this storytelling going to last?' Shyam demanded one day.

'I don't know,' I said. It was the truth. I wished it would never end. For as long as Uncle told his story, Chris was his captive.

'What is this? The Mahabharata? Why is he stretching it like one of those serials on television?' Shyam muttered.

Shyam was worried that he was losing money on Cottage No. 12. 'You realize that I thought it would be off season when I offered the cottage, don't you? But the season has been better than ever,' he said. 'We are having to refuse some bookings and turn people away. I don't like doing that.'

I shrugged. 'You know Uncle. He never says why he does what he does. He has his reasons, I suppose.'

It was not like Uncle to be difficult. I could see that this was hard for him. All his life Uncle had played characters whose actions were defined for him. Here he had to be both the creator and the actor, and it was his own history, his life, he was laying bare.

'What is wrong?' I ask Chris.

He scratches his chin. 'I was listening to the recordings of the past few days. I am not sure how much is true and how much he is making up.'

I see my printouts on the table. Every evening I take home the tape and bring it back the next evening with the transcript printed out.

'For one,' Chris says, picking up a page, 'there is the cycle ride. The burial urns, the brahmin villagers who eat pork. What is their relevance?'

I am not surprised by his bewilderment. I had listened to that episode and wondered too. What did it have to do with Uncle?

Later that night, it had occurred to me. Then everything fell into place.

Once again Uncle was creating an atmosphere where the real tussled with the unreal. If Sethu had met Saadiya after an insipid and boring cycle ride, the impact of that meeting would not have been so forceful or even poignant. Arabipatnam would have been just another Muslim settlement to him. But the unreality of the real world he passed through gave Arabipatnam a magic edge. It was an enchanted place, and Saadiya was the princess trapped there. I explain this to Chris. 'Do you see it?' I ask.

Chris crinkles his eyes. He has acquired a tan in a week's time and the ruddiness of his skin makes his eyes a deeper green. 'You have beautiful eyes,' I say.

He grins. 'I thought I was supposed to say that.'

I flush and look away, then take a deep breath and say, 'Do you understand what I am saying?'

'Not really. Why would he do it?'

'Actually, he's again using a technique from his art,' I say. 'Do you want me to explain it to you?' I hesitate to volunteer information. I worry that I am beginning to sound like I am lecturing him.

'Do you mind if I record this as well?' He inserts a new tape into the machine.

'There is a smallish episode in the Mahabharata. It is rather insignificant in the scope of the whole epic, but it is very popular in kathakali. It's called Baka Vadham. Which means the killing of Baka.

'Baka was this evil demon who was terrorizing a brahmin village. The villagers, who were incapable of defending themselves, pleaded with him to leave them alone. Baka agreed on one condition: every day a family would send him a cartload of food and the cart driver and the bullocks that pulled the cart as his dinner.

'Now, the Pandavas, who were in exile then, arrived at this village and were offered shelter. One evening, they came home from their wanderings to discover the host family in mourning. It was their turn to send the food and a member of their family to Baka. The family wept as each one of the male members offered to go. Bheema then stepped forward and said he would be the cart driver. Bheema, if you remember, was the strongest of the Pandavas, with a great love for food and battle.

'Now the libretto has a description of Bheema's journey into the forest that Baka lived in.

'Bheema hears the howling of jackals and the screeching of vultures. When he hears these ugly and terrifying sounds, he feels as if the animals are worshipping the demon. Bheema walks on and hears maniacal laughter and the blood-chilling shrieks of ghouls and other evil creatures. A breeze blows and it bears the stench of death, of putrefied human remains. Then Bheema sees shreds of the sacred thread that brahmin men wear and is even more furious.

'My point is, if the libretto didn't include such a lead up, then the Bheema–Baka battle would be an anticlimax.'

Chris whistles softly. 'All right. I buy that. But there is something else you must listen to...'

My heart skips a beat. I think of what he had said one night as we sat by the river. 'Sometimes I abandon a trail halfway through. Either the subject fails to hold me, or I discover that I have made a mistake and my subject is a load of bull.'

I worry now. Will he think Uncle is not worth the effort?

It is a warm evening. I lift my hair away from my face. I see his eyes cup my breasts and I straighten abruptly.

'May I use your bathroom?' I ask to break the mood.

'Here, put these flip-flops on,' he says, kicking his rubber sandals off. 'I just had a shower and the whole floor is wet.'

I step into them. My feet draw in the warmth of his. I examine the shelf in the bathroom. I sniff his cologne and touch his toothbrush. I bury my face in his towel and breathe in his scent. Then I see myself in the mirror. What am I doing?

The tape comes alive: '*Saadiya loved that phrase. It represented all that she felt was true of life. Life demands of us that we have a Plank of Avidity. How can we have more if we don't raise our expectations? How can we be content with just what we have and know?'*

I feel a question gather on my brow. 'So what about it?' I ask.

Chris runs a hand over his face. He looks at me and asks, 'Has he travelled much?'

I nod.

'What does that mean? A yes or a no?'

Before I can react, he suddenly leans forward and touches my hand. 'Hey, I didn't mean to snap. I really don't know what's got into me...' He drops his head in his hands.

'It's all right,' I say. I am willing to forgive him his surliness. What is this magic he is weaving around me?

He looks up. 'That phrase...Plank of Avidity. Do you know where I came across it first? At the Viking Museum in Roskilde in Denmark.' His voice is quiet.

I don't know what to say. 'He's travelled a great deal,' I say.

Chris smiles. 'You think I am being impatient, don't you? It is his story. I should let him tell it the way he chooses to. Besides...' He pauses.

'Besides, what?'

'Besides, I get to spend time with you.'

I look away. I feel him near me. How did he get here?

I step back. He watches me.

'Uncle wanted to know if you would like to go to a performance tomorrow,' I say. 'He will resume his story the day after tomorrow,' I add.

He is amused by my embarrassment. He leans forward and with his finger gently caresses my cheek. 'What are you scared of? I will go, but only if you go too.'

I know I should object. Say something to disabuse any notion he may have of our relationship developing into something else. Instead, I ask, 'Is it the dance or me you want to see?'

He gazes at me with his green eyes and says, 'What do you think?'

It is a little past seven when I walk towards Chris's cottage. The moon in the night sky is bright enough, despite its blurred edges. I look at myself.

For the hundredth time this evening, I wonder if I should have worn something else.

I had looked at myself in the mirror. I had told myself that I was going for a performance and it would be insulting to the art and the artist if I were to appear in casual clothes. As if his performance was not worth the effort. But I also knew that I was dressing up for him. The kohl in my eyes, the flowers in my hair, the varnish on my nails, the perfume at my pulse points, the sari draped low to reveal the curve of my waist...I wanted him to look at me.

As I near his cottage, I hear music. What is he listening to, I wonder. The music pauses and begins again.

It is Chris playing.

I hurry. I climb the steps to his cottage carefully, quietly, so he will not know I am there. Then I sit on the veranda, listening.

I know nothing about western classical music, but I know when I respond to a piece of music. I feel that stirring now. As if all that lies buried in me is aching to be drawn out.

I close my eyes and let the music wash over me. I think of what Chris said on his first night here. 'Baggage! None of us is free of it.'

I have my baggage too.

How old was I? Twenty-two. So young, so full of adult possibilities, and so determined to live my way. I was ripe and ready to fall in love; he was a much older man, married and a senior manager in the company where I worked. Normally, we would never have met. I was a trainee in the HR department and he a senior technical expert. But there was a seminar organized by the HR department and then, in the evening, a cocktail party. He was there and I had lots to drink and as banter moved to innuendoes, I saw that he was an attractive man. I was flattered by his attention and charmed by his conversation. I let myself yield.

Is that what falling in love is? To concede, to relinquish, to be pliant, to comply, to give way. I did all that, knowing that he was a married man and that 'my wife and I have a marriage only in name' was the oldest and most banal cliché ever used.

I was too young and too yielding to realize that I made a perfect playmate and would never be more. For two years, he and I were lovers. 'As soon as my son leaves home, I'll get a divorce,' he said, and I believed him. My whole life stretched ahead of me. What was a year or two, I asked myself.

I believed him because he seemed to be as much in love with me as I was with him. So much so that he wanted to flaunt it. There was nothing hole-in-the-corner or clandestine about our relationship. We did everything that other couples did.

We went to pubs and restaurants. It didn't matter that we might meet people we knew. He would fork morsels from his plate into my mouth and sip from my glass and he did it as if he had every right to do so. I revelled in it. He took me to meet his friends and in their homes he would slip his hand into mine and sometimes absently twirl a lock of my hair around his finger. When we went to open-air concerts, he would lean against the car and hold me cradled to his chest. He kissed me in the lift and pushed the car seat back and made love to me in his car.

And always I knew that rush, the exhilaration that came of defiance. I was doing in adult terms what I had done as an adolescent: sneaking out of the all-girls' boarding school for a wind-in-the-hair bike ride with a boy I had met. Smoking grass and necking in movie theatres. But this is the man I love, I told myself and yielded even more.

We held nothing back. He told me his fantasies and I complied. Perhaps the compliance was what made it so exciting. He had my body fine-tuned to a fever of sexual energy and he evoked an appetite that seemed insatiable. He knew how to make love in so many different ways, masterful and tender at the same time. And since he knew that it wouldn't be for ever, he crammed a lifetime's loving into as many stolen moments as possible.

Then his wife came to see me. Perhaps she had done this before. At first she was very brisk and matter-of-fact about it, as if she were dealing with a broken sewer pipe: there would be some stench and mess involved, but it could be fixed. 'You don't think this is the first time, do you?'

I couldn't meet her eyes. She was so elegant, and I felt like a gauche teenager. 'He loves me. And I him.' I dared her to defy me.

She bit her lip. I glanced at her. She wasn't angry, not even unhappy, only utterly, desperately hopeless. 'He seems to choose younger and younger girls. What do you see in him? Don't ruin your life for him. What did he say—as soon as my son leaves home, I'll get a divorce?'

I flushed.

'I thought as much. Ask him, which son? The fifteen-year-old, the eleven-year-old, or the five-year-old?'

I felt a sob grow in me. I hadn't known about the younger children.

'I know he hasn't mentioned the younger boys to you. That, too, is part of the pattern. I pity him. It is as if he needs to redeem himself after each child is born. Steal back his youth, perhaps. I don't know. He is not a bad man, only weak, and he will never leave me. He needs me...and I him. He is the father of my children, you see.'

I did not hear what she was saying. All I knew was that I wanted to go home. I wanted to hide myself in a place where there was none of this deceit or compromise. I felt betrayed. I felt used. I felt foolish. More than anything else, I knew that if I stayed I would find a way to excuse his lies and continue to be his playmate. That was the measure of how much I had yielded to him.

For days, I lay in bed. Even getting up seemed an effort. I sank into lethargy—or was it hopelessness? What was there for me to wake up to? Even thinking was an effort. Then I discovered that I was pregnant. I didn't really have an option. I would have to have an abortion. There was nothing else to be done. I slipped a gold band around my ring finger and a black-bead-and-gold chain around my neck and smeared the parting in my hair with the redness of sindoor. I met the eyes of the doctor as fearlessly as I could, and said, 'I cannot have this baby; my husband and I are separated.'

'Are you sure?' she asked. 'It is a first pregnancy, and I would advise against termination. Have you asked yourself if this baby might help you reconcile with your husband?'

'No, that will not happen,' I said. 'He is with another woman now.'

'In that case...'

So I wiped out all traces of a love that was not meant to be, and went home.

When Shyam was brought forth as husband material, I hesitated. Then my father said, 'I have heard some rather disconcerting things about you. Are you determined to ruin my good name?'

I wondered what he had heard. I didn't care. It wasn't as if my father was of unimpeachable character. But I knew that if I didn't tie myself to Shyam, I would in a weak moment go back to my lover. I agreed.

I had saved my pride and kept my integrity. I could sleep again without seeing the image of his wife, with her hopeless eyes and the resignation in her voice. Three months later, I knew I had made a mistake, but I buried the thought in my mind. There it lay and turned into a kernel of dissatisfaction, corroding and sucking the marrow out of my life. Why had I said yes to this marriage? To living with a man merely because I longed to flee from my own conscience?

Again I sank into apathy. Days dragged into years and I was ensconced in my lethargy. What was there to look forward to?

'Isn't it time you had a child?' Rani Oppol asked in our second year of marriage.

I shrugged. 'We will have one when we are ready,' I said.

'There is no saying with these things. You don't know if you can get pregnant unless you get pregnant.'

I wondered if I should tell her. But I bit back my retort.

'Isn't it time we had a child?' Shyam said a couple of years later.

I thought a child might bridge the distance between us. It would fill our lives. I would welcome a child, I thought.

But I wouldn't get pregnant.

So we went to doctors. For some months it was another routine. 'Don't think about it and it will happen,' the doctors said.

So I didn't think about it. But I didn't get pregnant.

Then, one day, we went to visit Rani Oppol. Their neighbours, a brahmin family from Palakkad, were conducting a seemantham for their daughter. I would be expected to go along, I thought, so I wore a silk sari and put some jewellery on. It was a festive occasion, after all: the celebration of a pregnancy coming close to full term.

Then Rani Oppol said, 'I don't think you should come with us. You know how people are; they think a married woman who hasn't had children for so long is a macchi. They won't like it. It is inauspicious to have a barren woman at such functions...the evil eye, etc.'

I didn't say anything. All I knew was a freezing within.

Now, as I hear Chris's music, I feel a thawing. I cannot bear to bury the thought again. I wish to be free of it. I do not wish to wake up one morning twenty years from now and ask myself: how could you have thrown your chance of happiness away?

The notes fill my ears as I walk through the carefully preserved fence of propriety. If there is a thought that goes with me, it is only sorrow for what could have been.

I stand at the door. Chris sees me but does not stop. I watch him as he coaxes the instrument to be his.

He is sitting on a chair. The instrument is wedged ever so gently between his knees; its neck rests against his shoulder. His hands move, his left hand searching, the right hand gleaning. They have become one, the instrument yielding to his body, his touch.

I see myself in his arms. I am the cello. It is me he is caressing. It is I who am responding.

The intensity of my desire shocks me. I close my eyes to shut out the image.

The music stops abruptly. I open my eyes. He keeps the cello aside. He continues to sit on the chair with his legs still slightly splayed, his eyes intense. The music hangs in the air.

He looks at me.

I walk towards him.

Shyam

I have a Rotary Club meeting to go to. We intend to conduct a project discussion. There are three projects under consideration and tonight we will decide which one it is to be. I wish Radha would go with me. All the other office bearers will bring their wives. I like looking at Radha when she is with a group of women. My Radha shines.

When we are out together in company, I watch her. I see the way she tilts her chin forward when she is listening, and the way she throws her head back as she laughs. I see her cover her mouth with her hand and toss her hair from her face. And I know again that sense of pride. She is mine. I see a burst of admiration in the eyes of the other men and a wave of envy on the women's faces. My Radha shines.

'Are you sure you are not coming?' I ask.

'No, I told you that I am going out with Uncle,' she says. I read the irritation in her voice.

'Is the Sahiv going too?'

'I think so. Uncle thinks it will help Chris to write his piece better if he were to see a few performances.'

'I see.' But I don't. I understand why Chris has to see kathakali being performed. What I don't is why Radha has to go along. I think of my mother's stock of sayings: sesame seeds need to soak in the sun so that they yield more oil, but why is the silly beetle doing the same?

'What are you muttering?' Radha asks.

'I was just wondering, won't you be tired if you stay up late? You know that we have to attend the SP's daughter's wedding tomorrow, don't you?' I try again to dissuade her.

She frowns. 'It isn't the first time I have stayed up late. For heaven's sake, what's wrong now? No one's going to gossip, if that's what is worrying you.'

It hadn't occurred to me, but now that she's put the thought in my head, I do worry.

'If you need me to pick you up, just call and I'll come,' I say.

She looks at me for a moment. I don't understand the import of that look; is it sorrow? But why?

'No, I'll be fine.' She touches my elbow. 'Uncle has booked a taxi. He will drop me back.'

I smile. Perhaps everything will be fine, after all.

I watch her as she fastens her earrings. She is even more beautiful tonight. She is my Syamantaka gem, I think. But I dare not tell her. She will laugh at me and ask, 'Syamantaka gem? What do you know of that?'

Both Radha and Uncle prefer to believe that I know little or nothing of mythology, or anything that makes an attempt to appeal to the unconscious. That is their realm and they guard it fiercely. In their minds they have divided the world into two: those who belong and those who don't. As far as they are concerned, I am a businessman and the only music I hear is the ringing of cash registers, the only literature I read is the writing on currency notes; my favourite paintings are stacks of industrial chimneys and my sense of rhythm is derived from the grinding of cogs and wheels. I don't belong in their world and they prefer that I don't try and trespass.

When we were first married, I tried to join a discussion that Uncle and Radha were having about a character in the Ramayana. They stared at me as if I had said something really stupid. Then Uncle sniggered and Radha said, 'Don't be foolish. It isn't like that.'

What isn't like that, I wanted to demand. Mythology is like poetry. It is fashioned by its telling. Uncle and you talk about the importance of interpretation, but you are such snobs. I may not be an artist or an art connoisseur, but that doesn't make my opinions invalid. Are you saying that you think only those steeped in art ought to be allowed to express their views? And that your readings are acceptable and mine foolish? But I was intimidated by the newness of our relationship and held my anger back.

So, how then can I tell Radha that she is my Syamantaka gem, 'yielding daily eight loads of gold and dispelling all fear of portents, wild beasts, fire, robbers and famine'? When you are with me, I want to tell her, I am the sun wearing a garland of light.

Instead I say, 'Why don't you ever dress like this when we go for dinner at the Club? Then all you wear are your stiff khadi kurtas. I hate them; they remind me of those activist women burning with vitriol and a cause. Women should wear silk, jewellery and flowers in their hair.'

She is silent.

I see the surprise in Shashi's eyes when he opens the door for her. And admiration, too.

'Madam is going for a kathakali performance. Which is why she is all dressed up,' I say. He grins.

'I'll drive. You can go home,' I add.

Radha snarls at me as soon as I start the car. 'What do you mean, all dressed up? You make it sound as if I am doing something extraordinary. Can't I wear a silk sari without your having to discuss it with the driver?'

I wonder why she is so upset. What did I say?

I stop at Uncle's gate. 'Are you sure the taxi has been booked?

Do you want me to check?' I ask.

'Don't fuss,' she says, getting out.

'Radha,' I begin.

'What?'

'Nothing. Have a good time.' I wait for Uncle to open his door and for Radha to step inside. Then I reverse and drive away.

Her perfume lingers in the car. I know that sense of loss again. Why is it that my hold over Radha remains so ephemeral, even after eight years of marriage? Why can't I reach into the substance of her being? Is it because she doesn't let me?

My father and Radha's mother, Gowri, were cousins. They grew up in the same house. When my father turned eighteen, he joined the army. He survived two wars and then, when I was nine years old, he was killed in a freak road accident. A lorry carrying a load of iron pipes took a curve too fast. One of the pipes bulleted out and knocked my father off his scooter into the path of a bus. I lost a father and acquired an unshakeable belief in destiny.

My mother didn't have a family to turn to, so we went to my father's house, where my grandmother still lived. That the house would go to Gowri ammayi when my grandmother died was understood, but she didn't need the house. She had married well. So we continued to live there even after my grandmother died. Gowri ammayi persuaded her husband to help us out. We wanted for nothing but self-respect.

My elder sister, Rani, was sixteen. A relative's son who worked in the railways married her. All the money we had received on my father's death was spent on her wedding.

My father had had great hopes for me. My son will be a doctor or an engineer, he used to say. Neither my mother nor I dared ask Gowri ammayi's husband for money to fund an education in a professional college. So I acquired a BA in economics and found myself a job in sales. We no longer needed his handouts.

When I was paid my first salary, I bought him a shirt. I took it to his house.

I heard him tell my aunt, 'Your cousin's chekkan is here.'

I flinched. Chekkan. Boy. I am a grown-up now, I wanted to tell him.

'What is this?' he asked, peering at the package I offered him.

'A shirt. I was paid early this week and I wanted to buy you something with the money.'

'You must learn to spend wisely; then you won't have to depend on others,' he said. 'Gowri, see what this chekkan has brought me.'

Why couldn't he use my name?

I never saw him wear that shirt.

I was good at my job, and ambitious. I took a management degree from the open university and switched jobs.

My mother saw that my prospects were bright and brought forth the subject of marriage. 'What are you waiting for?'

'How old is Radha?' I asked.

'Radha? What has she got to do with your marriage? I hope you are not nurturing any desire of marrying her.' My mother sounded querulous.

'Why not? What is wrong with me?'

'Don't be foolish. Only a child cries for the moon.'

'I am sure Gowri ammayi will agree,' I said.

'She will, but he won't. He expects his daughter to make a brilliant marriage into a family that will match them in status and wealth. We are nobodies. We don't even have a house of our own.'

I kept quiet. It was true. We had nothing to call our own, not even this roof over our head.

The next time she talked about marriage, I said, 'Amma, I will get married only when we have a house of our own.'

Then I received a letter from my mother. It said: Take two days off and come home immediately.

I was working in Trivandrum in those days. I wondered what it was about, but I went. Besides, I had news of my own. I had a letter of contract from a trading firm in Dubai. I was finally going to be making serious money. I was finally going to be somebody.

'Your uncle will be here by about ten to see you,' my mother said, even as I walked in. She looked fraught with anxiety. What could be wrong? Was he planning to sell the house?

'What's wrong?'

'Wrong?' Her face broke into a smile. 'It is good news. He came with a proposal of marriage last week.'

'Didn't you tell him that I don't plan to get married yet?'

'Wait till you hear who the girl is...It is Radha.'

My mother hustled and bustled. She wrung her hands and wiped her face with the end of her sari. She clucked and nodded, smiled and frowned, and was in a state of nervous excitement.

'Fetch me a cup of tea,' my uncle said, not bothering to hide his annoyance.

I was leaning against the wall. I straightened and I don't know how, but I found the courage to say, 'I don't want you to use that tone of voice to my mother, ever.'

He looked at me as if he was seeing me for the first time. I wasn't any more the chekkan he could dismiss with a tilt of his chin. I was thirty-one years of age, with two degrees and soon, a job in Dubai.

'Oh, I didn't mean it that way. She is like my younger sister,' he said slowly.

'You wouldn't ever talk in that tone to your sister if you had one. My mother is not your maid...I know that you took us in when we had no one else. You didn't have to. We are your relatives only by marriage. You have my gratitude, and hers, for that. But it doesn't give you the right to talk down to her or me.'

'Shyam,' he said. How easily he spoke my name now. 'Shyam, if I thought you were not my social equals, would I come here to offer you my daughter in marriage?' He came to stand near me. But his gaze was shifty.

I had known as soon as my mother gave me the news that something was wrong. Suddenly Radha was not the moon but the mango ripe for plucking.

I sat down then. I had never done this before—sit with him. I was expected to stand or perch on a step. Only equals sat down with each other. He stared for a moment and I saw him try and mask his displeasure.

'Is there a problem with her horoscope?' I asked.

'No, no, her horoscope is very good and it matched very well with yours.'

'Does she have a disease then? Leucoderma, or maybe something is wrong with her uterus?'

'What a thing to say! She is perfectly healthy.'

'Then she must be pregnant,' I said. My voice sounded cold to my own ears.

'Shyam, what is wrong with you? How dare you be insolent? To insult your own uncle who has been so kind to us...' my mother's horrified voice burst from the doorway. The cups on the tray shook with the force of her emotions.

'Amma,' I said. 'I have to know why I, a nobody with not even a house of my own, am being asked to marry Radha who you said would make a brilliant marriage. We are not in their league, you said. So why is it different now? I am sure it is not because they have realized that I may not be their equal in status or wealth, but am still the best man for Radha.'

'Let me talk to him,' Radha's father said.

My mother left us alone. He took the cup of tea and sipped it. He drew out a pack of cigarettes and after a moment's hesitation offered it to me. 'Would you care to smoke one?'

'No,' I said. I looked away. I felt deeply ashamed. He was willing to let me wipe my feet on him. He had no pride left, and I was still trampling him into the ground.

'What is wrong?' I asked as gently as I could.

'She's been involved with a man.'

'So why don't you get them married?'

He wiped his face with a handkerchief. 'I wish it was that simple. He is a married man with three children. His wife wrote to me saying, take your daughter away before he ruins her life and she my family. Knowing this, how can I delay her marriage?'

'So you are afraid to thrust soiled goods on to somebody else and decided to come to me. Shyam will do what we ask, because he is bound to us by a debt of gratitude—is that what you thought?'

My mouth tasted bitter. Radha would be mine because no one else would have her.

'Don't say that. It was an innocent relationship. A young girl's fascination for an older man.'

I could see he thought otherwise, but hoped I wouldn't.

'You have to save my reputation, my standing in society,' he pleaded. 'Shyam, you are my lone hope.'

So much for innocence, I thought. I stood up. 'You have to know something. I have always been in love with Radha. My mother said I shouldn't have foolish dreams. But I knew that she was destined to be mine. It doesn't matter to me that she had a relationship with another man. I shall be happy to marry her. But will she?'

'She will do as I tell her to,' he said.

'I have a job offer from Dubai,' I said. 'I will have to leave soon, so you must conduct the wedding before that.' I was suddenly afraid. What if someone else more suitable than me turned up?

'Will she be able to go with you?' he asked.

'Not immediately. Maybe later.'

'Oh,' he said. He looked away, unable to meet my eyes. 'Why not do something here? Young wives shouldn't be left alone.'

He took my hands in his. 'All that I own is hers, and therefore yours,' he said.

'Is that a bribe?'

'Shyam, you are my son,' he said.

'In which case, I would like you to advance me some money. I have an idea for a business venture. But I will pay you back every rupee with interest,' I said. Then I added, 'But there is one thing you must promise me. That you will never ever mention to Radha what transpired here today. I don't want her to know that I know about her past. Or that you put up the money for me to start a business.'

My mother approved of the alliance thoroughly. Only Rani Oppol wasn't so welcoming. She was suspicious that I had been forced to agree. 'Are you sure this is what you want?' she said when the marriage was fixed.

I smiled at her. She was so protective of me. 'Don't worry. I am sure.'

'You can get any girl you want. You don't have to be saddled with her just because we owe her father a debt of gratitude.'

'I like her. I like her very much, Oppol,' I said. I wouldn't dare use a word like love with Oppol. She wouldn't like it, I knew instinctively.

On our wedding night, Radha waited for me in our nuptial chamber with a face that seemed hewn out of stone.

'Why do you look so serious?' I tried to joke.

'I am not a virgin,' she said. 'I want you to know that I have had sex.'

I tried not to flinch and instead, peeled a banana. The bedside table was laden with the mandatory first-night accessories. My aunt saw too many movies, I thought. A plate of fruit, incense sticks, a glass of milk, and the bed draped with flowers.

'All this is a farce,' she said, sweeping a string of flowers away.

I offered the fruit to her. 'Have a banana,' I said.

She stared at me. 'Do you think this is a joke?'

'No, I don't,' I said. I had thought very carefully about this. I knew Radha well enough to deduce that she would want to confess to me, bare her soul before we went any further. I knew that to affect nonchalance was the only way to play down the significance of her confession. 'It doesn't matter. I have had sex, too. I have slept with other women, too.'

'Did my father offer you money to marry me?'

I looked at her carefully. 'You are insulting me,' I said quietly. I wouldn't allow her to provoke a quarrel. Not tonight. 'I don't need to be paid to marry you. Don't you know how beautiful you are?'

She wouldn't meet my gaze.

'But why did you marry me? You don't seem very pleased with this marriage,' I said.

She stared at the floor. 'I didn't know what else to do,' she said, and wept.

I did not know what to say. Perhaps I should have told her that I loved her. That I had always been in love with her. That it didn't matter what she had done before, what counted was what we made of our life together.

I did the husbandly thing. I made love to her and she let me do so without protest. When she responded to my touch and I knew that she was trying to block a memory, I closed my mind to it. That was then. This is now. You are mine, I thought as my hips locked with hers and my mouth sought hers.

I lie in bed, on my back. It is a quarter to eleven. Where is Radha? I look across at her bedside table, where a book lies face down. It has the picture of a woman sitting inside a train compartment. I turn it over and read the blurb on the back: 'The story of a woman's search for strength and independence...' I fling the book down. Is that what it's all about, the midnight wanderings and the hours closeted with the Sahiv?

I insert a CD in the player. A.R. Rehman's *Jana gana mana*...Radha dislikes most of the music that I listen to. She thinks my tastes are plebeian. She thinks it is disgraceful that I enjoy Baywatch and WWF. 'How can you even bear to watch?' she says incredulously. 'It is so unreal. Do you think lifeguards look like that? As for those wrestling matches, everything about them is make-believe!'

I think it is she who is living in an unreal world with her *F.R.I.E.N.D.S* and *Whose Line Is It Anyway?* What is it that the host, the fat man Drew Carey, says about the show…Where the points don't matter! That's what all her preferences are about. Things that don't matter.

But she couldn't fault Rehman, I had thought.

'He's got all the best names roped in, listen to this,' I had said, playing the song for her.

She listened for a few minutes and then rose to go.

'Why? Don't you like it?'

'It's too clever by half. How can you stand him?' She wrinkled her nose.

'He is brilliant. He scored the music for a London musical. Andrew Lloyd Webber's *Bombay Dreams*.'

'So?'

'The whole world thinks he is terrific.'

'That doesn't mean anything to me.'

So now I listen to the music I like either in the car, or when I am alone at home.

The clock strikes. It is half past eleven. I wonder if I should talk to the SP about Chris. Some years ago, a young Polish woman came to study with Uncle. She was his private student and he seemed to be getting rather too fond of her. I don't think the old man felt any passion, but he seemed to have a great deal of affection for her. I wouldn't have intervened but for the fact that the piece of land he lives on is worth a goldmine. When he dies, it will be Radha's. I don't want anything jeopardizing her inheritance. So I dropped into the SP's office and had a word with him and he saw to it that the woman's visa was not renewed.

I hear a car. She is back. I sit up. Then I lie down again, turn the light off and pretend to be asleep.

Uncle

The night scents fill the air. I walk slowly, humming *Sukhamo nee devi*...Are you well, my mistress? Hanuman's address to Sita when he meets her by accident many years after she has been banished from the kingdom. The words of that padam have always brought tears to my eyes, but tonight I hear the words in my head and I know they are for Maya.

For the past ten years, Maya has telephoned me every second and fourth Tuesday of the month at a quarter to eight. Her husband has a bridge game then and she has the house to herself. We speak to each other as if we are together in the same room. In the last ten years we have arrived at an ease of conversation that I have never known with anyone else. She tells me it is the same for her.

When Maya called earlier today, I decided that I would tell her about Radha and Chris and what was brewing between them. 'What do you think?' I asked.

'I don't know, Koman. Who is to tell? They are both old enough to know what they are doing, and its consequences. Like us, Koman. We knew, didn't we?'

'I worry that Radha will let it languish in her thoughts and not do anything about it.'

'Koman, you sound as if you want her to commit adultery. It is not an easy situation to be in.'

'Maya, you have to see Radha. I cannot believe the change in her. For the first time in many years she looks like she has found a reason to go on.'

'Why doesn't she divorce him then? It isn't as though they have children.'

'Shyam isn't a bad man. He can't be faulted as a husband. But I can see that Radha isn't happy with him. To divorce him because he bores her—what court of law would hear of it?'

'They have a phrase for boredom. Irreconcilable differences.'

'I don't know, Maya, I don't know where the three of them are heading.'

'Koman, I know you love her very much. But it is her life. You cannot live her life,' Maya said, and I knew she was right.

Then Maya said what I had hoped to hear her say seven years ago. 'Koman, I would like to see you,' she said.

I could hear the need in her voice. I would have liked to see her, too.

But I knew a stab of fear as well. To start everything all over again: did I have the courage? Did I have the stamina?

I tried to bridle her yearning. 'Maya,' I said. 'I know it's been very long since we met. But I seldom travel these days.'

'I will come to you. I just need to be with you,' she said and her voice broke. 'Just for a few days.' I heard the plea in her voice. 'Don't make me beg, Koman. Allow me that much dignity.'

I was silent. What was I doing to her, I asked myself. This was Maya. This was the woman I had loved for the last ten years. I smiled into the phone. 'Then come. You know that I would like you always by my side.'

What have I done? I wonder.

I think of what Shyam said to me a few months after he and Radha were married. 'I have always believed that if you want something badly enough and you wait long enough, it will come to you. I always knew that Radha would be my wife. I was prepared to wait and so it happened.'

Is he a wise man or an incredible fool, I had wondered. Then curious, I asked, 'But does it feel the same? Don't you think the waiting ruins the dream?'

'What do you mean?' He shot me an aggrieved look. 'I feel the same way about Radha as I did nine years ago.'

'You are fortunate,' I said, 'to be able to preserve your dream as you dreamt it, to want it despite all the years of waiting.'

I know that my dreams have acquired a blurred edge with all the ands and buts I have been forced to make place for.

I had expected to find Radha and Chris in the lobby. But it was empty, so I decided to walk to Chris's cottage.

Radha looked beautiful when she walked in earlier this evening. I had looked at the vision she made and said, 'You should dress like this more often.'

Radha made a face. 'Not you too, Uncle. What is wrong with men? Why do they so enjoy seeing a woman in silk? I really don't understand.'

I propelled her towards a mirror that hung in my bedroom. 'Look at yourself,' I said. She smoothened the pleats of her sari.

I smiled. 'I think it is because men like to think that women have made an effort to please them. It shows, when you wear silk and jewellery and flowers in your hair. I love flowers in a woman's hair.'

'For an old man you are very romantic,' Radha teased.

'I am not old,' I said. 'I am only sixty-four. That's not old.' I looked at myself in the mirror. I still had all my hair and most of my teeth. My face wasn't lined, except for a few lines near my eyes and mouth. My flesh hadn't sagged, nor were my muscles loose. 'Do I look old, Radha?' I asked.

'There, I knew it. You are vain.'

I pinched her cheek. 'You are very happy tonight.'

'I am happy,' she said, as though it had just occurred to her.

'Good.' I walked back to the veranda. 'It pleases me. Now listen, I am expecting a call. So why don't you go ahead and wait for me with Chris? Remind him to bring his video camera. And do me a favour. Tell him a little about Kalamandalam Gopalakrishnan, who he is and why it will be a treat to watch his vesham.'

The moon has gone behind a cloud. I look at the sky. Will it rain? Where are these two? Then I see them. Radha and Chris. Wrapped in each other in a tableau of intimacy.

He is sitting on a chair and she stands between his legs, facing him. The pallu of her sari lies over his knees and trails on the floor and over his instrument. He buries his face in her midriff, and his hands splay over her buttocks, gathering her closer to him. She throws her head back and I see her parted lips and the shuddering of her body. I see her hands plough his hair...

My breath catches in my throat. I stand there, unable to move away or even shut my eyes. I know I should, but I can't. My feet are like stone. I have never seen a man and a woman so completely drawn into each other's need.

Then I know I have.

In Uttara Swayamvaram, there is a scene that nobody attaches much importance to. It is a love scene like many others that speckle kathakali librettos. But tonight I understand what the scene is truly about.

Duryodhana, the cruel Kaurava prince, and his wife Bhanumati are in a beautiful garden. It is night. The combination of the beauty of the moment and the loveliness of his wife arouses in Duryodhana a great desire to make love to her. He turns to her with the nakedness of his desire showing. Kalyani, he tells her, gazing at the fullness and perfection of her breasts and letting his eyes rake the curves of her body, I can't think of a more perfect place or time to make love to you.

Bhanumati doesn't act coy or hide the intensity of her longing, either. I feel the arrows of desire, she tells him. We are all alone here. And I am yours. Can't you see how much I long for you? Bees, they say, will suck nectar from even half-open buds; why are you waiting, my beloved? Don't you see how much I thirst to drink deep of your lips, to feel you against me? Hold me...make love to me.

The completeness of desire. Chris and Radha. I feel humbled by the intensity of their intimacy.

I walk away to a little bench under a tree. I sit there and try to collect my thoughts. What are you doing, Radha? I am worried. Do you realize what you are starting here?

I walk back to the cottage. I cough and shuffle my feet to announce my arrival. They fall apart, hurled separate by my presence.

I do not step in. 'We should be going.'

They look at each other. Did he see us, their eyes ask.

I get into the front of the car so they can sit together at the back. There is enough electricity between them to light up the entire town.

I do not know what they will take in of the performance. My mind, too, is full of Maya.

I do not like open endings. There is nothing clear-cut about their relationship. It occurs to me that there is nothing definite about Maya's and mine, either.

I feel a great fear grow in me. What will happen to this love?

Then I think, I will tell them of another time and another love. I will tell them about Seth and Saadiya, and about love's consequences.

1938–1940
The Weight of a Glance

I, Saadiya, good girl, descendant of the Sahabbakal, descendant of the incomparable Malik, descendant of the leader of Kahirs, with the purest of Arab blood in my veins, lie here felled by the weight of a glance.

Where does it come from? This pain, this torment. I feel it now as it rises again to clutch me. Twin metal claws that extend from behind my spine and embrace my innards, smashing my resolve not to scream, ripping my flesh, pulling my hip bones apart. I bite my lips as the pain poles into me.

I am all alone in this room that is heavy with the reek of disinfectant and the darkness of blood effused and screams spilled. All of it has seeped into these walls, I know. I can smell it like I can smell my fear. I wish they were at my side—my sisters, Ummama and Zuleika. They would have stroked my brow, wiped the sweat off my face, given me a hand to cling to and smothered my pain with their caring. I have never felt as lonely as I do now.

I am paying my dues as I have in the past two years. I am paying my dues for letting the weight of a glance negate the weight of my ancestry.

Zuleika did what was expected of her. She told Ummama that she found me in the common alley coming in from the road. Ummama did what was expected of her. She threw up her hands and beat her heaving bosom. 'What have you done, Saadiya? When I tell your father, he will be furious.' She turned to Zuleika and pinched her forearm. 'And you? Who else saw her there? Tell me the truth, you lazy cow. Where were you when she decided to put the honour of the family in jeopardy?'

Zuleika rubbed her forearm where Ummama had pinched her and wept, 'No one, no one was there. I swear by all that I hold precious. No one saw her. No one knew it was her but me.'

Then my venerable Vaapa Najib Masood Ahmed did what was

expected of him. He had Zuleika heat an iron rod till it blazed a fiery orange and, with tears in his eyes, he laid it on my calf. 'This hurts me more than it will hurt you,' he said. 'But I can't let you go unpunished for risking the honour of my family.'

Through my pain, I saw him raise the rod and place it a second time by the line of burnt flesh. I screamed. He looked away and said, 'It is your age, I know. You feel the need to break rules. This, my Saadiya, good girl, is to still the restlessness in you. The next time you feel the need to break your reins, remember how your flesh melted and how my heart broke.'

Then for the final time, my venerable Vaapa pressed the now not so hot rod alongside the two bars of burnt flesh and uttered in his coldest voice, 'This is a lesson for you as much as it is for me, that it is unwise to give girls even a little rope. That it isn't in women to understand the nuances of freedom. Henceforth, these welts on your calf will help you remember your place.'

I did what was expected of me. I fainted with the pain. When I regained consciousness, I wept. I wept for the anguish in Vaapa's eyes and for causing him hurt. I wept for my flesh that was marked by his anger. I wept, for I knew that even though Vaapa had done all he could, I couldn't stop thinking of those heady moments of freedom. Of a sky that was not bound by grey walls. And of him, Malik, for that was the name I gave him, and of how he had caressed me with his eyes.

That night as I slept, Vaapa climbed the stairs and came to my room. He carried in his arms his precious Bulbul-tara.

He flung the door and windows open. Vaapa couldn't stand to be in a closed room. Then he sat down at the foot of my bed and began to pluck the strings of the musical instrument. The soft notes of the Bulbul-tara echoed a lullaby and Vaapa sang in muted tones the words of the song. I did not know the meaning of the words, nor did Vaapa. Perhaps in the many years of it being passed from father to son, the words had been corrupted. But the melody was that of a lullaby and when I was a little child and ill, Vaapa would sing it to help me sleep. As the words and music swirled around me, I felt a rush of tears in my eyes.

Vaapa set so much store by this lineage of ours. He sang only the songs his ancestors had bequeathed him. Vaapa loved me more than all his other children, but he loved his ancestry more.

The music was his way of asking forgiveness. But Vaapa, I wanted to cry, it is I who must ask your forgiveness.

For I am not sorry for what I did.

Vaapa, stop the music. Vaapa, go away. Your music makes me think of all that you want me to forget.

As much as you love your ancestry, so do I. When I close my eyes, I see the stories of my ancestors taking shape.

I see the ship with the billowing sails. I see the horse. The white steed galloping down the gangplank and racing against the wind. I see the rider…and there I pause. For it is him I see. But I let the story go on and he plucks me from the roof of my prison and takes me into a world where the sky has no end.

My bodice feels tight. My insides quiver with a queer churning. My breath quickens. I do not understand any of this. Vaapa, you ought to have branded me so that I could never dream again.

Vaapa, go away and take your music with you.

They spent the night in a room attached to the dargah. Dr Samuel watched Sethu unfold the bedding that had been provided.

'You probably think this is very ill-mannered of them,' he said, trying to fathom the set cast of Sethu's features. 'But let me tell you, it is an honour. They seldom let strange men in, yet the two of us who are not of their faith are spending the night within the gates.'

Sethu looked up.

'Yes, in fact, they were very reluctant to let you stay at first. But once I explained that you were my assistant, they agreed. You see, they need me and my medical prowess. They know that, and they also know that if they upset me, I might not make my periodic visits here.'

Sethu lay in bed unable to sleep. He lay with his eyes closed, feigning sleep, because otherwise the doctor wouldn't shut up. And all Sethu wanted to do was explore the wondrous sensation the girl had evoked in him.

It came to him again and again, the beauty of that face. He had never seen a face so untouched by life. The naked hope in her eyes. The slender lines of her throat as she raised her face to the breeze. The slight parting of her lips as if to draw in the wonder of the moment. And when her tongue had appeared and licked at the curve of her lips, he had felt a desire to be that lip, to draw that pristine being towards him and make her his for life.

'One of the major health hazards in this little settlement is polio,' the doctor said as he checked the contents of his bag.

Sethu watched the doctor as he counted the vials of medicine. Sethu had packed the bag as Hope had taught him to. But the doctor was never satisfied till he had personally checked that everything was as it ought to be. Sethu tried to stem his irritation. There was no point in saying it was all there. More and more, it seemed that the doctor and he were having little skirmishes. The doctor's will prevailed because Sethu knew he needed the doctor more than the doctor needed him. That, Sethu reflected bitterly, was the measure of the doctor's strength.

'All of them are in-bred a thousand times over. Not to mention the damp—you can see it for yourself. The absence of fresh air in their houses makes them a breeding ground for the disease. And to think the beach is just outside their thresholds. I have been trying to persuade them to let the women go for a stroll everyday, and they say yes to please me but I know that it won't be allowed,' the doctor muttered as they walked.

He turned to Sethu and said, 'Please remember that you will have to wait in the outer room. And that at no point must you make eye contact with any woman, even if she is old enough to be your great-grandmother.'

Sethu nodded. All he could think of was, would he see her again?

In the first house they went to, Sethu sat in the outer room, silenced by the oppressiveness of its insides, the wooden ceilings and the narrow windows. The weight of the confined space pressed down upon him. The doctor emerged a few minutes later. 'Nothing complicated here. I have an elderly patient with sciatica. But we must go now to Pasha's. His son has a fever, they tell me. I hope it is not a resurgence of polio. If it is, heaven help us. And He will. That I am sure of. "It is God that girdeth me with strength, and maketh my way perfect. He maketh my feet like hinds' feet, and setteth me upon my high places. He teacheth my hands to war, so that a bow of steel is broken by mine arms."'

The doctor waited for Sethu to respond. 'Psalms,' he prodded.

But Sethu wasn't listening. All he wanted to do was move on. She was here somewhere, he knew that. 'Do we go this way?' he asked, moving towards the common alley.

'No, no,' the doctor said, trying to hide how vexed he was. What was wrong with Seth, he wondered. 'We go this way,' he said, stepping into a narrow alley.

'This is the women's way. Only women walk this way. As a doctor, I become an asexual being. For now, you are one, too,' the doctor said, threading his way through what Sethu thought was a maze.

Even though the doctor had said he shouldn't, Sethu searched the face of every woman surreptitiously. Was it her? Was it the girl?

'We are to dine at the Haji's. He lives with his mother and youngest daughter. But before that we must go to Razia's. She is his second daughter and is eight months pregnant. She has had two miscarriages before and I am not sure I like the way this one is going,' the doctor said at about six in the evening.

Sethu wiped his brow. The day had been long and tedious for want of anything to do. All he had done was wait. He felt more trapped than ever. A curious weariness entered him, and a deep loneliness. If she did exist, where was she? Was she someone he had conjured up out of his own need for somebody to touch and hold? For someone to lay his cheek upon and rest his head against?

My leg felt as if it was on fire. My petticoat brushed against the blisters and every movement was agony. Was this the hell Vaapa talked about?

There was much hustle and bustle in the kitchen. Zuleika was cooking mutton. And chicken. There was to be rice and idiappams, and rotis made of rice flour. Who was coming, I wondered.

Zuleika and Ummama darted glances at me as they went past, but they didn't say anything. Their silence caused me more anguish than the rawness of my wounds.

I thrust away the plate that Zuleika brought. 'Come Saadiya, pet, darling,' she cajoled. 'Eat something. You haven't eaten since last night.' She averted her eyes from mine. 'Who are you angry with? Me?'

'Talk to me,' I said. 'Then I will eat.'

She sighed. 'But I am talking to you.'

'No, like you normally do,' I said.

'What do you mean, normally? Listen to this girl, bibi,' she said. 'She says we are not talking...That is what she says.'

That was Ummama's cue to break her silence. She came towards me. 'How can we not talk to you, darling child?'

'Are you angry with me?' I asked.

She folded me in her arms in reply. The warmth and cooking smells of her embrace, my relief at being included in the circle of her love, made me feel weak. I went limp in her arms.

They sprinkled water on my face. 'She's fainted because she's hungry,' Zuleika said.

'Poor thing,' Ummama murmured.

'My leg,' I whimpered. 'It's on fire.'

Zuleika raised my petticoat. She sucked in her breath. 'I don't like this. What if it gets infected? I wish I hadn't said anything to you.'

Ummama peered at my leg. There was guilt in her eyes. 'Forgive me, my child,' she wept. 'I do not know what came over Najib.'

I said nothing.

Zuleika wiped a tear and said, 'Bibi, let the doctor take a look. He will be here soon. He's gone to see Razia first.'

Ummama nodded. 'I will tell Najib that the doctor has to attend to her.'

Ummama didn't tell me what she told Vaapa, but just before dinner, when the doctor arrived, she ushered him in.

'Show the doctor your leg,' she said.

Doctor Samuel looked at my blisters. 'Please call my assistant here,' he said.

Zuleika and Ummama looked at each other. 'Can't we do what is required?' they asked.

'If you could, would I have asked for him? Please fetch him. This is important. She has second-degree burns,' the doctor snapped.

They ushered you in. You whose glance had stoked in me a thousand desires and sucked away all thought of propriety. They ushered you in silently and the doctor said, 'Seth, I need you to prepare a sterile pad dressing for me.'

You didn't raise your eyes from the doctor's bag. He has tutored you well in our ways, I thought. Suddenly the doctor asked, 'How did this happen?'

Vaapa, who had come in just then, said quickly, 'I think she stepped too close to the wood fire and a burning twig fell on her.'

The doctor stared at Vaapa and said, 'If you insist. Though I must tell you that this is the first time I have seen a twig fall so uniformly in three adjacent bars.'

Vaapa said nothing. And I swallowed my despair. The doctor knew I had been punished, but even he didn't dare probe any further. Unbidden, I darted a glance at you. You were looking at me. Again that glance.

Pity. Sorrow. Sympathy. Anger. I saw all that in your glance. And something else.

I knew a sense of inevitability. The weight of your glance was such.

The doctor took the pad from Sethu. He cleared his throat and spoke in English. Later you told me what the doctor said. 'I wonder what the girl did. What could she have done that needed such brutal punishment?'

Sethu felt rage cloud his eyes. He looked at the old women and the elderly man and said in a voice that bespoke a suppressed rage, 'I think she took a walk by herself. I saw her for a brief moment by the road yesterday evening. She stood there doing no harm to anyone. Just stood there looking.'

'How do you know it was her?' the doctor murmured as he applied an ointment very gently over the blistered area.

'I saw her face,' Sethu said very quietly.

The doctor was silent. Then he said, 'My, she is very brave. If they knew that she had shown her face, they would have branded her face as well. As for you, next time you see one of the women in an alley or on the road, for heaven's sake, remember to turn your face to the wall.'

Sethu raised his eyes and let them slide towards the girl. They had spoken in English, but on her face was an expression that said she had understood it all.

Sethu, who seldom took chances in his life, looked into her eyes and said in Tamil, 'Are you asking me to close my eyes to the beauty of the moon? How can I?'

The doctor snorted.

But as all beings who take chances discover, there is a recompense even for being foolhardy. Sethu was rewarded with a faint bloom in her cheeks, a covert smile and a dropping of her eyelids. An acknowledgement of more than just their shared deceit.

And Sethu felt his senses quicken.

Who would have thought of Dr Samuel as Kama Deva incarnate? The god of love with his bow of sugarcane, a line of bees for a bowstring, and arrows tipped with the most fragrant of flowers.

Except that instead of a parrot, Dr Samuel rode a bicycle and had as his attendant nymphs Hope, Faith and Charity.

But Kama Deva, it is said, chooses the strangest of hiding places. It doesn't matter how he does what he sets out to do, as long as it is done. And so it happened with Dr Samuel. For only Kama Deva could have made Dr Samuel say, 'Razia's baby will need to be born in the hospital. I would suggest that you send her to Nazareth as soon as possible. Rent a house or something. In fact, there is a house near the hospital that is vacant, I hear. I can't be responsible for her life or her baby's if she delivers at home.'

Dr Samuel added as an afterthought, 'I'll need to look at her leg. So she might as well as come, too.'

The Haji didn't seem happy at the suggestion. But remorse overrode his worry about impropriety. He nodded gravely. 'I will arrange it. Maybe their aunt or their grandmother could go with them, and I will send Suleiman, my son, as well.'

The doctor washed his hands in readiness for the meal. He gestured to Sethu to do the same. Sethu wore a faraway look. If he had looked at Saadiya, he would have seen the same expression on her face. It was as though both Sethu and Saadiya knew that what was to happen was preordained.

I, Saadiya, good girl, with the purest of Arab blood in my veins, branded by my Vaapa and a glance, lay awake. I did not know what it was that nagged at my flesh so. Was it the imprint of Vaapa's anger? Or was it your burning gaze? Or was it the thought that in a day or two I was to be allowed to glimpse the world that existed outside the gates of Arabipatnam?

I was not yet sixteen. How could I have known that the call of the flesh has its price? How could I have known what I was doing?

There were seven of us in the horse carriage. Suleiman and the driver in the front, and Zuleika, Ummama, Nadira, Razia and I at the back. Vaapa wanted his women to be together, Zuleika joked. But it was Razia who clamoured for her family to be with her. 'I want all of you around me. What if I die? Do you want me to go all by myself, as if I were an orphan?' she wept when Vaapa said, 'But what is the need for all of you to go to Nazareth?'

Even when Razia was a baby, Zuleika said, she was the one who wept the loudest. It was as if, when she was only a few seconds old, a farishta had whispered in her ears, 'Cry hard, little one. I am your guardian angel and I'm telling you this secret that will help you in life. Cry hard and loud. Only babies who scream and rage their protest get fed, so cry, cry, cry when you want your way.'

So Razia wept and Vaapa who fretted that all this wailing would hasten the baby's arrival in the wrong way, quickly agreed.

There was hardly any light or air in the confined space. I felt faint. On the driver's side was a thick cloth screen that shielded us from him and on the farther side was another thick sheet that hid us from the world. There were peepholes, but after a few minutes of trying to peer through them, I leaned against the side of the carriage and thought that if it weren't for the rocking of the carriage, I might as well have been at home. I could smell Nadira's talcum powder, Razia's attar, Ummama's odour of mothballs, Zuleika's sweat and the mustiness of the horse carriage. I willed my churning stomach to settle. How much longer, I wondered.

Then we were outside the house that Vaapa had rented. Suleiman jumped off the carriage and opened the gate in the high wall. I followed him, drinking in everything I saw around me. How I stared. I couldn't believe that houses such as this existed. A house that stood by itself. A house that was flanked by land on all sides and had a little path leading from the gate to the front door. A house with windows that could be flung open and a little terrace on the roof with a wall that stood just waist high. The sky over the house had no boundaries. I felt my heart flower. I wanted to spread my arms and gather the world to me.

Suleiman glanced at the neighbouring house and said, 'This is right next to the doctor's house. So we won't have to worry about prying eyes.'

I sat on the stone step. Would I see you then? Destiny was dictating the path of my life and there was nothing I could do but follow.

But soon there was no time to think of destiny or its dictates, for Razia moaned and demanded that she be allowed to lie down.

Zuleika rushed to the kitchen to light a fire and cook a broth to revive Razia and her unborn child. Ummama lay on a hastily made bed alongside Razia, complaining of pain in her back. Nadira and I worked together quietly. Nadira spoke little. She wasn't pleased about being dragged from her home. She hated to be away from her husband, unlike Razia who spent more time in Vaapa's house than in her own.

When we had unpacked, helped Razia wash, and eaten our dinner, Suleiman said he was going out for a stroll. 'I miss the sound of the sea,' he said.

I bit my lip to stop myself from saying, 'How easily you speak of missing the sea. Though we live so close to it, we don't get to see it ever.'

All the men in Arabipatnam went to the beach every day, like they went to the mosque. It was part of their routine. We were allowed out perhaps once a year. At other times, we knew the sea existed only when the breeze set in at early noon, bringing into our homes a whiff of salt and on hot days a brackish odour, part fish, part decay, part mystery.

I stood at the window and saw Suleiman pull the door shut in the high wall. I heard him locking the gate. With the key in his pocket, he was assured that his womenfolk were safe. My sisters were talking in low tones. I turned to Ummama and asked, 'May I go up to the terrace?'

Ummama looked at me with a worried expression. 'Saadiya, child, Vaapa...'

'Oh, let her,' Nadira said. 'Who is to see her there? There is no one next door but the doctor. What is the harm?'

'Yes, what is the harm?' Razia said.

The staircase ran up a side wall outside the house. I went up slowly. The night sky stretched as far as my eyes could see, my mind could imagine. A night sky speckled with a million stars. A breeze blew. Not the sea breeze I knew, robust and brimming with salt. This was a soft breeze laden with the fragrance of jasmine from the doctor's garden. I turned to the side where the doctor's house was.

In the darkness, I saw a glowing tip. It swung in an arc every few seconds. I felt my heart flutter. Then I smiled. This was no imp setting out to do evil as in Vaapa's stories. This was someone smoking.

The red tip glowed as the smoker sucked the cigarette. Then slowly, the red tip came closer to the wall.

'Is that you?' your voice asked.

I felt my heart singe.

I fed myself the cast of your features, the length of your body, your loose-limbed gait and the slow radiance of your smile. By day I devoured your line and form and even the blurred outlines of your shadow in the morning sun. And at night, when all I had was your voice that slithered around and over me in coils of forbidden feeling, I let the memory of my daytime marauding feed the hunger to see you.

Every morning we went, Razia, Nadira, Suleiman and I, to the hospital. There was no need to go every day, but the doctor said the walk was good for her. I insisted, because you were there. 'No, Razia,' I would nag. 'The doctor said if you don't walk, the baby won't come out easily and then they might have to cut you open.'

Razia loved the attention; her greedy little mind demanded more. However, even she wasn't willing to endure the pain of surgery, notwithstanding all the attention it would fetch her. So she agreed and we went to the hospital, each one of us bearing the weight of our individual lives: Razia her baby; Nadira her resentment and sisterly duty; Suleiman his vexation at having to waste time; and I, only I, bore my burden easily. How could I call this great hope, this sense of expectation, this knowledge that you waited for me, a burden? This was joy; this was even more than Vaapa's stories had led me to expect.

Then I would think of Vaapa and this feeling, this great joy would seem like a weight that warned me: Saadiya, good girls know no such feelings. And I would begin to despair. But then I would see you. My incomparable Malik. My sahib. Your lips would part in a slow smile that was only for me, and you would come forward to greet Suleiman and take his hands. And it was I who felt the caress of your skin against mine. You would say, 'I was wondering where you were…'

Behind my veil, I would gleam. That first morning, when no one was looking, I dropped a handkerchief that I had spent the previous night embroidering and then held to my cheek all night as I slept. You picked it up and placed it in your pocket. Later, you said that all day you drew it out and breathed deep of my fragrance. And that you slept with it against your cheek. The next day you held it up and said, 'One of you dropped it here. I kept it so I could give it to you.'

I rushed forward before anyone else did and stretched out my hand. 'It's mine.'

You gave it to me and even though our fingers didn't so much as brush each other's, I felt your fingertips trail my soul.

That night your voice said, 'I know your fragrance.'

I whispered, 'And I yours.'

On that little square handkerchief with scalloped edges, our fragrances married and when I held it to my face, I felt a great yearning. For you were my husband and I your wife and this fragment of white cloth our nuptial bed.

'I couldn't sleep all night thinking of you,' you said.

'I couldn't sleep all night thinking of you,' I said.

'What are we going to do?' you asked.

'What are we going to do?' I asked. What else could I have said anyway?

'I have never felt this way about anyone,' you said.

'I have never felt this way about anyone or anything,' I said.

'Are you a parrot or what?' Your voice was querulous.

I stared at the darkness till I remembered a heroine from Vaapa's story. It was her words I spoke. 'I am the mirror of your soul,' I said. 'I see all you see. I think your thoughts. I feel as you do. I am you.'

'If this isn't love, what is?' you said.

'If this isn't love, what is,' I agreed.

How could I have been certain? I knew nothing of love and life. And yet, I knew. There could be no love like this. How could anyone else know what it is to love, except you and I?

We created love. We birthed it. We fed it and nurtured it. This was our love. And no one else's.

'I must go now, my love,' you said. A voice from the shadows.

When you were gone, I stood there on the terrace, all by myself, with the wonder of this magnificent love.

For six days we fanned our love, with words and a thousand sighs. For six nights, you and I bared our souls. For six days your need for me woke a need in me. On the seventh night, when I could bear it no longer, I said, 'Will you come here?'

There was a long silence. When I heard no response, I felt a shame like I had never known. I had let you see my hunger and you were disgusted, I thought. I felt tears gather in my eyes and my head lowered with the weight of their salt. When the first drop fell, you caught it in your palm. 'Why?' you asked. 'Why are you crying?'

I was so relieved to know you hadn't forsaken me that I forgot to be frightened.

You drew me towards you and I let my head rest against your chest. I heard your heart beat. Or was it mine?

'I had to hold you in my arms,' you said.

I snuggled closer, my fists against your skin.

You unclenched them and raised my chin to look into my eyes. 'And now…' you said.

'And now…' I prompted.

'And now I can't rest till you are mine for life.'

Then the moon emerged from behind a cloud and you moved towards the shadows that would cloak you. Again you were two beings. The man. The voice.

I reached for you. To hold you once again so that at least for a moment you would merge, the man and the voice I knew so well.

You took my hand and gathered me in your arms again. You laid your lips against mine.

Then you were gone, leaving the memory of a faint pressure on my lips. I heard a soft thud as you dropped from the high wall to the ground.

I knew relief. You were safe.

I wondered, what next? But you would know what was next, I thought. You would lead the way and I would follow.

Sethu stared at the ceiling. These days he was given to staring at the ceiling and other vacant places as if to project into their emptiness the colours of his desire.

Where does this come from, he asked himself in bemusement. The weight of this feeling for Saadiya. The need to breathe the scent of her skin, twine her hair through his fingers, cup her chin and drink in the innocence of her. Words that he didn't know existed tripped effortlessly from his tongue. My love, the little bird of my heart, my pigeon, the singing in my veins, pretty phrases that he had jeered at when he heard them in the talkies. Now when he spoke them, they seemed to echo his feelings.

She said she was the mirror of his soul. You are my soul, he cried.

Then came the grim sense of foreboding. How could this love be? He had nothing, not even his real name. How could he have allowed this to happen?

Sethu told himself, no one need know. He would be Seth, the doctor's assistant. He would have Saadiya even if it killed him. That was the measure of his love for her. For Saadiya he was willing to die.

I am almost twenty-five. I am not a silly boy; I am a man. This is a mature love, he would tell anyone who protested. Most of all, he told the voice in his head. Then be careful, the voice said. Be cautious. Tread carefully. Your love is no good if you are dead. Besides, it is time you told her about yourself. You can't build a love on sand, the voice added, and he knew a dread that turned to fear. When she knows who you are, only then must you think of the days after, it said.

That night you were quiet. Silent as if all the words that waited on your tongue were paralysed by a strange fright. I could feel the weight of that silence.

Inside my bodice, nestling in the shallow hollow between my breasts, was the sprig of jasmine buds you had so artfully placed on your table. The jasmine grazed my skin. I felt you with every breath I took.

Your voice when it emerged was even quieter than your silence. 'Do you know who I am?' you asked.

I said nothing.

'I am not who you think I am,' you said.

'Does it matter?' I asked.

'It does,' you said. 'I grew up in Kerala. Do you know where that is? On the other coast. When I was fourteen, I ran away from home. I found my way to Colomb,' you said and paused. Then you gathered your breath and said, 'Colombo.'

I stared at you and said, 'I don't understand.'

'It doesn't end with that,' you said, impervious to my question. 'Later, when I began to work, I moved away. I was based in the Pamban quarantine camp. There I had a quarrel with a man. I stabbed him. If he's dead, I am a murderer.'

I felt more love for you than I had ever known before. How hard it must be for you to tell me this. I didn't care. I knew you. I had laid my cheek against your chest and heard your heart beat. I had known your lips on mine and tasted love. All I could think of was how bereft I would be if I was parted from you.

I touched your arm. You stood in the shadows. I could barely see you. But I knew you were just inches away from me.

Then you turned towards me and said, 'Listen. I have one more secret. My name isn't Seth. It is Sethu. Do you know what that means?'

I didn't speak. I did not understand.

'Saadiya.' Your voice was urgent. 'I am a Hindu. What is the word you use, a kafir…Our love will never be accepted.'

I knew then that you were asking me to choose. The weight of my ancestry, or the miracle of our love.

'Then we must find a place where our love will be allowed to live,' I said.

If the Venerable Haji Najib Masood Ahmed had a will wrought of iron, Saadiya Mehrunnissa's was cast in steel. Immune to heat and pain, resistant to corrosion and pleading.

When Razia's baby was born and the festivities to celebrate his arrival were over, Vaapa set about organizing Saadiya's nikaah.

The days away from home had turned her into a woman, he thought. She was a child no more. Her eyes and the unhurried movements of her body bore the languor of a woman, of a creature who hugged close to her a secret, he thought one morning as he watched her come down the staircase. To have left her unmarried so long was a mistake.

Then one night Saadiya went to him as he sat in the front room of the house. What he saw on her face unnerved him. It was a resolve that befitted a mutineer.

'Vaapa, I do not wish for this nikaah,' she said, not bothering to even lead up to the subject.

The Haji looked at his Bulbul-tara. It was as if, instead of its soft notes, it had boomed a drumbeat. He pretended not to hear Zuleika's gasp.

'Vaapa, I do not wish to marry Akbar Shah's second son.'

Ummama burst into the room and pulled Saadiya's arm. 'Come away, girl. What's wrong with you?'

But Saadiya shook her arm free. 'Vaapa, you can pretend that you don't hear me. But I will tell the Qazi that I am not willing to marry the man you have chosen for me.'

The Haji raised his eyes from his Bulbul-tara. He put it down gently. 'What is wrong with Salim?' he asked in a mild voice.

'I don't know Salim. I don't want to know anything about him. You see, my heart will not accept him,' Saadiya cried. Her face flushed and beads of sweat raised themselves on her forehead.

'Your heart! Your heart will accept who I ask it to. Do you hear me? I have no time for your silliness,' Vaapa said without raising his voice. He waved his hand as if to dismiss her and rose from his pile of cushions.

'I will not, Vaapa,' Saadiya said. Her voice was as soft as his. 'You cannot make me.'

Ummama pleaded. Nadira cajoled. Razia wept. Suleiman threatened. And Vaapa: he administered beatings and threats, gave orders to starve her and then sat with his face to the wall and wept. They tried all that they thought they ought to, so that she could see sense and the error of her ways. But Saadiya was inviolable.

Nadira crept to her father's side and said, 'There is no use, Vaapa. She only grows more determined by the day. There is hardly any life left in her, but she refuses to change her mind.'

Vaapa turned to his eldest daughter. 'What are we to do then?'

'Let me find out what is on her mind,' Nadira said, wiping her father's tears.

All day, the next day, Nadira avoided her father's gaze. The Haji waited for Nadira to come to him. But she stayed away and so the Haji sought her out, unable to contain his dread any more.

'What can I say, Vaapa?' Nadira cried.

The Haji tried to read the face of this daughter who so resembled his wife. 'She said something? What did she say?'

'She talks of her Malik. A man she has lost her heart to. He has her soul, she says.'

'Has she gone mad? What man? Who is this Malik?'

'Seth. The doctor's assistant,' Nadira said, her voice cracking.

'But how can it be?' The Haji frowned. 'How can it be?' His voice rose.

'I don't know, Vaapa, I don't know,' Nadira cried, afraid that she would be held responsible.

'Is he one of us?' The Haji spoke aloud to himself. 'But even if he is, how can it be? How will I face our kinsmen? How will I live with their scorn?'

'Vaapa, he is not one of us,' Nadira murmured. 'He is a Christian, I think.'

Then the Haji fell to his knees and wept. Great sobs that tore through his soul and shook the thin walls of the house. When it seemed that he could cry no more, he went back to his house and locked himself in a room.

They huddled outside and pleaded with him to come out. Nadira and Razia. Suleiman, Ummama and Zuleika. Only Saadiya stayed in her room, unmoved by Vaapa's distress.

Vaapa stayed in there for many hours and as abruptly as he had shut himself in, he emerged. He looked at the faces of his family as they stood there: eyes and cheeks ravaged by tears, voices despairing, hands wringing, clothes dishevelled and hair unkempt. Then he searched again to see if she was there.

'Bring me hot water for a bath,' he said. 'I am hungry. I wish to eat after my bath.'

They looked at each other, shocked by the ordinariness of his words.

'Vaapa,' Suleiman began.

The Haji held up his hand. 'There is nothing more to discuss.'

When it was twilight, the Haji went to the mosque. When the prayers were over, he said to the men gathered there, 'I have something important to tell you.'

They looked at each other. They had already heard a rumour. But since it was about the Haji's daughter, they had dismissed the rumour as baseless gossip.

'My brothers,' he said, trying not to show how much it hurt him to stand before them with the shadow of humiliation. 'For as long as I can remember, I have professed the importance of our ancestry. For as long as I can remember, I have sought to keep intact the purity of our bloodline. Our ancestors came only second to our faith, but it was a close second. So when you chose to make me your leader, I knew I was vested with a great responsibility. For as long as I was your leader, I would have to be the custodian of all the values our ancestors deemed fit to uphold. I would be the one to ensure none was violated, and if it did happen, that the violator was suitably punished. But now, within my own home, in my own bosom, I have without knowing nurtured an evil. A creature who seeks to transgress the tenets of our law, destroy all that we hold precious.

'It is fitting, therefore, that I step down from the honour of being the head of the clan.'

The men looked at the floor and then at each other. Suleiman clasped his hands to stop them from covering his face.

'All my life, I have lived true to our faith and ancestry. All my life I have never asked Allah for anything but to be given the strength to be an honourable man. My honour lies in shreds, but allow me this last vestige of self-respect. Allow me to apologize to you and know that in your heart you will find the generosity to forgive my family for the dishonour she has brought us.'

The murmurs grew louder. 'Speak clearly, Haji,' someone said.

The Haji gazed at his feet and said, 'My daughter Saadiya says she will not marry Salim, Akbar Shah's son.'

'Is that all?' someone else laughed. 'Find her another groom.'

'No, that isn't all,' the Haji said, his face paling in anger, his nostrils flaring. 'Do you think I am a silly girl to stand here before you, enacting a scene? My daughter wants to break every single law of our community. She wants to be a kafir's wife.'

'Who?' The voices rose in unison.

The Haji had pondered on what he would say if they asked him to name the man. The doctor was not to be faulted. If he were to name her lover, the doctor would never be allowed in again. And it would be the women and children who suffered. Saadiya, you do not know what your treachery is costing me, us…

'Does it matter? the Haji asked. 'She refuses to mention his name.'

'Beat her,' someone said.

'Brand her and starve her; that will cure her,' Mohammed, the Haji's brother-in-law, cried.

'Tell her that you will kill yourself,' an old man said.

'I tried. Believe me, I tried,' the Haji said quietly. 'But she remains adamant.'

'Then let her remain a spinster.'

'She says she will kill herself then.' The Haji's voice broke.

'What is wrong with the girl? Perhaps there is a djinn in her. Perhaps she needs to be exorcized,' said Mohammed.

'What will you do?' Akbar Shah asked.

'I will disown her. Tomorrow morning she will be left outside the gates and thereafter, neither I nor anyone else in my family will have anything to do with her. We will wipe her from our lives and memories. As penance for dishonouring our ancestry, we will accept whatever punishment you see fit to give us.'

The Haji waited while the elders held a council. It was Akbar Shah who spoke their decision. 'Haji Najib Masood Ahmed, we have heard your decision. Now hear ours. What you do with your daughter is your affair. As the head of the household, you may choose to do as you think fit. Keep her at home, or sever ties with her. That is your choice as the head of your family. However, we see no need for you to step down from your position. You have maintained your position as head of the community with dignity. You have fulfilled your duties flawlessly. Your character is unimpeachable. Why then should we deprive ourselves of your sagacity and wisdom? We wish you to continue to be our headman.'

The Haji rose from where he was seated. 'How can I who can't teach the greatness of our ancestry or faith to my daughter uphold it for the rest of the community?'

Suleiman groaned. The council was doing what they had never done before, by allowing the Haji and his family to go unpunished and wanting him to continue as headman, and here was Vaapa arguing with them.

'Please, Haji,' one of the council elders said. 'We trust you. Do we need to say more?'

Haji Najib Masood Ahmed shook his head gravely. He understood. That was to be his punishment. Henceforth, he would have to accept the council's decisions without questioning them. Turn a blind eye to transgressions, offer clemency where none was required. He would have to witness, unable to protest or voice his disagreement, the breaking of laws and the making of new ones. He would not be allowed to be guardian of their lineage. He would be a titular head and no more.

Haji beckoned to Suleiman. 'I want you to go home now. Tell Saadiya that she has all night to decide. At the crack of dawn, she will have to tell me what her decision is. Make sure you tell her what lies ahead if she chooses to go her way. Tell her clearly, so that she knows what she is forcing us to do.'

'Vaapa,' Suleiman asked, 'what if...'

The Haji looked at his son. 'We won't consider that now. If there is a what if, it doesn't concern us any more. Go now. I will remain here till it is time. I will pray to Allah that He grant her wisdom and bestow mercy upon me so that it is never said that Haji Najib Masood Ahmed's daughter destroyed the purity of our bloodline.'

BOOK 2

Kaananamithennalenthadhikam bheethithamalle,
Kaanenam thelinjulla vazhikal,
Noonamee vazhi chennal kaanam payoshniyaarum
Enaakshi, dooreyalla chenaarnna kundinavum

Though this is a forest, it is not that fearful
we should be able to find clear (trodden) paths
If we go this way, it is certain, deer-eyed one
that the river that quenches hunger and thirst
and famed Kundinam too, are not faraway

—Nalacharitam [Second Day]
Unnayi Warrier

Raudram

h, and so we come to raudram. The common fallacy is to think raudram is a synonym for anger. Nothing wrong with that, for raudram wears the countenance of anger. Wrath, even. Look at this: you start with the eyes. Widen them so that they open fully, until your head tilt backwards, the nostrils flare, the mouth sets and your jaws clench. You must inhale as you usually do, but try and exhale through the eyes. Intensely. Powerfully. Then the cheeks will acquire a mobility of their own.

Now do you see what I mean? This is the face you wear when you are angry, when you feel wrathful, and this is also the face you wear when fury rides your mind. So what is fury?

There are degrees of fury. Let me explain.

Previously I told you how the rain in karkitakam symbolizes sorrow. But there is another kind of rain. It begins with a gathering of grey clouds as the afternoon wears. There is a hush punctured only by the rasping croak of crows, the rumble of thunder, an old man heaving and snoring as he sleeps. The leaves resonate with silence. Then the rain falls. On leaves, on tree tops, on dried palm leaves. Rain through the undergrowth. Rain dripping down the eaves. The fat plop. The crystal drop.

In the night, the darkness is a thick velvet drape, muffling stars and noises. Only the steady drip of the rain penetrates. For this is the rain riddled with fury. When thunder rules and clouds burst. When jagged flashes of lightning tear the sky, striking trees, ripping through the trunks browning leaves...The end of October brings the thulaavarsham. And this is the rain that doesn't fall quietly, but rages and roars.

There is another version of raudram. For this you must go to your kitchen garden and pluck a cheenamolagu, those tiny green and white chillies with waxen skins, seemingly so innocuous. You might need to persuade yourself to take a bite. Almost instantly your mouth will be on fire with a burning sensation so intense that your heart beats faster, your mouth salivates, the nose sniffles and your head and face break out in a torrential sweat. So you see, you don't have to feel anger or wrath to know fury.

Now close your eyes and listen to the sounds that come from the trees. Do you hear that? The tuk-tuk sound? Don't you wonder who the aerial carpenter is? It is the maramkothi. Are you wondering what a woodpecker has to do with raudram? Listen. Do you hear it? The notes like a drum roll. Slow at first, then intense, as if driven by fury. And yet, the fury is not such that it makes earth crumble or blood fall. This is the fury of passion. For, while other birds have mating calls to attract the mate, the woodpecker has only its drumbeat with which to beckon and call. It is a quiet fury, not any less intense or raging in its power, but locked within you, so that only you know it. For only you hear it in your heart. Such is the fury of a passion that rules you.

Shyam

I lean forward and tug the curtains aside. I wonder if I should get up and wash my hands. God knows what has been wiped off on these thick ugly curtains—tears, snot, grease from food, chewing gum…I repress a shudder and look through the glass. I feel the wheels of the train beneath me, the crunching and grinding, the slow movement. The platform begins to recede. I think I see a face I recognize, but it is hard to say as the tinted glass in the window is grimy.

The door opens and a gust of warm air comes pouring in. Two pesky children walk down the aisle, giggling and pushing each other. They have a banana, a giant bar of chocolate, a packet of chips and a cup of Coke each in their hands. What are they preparing for? A siege? With them is a man wearing shorts and sunglasses, clutching a bag and a bottle of mineral water. Out of towners, I decide. I hope their seats are at the other end of the compartment. A baby wails from somewhere behind. A woman laughs. The wheels of a trolley bag squeak. There is a rustle of biscuit wrappers. Then the hum of the air conditioning resumes.

I like trains. I always have. When I sit in a moving train, I feel a great sense of hope. An energy that isn't mine is leading me to a destination. In a train, my mind races along and only my body remains where it is. Seat 12 A.

At home, I am never allowed a moment of respite. There is always someone around. Asking a favour, soliciting a comment, stating an opinion, demanding my attention. Some days, when I would like to just let my mind wander, I hide behind a newspaper. It is during these aimless wanderings that I have my best ideas, but who is there to understand this?

Once, Radha shot me a look that could have been interpreted as amusement or disgust, and said, 'Have you learnt to read upside down? Look at how you are holding the newspaper. What plots are you hatching behind it?'

I look around. The compartment is almost empty. Schools have opened and it isn't yet the season for Sabarimala pilgrims to fill roads and trains. Moreover, the monsoons have begun and very few people would want to travel by AC chair car now. It is, after all, the month of karkitakam. The month of penury.

I think of M.T. Vasudevan Nair's story 'Karkitakam'. I am not a great reader, but this is one of my favourite stories. The little boy Unni could have been me. Perennially hungry. Perpetually proud.

When my mother and I were living on the crumbs Radha's father tossed our way, my mother wouldn't tolerate my using the words hunger or pride. I was not allowed to speak of either need.

If I ever asked my mother for food, she would snap, 'How can you be hungry? Didn't you eat some hours ago? Aren't three meals enough?'

My mother rationed our food carefully, but I was a growing child, and all day and sometimes at night, hunger with rat-like teeth gnawed at my intestines. My mother dosed me for worms and said I must have monsters living within me, who demanded to be fed all day and night. My poor mother did her best to make ends meet, to make do with what was offered to us. My hunger threw her planning asunder, and the only way she could deal with it was with fury. 'Hunger? What kind of demonic hunger is this? It's the kind of hunger that reduces a clan into a family, do you hear me?'

My mother might have lacked for food to feed my hunger, but she was never short of folk wisdom. As her desperation grew, so did her repertoire of sayings, each more viciously deprecating than the one before. And yet, it wasn't that she was an unkind or callous woman. She was a woman forced to take on a man's responsibilities and her impatience stemmed from the fact that she was burdened with financial worries and the guilt that she was not doing her best for me. Apart from me, there was my grandmother to take care of. 'Do you see this?' She would show me a piece of paper on which were written the household accounts. 'Where is the money?'

I can still see those little scraps of paper she did her accounts on. They are pasted forever in my memory. Rations, kerosene, electricity, school fees, medicines; little scraps on which she wrote and crossed out, juggled and moved sums this way and that...coping, coping, surviving.

I was too young to help her out or even shoulder some of the burden. Instead, my young pride reared its head and all she could do was nip it so that we could survive. In retrospect, I understand. But I never did then, and sometimes my fury at her insensitivity was so laced with bitterness that I wished she had died instead of my father.

Some days Amma would have me milk the cow and take the milk to the teashop. At first, I refused. My fragile ego balked at the thought. 'I can't be seen doing this,' I protested in my quavering adolescent voice. Those days, everything in my life seemed ruled by chaos, including my voice; it was like a length of garden hose. Unwieldy, slithering, and beyond my control.

There were four or five louts who occupied the bench outside the teashop, keeping tabs on all who came and went. I was a special object of ridicule for them ever since my mother in an argument about a broken length of fence told our neighbours that she didn't care for their menfolk walking through our garden. 'We may be able to mend the fence only next season, but that doesn't mean your men can use my garden as a thoroughfare. We are poor, but we have a noble lineage.'

The neighbours didn't like the implied slight. They thought we were pretentious. One of the louts outside the teashop was the neighbour's son. And he exacted revenge any which way he could.

'I can't take the milk to the teashop. I'll milk the cow. Can't someone else take it? Nayadi can, can't he? I just can't...' I tried to explain.

My mother's face darkened. 'Nayadi has enough to do in the fields. What is wrong with you? Why can't you take it? Do you think you are too high and mighty to do so? People who have nothing can't afford pride. Do you hear me?'

The louts guffawed when they saw me with the milk can and said, 'Look who is here. The Maharaja of Cochin. His Highness Shyam. And what is this in his hand? A sceptre...oh no, it is a milk can.' They slapped each other's backs and laughed at their asinine joke.

Every day, they had a new comment to toss my way and injure my self-esteem. I had neither the brawn to beat them up nor the wit to match their quips. So I did the only thing that was left for me to do: I pretended not to hear them. Maharaja. What was I king of, except my hunger and pride?

The louts work for me now. Perhaps they don't remember that they made my teenage years a torment. They probably don't connect that timid stuttering boy with me, their modalali, their lord and master, but I know, and that is enough.

A vendor stops by my seat. His tin tray rattles me out of my reminiscences. I know many people who talk of their childhood fondly. A wave of nostalgia creeps into their voice as they talk of times gone by. When I think of my childhood, all I feel is relief. The kind you feel when you finish watching a horror movie everyone has been raving about. Now that you've endured it, you don't have to put yourself through it again. Thank god I have got past those years. Thank god I will never have to live them again. I am happy to be an adult and in control of my life.

The vendor looks into my face and bleats, 'Masala dosa.'

The train stops. We are in Thrissur already. The door opens and a man comes in. He looks familiar. He takes a seat in the row ahead, across the aisle.

I wave the vendor away and stare out of the window. The rain continues to beat its rhythm.

The kitchen smells from the vendor's uniform linger in the air. Why is it, I wonder, that perhaps more than any other of our senses, it is the sense of smell that propels us through time and distance? The smell of oil heating, of deep-fried gram flour, stir up the past. Memories line up again.

I was fifteen when Amma came bearing the news of the army recruitment. 'Janu's son Murali is going. I suggest you rush there and get all the details from him. You will have to start at the bottom, as a sepoy. But the army is a good mother. It'll take care of you. That's what your father always said.'

I stared at her. Did she really believe that? But perhaps the army was not to blame. My father died before he made anything of himself. I thought of him then, of Subedar Gopalan. With a red stripe on his shoulder, a single star, and a wristband that proclaimed his rank. His boots shone, his buckles gleamed, his khaki rustled with starch, and when he died my dreams went as limp as his body.

'Sepoy,' I growled. 'I don't want to be a bloody sepoy.' My voice emerged shrill and high.

'Nothing wrong in starting off as a sepoy. What do you know of the army anyway? Your voice hasn't even formed.'

'I am not going,' I said.

'What do you plan to do then? I can't afford to send you to college. Where is the money? At least with the army you have a future. No point in letting go of what's in your lap, trying to catch what's in the sky.'

'A future in which I have to salute every Chathan and Pothan,' I said, matching her ire with an aphorism.

'Do you prefer to live off your uncle for the rest of your life? Go join the army, son. It is for people like us who can't aspire for more. When we have nothing, we can't afford pride.'

I walked away. I knew I had to do something. If I didn't resolve my future, my mother would force me into a life of salutes, brass buckles and eternal sepoydom.

There was no point in asking my sister for help. Her husband was only a clerk in the railways and they had three children. That evening I went to see my aunt Gowri. I chose an hour when I knew her husband would be away. My mother was right, after all. My pride would take me nowhere. I threw away pride and asked my aunt for a loan.

'My mother would like me to join the army. Become a sepoy. But I know I can do better. I believe that. And I promise to pay back every rupee.'

My aunt reached across and patted my shoulder. 'Is that all? How much do you need?'

I showed her my calculations. I had learnt well from those little scraps of paper that festooned my childhood. I had worked it out to the smallest detail, checked and rechecked the figures. Fees. Bus fare. Books. I had been very stringent and allowed myself only the barest of necessities.

'I will give you the money,' she said. She looked at me with an expression that many years later I fathomed to be prescience and said, 'But...'

My hopes dangled from that word. I thought of all the excuses she could make: I must ask Radha's father. We have had great losses this year. Your mother will be furious.

'But what?' I asked.

'But you will have to work for it. I will ask Radha's father to find you something to do during the vacations. I don't want the money back, but I want you to understand that you mustn't expect anything for nothing. And likewise, give nothing till you are sure you will receive something in return. The money, the object, whatever it is, will acquire greater value and respect then.'

I agreed, and to this day I have done as she said. I give nothing till I am sure I will receive something in return, and I ask for nothing till I am sure I have something to offer.

It was the month of karkitakam. Like Unni in MT's story, I feared the onslaught of the monsoon. It wasn't getting wet that terrified me. I had sandals made of recycled rubber tyres that would easily survive a soaking in the puddles, and polyester shirts that dried on my back. What I feared was my craving for a cup of tea and a piping hot bonda from the Mudaliar's tea shop adjacent to the college. As it is, one little act of extravagance would to ruin my monthly budget. The Mudaliar's bondas were the best I have ever eaten in my life and during the wet month of karkitakam, I scrimped on bus fares and college guides and indulged my hunger for the bonda and tea as often as I could. For the rest of the year, I feasted on the memory of that meal.

I would sit on the bench, sipping my tea and punctuating every sip with a nibble. The gram flour covering was crisp and golden and the stuffing of potatoes and onions perfectly cooked. I savoured every mouthful, willing it to go on and on.

I kept my eyes on the food. I didn't want to meet anyone's eye. I made no friends and chose not to. Friendships at college demand sharing, doing things together. In my first year at college, the student unions came to me soliciting membership. The Students Federation of India. The Kerala Students' Union. There were at least three or four unions, each professing to make student life better. You have to belong to a party for an identity, they said. What are your politics, they asked. Survival, I said. Will joining your union help pay my fees, I asked. But there are other benefits, they said. Leave me alone, I said. I am not interested in student politics.

My university years passed without adding to my memories, save that of Mudaliar's bondas.

Once in a while I encounter a batch-mate or a junior, and then it occurs to me that I studied in the same college. A batch-mate is the president of a panchayat nearby. I see him now and then in Shoranur. Another one, a girl, is a writer. Her books have been translated into many languages, I read. I see her face in the newspaper and wonder if she too sat on Mudaliar's bench. In a newspaper article, she once professed a great fondness for his bondas. Neither of them will know me, the man I have become. I wear only linen, and even on the wettest of days, I shod my feet in leather. I have an AMEX gold card and a cellphone with Bluetooth. In the mirror, and in other people's eyes, I see a man who doesn't fear hunger or suffer the indignity of having to swallow his pride.

A vendor pauses beside my seat. 'Pazham pori,' he cries in a strangled voice.

I snap out of the golden brown casing of memories and eye the banana fritters. They look very tempting. Plump, with knobbly bits of batter fried golden crisp.

I see the man across the aisle look at them, too. I know I should recognize him.

Another vendor arrives. 'Bread omelette,' he cries, in yet another version of that strangled call all railway vendors seem to fashion their voices into.

I look at my watch. It is a lower end Rolex, but it is a Rolex. Another hour to Kochi. Lunch was a long time ago. My stomach rumbles. I point to a fritter and then ask the other vendor for a bread omelette. 'Ask one of the tea boys to come here,' I say.

The vendors rush off to do my bidding. I feel the man's eyes on me, and on the plates and paper napkins laid out on the tray. Then I realize who he is.

How could I have not recognized him? He is a finely built man with a face like the moon's surface. On the movie screen, you see each one of these indentations magnified. A crater for every contact his foot has made with the ball, I think.

I.M. Vijayan. The football hero turned movie star. I have seen him play and I have seen him act. He is brilliant on the field and competent on the screen, but what I admire most about him is his tenacity. He is a survivor.

I was there in the stadium that hot day in Coimbatore when he was playing against Kerala in the Santosh Trophy. I was with a group of salesmen, all baying for his blood. Those days I covered the Tamil Nadu region.

'He is a traitor,' one of them growled.

'How can he play against Kerala?' another snarled.

'Give the man a chance,' I said. 'He must have left the Kerala team for a reason.'

'What reason could he have? Greed, that's what it is,' someone else said.

'Do you call a man wanting to better his prospects greedy?' I asked, incredulous. How could they be so judgemental?

When he failed to shoot a penalty against Kerala, my companions rose in excitement. Vijayan had failed. The traitor was punished. They booed and jeered and thumped each other's backs. I joined them. To not do so would have been to incur the crowd's wrath. But I felt pity for the man. I watched him stand there, his eyes downcast. Just for a moment he looked up, unable to comprehend this mass hatred. What did I do wrong, his eyes seemed to ask the crowd. This is a game, not war. I am a football player, not the enemy.

I look at his profile. Should I introduce myself to him?

Perhaps I could invite him to the resort. I wonder how I should address him. Vijayan would be too presumptuous. Sir would be too servile. I glance at him. His eyes are closed. I decide not to bother him. There is time enough.

My phone beeps. A business call. I settle it with a bark. 'We'll talk when your quote is more realistic.'

I eat my snack slowly. My mind churns. Is this making of plans what Radha calls ambition? Is this looking ahead what my business partners term acumen? If I didn't have either, the resort would have had to close down, like so many enterprises in the region. I will never let that happen. My resort is my kingdom.

Four years ago, when I heard the summer palace by the Nila was up for sale, I rustled up the money to buy it. I put in all my savings and borrowed as much as I could. I have a loan liability that would cripple ordinary men for the rest of their lives. But I manage. I always will. I am a survivor. From an old issue of *Reader's Digest*, I forged a mantra that I start my day with. I stand in front of the mirror every morning and as I peer into the eyes of my image, I mouth, 'Every day and in every way, I am getting better and better.' I believe it. I have to, or I will go under.

I wonder what the next couple of days will be like. I have several things to attend to. A meeting with a tour operator. A discussion with a website designer. A preliminary discussion about advertising on-site at the Nehru Boat Race. A meeting with Sankars, the book people. They used to have a bookshop in a hotel in Palakkad and there is a new one now, on MG Road in Ernakulam. We don't have the room or the custom for a full-fledged book shop, but a kiosk would work very well. And then I have to attend an introductory lecture on the Art of Living.

I have no intention of attending the full workshop. I am content with my life, but it would, if the facilitators agree, be a great draw at the resort. I could work it into the package. I can see how much it would appeal to my foreign guests. I have to offer them something in this godforsaken place. God's own country, they call it, but even God wouldn't come to my part of the state on vacation. The resorts in southern Kerala have so much. Backwaters. Karimeen. Chinese fishing nets. Beaches. Plantations. Wildlife sanctuaries. What do we have here?

A river that's mostly dry, and a little railway town. On the Net, I once encountered a phrase when I was researching tourism in Italy. Agroturismo. For a moment I wondered if I had stumbled on a gold mine. Then I let go of the thought. Agricultural tourism might work in Italy. Picking grapes or harvesting fruits under a blue temperate sky was vacation work. One could play at being farmer. How could I ask my guests to stand ankle deep in slush under a blazing sun, transplanting paddy seedlings into a neat row? It wouldn't work.

The temple circuit would have been an ideal take-off point for the tourists. I even had a line for it: God's own Capital. Guruvayur, Kadampuzha, Vadakkanathan, Thiruviluamala, Molayan Kavu, Padirikunnathu Mana—so many temples that could be done as a day trip, but they are so cussed about not letting non-Hindus in that it has to be the Art of Living or some such thing.

The SP's brother-in-law who lives in Bangalore couldn't stop talking about it. 'In these times, we need something to help us keep our sanity. The Guruji inspires such faith,' he said.

I thought of the white-robed, hirsute man with his soft voice and outstretched arms. His reach was unimaginable. Even corporate heads and business tycoons seemed to surrender themselves to him. He has kind eyes, I can see. But what did they see in him or his teachings?

'But what is it?' I asked, suddenly struck by the business opportunity it presented. Spirituality is still a great lure. In fact, it would be a terrific slogan for the resort. Near-the-Nila. The Art of Living.

The man's face curled into a beatific smile. 'Let me put it very simply. It helps you block out all the unpleasantness and think only of the pleasant and the positive.'

'Tell me more.'

'Why don't you attend one of the workshops and find out for yourself?' he said.

I grunted. I didn't buy it, but I knew my guests would. So I decided to attend the introductory lecture and take it from there.

I know that if I didn't have the unpleasantness of my past to push me, I would have remained where I was. Selling milk or working as a sales boy even when I was fifty years old, in some little store somewhere.

I think of what the man said: block out the past and think only of the present. When an unpleasant thought crosses my mind, I shut my eyes and will it to leave. It usually works.

But two nights ago, I couldn't stop thinking of how the Sahiv let his eyes caress Radha. I did not like it. The man's a lecherous beast, anyone can see it. Why did she have to welcome his glances with her smiles and coy fleeting looks? Each time I sat with them, I felt excluded. I wanted to tap her on her shoulder and say, hello, I am your husband and those glances from the corner of your eye and the pouting of your lips all rightfully belong to me.

But I held my tongue, knowing that if I were to rebuke her, she would continue to do exactly the same, just to spite me.

I wondered if I could talk to Uncle. The old man was strange. But he listened to anything you had to say without offering an opinion, and that was rare in most listeners. But what could I tell him? That I didn't like Chris? That I didn't like the way he looked at my wife? Or that I didn't like Radha seeing so much of him? It sounded pathetic even to my ears.

When Radha came home from the kathakali performance, it was close to midnight, and something in me snapped.

One of the servants opened the door for her. I heard our bedroom door open. She padded in quietly. The lamp on her side of the bed was on. She took her sari off and draped it on the back of a chair. Then she began to take her jewellery off. 'Don't,' I said.

She turned with a jerk. There was surprise in her voice. 'I thought you were asleep.'

'I am not.'

She raised her hands to her ears.

'Don't,' I said. 'Come here.'

She sat on the bed. I touched her shoulder. The blouse she wore had a deep neckline. I ran a finger down her back. She shrugged me off. 'No, Shyam, I am not in the mood,' she said.

'I'll get you into the mood,' I said and brushed my palms against her breasts. I nuzzled her earlobe. Her earring jostled with my tongue.

She pushed me away. 'I told you I don't want to.'

'You are mine,' I said.

'You are drunk,' she said. 'And I am not a bloody object.'

I felt a dark rage gather in me. 'You are my wife.' My voice rose.

'Do you have to shout? The servants will hear us.' Her voice was low.

'You are my wife. I want you to show me some respect.'

'What do you want me to do? Lick your feet?'

'Just show me some respect. You strut about the place with strange men, you come home at midnight and expect me to say nothing. No husband would tolerate this. What do you think I am? A fucking eunuch?'

'Shyam.' She stood up. 'I will not listen to this.'

'You fucking will,' I said. I stood up and pushed her down. 'I have my rights,' I said.

'Don't I have a right to say no?' she demanded furiously, trying to get up.

'Not tonight,' I said and shoved her back on the pillows.

I felt her go rigid. She lay there like a wooden block, immune to all my caresses. But I was past caring. I kneed her legs apart and tore her panties away. She was dry and arid. I felt anger cloud my mind again. I spat into my hand and smeared her with my spit. 'You are mine, do you hear me?' I muttered.

Then I fucked her. The resentment I felt for being tolerated rather than loved, the yearning I had suffered, the loneliness of these eight years, all fused to become a consuming desire to possess her. To make her mine. To reach within and tear down that film of indifference that coated her eyes each time I took her in my arms.

'You are my wife, you are mine,' I said, and searched her eyes to see if I had finally managed to break through.

In the early hours I found her asleep in the swing seat. She had never liked the swing seat. When it was delivered to our home, she had laughed at its red-and-white candy-striped cushions and awning. 'It looks like something out of an old Tamil movie,' she had sneered.

I had wanted it placed in the front veranda.

'You must be out of your mind,' she said.

'Why, what's wrong with it? I think it looks grand,' I said, touching the frame painted a brilliant white.

'It looks like a prop in a stage set. It is embarrassing.' And so it was relegated to the eastern side of the house and tucked away in a corner.

I thought of waking her up and taking her into our bed, but I was scared it would provoke a scene. So I left her there.

When I woke up, she was at my side, all bright and chirpy. And suddenly it occured to me that that was what she had really wanted: a good fuck. It shames me to think it, but I realize it is the truth. Women like to be made to feel like women, dominated and put in their place. Even my Radha. So I wasn't wrong, after all.

Instinctively, I had known what to do. Now I know what else I will do. I will buy her a pair of emerald earrings. The flash of the green stones will please her.

What woman can resist the sparkle of jewellery?

The footballer's eyes are open. I lean forward and say, 'Excuse me…' He turns. He looks pleased. He is a man who likes to be recognized. No pretence of false modesty. I think I like him even more.

Radha

It is only half past three in the afternoon, but already this corner of the house is bathed in shadows. The rains have begun again. Shyam left a little while ago. For the first time in two days, I feel safe.

The swing seat creaks. I put my hand on the frame to steady it. I have never liked it or the corner it sits in. Now it is the only part of the house that I can bear to be in. Two nights have passed since Shyam plundered my body, seized and took away my right to say no. Time hasn't made it better, only worse.

Rape. The word grows fur and fangs, claws and talons. Its eyes are cold and its tongue is forked. Its touch is clammy and its smell the putrid stench of sweat, offal, force and brutality. I feel bile rush into my mouth.

Rape. I look in the dictionary again. Rape: a noun. A sexual act committed by force, especially on a woman.

There are no categories of rape. Rape is rape, even when sanctified by marriage. And the rapist doesn't have to be a stranger emerging from the shadows. He could be your husband. What Shyam did was to rape me.

I close my eyes, willing myself to forget. But I cannot shut my mind to the expression in his eyes as his body bucked and heaved over mine. His eyes seared and burnt. They said: you are mine, you are mine. Shyam's eyes branded me more than his body did.

Later, he drew me into his arms as if nothing had happened. His lips brushed my forehead. I flinched. I waited for his breathing to settle, then I turned on my side and curled into a ball. I tucked my knees into my chest and shoved my fingers into my mouth so I made no noise as I wept.

I felt sore and bruised, invaded and robbed. Is this rape, I asked myself again and again.

Then I knew I couldn't lie there any more. So I rose and went seeking a quiet corner where I could wrap my arms around myself and cry loudly. I went from room to room. I paused in the office room to find the dictionary. If I know what it is, I thought, I will feel better. If I can give this attack a name, I will know how to deal with it.

I woke at dawn and crept back into bed. My mind was made up. I would pretend that nothing had happened. I would cheat him of the pleasure of having imposed his will.

We went to the SP's daughter's wedding. I wore a silk sari and jewellery and flowers in my hair. I let my bangles sing my gestures. The bells on my anklets punctuated my steps with their chorus. I felt Shyam's eyes on me, watching. If he thought that he had forced me into submission, he was wrong. I pretended gaiety and life and somewhere within me the core of pain grew.

That evening I saw Chris and I felt a ray of calm suffuse me. Shyam might think he owned me, but he didn't. I was never his. And I never will be.

My eyes spoke to Chris: I remember. Do you?

His eyes glanced their reply: I do.

Tomorrow, my eyes said, tomorrow there will be more. That is all we can hope for. That is my prayer.

I know, his eyes confirmed.

I went home that night feeling strangely tranquil. Shyam looked at my face and began to say something. Then he paused.

'What were you about to say?' I asked in an even voice.

He stared. All day long he had expected anger, but I felt no anger. Revulsion, yes, and disgust. But not anger.

I saw his face clear. When he left home, Shyam thought all was well. I let him believe it. For there was Chris now.

I let the swing seat cradle me. I think about Chris. When I think about him, I do not have to think about Shyam. Everything ceases to be, except that long-drawn moment when Chris held me in his arms as if I were his precious instrument.

The phone rings. It is Chris.

I don't know what to say to him on the phone. We haven't been alone since that night.

'Will you be coming to the resort this evening?' he asks.

I hesitate only for a moment. 'Yes,' I say.

'In that case, will you have dinner with me? I would really like that.'

I wonder what I will say to him when I see him. Then I think, it doesn't matter. I will know what to do when the time comes.

Shashi twists his body around so he can see my face. 'Would you like me to stay?' he asks. 'It is no trouble, really. With Sir away, I don't feel right about leaving you here.'

'It's all right,' I say. 'I will come back only tomorrow morning. Uncle isn't feeling well. I need to be here.'

Shashi frowns. 'Isn't it better that you take him home?'

'He refuses to move from where he is,' I say. The lies trip from my mouth. I add one more. 'His roof leaks and he is scared the house will be flooded by the rains if he stays away.' And then one more. 'Besides, there is his parrot.'

Shashi doesn't say anything. But I can see he isn't pleased. I swallow the lies that flood my mouth. I don't need to convince him. He is the driver, not my husband.

'I'll bring the bag,' he says.

'No need for that. I can take it myself,' I say and step out of the car. 'Be here by nine in the morning.'

As I walk into Uncle's house, I hear the car drive away.

Uncle joins me on the veranda. Malini hops on one leg inside her cage. 'Why haven't you taken her in yet?' I ask.

She screeches a welcome. I tap the bars of her cage. 'Bad girl,' I say.

Uncle looks at me. His eyes question what I am doing here. I drop into a chair. I let my head fall back and then I muster an airy voice. 'I thought I'd spend the night here. Shyam is away.'

He leans against a pillar. I stand up.

'You are very restless. What's on your mind?' he asks.

'Nothing,' I smile. 'Nothing at all.'

Then I take a deep breath and say, 'I am going to the resort. I thought I'd have dinner with Chris. I'll be back a little late. Is that all right with you?'

His face is expressionless. 'I'll leave the door unlatched. I'll make a bed for you in the front room,' he says.

I nod and go inside to put away my overnight bag.

When I come back to the veranda, I see that he is still standing there with his back to the pillar. His eyes seek mine. Be careful, they say.

At the top of the steps, I turn. 'Who is Saadiya?' I ask.

'My mother,' he says.

I feel my eyes widen, my jaws slacken. Uncle is my father's half-brother. I had always assumed that he was a child from my grandfather's first marriage.

'I didn't know…' I say.

'No one did, except my father, my brothers and your grandmother. And the doctor. My father preferred to bury his past.' His face twists into a grimace. 'And mine.'

I see him pull himself together. I see the tension leave his face. 'My father, your grandfather'—his hands seek mine. He seems to need to hold something warm and alive to reassure himself that he does exist despite a buried past—'often said it is wise to bury the past. It was his way of coming to terms with life. To suppress remorse and regret. There are times when I think my father was a very wise man. Forget, forget…we must do that if we want to cling to our dreams and hopes. But you see, there is also who I am. A veshakaaran. An actor. Every character I am is influenced by what I know of life, so how can I forget or bury my past? That is my conundrum. But you, you ought not to let what has been rule you.'

He lets my hands go. Then he moves his right hand in an elaborate gesture. 'See this,' he says, letting his middle finger and thumb meet in a resounding click. 'Tell me, what is now? The thought that ran as an impulse to the brain, or the movement of the fingers, or the contact of skin against skin, or the trapped air escaping, or the echo of that escape…What is now? All of it, or merely the click?'

I repeat his gesture. 'I am not sure…'

'The click is now. That's what you need to accept. The before and after is of no consequence.' He takes my hands in his again. I realize there is a coded message in this, somewhere. An intimation I ought to be able to read.

Is he telling me to seek out Chris, or is he asking me to be content with Shyam? I do not understand.

'I must be going,' I say and slowly withdraw my hands from the warmth of his clasp. I step out into the night, away from the length of light cast by the bulb in the veranda.

I walk to the reception area.

On a wall painted a deep mustard yellow, more gold than yellow in the evening, is a cluster of photographs. Against the wall are potted palms in brass planters and a huge verdigris-muted bronze uruli in which water lilies float. A Lakshmi lamp with single wick lights a corner. Classic Kerala resort décor. Shyam has turned this decrepit old palace into a showpiece. Even buildings have to submit to his will, I think bitterly.

Chris is sitting on a cane sofa, glancing idly through a magazine. I stand in the doorway looking at him. He is the gold of the walls. His hair, a deeper gold in the muted light, is slicked back. He is wearing clothes that are unusual for him: a cream-coloured half-sleeved shirt and beige trousers. He is glowing as if the days in the sun have suffused his body with a light that blazes from within. I stand there drinking in everything about him.

The intensity of my longing must have touched him because he looks up suddenly, as if a finger had tapped him. 'Hey, Radha.' He smiles.

I sit on the sofa opposite him. 'Have you been waiting long?' I ask, trying to wave away the awkwardness that has suddenly crept into my voice.

'A few minutes.' He shrugs.

'Are you hungry?' Everything I had planned on telling him dries in my throat. Only banalities fill my mouth.

'You look beautiful,' he says.

'This is an old sari.'

'I wasn't talking about the sari. I said you look beautiful. You, Radha, you...' His eyes crinkle.

I feel heat gather in my cheeks. I look away. I can smell his fragrance. Crushed marigolds. Turmeric roots. A golden yellow fragrance. My fingers ache to touch that golden magnificence.

I see Unni looking at us. Behind that blank expression, I know Unni must be straining his ears to hear very word, making a note of every gesture, every smile, every detail, from the cut of my blouse to Chris's footwear. Suddenly I feel overwhelmed by Shyam's presence. His walls, his people, his ambitions, his ruthlessness, they press in on me.

'Let's go to the restaurant,' I say. I want to be some place where we are not the focus of attention.

'Who are these people?' Chris asks, rising from the sofa. He points to the cluster of photographs. 'Your family? Sham's?'

I try not to smile. Despite our best efforts, Chris still can't say Shyam.

'This,' I say, pointing to a studio portrait of a couple, 'is one set of my grandparents. The man, by the way, is Sethu. Sethu from Uncle's story. These,' I say, pointing to another one of a boyish young man and a girl with her hair in a little bun and a great deal of jewellery, 'are my parents. This is their wedding photograph.'

I move my finger to the left and point to the photograph of a man in uniform. 'This is Shyam's father. He was in the army.'

'And the others? Are they your extended family?'

'I really don't know who they are. Some minor royalty, I guess.' There are photographs of men in turbans and women with stone-studded brooches pinned to their saris. In the centre is a largish photograph of an imperious man seated on a straight-backed chair. He is holding a walking stick and the fingers of the hand holding the stick are studded with rings. A dog is sitting by the chair; both man and beast stare into the camera's eye. 'Shyam bought them from an old photo studio and had them framed and mounted.' I try to hide my embarrassment.

Chris is quiet. I can almost hear what he is thinking. I am thinking it too: He really is a sham. Old photographs are one thing. But what kind of man puts up strangers' pictures on his wall and pretends they are family?

We walk into the restaurant and sit at a table in the corner. The river is visible from here. We make desultory conversation. Chris drums his fingers on the table. 'I have never seen rain like this. Not even in Indonesia, which is very much like Kerala.'

'You should see the October storms. They are frightening. Thunder comes rolling in, and lightning tears the skies.'

It occurs to me then, that he may not be here to see the October storms.

I see that he is thinking the same.

His fingers brush mine. 'No,' I say, moving my hand away. 'Someone will see us.'

'Later,' I add, afraid that I have upset him.

He crinkles his eyes again and asks, 'Will there be a later?'

I drop my eyes.

I toy with the food on my plate. He eats with the absorption he seems to imbue his life with.

'Aren't you hungry?' he asks, forking a piece of chicken from my plate.

I see Pradeep staring at us from across the room. More notes to take to the master, I think. I decide to brazen it out. I catch Pradeep's eye. He rushes forward. 'Anything else, madam?'

'The Sahiv can't seem to get enough of our cooking,' I joke in Malayalam with an inflection that suggests indulgent mockery. I know what I am doing. I am wilfully drawing little walls around Chris, segregating him from me. Pradeep grins. I see his eyes clear. Suspicion dissolves.

Chris frowns. 'What did you say?'

'I told him that you are enjoying the food very much.'

'Don't do that. When you speak your language, I feel so excluded.' Chris leans forward.

'Do you want dessert?' I ask.

'Mocha Radha.' His eyes glint.

I smile, but look away. His flirtatious banter amuses me. It also scares me. He seems to do it so effortlessly.

'Do you have the tape for me?' I ask as we stand in the doorway. I can see that Chris is hesitant to suggest we go back to the cottage.

'It's in the cottage,' he says.

'In which case, I'll go with you.' I start walking.

'Are you sure?' he murmurs.

I know that he is not talking about walking to the cottage with him.

It had rained all afternoon and suddenly at dusk the skies had cleared. The night is resplendent with the stars in the skies and the fireflies in the trees. His hand reaches for mine. I let my fingers remain in his clasp.

Is this what it means to take your life into your hands?

I feel a shiver curl my heart into a roll of ash, grey-rimmed and crumbling. Cold that burns. Flames that freeze. I feel…I don't know what it is I feel any more.

I hear a hovering voice of caution: Uncle's. Is this why he is telling us the story of Sethu and Saadiya? Is he asking me to be prudent?

But Saadiya was only sixteen. At that age, the word 'consequence' has no bearing. I am thirty-two. I know where all this might lead. Yet, like Saadiya, perhaps like Sethu, I don't know what I can do to trim this fury of passion.

The cottage is dark. We walk hand in hand and it is in darkness that we take each other's clothes off. The night heightens every sound. Is it his breath, or mine that is rasping?

He is gentle. Very slowly, he turns me to him. His mouth erases the humiliation, eases the ache in my soul.

I reach for him, eager and hungry. His spine is knobbly under my fingers, the curve of his buttocks cold and smooth. Hair crackles. Static electricity. His mouth douses and then feeds the fires. I feel again that I am an instrument in his hands. Luring him with my curves and hollows, yet compelled to do his bidding.

An owl hoots. Sheets rustle. And I welcome him into me, again and again, a countless times.

Fireflies come in through the window. A firefly emits light as it sits on the bed frame. Another one is trapped in my hair. Yet another wings its way through the room, a darting green gem.

Chris reaches across and catches the one in my hair. 'Are you squeamish?' he asks.

I look at him. 'Why?'

'Don't be,' he says and lets the insect loose on my body.

It lights a path which Chris follows with his mouth and hands. He is Ravana, the demon king who sets aside his pride and confesses his longing to his wife Mandodari. He is Ravana, with twenty arms and ten heads, who cannot touch me enough, kiss me enough; his hands and mouths vie with each other to be the first to explore me. In their explorations I know the extent of desire. I feel within me joy, sheer joy. Then I know a sudden sorrow, for how long can this last? This fury of passion, how it thunders in my veins, daring obstacles, letting courage lead the way. Stop thinking, the voice in my head complains. Just be…Beacon-bearing insect and insatiable man: I feel every nerve end wake up and sing. I tremble. I ache. I reach for him again, unafraid to show how much I desire him.

The firefly flees into the night.

Chris looks at me. He is propped on his elbow.

'What do you call them?' he asks.

'Minnaminungu,' I say.

He tries to repeat it. But he can't get his tongue to curl around the word. The consonants weave in and out like the firefly's arc of light. 'I give up,' he chuckles.

'I think that's what I will call you. That's what you are. My min-min…whatever…' He traces my profile with the tip of his finger.

In the dark I glow, a blaze of green brilliance.

I rise from the bed. His bed. Our bed.

Chris lies with his limbs sprawled all over the bed. His arms rest on the pillow; his elbows form a parenthesis around his face. One of his legs is stretched out, the foot turning outward. The other is bent at the knee. A sheet, twisted and bunched, covers the top of his thighs. Wrinkles flare on either side of him.

I pause from picking up my clothes on the floor and look at him again. He is a painting, I think. A portrait of satiation, of a night of abandon. A moment of languor frozen. I feel a joy: he is mine.

I dress quickly. I see bruises on my neck and thighs. I touch them. My love lives on my skin. The fury of a passion I have never known before.

I sit by his side. I run my fingers through his hair. 'Where are you going?' His voice is soaked with sleep and sex.

'I have to go,' I whisper.

'Do you have to?' His fingers run up the inside of my arm and splay on my waist. I shiver.

'I have to go,' I say. 'I am sorry.'

'Okay, will you give me the eye cloth? It's somewhere here.'

I search for the eye cloth, a full-length sleeve scissored from an old flannel shirt.

'That's my eye cloth. I can't bear light in the morning. It makes my eyes water,' he had said when I first offered it to him to wipe his cello, thinking it was a rag he kept for the purpose.

'If you stay...I could drape your hair over my eyes and sleep with my arms around you...and when the sun gets stronger, I could hide my face between your thighs.'

I shiver again.

I drape the eye cloth over his eyes, switch off the light and walk to the door. I pause again. Good night, I whisper and, only for a moment, a small voice in me murmurs: you could have stayed awake till I left.

Uncle

I hear her come in. She is humming under her breath.

I glance at the clock on the wall. It is a quarter past eleven. Did she walk here by herself? Or did Chris walk with her? Which is worse? I don't know. Shyam will hear about this. He has eyes everywhere. Informants who keep their lord and master posted about all that goes on in his absence. My poor Radha. Does she realize what she is taking on with this new love she has found?

All day yesterday I worried about Radha. I was disturbed by what I had seen just before we went to the kathakali performance—Radha and Chris in each other's arms.

The next evening, Radha and Shyam had come to see me. Radha looked tired and wan. Her limbs dragged and her face was wiped clean of all animation. Could this be my Radha?

On the night of the performance, Radha had blazed with a thousand suns lighting her from within. She had been resplendent in her silks and new-found love. But the Radha before me was a woman crouching in a shell. A woman suffering. What could it be? Guilt or hopelessness? I felt anxiety cloud my eyes. Daylight had a way of leaching magic away.

Then I saw Shyam. He was smiling. It was a smile filled with arrogance and triumph. It was the smile of a conqueror.

He was Ravana in Bali Vadham. The ultimate picture of haughtiness. Ravana assesses his own success by asking himself: Why shouldn't I be happy with myself? I appeased the Lord Creator Brahma and made him offer me boons that I needed. I defeated kings and gods and founded an empire. I wrested away the heavenly chariot Pushpak from my half-brother Kubera, the god of wealth, and I amused the supreme destroyer, easy-to-anger Shiva by flinging the mountain Kailash down. My fame has spread everywhere and in all three worlds, there isn't anyone who doesn't know me or my powers.

The arrogance on Shyam's face worried me. It was Ravana's face reproduced: the face of a man who takes what he wants. Every fibre of his body pulsed with the measure of conquest. What had he done? What had he done to Radha?

Shyam flung himself into a chair. 'We met some of your comrades this morning,' he said.

I stared at him. Comrades. I had forgotten all about that period of my life. My brothers had hunted in the forests and drunk illicit liquor and experimented with marijuana; I experimented with communism. I wasn't a card-carrying member, but I was a sympathizer who believed enough in the movement to transport pamphlets and posters and other 'inflammatory materials' as the government called them. It was a risk, but I was willing enough.

No one suspected me, a dancer, of being connected with the movement and we had even evolved a password. A comrade would come backstage and ask, 'Is there a chuvanna-thaadi vesham tonight?'

Chuvanna-thaadi was red-beard and signified the vilest of characters, but the password worked, and it was only when I moved to Madras for a while that my comrades and I parted ways.

'Why do you look as if you have seen a ghost?' Shyam asked. 'I was referring to Kesavan. Didn't he perform with you?'

I nodded. 'How is he?' I asked.

'Well enough. His son is in Muscat, he told us.'

Shyam rose to leave. He looked at the table on the veranda, on which a few magazines were strewn about. He tidied the table and stacked the magazines into a pile. I watched him. I knew that sense of disquiet again. Why did he feel the need to lay his imprint on everything? Was he the same with Radha? What would he do if he ever found out about Radha and Chris?

When Shyam left, I asked Radha, 'Are you unwell? Or did Shyam and you quarrel? You look wrung out.'

'Shyam never quarrels. He has other ways of making his point,' she said. 'No, it's nothing.' Even her voice bore the fatigue that was in her eyes. I wondered again if it was fatigue or hopelessness.

I saw her eyes dart to the gate. I heard her start at every footstep. I knew she was waiting for Chris.

Then Chris lifted the latch of the gate and walked in. I saw Radha emerge again. Radha, alive and aware.

Their eyes met and locked. I saw the burden of waiting rise and dissipate.

I rise and walk to the window. I cannot sleep. I feel too wound up. In the morning, Maya will be here. I am not sure if I am prepared to cope with all the emotions that will rise to the surface when I see her again.

I hear a long-drawn yawn. Radha. She can't sleep either, I think. Should I go and talk to her? Perhaps it is best that I leave her with her thoughts. She is a woman in love again. I can see that. I think of what I said to her earlier. Of how there is only now.

What I failed to tell her was that the walls of 'now', her 'now', demand that they be built on deceit. The reality of deceit is that it has a way of sneaking into the past and the future. Will Radha be able to cope?

The curse of deception is that we can never erase it from our minds. I haven't led an exemplary life. It isn't as if I have a clear conscience. I have been deceitful. And I know the price I have had to pay for it.

I think of the only vesham in kathakali I have never been

enthusiastic about. That of Rama in Bali Vadham. It isn't an important role, nevertheless the degree of deception that the role demands unnerves me. In fact, the whole episode makes me uncomfortable. There is nothing inspiring or redeeming about it. Frankly, this is a section that ought never to have been made so much of. Everything in it reeks of chicanery and connivance.

I close my eyes and think of the chapter that is drawn from the Ramayana. Bali, the monkey-king, ruled Kishkindhya, a kingdom in the southern part of India. When Bali was very young, his father Indra, the king of gods, blessed his son that no matter who battled with Bali, the opponent's powers would be reduced by half and would shift to Bali during the battle. That was the first deception.

Soon, no one could vanquish Bali. Once, the demon Dundupi challenged Bali to a duel. Furious at the demon's effrontery, Bali decided to teach him a lesson. He began to wrestle with Dundupi. But the demon managed to free himself from Bali's clutches and flee. Bali, not about to let him go, chased the demon into a cave. He stood at the mouth of the cave and called to Sugriva, his younger brother, 'I am going after the demon and when I get him in my hands, I will break every bone in his body. I want you to wait here till I come back. If milk flows out, you will know that I have succeeded. But if blood flows out, you must leave immediately and protect our families and kinsmen.'

Sugriva waited outside the mouth of the cave. Some time later he heard Bali yelling, 'Help! Help! I'm being killed!' Then, to Sugriva's horror, he saw a rivulet of blood flowing out of the cave and he knew that his brother had been vanquished. What had really transpired was that the demon, realizing he was about to die, had played a final trick. As he struggled, he called out in a voice like Bali's, and when he saw Bali invoke a rivulet of milk, he conjured it to look like blood. That was the second act of deception.

In anger and grief, Sugriva sealed the mouth of the cave with a mighty rock. Then he went back to the kingdom and assumed the role of the king.

Bali was unaware of the trick and set about beating the life out of Dundupi. After killing the demon, he came to the mouth of the cave and found a huge rock blocking his way. He stared at the rock in surprise and then pushed it aside. 'Where are you, Sugriva, my dear brother?' he called. But there was no one there. Bali began to get anxious. He rushed to his palace and there he found his brother seated on the throne.

Suddenly Bali knew what had happened. His brother Sugriva had wanted to kill him and had sealed the mouth of the cave to ensure this. He stared at his brother angrily. 'So this is what you wanted. All this while you were pretending to be a loving brother and in your head you were plotting my downfall. You are a traitor!' he said. Bali must have nurtured a secret fear of his brother wanting the throne for himself. Isn't that why he was so easily deceived into thinking that his fear had come true? What then was the reality of the love he had for his brother? That was the third deception.

Bali banished Sugriva from the kingdom and Sugriva went to the forest with a band of faithful followers, which included Hanuman, the son of Vayu.

Later, when Rama and Lakshmana passed through the forests seeking Sita, they met Sugriva, who told them the story of his banishment. He narrated how Bali had seized the throne back and, to make matters worse, had married Sugriva's wife, thereby depriving him of his home and family.

'Everything I have is yours. But I have nothing to offer you,' Sugriva told Rama.

'Do not lose heart. I shall ensure that you find justice,' Rama said.

'No one can defeat Bali, he is so powerful,' Sugriva said. 'Besides, his father's boon ensures that in a battle his opponent's powers will be reduced by half.'

'Listen to me. I have a plan. This will not be a battle in the conventional sense,' Rama said.

The fourth scene of deception. It is here that I feel ashes coat my tongue. This righteous man, the epitome of all that is good and noble, wasn't above deceit.

Sugriva went to the palace doors and challenged Bali to a fight.

Bali looked up from what he was doing and said, 'What is wrong with that fool, Sugriva? Has he gone mad? Does he think he can defeat me?'

Bali screamed, 'Go away!'

But Sugriva continued to holler challenges. Bali lost his temper and stepped out of the palace and they began to wrestle. Rama, who was hiding behind a tree, shot an arrow which pierced Bali's heart and killed him. The fifth act of deception.

Thus Sugriva became king again, and his monkey army helped Rama in his battle against Ravana.

In the story there is no mention of the remorse Sugriva and Rama should have felt. How did they reconcile themselves to the deception they had carried out? That is the sixth and never discussed act of deception. Did they put it out of their minds and carry on as if nothing had happened? If so, they were without even the trace of a conscience. And these are the gods we have venerated for centuries. It frightens me to even think about it.

How do you live with such deceit for the rest of your life? How do you not let it haunt you? How do you balance all the acts of goodness you may do against that one act of deceit?

This is what worries me. How will Radha be able to live with herself? Or, for that matter, I?

Tomorrow morning I will begin my pilgrimage of deceit. Maya and I will seek stolen moments concocted with lies and complicity, and compromises we make with our conscience.

As I lie in bed, eyes wide open to darkness and deception, I think it is time I introduced reality into the fairytale world of Sethu and Saadiya.

Only then will Radha and Chris, and my Maya—for she too will hear this story—understand the gravity of what they have chosen for themselves.

1938–1940
The Grammar of Deceit

The delivery room was in a block that stood apart from the main hospital building. As if by positioning it there, the natural and joyful phenomenon of childbirth could be distanced from the horrors of disease and trauma. Whatever might have been the original reason, Dr Samuel approved wholeheartedly of this segregation. Shrieking women needed to be kept in their place.

But now, as he looked at Saadiya's wan face, he wished she would scream, shout, shriek, call her husband a few choice epithets as some of his patients did and, with the brutal force of that rage, push the baby out.

Instead, Saadiya lay there, her face contorting every time a contraction seized her, but not crying, not uttering a sound, not even a whimper. 'You don't have to bite down your pain,' Dr Samuel said. 'You may scream and shout; no one will hear you. Except me, and you know me. Don't you? Dr Samuel Sagayaraj. You are allowed to scream as loudly as you want, you know,' he tried to joke.

Saadiya turned her eyes to him as if she couldn't comprehend his meaning. The doctor met her eyes and what he saw filled him with unease. There was resignation there, and hopelessness. She should be trying to fight the pain, he thought. Instead, she lay there as if suffering the pain was penance for a crime she had committed. The doctor knew fear then, like he had never known before. It was as if the girl was willing herself to die.

Where was Seth, Sethu, he corrected himself. Sethu would know what was wrong. Why did she seem so disengaged from what was happening to her body?

A huge old neem tree stood outside the delivery ward. Sethu stood beneath the tree, chewing on a stalk. Its bitterness flooded his mouth. How much longer would it be, he wondered.

Usually there were at least a dozen people huddled beneath the neem tree. Expectant fathers and soon-to-be grandparents, to-be uncles and aunts, bystanders who could do nothing but flinch at the thought of what was happening within the labour room.

But this day, the neem tree stood all by itself and the long corridor that flanked the labour ward was wreathed in evening shadows unmarred by human presence. Sethu walked towards the wooden staircase. He sat on one of the steps, still chewing on his stalk. She had been in the labour room for more than five hours now. Dr Samuel was with her. All would be well. But he felt again that strange feeling—part fear, part joy, part uncertainty and horror.

To quell the sensation, he counted the steps. Six steps. How few they were. Just six steps and yet, when he had walked in, he had felt as if they went on for ever. Like time, he thought. Yesterday seemed so long ago, and the day before that even farther.

At first Sethu had wondered how he would cope with this ache deep within him. Saadiya had returned to Arabipatnam and he didn't know when he would see her next. A few weeks later, the intensity of the ache lessened. At times, Saadiya seemed distant, almost a dream. Perhaps it was best this way, he told himself. What hope was there for a love like theirs? What future? It was best that it died even before it began.

At twilight, Sethu heard a knock on the door. The doctor was in Madurai. He was to return only the following morning. Who could it be, he wondered.

She stood there on the side of the road, her hands at her side, her face forlorn and afraid. He stared at her, unable to believe his eyes. Her face was naked for the world to gaze upon and she was all by herself. 'What?' he stammered, suddenly struck by the enormity of her presence at his doorstep.

'I chose to come to you,' she said, and slid into a little heap at his feet.

The next morning, the doctor arrived beaming. What is he so smug about, Sethu wondered when he opened the door.

'It is wonderful to be back,' the doctor said in greeting. Unable to contain himself any longer, he burst out, 'I am to be married. I have found a help meet. Bone of my bones and flesh of my flesh. She is a relative—her father is from my village. In her home, they eat the same rice as I do. In fact, she won't eat anything else. She's educated. After all, she is a doctor's daughter, and her father said that he has taught her to assist him. What more can I ask for? My mother decided that we should announce the engagement right away and, after the dinner, she and I met the minister and do you know what she said to me? She said, "I would like us to call our home Rehoboth. For now the Lord hath made room for us and we shall be fruitful in this land." You probably recognize that easily enough. Genesis 27. 22. It made my heart sing to know my help meet is a woman who lives by the Holy Book.'

Sethu smiled. He recognized the help meet as well. Genesis 2. 20.

He didn't know what he felt about this new development, though. Astonishment that the doctor who he thought was destined to be an eternal bachelor had finally chanced upon someone suitable, relief that the doctor would now perhaps understand his situation.

Then the doctor spotted Saadiya, who was trying to merge into the shadows that veiled the veranda. 'Who is this?'

Suddenly he recognized her and his voice rose in incredulous fear. 'You are the Haji's daughter. What are you doing here? I don't understand.'

Sethu took the bag that had dropped from the doctor's hand. 'I will explain,' he said, leading the way into the house.

The doctor listened, his bafflement turning into fury as Sethu used words he couldn't even begin to comprehend. Love. Life. Soul. These were concepts one used to describe one's relationship with the Heavenly Father, not the Haji's youngest daughter.

'I will not even try to understand what you are saying. How do you expect me to? It has no meaning. You say love. What do you know of love? What you call love is lust. Yes, I say, lust. Do you realize that you have dragged a girl out of her home and family? And for what?'

'But I didn't,' Sethu protested, cutting the doctor off.

'You do realize what this means, don't you?' the doctor said. He polished the lenses of his spectacles as if to give his hands something to do. He fears he might throttle me otherwise, Sethu thought with a laugh.

Why wasn't he worried? Here he was with a girl who had chosen to trust her life to his keeping. He had no visible prospects except for his job with the hospital, and that was in jeopardy from what he could gauge from the doctor's anger.

The doctor saw the young woman step outside the veranda. He saw her walk towards a mango tree by the well. He swallowed. The girl seemed so much at ease here in his house. How long had she been staying here, he wondered. Perhaps he could persuade her to return. How could Seth have been so impulsive, so irresponsible?

It isn't the way you imagine it to be, Seth was saying. What did he mean? The doctor felt his anger return a hundredfold. He averted his gaze and said, 'Look at her. She is a young girl with silly fancies in her head. This can only be your doing. She would never have had the courage to walk away from her home if you hadn't encouraged her. This is a small town. Do you realize the implications of what you have done? But you never think, do you? You are always rushing around in a hurry to get things done, to prove how capable you are. Do you think I don't know that you broke into the quarantine camp and stole supplies from there? You put my name in jeopardy then and you do so again now.'

Sethu stared at the doctor, aghast. The ugliness of anger marked his face with a bestiality that was unnerving him. His eyes were narrowed slits; his teeth were pointed and sharp; his mouth snarled...who was this man?

He felt rage gather in him. 'You were glad enough then, when I brought the medicines. When it suits you, you call it God's hand and when it doesn't, it is my wilfulness. You are a hypocrite, do you know that? A sanctimonious hypocrite and a coward.'

Samuel Sagayaraj's face paled. He stared at Seth's face. This man who spewed such venom, was it Seth? For how long had he nurtured these feelings within him? He must hate me so, Samuel Sagayaraj thought. Which is why he cares not a bit about how all this will affect my reputation. And it was the sense of betrayal that tore away the mask after all and made him say, 'You broke my trust. This practice, this hospital, my reputation, everything is at stake because you want to fuck the Haji's daughter.'

Sethu felt his eyes widen. FUCK. Had the doctor actually used the word? He hadn't thought the doctor knew the word. From lust to fuck had taken two minutes.

'Fuck,' Sethu repeated in bemusement.

'Yes, fuck. That's all there is on your mind. You wanted a fuck but why did you have to choose this girl? Aren't there any whores around? What does she have that the women here don't? A cunt lined with pearls?'

Sethu began to laugh. Fuck. Cunt. Was this Dr Samuel Sagayaraj, the man with the keys to the kingdom of heaven?

The doctor stopped, stricken. What was he saying? When he lost his temper, unbidden, epithets from his university years fouled his mouth. He wiped his mouth with the back of his palm.

'I am sorry. I shouldn't have used foul language. There is no excuse...' Samuel Sagayaraj's voice was contrite. Sethu stared at him for a long moment. 'Yes, there is no excuse for what you said. The girl is to be my wife.'

'Seth.' The doctor reached forward to grip Sethu's wrist. 'You can't be serious. Send her back and everything will be all right again. I'll tell you what. I'll take her back. The Haji will listen to me. He will take her back. No one needs to know about this sordid business.'

One by one, Sethu prised away the tentacles of that grip. 'I will not let her go. And she will not agree to it, no matter what you say to her. You don't understand, do you? We love each other.'

In the silence that followed, Sethu knew once again the stirring of freedom he felt when he held Saadiya in his arms. It was time to end the pretence.

So, when the doctor, all traces of emotion wiped from his face said, 'In which case, you have to go. You have to leave my home and the hospital right away', Sethu welcomed the rejection.

There could never have been an amicable parting, he realized then. No matter what the reason for his leaving, the doctor would have seen it as a betrayal. Acolytes, he thought, are not allowed to have a mind of their own.

The doctor went to sit at his writing table. The room was a replica of his office at the hospital. His fingers drummed on the sheet of glass that spread itself on the wood top of the table, for a moment. Then he clasped his hands as if to rein in his unruly thoughts. 'You do realize, don't you? That you have betrayed my faith in you.' His voice was low, even and harsh.

Sethu felt sorrow sweep over him. Who was this man, he wondered again.

'I made you what you are and I didn't expect gratitude, but I did expect loyalty. So there is nothing I will do to help you.' The doctor removed his glasses and wiped them carefully. 'You talk of marrying her. But who will marry you? You are of one faith and she of another. In the eyes of your God and hers, this will never be a marriage. Of bodies, perhaps. But never of souls. And what of your children? Which faith will you follow in your home? Hers? Yours? As for your children, they will grow godless.' The doctor shuddered at the thought of young minds that could seek no comfort in the thought of a benevolent, all-forgiving father. 'Every day you will discover differences. You will find that you have no meeting ground. How can there be one? Thorns, sweat, dust, that will be the sum total of your life. Every day, you will regret what you have done, and the sorrow that it will cause will leave no place for happiness.'

Sethu flinched. The calculated girth of the words spoken caused a distance between them that they would never be able to bridge. If this was how it was to end, so be it. He met the doctor's gaze and said, 'I know you are angry. You have every right to be. Just as I have the right to want to make a life with Saadiya. I will leave. I did expect you to understand, but I was wrong. I bear you no malice, no anger. You helped me when I had no one else and I will never forget that. God be with you and...' Sethu fumbled for the phrase, 'your help meet in your Reheboth.'

He turned to go, then stopped. 'There is one other thing. My name is Sethu. Not Seth. I am a Hindu. Not a Christian, as you thought. But I believed every word of the book. I believed that your religion taught love and forgiveness. I believed that you would find it in you to offer us some of that precious Christian charity of spirit you talk so much about. But then, you always draw from the Bible what suits you and ignore the rest. So I will now do as it is advised in the Book of Job in your Bible. "I would seek unto God, and unto God would I commit my cause." It doesn't matter whether it is her God, or mine, or even yours. If there is a God, that God will take care of us.'

When Sethu and Saadiya were gone, Samuel Sagayaraj sat with his head in his hands. He felt drained and bereft. But what else could he have done? To help Seth and the girl would have been to show approval, and he didn't approve. As for his not being a Christian, what Seth—Sethu, he corrected himself—had done was unpardonable.

The doctor wiped the sweat off his face and drew his writing materials out. He began a letter to the Haji. He had to explain, make amends, distance himself from all that had happened. The man cheated me as well, he began. Henceforth, it will be my wife who accompanies me, he finished.

'You are not to worry. Everything will be all right,' Sethu said.

They were in a horse cart. Saadiya sat opposite him. Their knees met and parted with every movement of the cart.

'Malik, I am not,' she said.

Sethu straightened, startled. 'Malik? Why do you call me that? My name isn't Malik.'

'But it is!' Saadiya whispered. 'You are my Malik. The incomparable one who came from across the seas. Strong and straight, a leader among men, one who could be trusted to brave the ocean and winds and unknown ways. You are Malik. Don't you see?'

Sethu looked at her with a great surge of love. She made him feel ten feet tall. Nevertheless.

He caressed her cheek with a finger. 'I am Sethu. Not Seth. Not Malik. I have had enough of play-acting,' he said, trying to be as gentle as he could. 'You must think of me as Sethu.'

Saadiya smiled. No matter what he said, he was her Malik. The incomparable.

Sethu saw her smile. An inward smile that seemed to shrug his words away. He felt a sudden fear. Was this the difference the doctor had predicted, no, cursed him with?

'It is a village only in name. It's just a few streets and the sea,' James Raj had said. 'Very few people live in that area. And those that do won't bother you. They have their own secrets and lives. I built the house thinking it would be nice to live by the sea. The sea has given me all that I have. But my wife refuses to leave Nazareth. She wants people and streets and she is a great churchgoer...so the house lies vacant most of the time. Once in a while she consents to go there with me, but even then she begins to get restive. You can stay there till all this has settled down and if you like it as much as I do, you can continue to stay rent free. Do you understand?'

Sethu tried to read the man's face. What was he expected to do in return? Then Sethu remembered his lesson from the sea: Don't fight it. Let it be.

So he agreed. As he did to James Raj's offer of a job. 'I need a man like you. Someone who can speak English, do the accounts and help me with my business.'

The word business worried Sethu. No one knew what James Raj did. Some said he had a fleet of fishing boats. Others said he traded in diamonds and precious stones. But he was accorded as much respect as the doctor. For James Raj was the richest man in Nazareth. Perhaps the doctor resented this, for he referred to James Raj as an upstart and when he was vexed with a story of James Raj's inordinate kindness, he would mumble, 'The upstart smuggler can afford to give it away. After all, it is ill-gotten money, easy money.' James Raj was also the only being in all of Nazareth who was not awed by the doctor. Which is why, when Sethu and Saadiya walked out of the doctor's house, Sethu thought there was only one thing to do: seek out James Raj and ask for his help.

Sethu knew he was exchanging one master for another. But James Raj had asked no questions when Sethu said, 'I need a house and a job. The doctor doesn't need me or my services any more.'

James Raj nodded. He had already heard, but he pretended that he knew nothing. James Raj knew the power of discretion. Besides, it made him feel good to score one over that Bible-thumping quack who behaved as if he was the Lord Jesus's apostle.

'Go to Manappad. You can use my horse cart to get there,' he said. 'You will find peace and quiet. In a few days I will send for you.'

So Sethu and Saadiya went to Manappad, to home their love in a mansion that sat on the sands of a wild sea.

Saadiya was enchanted. How could anything be more perfect, she said again and again. She flung the windows open and the sound of the sea spread itself through the house. There was nothing between the house and the sea except creamy sand. The breeze blew all day.

'We will have to leave when the summer begins. It will be hot here,' Sethu said.

'I don't care how hot it gets,' Saadiya dimpled. 'Just to be able to see the sea...just to see the horizon day after day, what could be more perfect? This is my jannath!'

Sethu's brow wrinkled at the unfamiliar word. 'Jannath?'

'Paradise. That is what it is called in the Holy Koran.'

Sethu saw the pleasure in her eyes and knew pleasure himself. God was good. Long ago, the astrologer who had cast his horoscope had said, 'This boy is fortune's child. No matter what, he will always fall on his feet.'

It was true. First there had been Maash. Then the doctor. And now James Raj. Each of them arriving at a point in his life when he didn't know which way to go. He had to pay a price for their succour, but that was to be expected: nothing in life came without a tag. Not even love. For even Saadiya wore the vestments of difference.

Sethu peeled a plantain for Saadiya. 'This is all I could find,' he said, pointing to a hand of plantains that he had managed to buy from a vendor. 'Tomorrow I will find us all we need. Chairs and a table, utensils for our kitchen and provisions for you to cook with and...' he paused slyly, 'a bed.'

When Saadiya coloured, he gleamed.

'For now we have to settle for this,' he said, pointing to the palm-leaf mat on which he had spread a thick cotton sheet. 'This mat will have to be our mattress and for a pillow you can use my arm.' He smiled.

Her gaze widened and dropped. 'Come,' he said, sitting on the floor on their makeshift bed.

She stood, unsure and afraid.

'Come,' he said again.

When she didn't move, he rose and stood before her. 'What am I to do with you?' he asked gently, raising her chin with his forefinger. Above her upper lip was a line of sweat. She is frightened, he thought. Lowering his head, he gathered with his mouth the beads of sweat as if they were rice pearls. I have tasted the salt of her skin, he thought with growing pleasure. She trembled. Was it the feel of his mouth on her skin, or the way he stood so that not even a whisper of silk could pass between their bodies?

He felt her lean into him. Then he led her to their bed and drew her down with him.

She lay on her back, stretched out and still, her eyes closed. Sethu gazed at her and swallowed his disquiet—was this the spectre of difference? Then he felt a wave of love exorcize his fear. How beautiful she is, he thought. And she's mine. My own.

She let him caress her, but when his hand cupped her breast, she sat up. 'No, you can't,' she said, in a voice striated with terror.

'Why not? I am your...' Sethu paused, then spoke with as much conviction as he could muster, 'your husband.'

He saw her look at him. He saw the fear in her eyes dissipate. He took her in his arms again. Slowly, he ran a finger along the line of her neck and traced circles on the skin at the nape of her neck. He felt her body relax against his. He pressed his lips against her forehead. She snuggled even closer to him. Drawing courage from this, he ran his tongue along the curve of her closed eyelids. She shuddered in his arms and as if she couldn't have enough of this, enough of him, he felt her arms wrap around him. He smiled against her skin.

'I don't understand what is happening to me,' she murmured.

'Hush, hush,' he whispered. 'There is nothing to understand. It is just you and me and how we feel about each other.'

'Now unbutton my shirt,' he said.

Her hands shook as she slipped a button through the button-hole.

'Are we to stay like this all night? Oh Saadiya, how you waste time!' With a little laugh, he helped her take his shirt off.

He waited for her to protest when his hands fumbled with her clothes. But she lay against him and let him remove, one by one, each piece of her clothing. He unwound the long scarf she had draped around her shoulders. He snapped apart the buttons of her long-sleeved blouse and gently eased open the knot at her waist. Her skirt slithered away from her.

'What is this?' Sethu mumbled, when his fingers encountered fabric instead of skin.

Beneath, she wore a long chemise and when Sethu's fingers lingered at its neckline, she covered his hand with hers.

'Don't,' he whispered.

'Let me look at you,' he said and watched with amusement as Saadiya covered her face. She who had never shown her face to a man lay naked before him.

He gave her a sidelong glance, and felt again a tide of love. His. She was his. Her disarrayed hair and clothes showed the extent of his trespassing hands and mouth.

'Don't,' he said, drawing her fingers away from her face. 'I am your husband. You are mine. There is no need to feel ashamed or even embarrassed.'

As he swooped down to cover her mouth with his, he felt the hard nubs of her nipples graze his. He felt her lips part. The wetness. The glorious liquid wetness in his mouth, on his fingers, gathering him into her. He laughed again in triumph, knowing the extent of her desire.

What does it matter, all these differences between Saadiya and me? What does it matter, for I have this, he thought. How can anything be more perfect than the soft skin of her inner thighs? Or anything be more comforting than to lie as I do, pressed against her back, my breath fanning the back of her neck, my hand cupping her breast, and knowing myself held in the grasp of her love?

How it enfolded him, that concave space between her inner thighs. A nest for him to lay his limpness and seek new strength. Mother. Hope. Comforter. As he felt himself grow and stiffen, that soft space became a wanton creature, urging him on with velvet paws, more, more, more...

As sleep came, he knew a quietness of spirit, an incredible calm, a peace.

So this is content, Sethu found himself thinking in the next few weeks. The thought came to him when he wasn't expecting it, and that made it so much more precious. It came to him when he raised his eyes from his plate of food and found her devouring him with her eyes. It came to him when he hurt his finger while hammering a nail into the wall and she rushed to his side with tears in her eyes and licked the drops of blood away.

Content. It came to him when they walked on the sands and she collected shells that she later lined on the windowsill of their bedroom. He watched the breeze toss her hair and make her eyes dance.

Content. It played in the songs that filled their home. Only he could have thought of buying such a thing, Saadiya laughed when he brought home a second-hand, or was it third-hand, wind-up gramophone and a stack of records. Only Sethu could have been so easily fooled, Saadiya grumbled when he found the stylus had no needle. Only Sethu could have thought of stripping off a branch of the acacia and taking from it a thorn to place in the stylus, Saadiya said in admiration as the acacia thorn coaxed out the notes from the record.

Content. It grew like the pomegranate sapling he brought home for her because she said that jannath was incomplete without a pomegranate tree.

Content. It flashed a multitude of colours for it was a tri-coloured lantern Sethu found in a junkyard, abandoned by a railway pointsman, or perhaps it had been stolen from one. Sethu cleaned the three pieces of glass, inserted a new wick, and showed Saadiya a new alphabet for togetherness: green when Sethu wanted her, red when she wanted him, yellow when either wanted a pause from loving. In those first weeks, the colour yellow never glowed.

But content is a demanding mistress with a rapacious orifice. As the extraordinary settled into routine, Sethu found himself getting restless. 'Do you think James Raj will send word today?' he asked every morning.

Saadiya shook her head. Who was James Raj, she wondered. Why did he have to send word?

One day Saadiya asked, 'Why?'

'Why?' Sethu looked at her in surprise. 'My dear girl, if I don't start earning soon, we'll starve. My money has almost run out.'

She looked at her feet. 'Oh,' she said. Money. They needed money to live. In Arabipatnam, everyone had money and no one ever used the word starve. For the first time in all the days that Saadiya had left home, she knew fear.

'Don't look so worried.' Sethu laughed, pulling her into his arms. 'I am here. I will take care of you. Don't you trust me? I'll look after you better than your Vaapa ever did.'

Saadiya smiled. But it was a smile to mask her uncertainty. What would life throw their way?

James Raj sent word. Sethu presented himself at his home in Nazareth. James Raj looked at Sethu as if he didn't recognize him. Sethu smiled hesitantly. What could be wrong? Had the doctor managed to dissuade James Raj? What would he and Saadiya do then? The older man shifted in his chair and from his breast pocket he drew a piece of paper. He studied it for a moment and said, 'Thy way is in the sea, and the path in the great waters, and thy footsteps are not known.'

James Raj waggled his eyebrows. 'Do you recognize that?'

Sethu looked at the older man in surprise. James Raj, he had heard, professed little faith, least of all in the Bible. But he nodded. 'Psalm 77.19.'

James Raj beamed. 'So it is true what they say. The youngest of the kondai sisters said that you know every word of the Bible. She came here secretly, asking me to help you. Their mother is a distant relative of mine. The doctor doesn't like them visiting me, but Mary Patti doesn't care what the good doctor thinks. The little kondai is the same. It's the older ones who are his slaves. But you are not a Christian. How is it then that you know each psalm, every word?'

Sethu allowed himself a smile. He felt relieved. 'I read it a great many times and I seem to remember almost all of it. I suppose I have a good memory.'

'Good!' James Raj stood up. 'You have a phenomenal memory, my boy. Do you know what that means? I can use your memory instead of ledgers. Everything will become so much simpler!'

'For the first time in a long time, I feel sure. As if I know what has to be done,' Sethu told Saadiya, who sat patting a mound of sand into a landscape of hillocks.

She looked up.

They were sitting on the sands by the sea. The twilight bathed the waves in a haze of colour and Sethu felt at peace.

He smiled. 'You are such a child. And I feel so responsible for you. I was afraid, horribly so. What if I had done wrong in taking you away? What if James Raj's job hadn't come through? So many what ifs…Everything scared me.'

'Why?' she asked. What could Malik have been scared of? Her incomparable, courageous Malik.

'Do you really want to know?'

'Tell me.' Her voice was softly persuasive. 'I might not understand, but tell me.'

Sethu stretched his legs and leaned back on his elbows. He looked at the horizon.

'Across the seas is Ceylon. This fear I have, it began before I went there,' Sethu said, his voice already tight with the memory of pain. 'I told you why I left home, didn't I? When I met Maash, I thought I had got past the fear of failure. Then it began again, only this time it was because of him. Maash. The man who took me to Ceylon.

'He was the nicest man I had met. He was kind and generous. He taught me all I knew and he even helped me get past my difficulty with arithmetic. But there was a side to him that I shut myself to. And once I left his home, it faded into an uncertain memory. Sometimes I even wondered if I had imagined it all.

'I moved away from Colombo and in Kandy I met Balu. Balu was perhaps my first friend. A little later, he was transferred to the Pamban quarantine camp. A year after that, I went there and we were together again. I loved him as if he were my brother.

'One night we were talking about our growing-up years in Colombo. Balu had been drinking steadily all evening and as he spoke his words grew more and more bitter. Then he said, "All of what I have done in my life I can live with; what I find unbearable is the thought that I sold myself. I was young and didn't know enough, and the man…" He stopped when he saw the horror in my eyes.

'"Yes," he said softly. "The man was persuasive—I'll be able to help you, he said, I'll find you a government job—and I thought, I won't lose anything. All he wants to do is hold me when he shags. He wants to kiss my penis and lick my balls. What does it matter, I thought, as long as I didn't care for any of it. I wasn't being violated. The man kept his word. He helped me find this job."

'"There was a back issue of a newspaper in the supplies that arrived today," Balu said after a long silence. "I saw a report that he is dead."

'And then Balu said, "He died in his home. He is from Kerala, like you."

'I felt my heart sink, Saadiya, I felt as if someone was ripping the veils off my past. It couldn't be, I told myself. "What was his name?" I asked.

'Then Balu spoke Maash's name and I knew horror again. It couldn't be true. I tried not to think of the nights Maash had crept into my bed. Of how he would put his arm around me and I would hear his fist moving. Up and down, up and down. It has to be the crudest sound ever. The sordidness of it repelled but, like Balu, I let it be. He was just holding me, I thought. I was neither a victim nor a participant. Later, when I was older, I realized that he had been using me. But I shut my mind to the thought.

'Balu was dredging out the coarseness of that memory; the stench and vileness of it…and I felt something smash into my brain. I was angry with Maash for abusing my trust. I was furious with Balu for making me see Maash for who he truly was. More than anything else, I was angry with myself for having allowed it to continue. How could I have been such a coward? How could I have been so afraid? I knew I had let it be because if I had protested, I would have had nowhere to go.

'I wasn't thinking straight, you understand. I looked around wildly.

There was a penknife Balu had left on a table. I grabbed it and I remember screaming, "Stop it, stop it!" and then I stabbed him.

'Why? I don't know. Perhaps because he tore that last veil off. Then I ran. I ran into the ocean where the fishermen were about to leave and I left with them. I have been running ever since, Saadiya. How can I shrug off my past? There is the sordidness of my association with Maash. There is Balu. I do not know if he is alive or if I am a murderer. And now...' Sethu paused.

Saadiya leaned forward. 'And now...' she prompted.

Sethu looked at her. He wondered if she had understood anything at all of what he had said—the murkiness of his past, his fears and anxieties. She was such a child.

He wanted to tell her how, with James Raj on his side, he felt secure and protected. And he saw that she waited for him to say that it was she who made the difference.

Sethu took her foot in his hand. How small it was, the arch high and curved. He stroked the instep, causing grains of sand to rain and said, 'Now it doesn't matter. When I met you, it was as if my life had come full circle. I was cleansed. And this job, it makes me feel that we have a chance.'

Saadiya smiled. Such was the triumph of their love, she thought. Sethu gleaned the smile and understood the measure of that triumph, for it was his as well.

So Sethu went to work and Saadiya cooked, cleaned, stared at the sea, and waited. This was what wives in Arabipatnam did and Saadiya did it easily enough. Till the waiting began to stretch late into the evening and sometimes way past midnight and into the early hours of dawn. In those silent hours, even the sea sounded listless to her. When she looked out of the window, the expanse of the skies and the glaze of the sand hurt her eyes.

Days stretched into months and Saadiya knew fear again. It wasn't the fear of poverty. This was the fear of another hunger. To be with her sisters and Ummama, Suleiman and Zuleika. To be with Vaapa. She felt sorrow creep into her mind. For her family she would never see again. For all the pain she had caused. She began to fear that she would have to pay a price for abandoning them. This was to be her punishment, she thought: to be lonely. To be trapped in a space as confined and as short of air as Arabipatnam had been. She wept and then hastily wiped her eyes, hearing the creak of the gate. Sethu would be furious if he knew that she cried for them.

Another night, when she lay by herself in her bed, wondering when Sethu would arrive, she remembered how Ummama had said that one could find solace in the Holy Koran. So the next day, when Sethu returned home, Saadiya asked him if he would bring her a copy.

Sethu felt a weight settle on his brow. Was this the difference the doctor had prophesied? 'Why do you need one?' he demanded, setting down his cup of tea. 'I thought we told each other that we don't need religion or religious teachings.'

'This has nothing to do with religion. I have so much time and I do nothing.'

'In which case, why don't you do some handiwork? Weave baskets, or make silk flowers, or sew. You could do some embroidery. I can bring you beautiful threads. Something other than read the Koran,' Sethu said quickly.

'You are turning this into something else. How many baskets can I weave? How many flowers do I embroider? I am alone all day. I am lonely. Don't you understand?' Saadiya snapped.

Sethu looked at her with narrowed eyes. That night she turned the yellow panel of the lantern on. Sethu sighed. Despite all their frequent squabbling, at night all was forgotten and her passion matched his. To punish him with the lexicon he had taught her was cruel. He turned the panel to green. She moved the panel back to yellow. 'Don't be cruel, Saadiya,' he pleaded.

She turned on her side in reply. Sethu smiled in the darkness and caressed her arm. She shrugged his hand away. He felt her stiffen. He thought he heard a muffled sob. 'Oh lord, Saadiya, why are you crying?' he pleaded. 'I'll fetch you whatever you want.'

When Saadiya turned to him, he felt his misery lift. He couldn't deny her what she wanted, but he would find a way around this unhealthy craving.

He brought her the Koran, and the Holy Bible, the Thirukkural and the Ramayana. 'I know you read the Koran in Arabic, but didn't you tell me that your community writes Arabic using the Tamil alphabet? So you can read Tamil, isn't that right? In which case, you can read all these books. You can have the religions of the world to fill your empty hours.'

Her arms laden with the books, Saadiya said, 'I like reading and I will read them all, but you can't expect me to forget what I have learnt ever since I was a child. The Koran is more than a book. The Koran teaches a way of life. Is that so wrong?'

'So does Hinduism,' Sethu retorted. 'Besides, it is an older religion.'

'You don't understand what I am saying.' Saadiya shook her head. Was it in exasperation or sorrow?

Sethu looked at her for a long moment and then turned away. He didn't understand her any more. Why was she being so difficult? He could see that she was miserable, but couldn't understand what caused the misery. Particularly when life had become so much easier.

James Raj was a good employer. He made no unreasonable demands and if Sethu worked long hours, it was because he volunteered to do so. As for the business without a name, Sethu called it trading, though there were no ledgers or written records of transactions. Some might even call it smuggling, but it wasn't really so. Besides, Sethu liked the challenge. He was making money, too. More than he had ever expected to. James Raj gave him a bonus for every successful transaction and Sethu was beginning to feel a confidence that had eluded him since he struck a knife in Balu's abdomen.

If only Saadiya wouldn't be so trying. She seldom smiled, and her eyes hurled accusations at him.

Sethu went to Nazareth. He needed to talk to someone. There was only James Raj. James Raj listened to him quietly. 'I don't understand her any more,' Sethu said.

'Here, drink some buttermilk,' James Raj said, gesturing to the glasses of buttermilk that someone had brought in.

'She is lonely. She is used to being with people. Here, she is all by herself most of the day. It fosters strange thoughts, peculiar cravings,' the older man said, wiping his mouth with the back of his hand. 'Once she has a baby, she will be all right. Find her a pet for now. A kitten, perhaps. It'll grow up quickly and won't need much caring for after that. By that time, if she is pregnant, she will have the thought of the baby to occupy her.'

Sethu grinned. This was why he liked James Raj. The man was

practical, unlike the doctor who would have quoted a verse from the Bible and asked him to pray for guidance.

When Saadiya missed her period for the second time, the midwife confirmed the pregnancy. Sethu swallowed his pride and took her to Nazareth, to Dr Samuel Sagayaraj. No matter what their differences, the doctor was the best man to help bring this baby of theirs into the world.

The doctor examined her, gave her a list of dos and don'ts, and patted her back with a smile. He looked through Sethu and acknowledged him just once, to explain the prescription.

Sethu was quiet on their way home. The doctor's rejection had hurt him. Once he could have talked to Saadiya about it. Now, it was as if she had withdrawn from him. Completely. Irrevocably.

Where was his Saadiya?

I could tell him. I, Saadiya Mehrunnisa could tell him if only he would care to listen.

I lie here in this bed. The doctor tells me that I should fight the pain. He has gone to look for Sethu. To bring him to my side to persuade me to shout my pain, vent my agony.

My anguish is like a ball of iron. It stays rooted and refuses to budge.

I see disdain. In the holy books that you brought me—yours, mine and others', I see contempt for a love we tried to tend. Ours is an unholy love.

I see contempt in the eyes of our neighbours. They will not let their wives or daughters associate with me. He is blameless; she is the wanton creature, they say. She is the one who ran away from home. What could he do? The poor man. He had to take her in. That is what they say.

Everywhere I go, everything I do, I hear the words: You are to blame.

When the baby kicks me, I hear the echo: You are to blame.

I try praying, but even God turns his head away.

You, my husband—but you are not my husband, for we are not wed—tell me I am silly. That these voices of contempt I hear are merely voices in my head.

But I know. My anguish blossoms from that.

Early this afternoon, as I waited in the hospital corridor while you went to fetch the doctor, I saw Vaapa and Suleiman.

I saw them look at my distended belly. I saw Vaapa's eyes narrow and heard Suleiman gasp. Then Suleiman's eyes met mine and I saw the uncertainty in them. I saw his love for me vanquish the hatred and his lips stretch into an arc of tenderness. I saw him lean towards me and I saw Vaapa touch his elbow with a finger.

They turned on their heels and walked away quickly. I wanted to run after them. I wanted to fall at Vaapa's feet and plead, 'I have sinned, Vaapa. Forgive me, please Vaapa. If only you would.'

The pain rips though me, but I clench my teeth. Not even the thought of the baby wills me to fight it. It would be best if the baby and I died here.

What kind of life would it have anyway, with no ancestry to speak of, no family, not even a religion or a god to call its own?

Why does the baby have to live? Why should I?

'You mustn't be like this,' Sethu says. I try to read his eyes. What does he want from me?

'Saadiya, my love,' he says. I feel myself relent at the emotion in his voice. If only he knew how much power he exercises over me.

'Saadiya, my precious girl, have you forgotten our dreams? This baby is a seal of approval from God. He wants our love to be. This baby is us, Saadiya. Saadiya, please, you must…' His words still. I know what he wants to say even if he doesn't.

I must fight. I must not give up. I must be more responsible. The baby's life is in my hands. But I don't want this child. Why bring forth a child that will have to pay for my sins? Our sins.

'If this baby is born, it has to be brought up as a true Muslim,' I hear myself say.

Sethu stares at me. He is shocked. 'Is that what it's about? Religion?'

I feel a contraction begin. I mutter through clenched teeth, 'Isn't that what everything is about? Faith. How can I allow a life to be born if I don't know what that life has to look forward to? Don't you see, I want my child to know God, my god. I want my child to belong.'

Sethu puts his hand on mine and says gently, 'Whatever you wish. Only let this child, our child, be born.'

The contraction grabs me from my hipbones and prises me apart. I scream. I scream again.

Veeram

Come then, this is not as difficult as you think it is. Veeram: you may think of it for now as valour, and that is the expression we will perfect here. Allow your eyes to widen. Yes, just as in raudram. Your eyes have to open wide, but do not glare. Let your nostrils flare, as though sensing victory. The mouth is set and the jaw is clenched. You must inhale as you usually do, but try and exhale through the eyes. Then the cheeks will acquire a mobility of their own...but you already know that. Now, to crown that valour, you must let your shoulders and chest and your gaze turn ever so gently this way and that to either side. You are the lord surveying your conquests and empire.

Now think. Where does valour derive from? Yes, you are right. It is courage. But what is courage?

For this we shall look to nature again.

Take the drongo. The aanaranchi. It is a common enough bird, small, with a glistening black body and a forked tail. What is uncommon about it is its courage. It will not let the crow anywhere near it, and will chase crows and even kites and peck them mercilessly till they flee. Why does the drongo do it? In the nesting season, it's to protect its babies, but what about the other times? Who knows? The timid birds—babblers, doves and pigeons—will all build their nests where a drongo does. For they know that the drongo will keep the marauding birds away and protect their young. Perhaps this is nature's way of teaching us to draw courage from our beliefs.

But to survive is also an act of courage. The afternoons and nights of the thulaavarsham, the October storms, are fierce and frightening, but it is the day that teaches you about endurance. The morning after the storm, the sky is blue. The air is cool and moist, even though the sun shines clear and radiant, finding its way through the undergrowth to light even the underbellies of leaves and gnarled stems. The paddy fields are squares of jade interwoven with emerald.

They gleam. The plants stand with their ankles in brown muddy water; waterbeds that reflect the sky in tiny patches. Dragonflies hover. In gardens, coconut clusters that have sagged from the assault and battery of the rain are propped up and tied. The land repairs itself.

But for the highest feat of daring, I would suggest the cashew apple. Look at it, rosy red and yellow, sometimes orange, as it hangs from the tree. Its purpose is to sustain the nut that grows on it rather than within. It is the nut that everyone wants. But somewhere within that fruit, in its fermenting ripe breath, is a need to prove itself. Which is why, even when it drops to the ground with the weight of its ripeness, it will still not let go of the nut. This is the courage to go on. Despite everything. And this, too, is veeram.

Shyam

My head hurts. A fierce throbbing that I think will split my skull and smash it into a thousand pieces. I clench my jaw to ride the spasm. There is a narrow chink of light sneaking its way through a gap in the curtains. Even that hurts my eyes. My mouth is dry, and my tongue feels heavy and wooden. I wish Radha was here to shut the chink of light out. I wish Radha was here to fetch me a glass of water and two aspirins. I wish Radha was here to sit at the head of the bed and rub balm on my pounding temples. I wish Radha was that sort of a wife. I wish I hadn't drunk so much last night.

I sit up. The world swirls. A sledgehammer slams the insides of my skull. I shut my eyes and hold the edge of the bedside table to steady myself. I have a meeting at ten in the morning. I cannot afford to miss it.

I go into the bathroom. In the mirror, I see myself, bleary-eyed and with mussed up hair and greying stubble. I splash water on my face. The smell of toothpaste churns my stomach. I feel last night's excess push its way into my mouth. I put the toilet seat up and crouch by the yawning mouth of the bowl. I retch again and again till there is nothing left in me. I can taste the sourness of vomit. I slam down the lid and flush. All the unpleasantness of the past buried, I think grimly.

The throbbing in my head lessens. I splash cold water on my face and brush my teeth again, then I call room service and order a tall glass of lime juice, black coffee and a few Saridons.

I lean back against the pillows and close my eyes. In a little while, the coffee will be here. I will drink it and begin to feel better. Only then will I confront Radha.

The coffee works its magic. I feel my eyes begin to focus again. I shower, dress and splash enough CK One to obliterate the memory of the stench of vomit. I look at my watch. It is a quarter past nine.

I pick up the phone and call home. There is no response. I stare at the phone for a moment. Do I dare to? Then I dial Uncle's number. Radha answers the phone.

'Where the hell were you last night?' I snap. The words seem to have emerged without my volition.

I hear her indrawn breath. When she speaks, I feel as if my head has been thrust into a bucket of ice cubes. Her voice is cold and edged. 'Here, at Uncle's. Where else?'

'I called last night at least half a dozen times. Shanta said she didn't know where you were. She said you went at sunset.' I try to explain my impatience.

'Shanta is an idiot and you are an even bigger one not to have called on my mobile. Uncle has been unwell for two days now and I came here because he refused to come home.'

I hear her, but I am not sure if I believe her. Everything she says sounds rehearsed. Even her indignation.

'Why didn't you tell me he was unwell when I was leaving? I wouldn't have gone then. He was all right when we met him the night before.'

'He seemed to be better when I spoke to him yesterday, in the morning. Then he called to say he was feeling unwell again. So I came here last night. But why didn't you call here?'

I don't say anything. How do I tell her that I was scared to? I had tossed and turned the thought in my head a million times: What if she wasn't with Uncle? What if she was with Chris?

It was then that I began to drink.

'What is wrong with Uncle?' I ask.

'A gastric attack. Vomiting and dysentery. He seems very weak.'

There was no point in checking with him. The old man will admit to rabies if Radha asks him to.

'I don't know when I will be home,' I say.

'I may need to stay an extra day or two,' I add. 'I might even go down south to Trivandrum.'

'Oh,' her voice murmurs. I feel disappointment. I had expected her to protest at my absence. Instead, she sounds very matter-of-fact.

'Do me a favour. Will you check if Padmanabhan has come? And give me a call, will you, to let me know,' I say. When I am back, I will have a valid excuse to check with Unni about Radha's comings and goings.

'Who?'

'Padmanabhan, the elephant,' I say.

'Oh!' I hear the displeasure in her voice. 'Anything else? Would you like me to check how many bunches of bananas he ate?'

I ignore the sarcasm in her voice. 'Yes, there is,' I say. 'Have you booked a new gas cylinder? What about the plumber? Has he come? Call him and remind him. And remind Shashi to check the air in the car tyres. Ask Unni to check on the new coconut saplings.' Each time I go away, I think when I call Radha, I will tell her how much I hate being away. That I feel lost without her. And then all I do is squabble or hurl instructions at her.

'I am waiting for Shashi,' I hear her say.

She is going home. I feel a coil of joy unwind.

'So Uncle is better now?' I probe.

'He is. But I will come back in a little while. I don't dare leave him alone.'

I don't like this. I don't even like the thought of it.

'Is that really necessary? You know how the servants will gossip about your going away in my absence.'

'For heaven's sake, Shyam, I am going to stay with my uncle.'

'I know. But...'

'Don't be silly. It's ridiculous, the way you fuss. Besides, what is there to keep me at home?'

When I put the phone down, I feel the sledgehammer at the back of my head. I swallow one more Saridon and call for a taxi.

I think of what Radha said. The bitterness in her voice chills. What is there to keep me at home? she asks.

How does she know? I have been so careful.

Four years after we were married, I began to worry. There seemed to be no sign that little feet would ever patter about in our home. We made love. Not as frequently as I would have liked, but enough to start a baby.

I wondered if she was doing something to prevent conception. 'Are you on contraceptive pills?' I asked.

She had a bemused expression, but she shook her head. 'No.'

'Well then...' I smiled. I felt as if we were starting on a project together.

As project leader, I had certain responsibilities. I rummaged through her bedside table drawer and her vanity case and even among her clothes to check if she was telling the truth. She was. A year later, we were still trying.

We went to see a doctor. She wasn't a gynaecologist, but we knew her well. She said, 'Don't think about it and it will happen.'

Rani Oppol wasn't so convinced. 'Maybe there is something wrong with her. You must go to a specialist and get it verified.'

Rani Oppol was angry with Radha that day. We were spending the day in my mother's house and I discovered that staying in Radha's house had spoiled me. I was used to clean tiled bathrooms, and found the bathroom in my house dingy and even a little smelly.

I thought of what Radha would think when she saw the clothes wedged over the tap. There were petticoats and saris, bras and panties, and my brother-in-law's Y-fronts. 'Do you have to keep these here?' I asked Rani Oppol.

Rani Oppol frowned. I saw the anger on her face. 'I suppose she asked you to tell me this. You can tell your wife that my daughter and I wear saris and we have that many more garments to wash. Not all of us are like her, wearing the same pair of jeans for months together, and as for those little blouses, I wouldn't let my ten-year-old daughter wear them. Every time she raises her arm, it shows her midriff. And all that hair left loose...The girl has no sense. And what about you? How can you let your wife dress like a slut?'

I kept quiet. If she knew Radha had nothing to do with this, she would be even more wounded. My sister is a very sensitive person. 'So now my brother doesn't like me any more,' she would say. There might even be tears. At the moment she was merely angry at being criticized. It was preferable to her being hurt. So I let it be.

Rani Oppol was right, of course. If we went to a specialist, we could find out exactly what was wrong. But I didn't have the courage to broach the subject with Radha.

So I read up as much as I could on conception and began to keep a calendar of her menstrual periods.

I knew Radha would be furious, so I didn't let her know what I was doing. Then one morning she came into the office room to ask me about a magazine subscription. 'I have a feeling that it ran out last month,' she said, drawing the desktop calendar towards her. I felt my insides shrink and shrivel.

'What is this?' she asked, frowning at the red crosses that appeared on every page. Then she understood. Her mouth tightened. She flipped the pages rapidly. When she looked at me, the expression in her eyes scared me.

'Isn't anything sacred to you?' Her voice rose. 'These red crosses are my periods, aren't they? Why are they here? On your calendar? If anyone should keep tabs, it should be me. Why are you like this, Shyam? You seem to want to rule me. You won't let me breathe. It isn't right.'

I heard the sob in her voice.

'It isn't the way you think it is,' I tried to explain. 'This way I know when you are ovulating and that's the best time…' I finished lamely.

The anger in her eyes unnerved me. I dropped my gaze, unable to meet hers.

She stood there for a moment. When she spoke, the distress that had run through her words was replaced by fury.

'I was pregnant once. So it isn't that I can't conceive. Perhaps you need to find out if you can father a child,' she said before walking away.

I was stunned. I did not know what stunned me more. The thought that she had been pregnant once, or the possibility that I could be sterile.

I chose to go to a fertility clinic in another city. I wanted the investigations to be done as quietly as possible. The doctor who had been recommended to me was one of the finest. She had an enviable track record and if anyone could help my cousin, it would be her, I was told. I had had to invent a fictitious cousin while I made my enquiries about a gynaecologist with experience in this field.

On my way to meet her after the tests, I stopped at the Kadampuzha temple and made an offering. Santhana-muttu. A coconut for a child. If the coconut split in neat halves, all would be well. The priest broke the coconut and it cracked evenly. I offered a prayer of thanks. All would be well now.

The doctor's smile gave nothing away. 'It is not good, but it's not bad either,' she said, shuffling the sheets.

'What do you mean?' This woman might look old enough to be God's mother, but she wasn't God. And God couldn't be wrong.

'Your sperm count isn't very high. It is about sixteen million spermatozoa per ml of sperm. It is not bad, but it isn't great either. Also, low sperm counts could be a temporary affliction. What is more serious is the sperm mobility—the sperm's ability to move. If the movement is sluggish or not in a straight line, it will have difficulty in getting past the cervical mucous or penetrating the hard outer shell of the egg.'

Why am I not surprised? Radha has not let me penetrate her soul in nearly six years of marriage, so what chance has my sperm to penetrate her egg? The fortress walls she hides behind are beyond my sperms and me.

'It is not uncommon. A recent study suggests that fifty per cent of men with infertility problems have double defects like you do.'

I looked at my reflection in the glass that covered the top of her table. I felt axed. How could it be? How could I have an infertility problem? I didn't even approve of her using that word. Women were infertile, not men.

'There are a few things you can do to improve your sperm count,' she said. 'Wear looser underwear for one. When you wear tight briefs, there is no air circulation and the heat is not conducive to sperm mortality. In fact, the testicles are outside the body because the body temperature has a direct effect on the sperm's chance of survival. You will be interested to know that Eskimos have the highest sperm counts because the cold temperature allows their sperm to live.'

I felt a sheepish grin fix on my face. This was surreal, I thought. Here I was sitting with a strange woman, discussing the state of my balls.

'Cut out smoking and drinking, avoid bicycling, but get plenty of exercise. All this should help.' I looked at her face. How could she not be embarrassed? I was so mortified that I couldn't even meet her eyes.

'I suggest you come back in a month's time and we will do a sampling again. Please do bring your wife. I need her to be present. Both partners have to be willing to co-operate. Only then can we start planning how we can make you parents.'

I took the reports, and on my way home I bought a medical textbook.

Sperms have to have an oval head and a long tail, I read.

The descriptions of abnormal sperms reminded me of the freak babies preserved in formaldehyde in specimen jars in the anatomy department of medical colleges. As I read, the word sperm blurred to become baby. Babies with extremely small, pinpointed heads. Babies with tapered heads and crooked heads. Babies with twin heads. Babies with kinks and curls in their limbs. What chance did a sperm with these defects have?

The textbook reassured me more than her words had. She hadn't said anything about the shape of my sperm, which meant at least my sperm morphology was all right.

I put the reports and textbook away in my locker with my important business papers. I didn't want Radha to discover the truth. I wasn't afraid of her scorn. If she knew that I was the one to blame, she would smother me with concern. What I feared was her pity. When Radha looked at me, I wanted her to see a full-bodied, red-blooded alpha male capable of fathering a hundred and one children.

The taxi driver clears his throat. 'We are here,' he says.

I sit up and roll down the window. The tour operator had insisted we meet at a resort. He wanted to show me a few things which he thought were very commendable and saleable.

'Is there a teashop nearby?' I ask.

'There is a restaurant inside the resort,' the driver says.

'No, not there. Somewhere outside the resort.'

'We passed one about two kilometres back.' The driver is puzzled.

'Take me there,' I say. I need some coffee to clear my head. I don't want to meet the tour operator feeling the way I do.

I sit in the teashop sipping my coffee. I watch a lizard scaling a wall.

From a school lesson, I remember a story. Of Tanaji, the commander of the army of the great Maratha king, Shivaji. He had thrown an iguana on to an enemy fortress wall and on the strength of its grip, he took his forces in and broke into what was considered an impregnable fort.

I would find an iguana, too. The doctor would help me find and nurture one. I would raise enough sperm to conceive an army. I would teach them to rush headlong and straight. I would impregnate Radha. I would give her a healthy, wailing, screaming, kicking and gurgling reason to stay at home. God couldn't be wrong.

Radha

Shyam's call leaves me feeling angrier than ever. I cannot take this any longer, I think. I cannot bear to be this insufferable man's wife. I bite my lip and try to repress my anger. Uncle's friend, Maya, is looking at me from across the room.

'Is everything all right?' Uncle asks.

'That was Shyam. And...' I stop. I do not want to criticize him in Maya's hearing.

'And?' Uncle prompts.

'He's upset that I didn't sleep at home last night.'

Maya rises from her chair and walks to the veranda.

'I said you were ill, which was why I came here last night. I hope you don't mind.'

Uncle doesn't say anything. He sighs. 'What am I ill with?'

'Gastritis.'

'Radha, do you know what you are doing?' he asks. His face is worried.

'I know, Uncle. Very well. I know the world would think it is wrong. There is no justification for adultery, I will be told. But I love him. He is a fire in my blood,' I say.

'I can see that,' he says wryly. 'What about him, Radha? Are you a fire in his blood as well?'

'Yes, Uncle. He cares for me. We are like twin halves of a being. We think the same way. I am not a sixteen-year-old girl. I know this love of mine is for real.' I try to explain how I feel about Chris, and his feelings for me. It is a relief to do so. What we have, Chris and I, is more real, I discover, when I talk about it. To give it mouth and eyes, heart and soul, is to give it form, breathe life into it.

'Be careful, Radha. Shyam has eyes and ears everywhere. They will think it their moral duty to inform your husband.'

'I don't care,' I say. 'My marriage is dead. And Shyam means nothing to me.'

'I don't think you mean that. You do, in your own way, care for Shyam. Are you saying that eight years of marriage mean nothing to you? But it is not for me to resolve your feelings. You have to do that yourself. Be careful, that is all I ask.'

On my way home, I stop at Chris's cottage. He is playing his cello. I stand there, letting the music soak into me. I will ask him for the name of the piece. I will buy a CD and play it all day when I am away from him. That way, I'll feel as if he is with me all the time.

I step back. I don't want him to know I am here. I merely want to reassure myself that last night wasn't a dream. No matter what the world thinks, as long as I have Chris, I will find the courage to be myself.

The resort is sunk in a soporific calm. I think of what Uncle had said: Be careful. I am. Which is why I walk in, seemingly guileless, and ask Unni, 'Has Uncle come in yet? He said he would wait at the Sahiv's cottage for me.'

Unni looks up from the computer screen. 'I haven't seen him. Do you want me to send someone to the cottage to check?'

'No, I'll go. I have to return some tapes anyway,' I say. I do not hurry as I walk to Chris' cottage.

He is sitting on the veranda, writing. I worry that I am intruding. He looks up at my footfall. 'I was waiting for you,' he says.

I feel all my worries dissipate.

He takes my hand and leads me into the cottage, and closes the door with a decisive click.

Last night, the darkness had allowed me to forget my uncertainties, hide my fear. Last night was a dream I had walked into. At half past three in the afternoon, I cannot tell myself the same. I feel unsure, afraid even, and a voice in my head holds me back: what are you doing here?

I look around and see the cello. I pretend a casual ease. 'What is that piece of music you play so often?'

'Which one?' He crinkles his eyes. I feel my heart somersault. It is an expression I am beginning to know well.

He opens the cello case and takes the instrument out. He moves to sit on the chair opposite mine and places the cello between his legs. He plays the opening bars of the piece.

'No, not this one,' I say hastily.

I hum a tune. 'That one.'

He peers at me, interested. 'You have a nice voice,' he says.

'A nice humming voice. Would you play it for me?'

Chris slides the bow on the strings. He plays it for me and a great yearning fills me.

When he finishes, he places the cello down carefully. 'I don't know much about this piece. I found it in the wardrobe of a lodge on the edge of Loch Tay in Scotland. I think it was called Ardeonaig Lodge. One of those places with a log fire, a stunning view over the loch of the surrounding mountains...I found this music score written for the cello. I know I shouldn't have, but it intrigued me and I took it away. I must send it back and ask them who T. Lavin is. That's the name of the composer. It is not often you find music written for the cello and this one speaks to me.'

'Oh,' I say. I know fear again. I feel so distant from his life.

'Radha,' Chris asks, 'what is wrong?'

'I don't know,' I say. 'All of this is so unreal. You, me, this...Our lives are so separate.'

Chris says, 'Come here.'

I go towards him and he takes me in his arms and holds me so close that all distances disappear and I know that flame in my blood leap and blaze again.

'We can't take chances,' I whisper.

'Why are you whispering?' he whispers back.

'Because we can't take chances,' I murmur against his skin, and then opening my mouth I nip his flesh.

'Ouch,' he screams.

The curtains shut out the day. In the semi tones of the room, in the welding of light and darkness, I can see bits of him. The corner of his smile. An upraised nipple. The ball of his knee. A line of shank. The curve of his little left toe. Dark spaces, too. The shallow cavern of his armpit. The silk of his skin. The salt of his sweat. The base note of his cologne. He is a jigsaw I am still putting together, day by day…I smile at the conceit.

'First she bites a piece of my flesh off, then she smiles. What is all the mystery?' Another piece falls into place, filling a dark space with defined edges. His voice. I would know it anywhere now.

'I mean it, Chris. We can't take chances,' I whisper again.

'Huh?' He cocks an eyebrow. In the darkness, the green of his eyes is a deep olive, the whites of his eyes whiter than they really are.

'You will have to use something.' I am too embarrassed to use the word condom.

'Oh, would you pick up a few?' His tone is careless.

I sit up in shock. 'What?'

No doubt in his country women think nothing of buying condoms. There are even vending machines, I hear. But this is India. And small-town India. How could he even ask me to do it? The horror of it makes me cringe.

And yet, when I speak, I hear myself say in a small and apologetic tone, 'I can't. What do you think will happen if I went to the chemist's and asked for condoms?'

He pulls me towards him. 'Hey, I was just teasing. Relax, Min-min.' His voice caresses me.

'I picked up a few this morning,' he says. For a moment, his face is serious. 'But what about yesterday?'

I settle against his chest. 'Last day of my safe period. So I should be fine.'

I didn't dare tell him that yesterday morning I had calculated frantically.

'Shall we test drive one?' he asks.

I giggle.

I like this new me. A giggling, glowing Radha. I feel as if I have retrieved the courage to be myself again.

Much later I ask him, 'Tell me about where you live.'

'It's a lovely neighbourhood,' he says. 'You wouldn't think it was Manhattan. There is a tree that overlooks my apartment. My bed is by the window and I can see the tree from there. It is an old apartment. My mother's friend owns it; she sublet it to me. It's filled with bits and pieces she has collected over the years. A whole wall of books. Many paintings, too. She is a painter, so there are some works of hers, and others she has been given or has acquired. There is a lovely tub. An old porcelain tub mounted on cast-iron griffin feet. There is a screen door that has wheels so you can move it around, depending on where you want it. Strange things, but nice. She lives there for part of the year and I live there for the other half. It's worked out to be a nice arrangement. There's place enough for both of us to keep our things and we have a home to go back to.'

I suppress a bolt of jealousy. I think of this woman he doesn't even give a name to. I imagine her to be a Glenn Close like creature. Chic and passionate, like she was in *Fatal Attraction*. All crimped hair and flashing fingernails. I see them sipping wine from tall-stemmed glasses with 'Madame Butterfly' playing in the background. I see him playing her instead of his cello.

'How old is she?' I ask.

I feel his gaze scald me. 'You are jealous.' I hear the laugh in his voice.

'No, I am not,' I protest.

'Don't lie. You are jealous. I can see it.' His voice is triumphant. 'She is my godmother. She is sixty-three and her name is Helen. And guess what, she's met your uncle. A long time ago. I must ask him about her. Helen doesn't do figurative work; the only figurative painting she has done is of him. It is a strange painting. Almost diabolic. The energy in it would sear you. Somehow I can't reconcile the man in the painting with the man he is.'

'He is not so young now,' I say. I am smiling now. Uncle's contemporary. Perhaps even an ex-lover.

'Is she good-looking?' I ask.

'She is charming when you know her. But when you see her first, you think what a little dumpy creature she is. She has a wart on her chin, badly cut hair, and no dress sense. And she smokes a pipe, so she reeks of pipe tobacco.'

I ache to grin, but feel I ought to be charitable. 'You are vicious. I wonder what you would tell your friends about me.'

He hoists himself on his forearms and looms over me. He is so close that his face is out of focus when I look at him.

'Let me see,' he murmurs. 'My Min-min is a piece of music that I am still learning to play. Her key signature is F sharp major with sharps and flats that would drive you nuts. Her time signature is adagio appassionato. Slow and passionate.'

I do not understand the complexities of his description. It is enough that he sees me so.

'Oh, Chris,' I murmur, for I do not know what else to say.

'Let me finish,' he says. 'I was just getting started.'

'Don't bother,' I say, holding my palm against his lips. 'I've heard enough.' And then, with a daring I didn't think I possessed, I murmur, 'Show me...'

He chuckles. His laugh salutes courage. His and mine.

'When did you know?'

'When did you?'

'I asked first.'

'Was it when we sat by the river?'

'Sat by the river...no, much before that, but I asked you first.'

We play the lovers' game of trying to retrace our footsteps. We play it with eyes and tongues locked, with hands clasped, and feet that curl into each other's. We take the time when we didn't know each other and turn it into a fiery orange ball. A boiled sweet in its cellophane wrapping, which we peel away. A hard confectionery ball we roll between our mouths, playing catch with our tongues. A layer of his time seeps into me, a chunk of my time rests in him. Back and forth we toss our memories. Our tongues and reminiscences, our saliva and our past collide, clash and then collude into a quiet calm, so that the time when we were strangers ceases to exist.

We lie back content. He knows that my teen years were overrun with the Beegees, while I know his were filled with Pink Floyd and the Grateful Dead; we both read Kafka and Camus and secretly dipped into thrillers to shrug existential angst away; we both smoked grass and experimented with drugs. We know that our parents embarrassed and enraged us by turns and sometimes caused us to bury our heads in a pillow wailing, why don't they understand us? That our formative years lived in two different continents were not so far apart...

Then we begin to poke and prod forgotten corners of each other's lives, seeking hidden recesses and ugly secrets. Only with such knowing can we possess each other truly.

'What is it you have never admitted even to yourself?' he asks.

'I have no secrets,' I say. 'I have told you everything.'

Then I remember. A memory I had discarded as irrelevant until now.

I drape my arms around him. 'I have never talked about this to anyone,' I say.

He wraps his arms around me. I draw comfort from his embrace.

'Listen,' I say.

I was seven when one afternoon I came back from school to find a stranger in the sitting room. A broad-shouldered, laughing stranger with muscles that rippled, hair that bristled and teeth that shone. He saw me hesitate at the doorway and was at my side in a few strides. He tossed me in the air, pinched my cheeks and then, dropping into a chair with me on his knee, filled my lap with toffees he emptied from his pockets. 'Who is this princess?' he asked.

My father looked grim and uncertain. My mother turned pale. My grandfather smiled as though he didn't know what else to do with his face. Then Uncle stepped forward, scooped me from the stranger's clasp and said, 'This is Radha. Gowri and Babu's daughter.'

He tucked a strand of hair behind my ear and said, 'Radha, this is your uncle Mani, your father's brother. He has just come back after many years of wandering the world.'

I wondered at the emphasis on the word father, but let it pass. I was much too enamoured by the stranger. He had a trunk filled with strange and exotic things. A Japanese umbrella and a fan. Crayons and hairbands and packets of chewing gum. He had stories to tell and adventures to narrate. In the evenings, he poured whisky into tumblers for my father and grandfather, and if Uncle joined them, for him as well. He took me for walks to the river and to Uncle's house. He was a playmate first, and only after that, my father's brother. Besides, I already had an uncle: Uncle. And I couldn't conceive of this stranger in that role.

One afternoon, as I raided the kitchen shelves for something to eat, I heard a rustling. It came from the patthayappura. The granary was on one side of the house and it was accessed from a passageway the kitchen opened on to. I heard a moan. I heard a sigh. Then I heard furious whispers. Uncle Mani and my mother. He had her pinned against the wall. His arms were on either side of her. 'She is mine, isn't she? Tell me. I can see it. She looks nothing like you or that runt brother of mine.'

My mother didn't say anything. He lowered his head and nuzzled her ear lobe. His whisper echoed: 'Does he do this to you? Can he please you like I did, like I do now? Does he?'

My mother stood there. There were tears in her eyes, but she didn't move away. She seemed to lean into him. 'We'll go away,' Uncle Mani said. 'You and I and our child. We'll make a life like we should have seven years ago.'

I turned away. Something in me wept. It wasn't right, I knew. My mother shouldn't let my uncle do this to her. He shouldn't be doing it to her. I felt a sense of outrage for my father.

That evening, I sidled up to my father and said, 'How long will he stay here?'

'Who?' My father frowned.

'Uncle Mani. When will he go away?'

'Why do you ask? Are you tired of him already? I thought he was your favourite person.' His smile was humourless. Even I could see that.

I dropped my eyes and said, 'He was telling Mummy that he wants me and her to go with him. I wish you and Uncle would come too.'

He grabbed me by the shoulders and stared at me. He was examining my face to see if I was telling the truth. I had been artful, but I had spoken the truth. Then my father thrust me away. 'Go play with your dolls,' he said.

The next week I was sent away to a boarding school in Ooty. I never saw Uncle Mani again. He died in a car accident a few weeks later, I was told.

'Didn't you ask your mother?' Chris asks. 'She could have told you the truth. She owed it to you.'

'I think I thrust it out of my mind. Now I wish I had been more understanding and less judgemental. My mother was desperately unhappy. Perhaps if she had gone away with him, she would have been happier,' I say quietly. I am beginning to know what my mother must have felt like, trying to divide her life between two men, each of whom seemed to have staked a claim to her.

'You were a child. Don't blame yourself.' Chris squeezes my shoulder.

'I know. But how easily we judge our parents and their lives.'

Chris leans back against the headboard. 'Last year, my father died. That's when my mother told me that the man I called daddy wasn't my father. When I asked her who my biological father was, she said she wasn't sure. I don't know: that was her answer. So you see, we have that in common, too. An uncertain paternity.

'They fuck you up, your mum and dad,' he quotes softly.

'Huh?'

'Larkin. Philip Larkin,' he says.

I smile. 'Children begin by loving their parents; after a time they judge them; rarely, if ever, do they forgive them,' I counter quote.

It is his turn to look puzzled. 'I know it, but I can't place it.'

'Wilde. Oscar Wilde.' I mimic his tone.

'There is an even better one,' I add. 'More appropriate. "All a child's dreads came true in worlds within her world."'

'I don't know that,' he says.

'Dom Moraes. Indian poet. I have his last collection of poetry. Typed with one finger. Would you like to read it?'

Chris looks at me. He draws me into the backrest of his chest. 'All measure, and all language, I should pass, should I tell what a miracle she was.'

'Donne, isn't it? Now let's see if you know this. "He was my North, my South, my East and West/My working week and my Sunday rest/My noon, my midnight, my talk, my song…"'

I pause. I don't dare mouth that last line: 'I thought that love would last for ever: I was wrong.'

He is silent for a moment. 'I know that. Auden. But why didn't you finish the stanza? You still don't trust me, do you?'

I shrug helplessly. 'How can you say that? If I didn't, would I be here?'

The gaiety of the afternoon is lost. For a while, as we swapped memories and quotes, I had felt spooned by his intellect. Our worlds nestled into each other. We belonged, he and I.

Then Chris takes my hands in his. 'Take courage, lover!/Can you endure such grief/At any hand but hers?'

I nuzzle his chest. 'Whose is that?'

'Robert Graves. He wrote *I, Claudius*.'

'I know. Don't patronize me.'

'I don't think much of his poetry. But my mother does,' Chris says.

'What is your mother like?'

'Flower-child turned pillar of the society. She did all that her generation did. Smoked grass, tripped on acid, listened to the Beatles and Ravi Shankar, travelled to India. She was here for a while. Then she went back, sorted herself out, got a job in publishing, met my father, married and lived happily ever after. I happened somewhere along the way. I have two sisters. Did I tell you that?'

I shake my head.

'Younger than me. The older one, Elizabeth, is a lawyer, and the younger one, Deborah, works with a bank. My parents retired to Bosham, a little seaside town. My mother still lives there in a house too big for her and a garden she can barely manage on her own. But she is happy, with her many committees and friends. Once in a while, she trots off to London for a literary lunch. The rest of the time, she is content to play respectable mum.'

'Tell me about Bosham,' I say. In my mind, I imagine a little town that is two parts Enid Blyton, one part Jane Austen and one part Barbara Pym.

'It is very pretty. You would love it. There is a lovely waterfront, with boats bobbing in the water. It was from Bosham that King Harold sailed to Normandy in 1064. The Borham church is very old. In fact, it's one of the oldest in England.' His voice bears the softness of nostalgia.

I feel fear gather in me. His life is so beyond my comprehension. 'Chris,' I murmur. 'Please hold me.'

In his arms, I feel panic stem. In the fold of his nearness, I feel nothing can come between us. Shyam, the parallel worlds we inhabit, guilt. Nothing matters. What feels so right can't be wrong. This is what I have to draw courage from, to go on.

Uncle

Two days, and already it seems like Maya has been here a long time. Our lives have fallen into a routine in just forty-eight hours.

Maya is sitting on the veranda, reading a book. Her hair, freshly washed, hangs down the back of the chair. There are streaks of grey in the black. 'Your hair is greying,' I tell her.

She peers at me over her glasses. 'I know. I keep thinking I should dye it.'

I see a flash of concern in her eyes.

'Does it bother you? That I am not what I used to be?'

I laugh. 'Don't be silly. I am not what I used to be, either. We are all ageing. We can't deny that.'

Malini squawks loudly. She is jealous. She begrudges the attention I give Maya. 'Even Malini,' I say. 'But age can't kill what we are, within. Look at her. After all these years you would think she would have calmed down, but she is still as demanding as ever, still as vicious, and so bloody possessive. Even though she knows that I am her slave, she resents your being here.'

I go to her cage and scratch her head. Malini closes her eyes in pleasure. 'Silly girl,' I murmur. 'Koman loves you, don't you know that?'

Maya shakes her head in disgust. 'You spoil her, which is why she is the way she is. You should get a dog.'

'I had one.'

'What was it called?'

'Ekalavyan,' I say.

Maya stares at me. 'What a strange name for a dog.'

'When I came back from London, I decided that I wanted to have nothing more to do with anyone. My guru was dead. My brother Mani had disappeared. My father was ailing, and there was no one I could talk to. The dog attached himself to me. He was a puppy when he started lurking outside the classroom. Each morning he would be there, and he would stay till I finished. He would be back in the evening when I began the theory class. He played quietly by himself and seemed to want nothing from me. Some days he would sit there with his head on his paws, staring at the class as they did their exercises. One evening, on a whim, I whistled to him when I was going home. He put down the piece of cloth he was worrying and followed me. And never left my side after that.'

'Is that why you called him Ekalavyan? For his steadfast devotion to you?' Maya is amused.

'Oh no,' I protest. 'I wouldn't burden a dog with such a name. My students named him Ekalavyan. They were vexed with him, and me, I suppose. I would scream at them saying, "That dog has more sense than all of you put together. He never misses a lesson, never disobeys me, and he does all I ask him to. He has learnt more by watching me than you ever will." It was their idea of revenge, I suppose, to name him after the ideal student from the Mahabharata. He would wag his tail furiously when they called him Ekalavyan and run towards them with his tongue hanging out and his ears laid back. They knew it annoyed me, but he seemed to like the name.'

'So did you call him Ekalavyan, too?'

'I called him Dog.'

'Why didn't you give him a name?'

'Dogs don't need names. Do you think dogs call each other by name?'

'What about Malini, then? Shouldn't you call her Parakeet?'

'Radha named her Malini. Left to myself, I would have called her Parakeet.'

'You are strange, Koman. I suppose I should be thankful that you don't call me Woman,' Maya laughs.

I like the sound of her laughter. It is low and throaty.

The evening is beginning to die. I look towards the horizon. The sky is overcast. It had rained intermittently all day. The river is rising. It has covered the last three steps already. 'Maya, do you want to go and sit on the steps?' I ask.

'Later. When the moon is out. I want to see the fireflies you talk about.'

I look at my watch. Where is Radha? And Chris? 'This evening I will tell you more,' I had promised. Suddenly, I discover I am impatient to tell them my story.

'Sometimes I wonder what you see in me,' Maya says, shutting her book.

The first afternoon she was here, we lay down together, Maya and I. All we did was lie in each other's arms. It was enough to be together, drawing sustenance from each other's presence. It was more intimate than making love. There would be time enough for that.

Her body has settled into a pleasing fullness that is more comforting than enticing. We lay with our bodies pressed together; my breath caused the tendrils of hair at the nape of her neck to rise and fall, my hand gathered the roll of flesh that padded her lower abdomen, her legs trapped between mine. All afternoon we lay cupped by each other's bodies, comforted by the intimacy of flesh against flesh.

'What do I see in you, Maya? Comfort,' I say.

Her lips part in a smile. She is pleased.

Maya touches my elbow. 'What do you think will happen to them? Chris and Radha. They are sleeping with each other.'

'I don't know about that. She spent the night here yesterday and the night before that.' I laugh.

Maya makes a face. 'Don't be facetious. You know what I mean.'

'I know.'

'They could, if they choose, make a life together. There's nothing to hold her back. No child. No responsibilities.'

'Is that what held you back, Maya?' I ask.

'Yes,' she says. 'And there isn't a day in my life that I don't wonder if I should have been more kind to myself.'

'We can still be together.'

Maya is sad. Sorrow sits easily on her face. 'I know you think that, Koman. I know that you don't make the offer easily, when you say you would be happy for us to live together. But you love your solitude too much. You like what we have even if you won't admit it. It's best we remain the way we are. That way, what we have will never dull or pale.'

One other woman had said the same to me. What was it that Lalitha had said? 'There is no room for another person in this world you have chosen to live in.'

I still do not know who I am till I am someone else. How then do I find the space to usher in another presence?

'For some years, my companion was a woman called Lalitha. I asked her to marry me, but she didn't want to. She was happy to come and go. She said the same thing. That it was best we remained the way we were.'

'Was she a dancer?' Maya asks.

'No,' I say. 'She was a prostitute when I first met her. She became my mistress. She worked in a tailoring unit and it was only in the last few years of her life that she would accept any money from me.'

'She must have been a very special person,' Maya says.

I get up and go towards her. I stroke her hair. It is this graciousness of hers that binds me to her. It is the relief that I do not have to pretend to be someone else when I am with her. Perhaps this is love.

'I listened to the tapes this morning. Can I ask you something?' She turns to look up at my face. 'I know that you don't like talking about yourself. So why are you doing it now?'

I shake my head. 'I don't know. I hadn't meant to. Perhaps I am trying to find myself.'

Maya laughs. She thinks it is a joke.

'I am not joking,' I say.

'You can't be serious. Don't you know who you are?'

'Maya, let me tell you the kathakali version of Ravana Udbhavam, the genesis of Ravana. The story begins with Ravana, king of all three worlds, whom neither weapons nor gods can destroy, revelling in his power. Why do I feel so triumphant about what I have achieved? he asks himself. He knows that he acquired his position because of his belief in himself. He didn't beg and plead for the boons that made him the lord of all three worlds. He acquired them by the sheer power of his penance. He lit around him four sacrificial fires and forbade the sun to move away; it was to be the fifth sacrificial fire. He stood on one toe in the blazing heat and offered his prayers to the creator for a thousand years. When the creator still wouldn't appear, he began severing his heads and threw them one by one into the sacrificial fires. Can you ignore this, he asked of the creator. One after another, he severed nine heads until he had just one head left. Even then he didn't hesitate. He was about to sever his remaining head when the creator appeared and granted him every boon he desired. Ravana knew himself. He knew what lengths he could go to. He knew the measure of his power. And his life. That is why he feared nothing and no one.

'I do not have ten heads to offer to this hungry creature called the inner me. But what I am doing is, laying bare my life. Perhaps then I will discover who I really am.'

'What happens now?'

I don't know. Some days the dredging of the past is easy. Some days it is painful. Henceforth, I realize it will not be accomplished so easily. I, who have always been someone else, will have to be me. Where do I find the courage to go on?

I begin to braid her hair. It is soft and silky. 'I happen,' I say. 'All those things I told you about my life and everything I didn't, you get to hear if you stay long enough.'

'How long, Koman?'

'Long enough. Remember, I've just been born in this story.'

1940–1952
The Crown of Hope

The boy stood on the wooden bridge, staring at the river. He held the wooden rail that served as a banister while the doctor chatted to a man. The wood dug into his palms; he felt a searing pain when a splinter pierced his skin. But he was unwilling to let go. It was the only thing that felt real; everything else, the station, the river, the bridge that groaned under his every movement, this town and the knowledge that here lived the man who was his father, all of this was unreal.

He heard the doctor come up the steps towards him, but he continued to stare at the river.

'It goes to the sea,' the doctor said. 'Not the one you know, another one.'

The boy turned.

'Koman would like to know, what is the sea called?'

'The Arabian Sea,' the doctor said. 'But didn't they teach you that in school?'

'Koman would like to know, what is the river called?'

The doctor shook his head.

'I don't know. You must ask your father that. Yes, he's here. And apparently, he's a big shot in this small town!'

The boy looked at the doctor's face. Was that sarcasm he heard? The doctor was seldom sarcastic and rarely mocked anyone or anything. But every time the doctor referred to his father, his mouth narrowed into grimness and it seemed even his eyes frowned. The boy touched the cloth he had wound around his head. It felt strange and it drew people's eyes, but at least they didn't laugh.

What would his father think of him when he saw him? What would he say?

'You do realize, don't you, that your father may not be so pleased to see you? He may even be rude. But you must understand that all of this, you and I at his doorstep, will come as a shock to him. And human beings react differently to sudden shocks.'

The boy nodded, the turban giving his nod a greater emphasis. He touched it again.

'We have to go now,' the doctor said.

The boy said nothing. There was nothing to say anyway.

So he followed the doctor over the wooden bridge that connected the platforms, down the steps, and into the small town called Shoranur where his father was a big man.

'Please wait here,' the man said. 'He's eating his breakfast. I cannot disturb him now. Modalali meets his visitors here, in his office room.'

For a fleeting moment the doctor's eyes met the boy's. They both knew what the other was thinking. He. The man spoke the word as if it was weighed with the authority of royalty. He might as well have said His Highness. Modalali. Owner. What did he own, they wondered.

The doctor looked around the room and bit his lip. He didn't know if he should be annoyed or pleased. The room was an exact replica of his at the hospital in Nazareth, from the table to the paperweight to the position of the waste-paper basket. Even the clock was a twin of the one that ticked in his room. Does the boy see what I see, he wondered.

The boy did. He saw that the room was like the one he had sat in two days ago, when the doctor explained the need to make this journey. He saw that the room exuded an authority like the doctor's did. He thought, now I know why the doctor has that strange note in his voice when he refers to my father. They must be rivals. Was his father a doctor too, he wondered.

Again he touched the turban on his head, feeling it slip.

'I should have got you a cap,' the doctor said.

The doctor tried to suppress the pleasure that came to him unbidden when he thought of how he would present to Seth, who he now knew to be Sethu, his twelve-year-old son wearing a cloth turban to cover his ridiculous crown of hair. That will put him in his place, if nothing else will, he thought.

The boy wondered how so many emotions could flicker on a face in the span of a moment. He saw the play of feelings first on the doctor's face as they waited. Then he saw it on the face of the man who walked through the doorway that led from within the house to the room. Amazement, affection, sorrow, anger, fear and then another...What was that? He narrowed his eyes and suddenly knew. Arrogance.

'Well, well, well, what do I owe this surprise to?' the man asked in a voice that was wiped clean of all emotion.

The doctor stood up. This couldn't be Seth, he thought. Who was this man with a fleshy face and a doormat of a moustache? He was wearing a gold watch and a silk jubbah and a gold chain that sat heavily in his chest hair. My Seth was a fresh-faced boy and this one is a—he groped for the word: Modalali. No less. Owner. Rich man. Arrogant beast.

Then the man dropped his eyes, and the doctor knew that this was Seth. Someone who still couldn't hold a gaze despite the obvious change in him and his circumstances.

'I suppose there is no need for me to ask how you are? I can see that you have done well for yourself.' The doctor was brusque. It wouldn't do to let Seth think he was overwhelmed by his obvious prosperity.

Sethu smiled. 'You haven't changed at all!' he said.

The doctor stared. Was that an insult?

'I can see you have, Seth,' he said. And he meant it in the most derogatory way possible. Then he added, 'But it's Sethu, isn't it?'

Sethu looked away.

'Oh, you may do this easily. Take new names and new lives as you go along. But what am I to do with him? He's your responsibility and he doesn't even have a name he can call his own.'

Sethu felt a line of sweat on his brow. Could it be him? He studied the boy, seeking in his face and limbs, the curve of his lips, the slant of the nose, a mole, a dimple, something in the terrain that would tell him the boy was his.

'You needn't worry that I would pass off someone else's child as yours,' the doctor said, trying not to let his irritation show. 'I am leaving Nazareth. We are going abroad. All these years your son was my ward...'

'I paid for his keep. Every month I sent a money order,' Sethu interrupted the doctor.

'I know.' The doctor looked up. 'But he needs more than that. He needs a family. I can't take him with me. And once I leave, who is there?'

'Faith is there, isn't she?'

'No, Faith isn't there. For the last three years, her mother has had him. Faith married and went away. It's not just you whose life changes, you know. Faith's mother is in her seventies. If she dies, the boy will be alone. I can't let that happen.'

'I didn't know,' Sethu said.

'I know.' The doctor was gentle. 'He is your son. You must keep him with you.'

'But what do I tell my wife?'

'The truth, or at least your version of the truth,' the doctor said, rising to go. That can't be too difficult for you, his eyes said.

'Look at him,' the doctor said, tilting the boy's chin. 'Can't you see your Saadiya in him?'

Sethu nodded silently. He put his arm around the child. The boy stiffened.

'This is your home,' Sethu said, suddenly tired of fleeing his past. Devayani would have to accept his past and his son.

'The bows of the mighty men are broken, and they that stumbled are girded with strength,' the doctor quoted.

Sethu stared at him blankly.

'You know it,' the doctor prompted. 'It has my name.'

Sethu waved his hand as if to ward off the words.

'Let it be. I don't think of those times any more. I have forgotten all of it. Or perhaps most of it,' he said, looking away.

When the doctor left, Sethu looked at the boy.

'What is this for?' he asked, tugging at the cloth around the boy's head.

The cloth came away in his hand and he saw that the boy's head was shorn clean except for a band of hair that ran around his skull like a circlet. A crown of curly hair that wreathed his head. A circlet of thorns offering penance. Sethu felt an iron fist clamp his chest.

'Omar Masood?' Sethu rolled the name around in his mouth as if it were a tamarind seed. 'Omar Masood. What does it mean?'

'It is a name. Just a lovely name. He has to have a name. For four days we have called him baby. But he can't be baby for life,' Saadiya said, fitting her nipple into the baby's mouth.

'Yes, but why Omar Masood?' Sethu said, feeling that familiar tug of pleasure when he saw Saadiya suckle their son.

'Omar is Arabic for first son, disciple, gifted speaker. Famous. And Masood means happy, lucky.' Saadiya looked down at the baby. 'I want him to have everything. Fame. Wealth. Happiness. Luck!'

Sethu smiled and reached to fondle the baby's cheek. 'So ambitious a name for so little a creature!'

'The names closest to Allah are Abdullah and Abdur Rehman. The truest are Harith and Hamman. Do you prefer one of these?' Saadiya asked, consulting a little book.

Sethu felt his face flush. He had allowed Saadiya to have her way this far. He had kept his word. A promise that Saadiya had clung to, to bring to heel her fleeing spirit as she fought to keep alive their son.

'You must come in as soon as you hear the first cry,' Saadiya had whispered through her pain. Sethu had looked at the doctor and he had nodded.

And so, when the first cry pierced his thoughts, puncturing dread and letting fear drain, Sethu rushed in. The room smelt of warm blood, of wet loam, of dark mysterious things and the sweetness of birth. Saadiya lay exhausted and wan. The baby was in the midwife's hands.

'Take him,' Saadiya said. 'Now in his left ear, whisper Allahu Akbar. It is the call to prayer.'

Sethu picked up the baby and into its left ear murmured, 'Allah is great!' Then, unable to help himself, he whispered a prayer from his childhood, invoking the mightiest of the trinity, with the third eye and the power to destroy. 'Om nama Shivaya.'

He bent to put the baby down but Saadiya said, 'No, not yet. Now in his right ear, you must whisper this prayer. Repeat after me.

Ash hadu an la laha llal lah
Ash hadu anna Muhammadan Rasulah lah
Ash hadu anna Aluyyan Waliyah lah
Hayya alas Salah
Hayya alal faleh
Hayya ala Khayril Anal
Alahu Akbar
La llala llal lah.'

Sethu felt something in him turn. But he repeated obediently:
'I justify that there is no god but Allah
I testify that Muhammad is Allah's messenger
I testify that Ali is protected by Allah
Hasten to prayer
Hasten to deliverance
Hasten to the best act
Allah is great
There is no God but Allah.'

Then again as he had, he murmured, 'Om nama Shivaya' and for good measure he added, 'Narayanaya nama, Achuthaya nama, Govindaya nama…'

He couldn't remember any more, but it was enough, he thought. Suddenly he knew a great sadness. The child was just a few minutes old, and already he had to balance the two gods that resided in him.

'You must leave now,' the midwife said. 'There is some work to be done here.'

He gave the baby to the midwife and over her head, his eyes met the doctor's. He thought he saw in them the words he dreaded: I knew this would happen. This difference!

Three days later, on their way home from the hospital, Saadiya and Sethu summoned the barber.

'This is so that all misfortunes may be removed,' Saadiya said. Sethu didn't protest, even though he flinched when he saw the barber's blade.

'He'll have a good head of hair.' He smiled.

'The Aquiqah is an important ritual in a Muslim's life. Now you must weigh this hair and give the same amount as alms,' she said, taking the baby back from the woman Sethu had found to help Saadiya with the baby.

Saadiya smiled. Her voice rose and fell as dainty bells. Her happiness lit the house. Sethu knew relief. His Saadiya was back. All would be well again.

It didn't matter what their son was called, he thought. Harith was nice; it seemed like Hari. However, she seemed set on Omar Masood.

'I like Omar Masood,' Sethu said.

Saadiya smiled again, pleased that her choice of name had been approved.

Saadiya put the baby over her shoulder and patted it so it burped. Her palm cradled its shaven skull.

'Now there is just one more ritual.'

'What is that?' Sethu asked absently. 'You know that I will be gone for two days. I have to leave early in the morning tomorrow.'

'It can wait till you are back. The Prophet advised that it be done on the seventh day, but I am told that we can stretch it to the fortieth day.' Saadiya held the baby in her arms and rocked it gently.

'Here, give him to me,' Sethu said. 'It'll be two days before I see him again, Omar Masood, son of Saadiya and Sethu.'

Sethu held his son in his arms and knew content, something that had eluded him for more than a year now.

'So what else do you have in store for this little rascal?'

'The khitan,' Saadiya said.

'What's that?'

Saadiya wouldn't meet his gaze. She looked away as she said,

'The skin on the end of his, you know, his thing, has to be removed.'

Sethu stared at her, puzzled. Suddenly he knew what she was saying. He felt a tingling within his penis, a cringing of his testicles. Circumcision. That was her khitan.

'Over my dead body,' he said quietly.

Saadiya frowned. 'You don't understand…'

'No, I don't,' Sethu snapped, tightening his hold around the baby. 'I don't understand how you, his mother, can talk of maiming him. What kind of mother are you?'

Saadiya stood up. Her eyes begged him to understand.

'Please, listen to me. There are five acts of cleanliness in Islam. Shaving the pubic hair, plucking the hair under the armpits, shaving the moustache, clipping your nails and circumcision. Only then is fitra achieved. Fitra is an inner sense of cleanliness, which will make him a good Muslim. Without the khitan his acceptance into Islam won't happen. You promised me that I could bring him up as a true Muslim. You promised. Don't forget that!'

Sethu moved away. He walked to the window and stood there. The tide was beginning to rise.

'Have I broken my word? I did all that you asked. I didn't understand any of it, but I didn't speak a word in protest. And even now, Saadiya, I am not saying he shouldn't practise his acts of cleanliness. Shave his head, clip his nails, do all that you have to do. But don't you see, when you talk of a moustache and pubic hair and hair in the armpits, you're referring to a man. Or a boy almost a man. Someone who knows his mind. But this, circumcision, I can't allow it. You must wait till he's old enough to decide for himself.'

Sethu paused. 'When I was growing up, I heard of the sunnath, but it was always performed on pre-adolescents. You must wait at least until then.'

Saadiya was silent. Then she said, 'I am a descendant of the original Kahirs. In me is the purest of Arab blood. Islam, as we practise it, is a religion that demands sacrifice. In your village, the Muslims are converts. No matter what, they will never know what it is to be a true Muslim. Everything is compromised to make it acceptable. My son is not a convert. He has my blood.'

'Will you stop this?' Sethu heard his voice rise as if it were someone else's. 'You keep saying, my, my, my…He's my son as well. My blood is in him. What's wrong with you, Saadiya? You sound like a fanatic; you sound like one of those idiots in Arabipatnam. You chose to give it up, so why are you inflicting it all on this little child?'

'I made a mistake. I can't allow my son to make the same.'

Sethu felt his rage evaporate. A cold sheath settled over his face, his heart, his thoughts. She looked cold and aloof. Like she had in the labour room. Only this time, he felt the same.

'If you think you made a mistake, then I will not insist you continue doing so. You may leave. You can go back to your family and your religion, but you can't take this child. You will not want a reminder of your mistake.' Sethu spoke quietly. He felt his insides hurt as if someone had struck him in the ribs.

He laid the baby in its colourful cloth cradle fashioned from an old sari and went to the other room. At the door, he turned and said, 'May God go with you. Your God, not mine, because in your narrow mind there is no room for any God but yours.'

I, Saadiya, sit on the floor. His words beat a tattoo in my head. He says, go. But where do I go? I have no place. No home…no one.

I take the baby out of its cradle.

'Omar Masood,' I say. 'Your Umma has to go. Your Vaapa wants her to.'

If he would take me in his arms, all would be right again. If only he would. But that isn't true. Nothing can change the fact that I have brought to life an infidel.

Omar Masood begins to whimper. I lay him on my shoulder. For the past five days, since I came back from the hospital, I have been in this room, resting from the rigours of birth. My legs feel unsteady. I feel cold.

The sea breeze lifts my hair. I feel a great longing to wash my feet in the waters of the sea. To lie in its embrace and never know a moment's confusion again. To not feel so torn between my ancestry and my lfe as it is now. To just rest.

Sethu didn't know what to do. Saadiya had vanished. Could she really have returned to Arabipatnam? They wouldn't take her in. He knew that as she did. But where else could she have gone?

The body washed up three days later. A bloated Saadiya whose funeral was devoid of all religious rites. Sethu held the baby in his arms as he lit the pyre. 'Please, God,' he prayed, unable to keep the tremor even out of the voice in his head. 'Please, God, accept her in heaven. Her version of heaven, whatever it may be. This is all I ask.'

Later, when James Raj came to see him, he broke down and wept. 'Why would she do this? That night, we quarrelled. I said some very harsh things to her, but I didn't ever think it would lead to this. If I had known, I would have agreed to anything she wanted. I wish I had known. If only…'

James Raj patted his arm and said what he said to grieving relatives all the time, 'Who knows? It is God's wish that she go away from us.'

Sethu wiped his tears.

'You must get away from here. Go somewhere your mind won't dwell on the unpleasantness of your memories,' James Raj added.

'Go where?' Sethu asked.

'Come back to work,' James Raj said, as if he had just thought of it.

'But what about the baby?'

James Raj scratched his chin thoughtfully. 'Do you remember Faith? She has left the hospital. She might be willing to take the baby into her care. You can pay her for it and I'll ask my wife to keep an eye on them. Mary Patti is there for advice as well. Mary Patti, I don't know if I've told you this before, is my relative by marriage.'

Sethu's eyes lit up. Faith. Jada Kondai. Plaited bun. The quietest of the three. Given to bursting into cries of 'Praise be the Lord', whether it was for a hen laying an egg or a thunderstorm, but otherwise harmless and cheerful. She would do.

'What shall I call him?' Faith asked, cradling the baby in her arms.

'Om…' Sethu began. Then he made a decision. With Saadiya, his promise too had died. 'I haven't thought of a name yet. For now, you can call him Koman.'

Faith wrinkled her nose. 'What kind of name is that?'

'It was my uncle's name,' Sethu said, dropping a kiss on the baby's head, and then he was gone.

Faith looked after the baby well. Sethu came back after three days, worried about his son. But the baby seemed to be thriving.

When he began to leave with the baby asleep on his shoulder, Faith said, 'Perhaps you should leave him here. He'll fret when he wakes up and you won't be able to cope.'

Sethu paused at the doorstep. He thought of the house on the sands. It was a mausoleum of Saadiya's dreams. Of her unrequited desires and their anger. It was also empty. He would be alone with no one to help him. And by the time he got the baby used to him and he had learnt its routine, it would be time to leave again. Faith was right.

He gave her back the baby and said, 'I feel so inadequate.'

Mary Patti smiled. She said, 'Don't.' She took a whorl of tobacco from the length Sethu had brought her. 'Babies need women. Boys need men. We'll look after him till we can, then he is yours. He is always yours. But you need to make a living now.'

Sethu sent them money. He went as often as he could to see them; then slowly, the time between visits grew. And each time a worm of doubt or guilt niggled in his mind, he trod it underfoot. They are good women. They care for him better than I would, he told himself.

On his last visit to see the baby, who was less than a year old then, Faith said, 'He said he would like to see you.'

'Who?'

Sethu was curious.

'He. The doctor.'

'Why? Did he say anything?'

Faith shook her head. Her eyes said: as if the doctor would ever tell me why. For a long time, Faith had nurtured an infatuation for him. Some day he would turn around and notice her, she had thought. Then he had brought home a wife and Faith, her heart broken, had resigned from the hospital. She couldn't bear to be where he was.

Sethu sat across the table. When he had knocked on the door, the doctor had grunted, 'Come in.'

When he saw it was Sethu, he had gestured to the chair and returned to the file he was looking at. He peered over his glasses and said, 'I will take just a few minutes.'

Sethu felt the smile on his face freeze. He had been prepared for the doctor's apathy, but as the minutes stretched, he felt a slow coil of anger uncurl. He looked at a point over the man's head. I must not lose my temper, he told himself. I must not forget that at one time I revered this man. He dropped his gaze to the doctor's face and encountered his eyes. It unsettled him, and he knew the doctor knew it.

'I am very sorry to hear about your troubles,' he said.

Sethu remained silent. Then it suddenly erupted out of him: 'You were right. It must please you to know that your prophecy came true. Our marriage was nothing. Our love was nothing. Everything was wrong. You were right!'

The doctor took his glasses off and pinched the bridge of his nose. 'Do you think that I called you here to gloat over your…' he groped for a word and let it remain unspoken.

'I am sorry that it had to end this way and believe you me, I would have wished it to be otherwise. But now my concern is for Faith and her family. And your son.'

'What of them?' Sethu asked. The women cared for the baby well. No matter what the doctor said, he knew that for certain.

The doctor leaned back in his chair. He wiped the lenses of his spectacles with a white handkerchief, inspected the glass and said, 'All things are lawful for me, but all things are not expedient; all things are lawful for me but all things edify not…'

Sethu stared at the doctor and asked, 'Corinthians I?'

The doctor smiled. 'Your memory is as superb as ever, but I would rather that you understood the wisdom of the words. I do empathize with your position, but the world won't.'

'What do you mean?' Sethu asked, puzzled by the veiled references.

'Do you know that your son is being brought up as a Christian?'

Sethu leaned forward. 'When he was born, you saw me whisper the Muslim call for prayer in his ear. What you and Saadiya didn't realize is that I whispered a Hindu prayer as well. So if Faith or Mary Patti want to induct another religion into him, it doesn't matter. One more religion won't hurt.'

'You think this is a joke, don't you? Never mind your son; I can't have Hope and Charity's name slandered. It affects my hospital's reputation.'

'What do you mean?' Sethu was even more puzzled.

'It is natural that you would want to see your child, but your visits to Faith's home are much speculated upon. Even her sisters are not spared. All this coming and going makes the world talk.'

'But Mary Patti is there,' Sethu said in defence.

'Mary Patti is a silly old woman. They say you have bought her consent with chewing tobacco and an occasional bottle of spirits.'

Sethu sank his head into his hands. Then he rose from the chair abruptly. 'I understand. What I don't is that you are doing nothing to stop this vile gossip. If you were to say you trust them, the town would take your word for it!'

The doctor's face was stern when he said, 'I do trust them. But how can I trust you? You destroyed my faith in you.' His eyes were grim and full of contempt.

Sethu walked out of the room. There would be no farewell, as there were no words of greeting.

He tried to explain to Faith why he would not visit again for a while. Faith wept. 'I don't care what anyone says. You must feel free to come here any time you wish.'

'Thank you, Faith.' Sethu smiled. 'But I can't ruin your chances of marriage.'

'It's all that Hope's doing. She still hasn't forgiven you for not telling us you weren't a Christian.' Faith wrung her hands.

'I'm sorry I lied. I didn't mean to. But at that point, that was all I could think of,' Sethu said quietly.

'You didn't lie, did you? You said your name was Seth. It was Hope and Charity and the doctor who decided you were a Christian.'

'It's called lying by omission. But that's all in the past now. It seems so long ago, my coming here, meeting Saadiya, and now I have to leave…Mary Patti,' he said, turning towards her. 'I do not want your daughters' reputation besmirched. When my baby is a boy, I will come back for him. Until then you must give him all I would have. Three years, not a day more, and you can be sure I will return.'

Sethu started travelling. He went everywhere that James Raj had business interests. One day, he was on a train that would take him past his old home. On a whim, he stepped off the train at Shoranur. The town was some distance away from where his home had been, but this was the nearest railway station. The same one from where he had boarded the train many years ago. Then, he had barely looked around him. Now, he devoured every little detail. The flowing river. The distant hills. The green paddy fields. The coconut trees. The blue skies. The beauty of it all made his eyes smart.

It took Sethu only a few moments to know that he would never leave again. This was home. From where he had fled, he had returned. He would have to sever ties with James Raj, who would have to accept that Sethu could no longer be parted from his home. Sethu began writing a letter in his head: It's been two years since I went away from Nazareth. 1940 to 1942. But in all these years I never wanted to stay anywhere for too long. Now I have arrived at one such place.

Then for the first time in his life Sethu dredged from memory a biblical quote from the Psalms, a prayer for what would be his home, his life, his future: Thou which has shewed me great and sore troubles, shalt quicken me again, and shalt bring me up again from the depths of the earth. Thou shalt increase my greatness and comfort me on every side.

Sethu did what he always did by way of getting to know new territory. He took a walk. The station was busy. It was the most important junction that connected Malabar, Cochin and Travancore to the rest of the country. The Shoranur station hummed with movement. Engines and passengers, porters and vendors…the trains and the junction determined the life of the town and its people.

Outside, there was nothing. A few shops huddled at the tip of the barren land across the station. Sethu paused and drew a deep breath. All he had with him was a little bag. He could carry it with him, but first, which way ought he to go? The road to the left seemed more alive. So it was to the left he set his course.

He walked slowly, gathering the names and shapes of all that he passed. There was just about everything a town of this size would need. Aboo Backer Bakery. Cheru's Grocery Store. Pappachan Textiles. Padmanabhan Nair's Swadeshi Handlooms. And Kunju Mohammed's Variety Store with stationery, shoes and toiletries.

There were schools. The Ezhuthachan School and the Basel Mission Lower Primary School. The St Theresa's Convent and the Shoranur High School for Boys.

Sethu, as he walked, discovered that the road ran like a ring around the town. By the time he had navigated the ring, his mind was made up.

He would have to reinvent himself all over again. For that the only thing to do was to become a Janmi. A landowner, representing continuity and old wealth. With land, he would acquire a lineage he didn't have, and respectability. He would buy fields where he would grow his own rice and tracts of land where he would plant teak and rubber and coconut. He had money enough to do as he pleased.

To announce his presence, he would also set up a talkies. The town only had travelling talkies. He would give it what would be its first permanent home for the talking pictures.

Sethu went to the man who ran the small bank in the town. He asked to meet the owner and announced his intention with a deposit of a thousand rupees. The owner of the bank widened his eyes in surprise. Sethu could read that look: who is this man who exudes such authority and worldliness?

Sethu smiled. He recognized the type instantly. They bullied their inferiors and sucked up to their superiors.

'I am Sethumadhavan,' he said. 'I come from Colombo. I am a businessman. I run a trading company, but I have always wanted to come back to my ancestral land. And this time I decided I would.'

'Where is your tharavad? Your family must still be there?' the man asked, in a voice striated with humility and curiosity.

Sethu looked into the middle distance. It was a look he affected these days when he talked of the past. It spoke of nostalgia tinged with some unmentionable sorrow. It usually left the questioner content with the answer he provided. But this one is wily, this beady-eyed shyster, Sethu thought, and in time will serve my purpose. So he waved his hand and said, 'My family was from hereabouts but there is nothing left here. My parents never wanted to return. It is only I who have nurtured a desire to return to my land...'

The bank owner nodded his approval. 'I am glad. This town needs people like you.'

So Sethu acquired land for fields and plantations and within the town he bought land to build his talkies upon. When it was built, he called it Murugan Talkies. The other big business in town was a bus service called Mayilvahanam. Sethu pondered on his choice of name for only a few seconds. Mayilvahanam meant peacock transport and the one who rode the peacock was the warrior god Murugan. By calling his talkies Murugan, Sethu thought the town would know that here was a man whose business was on a par with the Mayilvahanam people. Or perhaps bigger and better.

Then Sethu set about acquiring the other trappings of respectability.

The owner of the bank knew of a family who had a daughter of marriageable age. 'They live in a little village called Kaikurussi. The girl is older than someone like you would normally choose; she is eighteen, but very pretty.'

Sethu didn't let his relief show. Saadiya had been too young. That had been the beginning of their troubles. This time he wanted a woman and not a child-woman. He perked his ears to what the man was saying. 'Her uncle is determined that she marries a man of means. None of these sambandhams that result in nothing but a handful of kids, he is rumoured to have said.'

Sethu nodded. He agreed with the uncle of the girl.

Sethu was the result of a sambandham. His father was from northern Malabar. He had come visiting and fallen in love with Sethu's mother, whom he saw at a temple festival. He had asked for her hand and she became his wife.

His mother had never been a wife. She shared nothing of her husband's life, except his bed. The word sambandham was perfect to describe marriages of this nature, Sethu thought. A bond, a sexual bond, and no more. Sethu had grown up not knowing who his father was. He had moved on, and another man had taken his place. It was considered perfectly normal for a woman to change her husband, if it didn't suit either of them to continue with the relationship. A boy grew up looking up to his maternal uncle rather than his father, who was little more than a casual visitor, and the women sitting on the steps of the bathing pond talked about their sambandhams as if they were discussing glass bangles...It had made his teeth grit then and it did now.

'I don't think that will be a problem. I hope you have told them about me. Like the girl's uncle, I have scant regard for these sambandhams. I will be very happy to progress with this alliance.'

'Don't be so hasty. Shouldn't you see the girl first?' the owner of the bank said. Sethu may be given to making snap decisions, but this was a little too rushed, he thought.

'Should I?' Sethu asked.

'Yes, you must. They'll want to see you as well.'

Sethu, accompanied by three other men, took the train from Shoranur to Vallapuzha. A little trek through paddy fields, past a canal, and finally they were in Kaikurussi.

Sethu mopped his forehead and thought, when I come here next, it will be in a car.

So Sethu, man of means, owner of Murugan Talkies, married Devayani.

He came to the wedding dressed in a cream-coloured silk jubbah and a double mundu with a zari border. He wore a gold chain around his neck and two gold rings. The motorcar he sat in led the way, and at the back walked men bearing petromax lanterns. It was dark when they reached the village border. The car paused and the lantern bearers walked ahead. The entire village came to see this spectacle of a groom in a car, with lanterns leading the way. The villagers, who had never seen such sophistication in their lives, whispered, 'Did you see that? Who would have thought Kaikurussi would ever see anything like this?'

At the wedding, he noticed a boy and a girl who vied to sit next to him. He smiled. 'How old are you?' he asked the boy.

'Eight,' he said. 'She is eight as well.' He pointed to the girl.

'We heard that you have been to far away places. To Colomb across the seas,' the girl said.

'His father is in Burma. Tell him, Mukundan,' she prompted.

But Mukundan merely smiled.

'What's your name?' Sethu asked the insouciant girl.

'Meenakshi. Is Colomb better than Burma?'

Sethu smiled. 'I don't know. I have never been to Burma.'

'Oh.' The girl looked disappointed.

The boy raised his eyes and asked, 'What is it like outside this village? Everything must be so different.' His eyes willed Sethu to say yes.

Sethu knew a strange sense of disquiet. 'It is very hard to say.' He tried to be cautious. What if the boy decided to run away from home, lured by the magic of the picture he painted? 'Sometimes I feel it is the same everywhere. Sometimes I think just entering another room in a house is a different experience.'

The boy's eyes pleaded for more. Sethu wiped the sweat off his forehead. The night was warm and sticky. 'You must ask your father. What is his name?'

The boy mumbled, 'Achuthan Nair.'

'It will be nice for us to meet when he is here next,' Sethu told Paru Kutty, Devayani's cousin and the boy's mother.

She smiled. Six months later, Sethu understood the meaning of that uncertain smile.

Sethu and Devayani went to meet Achuthan Nair when he returned from Burma. 'He is a very impressive man,' Devayani gushed. Sethu wondered what Achuthan Nair was like. Would he consider becoming a business associate, he wondered.

Murugan Talkies ran full house, but the real money lay in the black market. There was a shortage of rice and sugar. The adventurous and not-so-finicky ones ate macaroni that came from foreign lands and was readily available, rather than the vermin-infested, worm-ridden rice sold in the shops. The poor ate boiled tapioca. Good rice could be bought only in the black market. Most people were willing to pay extra, for a meal without rice was almost inconceivable. Sethu's profits were quick and large.

'This will end when the war is over. Now is the time to profit,' Sethu told Devayani.

Sethu wondered how he would broach the subject with Achuthan Nair. 'This chap, Gandhi,' he began.

Achuthan Nair stared at him. Then he reached forward and fingered the fabric of Sethu's shirt. 'What would you know of Gandhi or nationalism, given the fact that you are still wearing these videshi clothes? Your shirt, your car…everything shows your indifference to the freedom struggle. Why else would you flaunt your lack of patriotic spirit in these times when people all over our country, even poor people, are making bonfires of their foreign goods? And you wear a foreign, mill-woven shirt!'

Sethu flushed. He looked at Achuthan Nair in his hand-spun mundu and wooden clogs. He rose. 'Devayani, it's time we left,' he said abruptly.

He could do without such pompous creatures. Sethu knew a familiar ire rise. He is worse than the doctor, he decided, and thereafter did nothing to further the acquaintance.

Sethu knew content again. Life was a plateau with no uneven slopes or pitted surfaces. Devayani was a good enough wife, loving and considerate, and not given to emotional excesses. She smiled easily and seldom lost her temper. She ate well, slept well and loved well. Sethu would often look at her and think: she is not Saadiya. And only occasionally, he couldn't decide if that was good or bad. He would think of his son growing up in Nazareth. I must bring him here, he would think. Then he would postpone the decision, telling himself that it would affect his reputation to do so at this point. Besides, he would need to introduce the idea to Devayani first. So time went by and Devayani gave birth to two boys and the moment to bring home the child in Nazareth never arrived.

Then came a whiff of scandal from Kaikurussi. The boy Mukundan had gone away to work in Trichnopolli and the father had taken a mistress.

An invitation came to visit Paru Kutty.

'May I go?' Devayani asked.

'Do you want to?' Sethu asked.

'She is very lonely and very unhappy. This mistress business is very humiliating.'

'What would you do if I took a mistress?' Sethu asked.

Devayani searched his face. 'I don't know…'

'Go and get ready. I'll take you to Kaikurussi.' Sethu smiled.

The boy's head came to his chest. Sethu pressed him against his breast and with that gesture, tried to erase the sin of neglect. 'Who did this to you?' he asked, touching the boy's crown of hair.

'Mary Patti,' the boy said. 'Faith Akka's mother. I was very ill some months ago. Then Mary Patti made an offering to St Francis Church on the cliff that she would have my hair cut. There are a few other boys in the village near the church who have a similar haircut. That's what Mary Patti said. But I heard Mary Patti tell a neighbour that she had prayed that if I was to be taken back into your care, she would have my hair cut.'

Sethu ran his fingers along the ring of hair. Do you blame me for this, he wanted to ask the boy. I am the reason you have had to endure so much in twelve years of life. This ring of hair must have come with enough torment and humiliation. How could I have been so irresponsible?

Sethu now did what he had never done before, when faced with trouble. He decided to confront it.

He tilted the boy's chin and said, 'First, I am going to send for the barber. He will shave your head so that you don't have to walk around with this ignominy of a haircut. Then we will go to Kaikurussi and pick up your...' Sethu wondered what he ought to say and then decided, 'your mother and brothers.'

Suddenly he asked, 'Is there anything you would like to know? You can ask me anything you want.'

The boy met his eyes for the first time and said, 'Koman would like to know the name of the river.'

Sethu stared at his son. Then he said softly, 'You must stop addressing yourself in the third person. It sounds weird. Say I. I want to know the name of the river. That's how you ought to say it.'

The boy's eyes fell. Then he raised them and looked again into his father's face as if seeing him for the first time. He said, 'I want to know the name of the river.'

Bhayaanakam

We arrive now at the sixth emotion with which we dress our faces. Bhayaanakam. Fear. Don't we all know fear?

The face of bhayaanakam requires that you remember to let fear show. Your eyes widen, your forehead wrinkles, your nostrils flare, your mouth droops, and your neck retreats into your chest, but it is the breath that you have to concentrate on. Let it emerge from either side of your eyes and you will see that the eyes move on their own, naturally travelling to the object causing fear.

The state of being frightened can stem from many things. A wild beast, an evil man, a natural calamity, a dark night. All these can fill us with fear. But there is yet another fear, which is what I would like you to reflect on here.

Let us begin with the wild pineapple. First, you need to cut it away from its nest of green sword-like leaves. You know a fear; something akin to dread coils itself around your ankles. You do not know what awaits you. Cuts and bruises, snakes that crouch hidden in the undergrowth, so many trials waiting even as your arms stretch towards the pineapple. When you have the pineapple in your hands, another kind of fear attacks you as you slice its prickly sides away to expose its flesh. The sweetness floods your mouth, but at the back of your mind, you worry: will this be the one that causes your body to swell, making your eyes recede in a welt of puffiness? Will this be the one that will drive you into a frenzy of itching, making you want to tear your clothes off and rake your skin with your fingernails and roll in the dust? You do not know, you do not know...

Like you do not know what to make of the cry at twilight. In that hour when light gives way to shadows and there lurks in every corner an imaginary ghost, a thin quivery call echoes through the shadowed skies. Poo-ah, poo-ah...the kaalan kozhi. The devil's bird, we call it, though it is merely a mottled wood owl. When the kaalan kozhi cries, death wanders, seeking another victim, our grandmothers teach us. They tie knots at the end of their mundu and thrust a ladle into the ashes of the wood stove, all to drive the kaalan kozhi away. Yet, the cries echo through the twilight and the heart beats faster: who is to be next?

So it is with the stillness of Meenam—the month of April. As it dawns, the heat wraps the day, stilling every moment, hindering every thought and breath. The fields lie brown and baked. Tufts of paddy splay out like brown flowers that crackle even as you look at them. Wells dry up. Sweat prickles every brow and rushes down the temple. Exhaustion lines every face and dogs every step. The nights are still. The fireflies have gone into hiding. In the morning, the heat reappears, a ghoul strangling the breath of the hour, harder and harder. In your heart you know a fear. The worst fear of all: Will this ever end? When it does, what next?

Remember, you can pretend all other emotions: courage or love, laughter or sorrow, disgust or wonder, contempt or calm, but you cannot pretend fear…you will give yourself away. Fear cannot hide itself. It emanates from you even if you try to conceal it.

There is one other aspect to fear. When you are afraid, you react in two ways—with utmost courage or cowardice. The choice is yours, but only fear can draw that decision from you.

Shyam

I sit and look at her. Again and again. There is a hollowness in the pit of my stomach. I know the density of the milky fluid that replaces the ligaments in my knees. I know the taste of the liquid that fills my mouth. I know this feeling. It used to court me once. It held me in its arms and turned my intestines into nothingness. It hollowed my knees and washed my tongue with bitterness. When I was fifteen and didn't know where to turn, I knew you then, old foe. I recognize you even though it's been a long time since we met. I know you, fear. I know you are back in my life again.

She is sleeping on her side. Her plait snakes across the pillow. She is sleeping like a child. She has a child's nightgown on, buttoned to her neck and pulled down demurely to cover her knees. Sprigs of pale pink flowers, scalloped edges and cap sleeves—she has clothed her womanhood and transformed herself into a child.

Her sleeping face is drawn into a smile. Once in a while she nuzzles her pillow. Who treads through her dreams and stretches her lips into a smile? Is it him she is seeking?

I sit there on my chair and look at her. Again and again.

In movies, in the final confrontation, the man tells his adulterous wife, 'Did you think I wouldn't ever find out? Did you think I didn't know? I knew the day it began. Don't you realize I know everything about you?'

I have seen this scene enacted in so many different ways by so many different actors. I have asked myself: Did he, really? Would I have known? Would I have been able to tell?

I didn't, did I, Radha? I never knew. I never realized. I was jealous, but then, I always am. Have always been, when I think that someone or something threatens my place in your life. I am jealous of your childhood friends. Of your uncle, who seems to command your loyalty and trust while I have to wait for crumbs to come my way. Of the music you listen to, the books you read, of even your memories that exclude me. Which is why, each time you said you were planning to do something with your time, I found reasons for you to not do it. I don't like sharing you with anyone. I don't like anything that draws you away from me.

Tell me Radha, when did this begin? How long have you been cheating on me? Was it the day you first met him or the day I went away? Was it when the sun was shining, or was it when the rain drew a curtain around your adulterous coupling? Did you seek him out? Or did he seek you? Was it on my bed or his? Did he take you against a wall or lay you down on a patch of grass? Did you scream and rake his back with your nails? Did you nip his flesh and wrap your legs around his? Did he draw your hair over your breasts and ply his fingers through your wetness? Did you open your mouth and ask for more? Or did you close your eyes and sigh your pleasure?

I sit here, Radha. I look at you again and again. And I think of when fear came knocking at my door…

I would never have known, would I? If I hadn't met Jacob and, on a whim, decided to go with him to the rubber plantation he works on.

'C'mon,' Jacob had persuaded me. 'Just for a day. It has been so long since we met. You can take the same train back tomorrow, from Kottayam. I promise to drive you to the station.'

Jacob and I had been room-mates in the house we rented with two others. We were room-mates till I gave up my job and started my own business. Four years ago, he had switched jobs and become the assistant manager of a plantation. 'It's not an easy job, but it has its advantages,' he had said, when we spoke last.

I could see the advantages. A hundred-year-old bungalow that overlooked a green valley. Fireplaces and mullioned windows. Antique furniture and servants to keep everything clean. A lawn and ancient trees. There was a giant manjadi tree, and in the grass beneath were hundreds of manjadi seeds, glistening like ruby drops in the emerald of the grass. I picked one up and rolled its red glistening smoothness between my fingers.

I thought of the emerald earrings I had bought you. And knew that here was yet another way to please you. I found a thing to do.

I gathered the red manjadi seeds. I would hide the red velvet jewellery box in a bag of red manjadis and let your fingers chance upon it.

'What are you doing?' Jacob called from the veranda.

'My wife will like these red seeds,' I explained, holding up the bag.

'I'll get someone to collect them for you,' he offered.

'No, I have to do this myself,' I said.

The sun was disappearing into the horizon. Fingers of darkness gathered the redness in the sky.

'It's going to pour tonight,' Jacob said. He winked. 'Shall I start pouring before that?'

There were snacks—murukku and fried chicken, peanut masala and tapioca chips. We talked. The whisky disappeared. A pile of bones grew. I leaned back in my chair and inhaled the fragrance of tobacco. I had quit smoking three years ago. I hadn't craved for a cigarette even once. But without the slightest hesitation, I drew out a cigarette from his pack when he offered it to me, and lit one.

The rain fell in sheets. On the veranda we sat feeling the lash of its wetness. The raindrops stung my face. 'Do you want to go in?' Jacob asked.

'No,' I said. 'Let's just move away from the rain. It is so beautiful sitting here. God knows when I last had such a restful time. No problems to solve, no calls to take.'

It was then I realized that my mobile hadn't rung all evening. You hadn't called me even once. What was wrong? I pulled my mobile out. The signal tower on the left of the screen was a flat brick.

'Is this a no-signal zone?' I asked.

'Yes. Didn't you know?'

I looked at my watch. It was a quarter past twelve. It was late, but I knew I had to call you. 'I must call Radha. She must have tried calling me all evening. She must be worried,' I said.

I went into the house. I dialled your mobile. Why did I? Why didn't I call home? Or Uncle? I don't know. I was drunk. Perhaps I was scared to call home and find you gone. I just wanted to hear your voice and reassure myself.

I imagined the phone ringing and ringing. I imagined the sleep in your voice. I imagined you would be angry at being woken up. And I chuckled.

You picked up the phone at the second ring. Your voice was low, but clear. You were awake, you said. You were at Uncle's. Where else, you asked. You didn't want to wake him up; he had just gone to sleep, you said. No, you hadn't called, you said. If there was anything important, I would have called, you said. I was not worried, you said. I really must go to sleep now, you said. Good night, you said, and your voice in my ear went dead.

Was it then I knew fear for the first time?

I imagined you in his arms, turning to snatch the phone and willing it to not be me. Arranging your voice so you wouldn't give away the fact that he was with you. I imagined him licking the curve of your throat as you dribbled your lies into the phone. I remembered all the love scenes in the books I had read and the films I had seen. I imagined you and him turning them into reality.

In the morning, the sun blazed. It was one of those hot July mornings when you think the monsoon never happened. The heat dripped down my back in rivulets of sweat. The servants brought a bowl of cubed pineapple. Sugar sparkled on the fruit. I bit into the flesh and felt the sweetness envelop me. I must stop drinking, I thought. It changes my personality. I become another man: insecure, suspicious, afraid. I begin to imagine the strangest of things, and let it shoot up my blood pressure.

The heat and the yellow sweetness enveloped me. That July morning I thrust away fear and gathered my manjadis once again. I found a thing to do.

Yet, beneath the rows and rows of brooding rubber trees, fear lurked in the shade. From the cut in the bark, fear flowed into little black cups. And without my knowing, I carried fear with me into my home.

So, did I know fear's presence when I walked down the railway bridge and saw the two of you drive past? Shashi was driving, and I wondered what he thought of the two of you sitting behind in the passenger seat. Did the line of your body trace his? Did your hands brush surreptitiously? Did he have his arm draped along the back seat and did it toy with the nape of your neck? Did you lean against him?

Did Shashi see and wonder? Was he asking himself, does Sir know? In his heart, is Shashi pitying me for what you are doing to me?

I knew fear for certain when I went to the resort and they, each one of my employees, took great pains to not let their outrage show when they told me that when I was gone, you were at the resort. Without actually saying so, they let me know you were here. Dining with the Sahiv. Talking. Laughing. Cavorting as if you didn't care who would see, what they would assume. I listened with a heart fit to break.

It trailed me, this fear, when I walked into our room and saw that everything was as it was, on your bedside table. A thin film of dust spoke of your absence. You had hardly been home while I was gone. I dusted the top of the table and your various possessions. I found a thing to do while I waited for you.

The rain set in early. I stood there on the veranda, waiting for you. You came in, the rain dripping from your hair and the edge of your nose. 'Why didn't you take an umbrella?' I asked.

'Oh, a little rain isn't going to hurt me,' you said. 'When did you arrive?'

'A while ago,' I said. I resolved that I would not ask where you had been. Anyway, I knew what your answer would be: at Uncle's. Where else?

I watched you towel your damp hair and dry it. The hot air hummed and the perfume you wore sprang to life. I watched you as you walked between bedroom and bathroom, taking off your clothes. You were never so confident about your body before. I stood there as you draped a towel around yourself. I saw your shoulders, bare and inviting.

'Sit down,' I told you.

You looked at me as if I had lost my mind. 'Can I put some clothes on?'

'No,' I said. Where did that hectoring tone come from? I didn't mean to, you know. 'Sit down. This can't wait.'

You turned pale. You bit your lower lip. I saw fear in your eyes. 'Shyam…' you said in a voice that shook.

You sat down. I sat down beside you. I took my bag out and said, 'I brought this for you…'

For a moment, only for a moment, I thought I would set the manjadis cascading down your hair and face. See them tumble over your body and into the folds of your towel. But it is not in me to make such flamboyant gestures.

'Oh, what is this?' you asked and held up the plastic bag. The manjadis rustled and tittered and within, the emerald earrings nestled in their red velvet box.

'Manjadis? Is this what couldn't wait?'

'Look inside,' I said.

You stuck your hand in. It might have been a sewage pit with frogspawn on top, you showed such reluctance. Your fingers settled on the velvet box. You drew it out and I watched your eyes.

They were flat and disinterested. 'How pretty,' you said and left them on the table. I waited for you to put them on. But you rose to go. I knew fear again. What more could I do?

All evening I waited to see them glow on your earlobes. Then I asked you, 'Don't you like them?'

'What?'

'Don't you like the earrings?'

'I do.'

'Why don't you wear them? They are so valuable and you leave them lying around…'

You frowned. Your mouth tightened. I knew I had said the wrong thing again. And you said, 'If they are so valuable, why don't you put them away? It isn't as if I asked for them.'

'I didn't mean it like that,' I tried to explain.

'What else did you mean? You are barely back home and you've begun treating me like an errant, wayward child already. I don't need a daddy. I had one.'

I sit here in my chair looking at you. Again and again. It isn't only you who have read the poets. I know some poetry, too. Shall I, like Porphyria's lover, take your braid and wrap it around your neck three times, round and round and round? I wouldn't want to hurt you. You would feel no pain.

I would like to kill you. I hate you for what you are doing to me. But how can I? To kill you would be to lose you. That I cannot bear. I cannot let him take you away. I cannot let you go. Nor can I let you do this to me…none of this I can bear.

I think of the other Radha. The cowherd husband herded his cows while Radha sneaked off to her trysts with Krishna. He seduced her with music and charm. But do you know what happened? Krishna went away. He had so much to do, so many things to accomplish, so many demons to vanquish, and sixteen thousand and more wives to tend to; time had staked its claim on him. But the husband remained. The cowherd husband herding his cows and waiting for Radha to come to her senses, to go back to him.

Am I to be that husband? Willing to close my eyes, willing to forgive and forget?

Fear courses through me. What am I to do next?

I sit here, Radha, looking at you. Again and again. And thus we sit together, fear and I. And all night we have not stirred.

Radha

I wake up with a start. I do not know what woke me. A light left burning. A gust of wind. An absence...I sit up.

There is a light in the room. Shyam's bedside lamp. His side of the bed hasn't been slept on. I turn my head. Where is he?

Then I see him, sitting in an armchair. He is sitting facing me. What is he doing watching me sleep?

I wish he would turn the light off and return to bed. 'Shyam,' I begin to call him. Then I pause. Something about him scares me. This is not the Shyam I know. The Shyam who squares his shoulders, sucks in his abdomen, holds his head up pert and straight, and would never be caught like this.

The man in the chair lies back with his feet splayed out and his abdomen slack and protruding. His hands lie curled in his lap and his head lolls to a side. There is a wet patch on his t-shirt. Saliva had dribbled out of his mouth. He looks like a man whose breath has gone out of him.

I feel a hand clutch at my heart. Is he all right?

Then I see his chest rise and fall; a little snore escapes his mouth. And I feel that familiar ire rise. Now what?

He shifts in the chair. I see the red velvet box in his loosened clasp. I shudder. Those ghastly earrings. They must have cost a great deal. I wish he wouldn't buy me jewellery. His taste runs to the ornate and florid.

Rani Oppol would love them. 'Look at them,' she would say, holding them up to the light. 'Such magnificent earrings. You are so lucky to have a husband like Shyam, who thinks of you all the time. In fact, if you ask me, he spoils you. I think mine would remember me only if his food didn't appear on the table. That's what I am, his cook and washerwoman.'

Shyam would be upset if I gave them to her. Or would he? She is his sister after all.

I touch my ear lobes. My pearl earrings crouch there, almost invisible. I suppose Shyam is trying to make amends for mauling me the night before he left. But it isn't just that. There is something else. All evening he has watched me. His eyes follow my every gesture, his ears weigh every word.

Then I know. It hits me in the pit of my stomach. Uncle had been right to warn me. Someone has said something to Shyam. He has heard of Chris and me. A wave of panic engulfs me. What am I going to do?

Uncle and Maya are away. They have gone on a little jaunt on their own. Uncle wouldn't tell me where. I wanted to ask him about Maya, but his eyes warned me off: later, later.

The night they left, Chris came over. 'Will he mind?' Chris asked. There was apprehension on his face.

'He knows, Chris. He knows about us,' I said softly. 'Uncle never judges anybody. He never does that.'

'That's because he is scared that his life will be held up for scrutiny if he were to pronounce judgement on others,' Chris said, examining the interiors of the house.

I looked up, surprised. 'Why, you sound like you don't like him very much.'

'No, I didn't say that,' Chris said. 'How can I dislike him?' There was a strange expression on his face.

I didn't probe. I began making the bed with fresh sheets. 'He is her lover,' Chris said.

'Do you think so?' I paused, stuffing a pillow into its case.

'You can see it. There is a familiarity they share that only lovers have.'

'Do we have it, Chris?' I asked.

'You should ask your uncle,' he said. I swallowed my retort. What was wrong with him, I wondered.

I sat on the bed. He lay beside me. For a moment there was silence. We were a man and wife going to bed. It ought to have made me feel content. Instead, all I felt was awkwardness. Had our passion, our all-consuming passion, dwindled to this? Perhaps Chris thought the same.

He leapt up from the bed. 'Let's sit on the veranda,' he said. 'It's too early to go to bed.'

We sat there holding hands. He told me of some of his travels. I listened. I told him family stories. He listened. The night lay around us, lovely and dark, shutting out everyone else and gathering us together, closer...

'I think I am beginning to fall in love with you,' I said.

He smiled. 'You do?'

I waited for him to respond. To tell me what he thought of me. He didn't. I knew an inkling of disquiet then. But I suppressed my fear. Don't hurry him, I told myself. He has been single for so long. He is scared of commitment. He feels the way you do. He just won't say it. Give him time.

'Come,' he said, and led me into the rain. We walked to the edge of the steps. The drizzle was gentle but steady. He walked into the water and I followed him.

We were the only two people in the world. Only the rain and the river saw us as we made love and pledged our troth to each other.

Later, he towelled me dry, and I him. When we went to sleep, we lay in each other's arms. Lovers, or man and wife. What did it matter? We could be one or the other.

In the morning, I woke to find him gone. There was a note: I woke at first light and decided to go back to the cottage. I didn't want anyone to suspect anything. xxx Chris.

He wouldn't even write the word love to sign off. I folded the note carefully and thrust it into my purse. It was the first letter he had ever written me.

I wrapped my arms around my legs and huddled in the bed. Were we to be lovers and no more?

In the evening, I did not let any of my insecurities reveal themselves. I was beginning to know Chris. I worried that to tell him about this kernel of fear in me would be to put pressure on him.

Instead, we sat on the steps of the river. I told him what I had planned for the evening. I was going to cook dinner for him. I thrilled at the thought of playing house with him.

'Uncle and Maya will be back tomorrow,' I said. Let us savour each moment of this precious time together, I meant.

Chris did his best to imbue our time with pleasure. And love, even if he wouldn't speak the word.

When, a little after midnight, the phone rang, I knew it could only be Shyam. It was. I felt uncomfortable, guilty, as I spoke to him, lying there with Chris.

When I had put the phone down, Chris spoke. 'Was it him?'

'Yes,' I said. For some time now, Chris had stopped mentioning Shyam by name. I turned to look at him. His eyes glittered in the dark.

'This doesn't feel right, Min-min.'

'What?' I asked. I was being deliberately obtuse.

'This...'

I chose to misinterpret him. 'In the circumstances, this is the only way. I know Uncle's house is rather primitive, but I can't spend the night at your cottage and I so wanted this. To sleep in your arms, to wake up to you. Two nights. That's all we have for now.'

'I know, Min-min,' he sighed.

I snuggled up to him.

Chris said again, 'I don't know how to say it, but this doesn't feel right.'

I said, 'I know.'

'I mean, I, in some way, am indebted to him. He's let me have this cottage for almost nothing. I see that now. I wish I never had accepted his offer. I wish I had found somewhere else to stay. I don't like feeling beholden and to add to it, I seem to have wrecked your marriage. I feel like I got you into this situation. This horrible messy situation.'

'It has nothing to do with you. My marriage was fractured even before I met you,' I tried to explain, to drive his discomfiture away.

'How can you say it has nothing to do with me? It has everything to do with my being here...God, what have I done?'

'Please, please,' I pleaded. 'Let us not spoil this night. This is all we have.'

'Sometimes I wonder if you really know what we have done.' His voice was flat. He turned to me and his face was grim. 'Is this a game, perhaps? Something you need to do to prove a point? To yourself. To your husband.'

I felt anguish cover me where his body had. How could he even think that?

'Chris, please.' I felt tears rise. 'Why are you angry with me? What did I do?'

'How do you think I feel when you speak to your husband while

I lie here beside you? I don't want to be involved in this deception. It makes me feel sordid and responsible.'

'What can I do? You knew I was married. I didn't spring it on you, all of a sudden. Do you think I like lying, or that I enjoy this deception? It makes me feel sordid, too. It kills me, this guilt over what I am doing to Shyam. He has a very frail sense of dignity and if someone found out about us, he wouldn't be able to handle it. But...'

'What a bloody mess!'

I felt my body repel him; all that had been beloved to me until then filled me with dread. I had expected him to hold me and reassure me that while what we were doing was wrong, it was right for us. I had wanted him to say that despite everything, it meant the world to him.

I felt myself curl into a ball. I realized he was asking me to choose. But it would have to be a choice of my volition, for he would offer me nothing to help me make the choice.

For so long now, my days have had a sameness. They have stretched vapid and dull, predictable and monotonous. Nothing would ever change, I thought.

One evening, a girl I knew at college and who now lived in Coimbatore, came visiting unannounced with her husband. They were driving to Wayanad, she said. A kind of second honeymoon, she implied. On a whim, they decided to call on me and see how I was. 'You look the same,' she said. 'Where is your husband?'

Shyam was out. He should be back any time, I said, and I prayed he wouldn't return till they had left. I worried what they would make of him.

I saw the ease that flowed between her and her husband. The casual intimacies of a marriage. He took her hand in his when he talked. She touched his cheek in a casual caress...I looked away. I was glad to see them leave. Any reminders of my past made me realize how drab and barren my life was.

Then Chris arrived. He took my days and turned them into something else. He gifted me a prism that caught light and threw a spectrum of colours. I saw that even grey could be refracted. Violet, indigo, blue, green, yellow, orange, red—Chris led me through the hallways of the prism. I followed, uncertain but happy. There was nothing predictable about my life any more. My nerves sang and an iridescence filled me. How could I go back to my grey world after this?

And yet, as I sit here wondering if I dare to wake Shyam, if I can harden myself to withstand the accusation in his eyes, shrug off my guilt and his anger, I feel a sudden longing for that time when I feared nothing and no one. My grey world was a shroud that kept fear away. I have colour and light now, but at a price.

There is only one thing to do: brazen it out. If I can persuade Shyam that nothing has changed, I can buy time.

I need time. I need it more than anything else now. I need time to make Chris understand how much I mean to him. I need time to let Shyam know that I can no longer live with him. That Chris's arrival has only precipitated my going; I would have gone anyway. When I smash this little world that Shyam and I live in, I will need time to clear the debris.

I need time. And I fear that I am not going to have enough. Someone will be hurt. Shyam or Chris. How do I choose? What am I going to do?

I tiptoe into the bathroom. I wash my face and brush my teeth. I unbraid my hair and put on the emerald earrings. Fear clasps itself around my ear lobes.

Fear makes one do things one would never do otherwise. Fear lets you compromise. Fear will even let you seduce your husband so that he thinks he imagined your transgressions, your betrayal, and that you still are his.

I walk to where Shyam sits. I trail my fingers through his hair and whisper, 'Shyam, Shyam…'

Uncle

In the car, I take Maya's hand in mine. 'So, did you have a good time?' I rub her hand between mine.

She smiles. 'The best!'

I think of what Radha would say if she knew where we had been. 'But Uncle, Guruvayur! What were you doing at the temple? I didn't think either of you was religious. You must be getting old.'

I chuckle.

'What is so amusing?' Maya raises her eyebrows.

'I was thinking of Radha's reaction when I tell her where we have been. She assumes that you and I sneaked off to some romantic place for a passionate reunion.'

'Why would we need to go anywhere else? Your house is in the most romantic spot I have ever seen,' Maya says, rolling down the car window.

'For you; not for her. She has seen it all her life. But tell me, would you have preferred to go somewhere else?'

'Of course not.' Maya shakes her head. Then she smiles at me shyly. 'If we had, would we be man and wife now?'

I had decided on a whim that we would go to Guruvayur. A friend called to invite me to see the swayamvara sequence from the life of Lord Krishna. 'My brother is rather concerned that no suitable alliance has come for his daughter and someone told him that organizing a performance of the swayamvaram sequence as an offering at Guruvayur might help. I don't know if it will, but he has money to spend, and it will be interesting to watch. Why don't you come if you are free tonight?'

'Would you like to go?' I asked Maya.

'Will it be good?'

'Krishnattam is supposed to be kathakali's mother. It will be interesting…'

Maya likes dance. She will never be able to discuss the finer points of a performance. That needs many years of orientation, but she is a true rasika, a worthy audience who would inspire any artist to greater heights. She is interested, she is involved, and she respects it enough to switch her mobile off, unlike many others I know. As I sat next to her, I saw pleasure animate her face. And I was glad that we had chosen to come.

When we went back to our hotel, Maya seemed bathed in elation. She couldn't stop talking about the performance. 'I never expected it to be so awe-inspiring,' she said, as we prepared to go to bed.

I lay in bed, hands crossed beneath my head. Maya combed her hair as she talked.

'The devotees believe that by watching a sequence of krishnattam you are blessed. It is an act of prayer,' I said, enjoying the sight of her combing her hair, rubbing cream into her skin.

Maya paused. Dots of cream studded her cheeks. She smiled and said, 'In which case, I am truly blessed. To see it, and with you by my side.'

I felt something in me turn. Her smile was suffused with such sweetness.

'We have to wake up early if you want to see the puja at dawn. I prefer to go then, rather than later in the day. The crowds aren't so dense and it's peaceful. It makes me feel as though I am truly in God's home and not in a commercial complex where God is sold,' I said.

'Do you have a whetting stone to sharpen your tongue every day?' Maya shook her head.

The temple corridors were dark. The crowds melted into the shadows and I knew again that sense of serenity, as though I was alone. There was only Krishna, and I. Then I felt Maya touch my elbow. It seemed appropriate that she was here. She, too, belonged.

We could hear chants of Narayana, Narayana, the devotees' fervour rising as the doors of the sanctum sanctorum opened and the priests raised the lamp. A fleeting glimpse of the idol's face and Narayana, Narayana, the God's name drummed into our ears...

Amidst such devotion, I felt humbled. Why was it I could never lay my troubles at God's door? It occurred to me then that arrogance too is a manifestation of fear. To ask God to intervene was to accept that I was incapable of resolving my life...to accept that I was weak. Would I ever learn humility? I didn't know.

I turned to look at Maya. Her hands were folded and her eyes were closed. What was she praying for?

Later, when we had worshipped and breakfasted and time hung on our hands, plentiful and easy, we walked back to the temple. 'Do you want to buy some knick-knacks?' I asked her. 'You can buy Guruvayur pappadum, copper and bronze kitsch, pictures of various gods, devotional music, banana chips, just about anything you fancy...in addition to Guruvayurappan's blessings.'

Maya giggled. 'You really are wicked.'

'No, it's the truth,' I said, pointing to the shops that clung to the side of the temple like burrs to a dog's fur.

'What are these?' Maya asked, pointing to the raised platforms in the long corridor.

'Marriage pandals. If we wait around here, we can see a few marriages. Would you like to?'

So we found a place to sit and waited. A procession of people arrived and another and yet another. Couples climbed on to the dais to exchange garlands. The music of the drums and the nadaswaram flowed, packing itself into the meagre spaces between people.

'What a crowd,' Maya marvelled. 'How do they know who is marrying whom?'

'I have heard of instances where the bride has garlanded the wrong groom,' I said.

'And?' Maya was incredulous. 'What do they do then?'

'Nothing. It is accepted as divine ordination. Krishna has decided, and who are we mere mortals to question his decision, etc.'

'Interesting!'

I looked at her face then. There was such contentment there that I wanted to grab it and make it mine. 'Maya, do you want to get married?' I asked.

I watched her head turn. A slow swivelling, as though she couldn't believe what she was hearing. 'Koman, what did you say?'

I clenched my features to not show any emotion. 'I asked if you wanted to get married.'

She started laughing. 'I would be committing bigamy. Remember, I am already married. So, sorry, no. I can't marry you. Thank you for asking.'

'This is not a joke. I am serious. Will you marry me? Who is to know that you already are?'

The more I thought about it, the better I liked the idea. To exchange garlands and be wed. No pomp, no ceremony, just the two of us and a god to witness our marriage.

'Are you serious?'

'I am. I really am.'

'But why, Koman? Why now? Why do we need to be married?' Maya placed her hand on my elbow.

'I don't know. Perhaps I am feeling my age. I long to belong to someone. I want to know that someone else has a stake in my life and well-being.' For the first time, I was beginning to feel lonely. I thought of how all my energies were now concentrated on Radha. That seemed to be the role in my life. Uncle. Much as I loved her, I wanted more.

'Oh, Koman.' Maya's voice was soft with sympathy. She paused and said, 'Do you think it will cause any legal problem?'

I shook my head. I wasn't sure, but as long as we didn't register the wedding, what legal value did it have? I prayed that we wouldn't meet a roving reporter from a Malayalam daily, gleaning titbits to fill column space. I remembered a news item from a couple of years ago, when an eccentric had done a thulabharam with pencils. He sat on one side of the huge iron weighing balance and the other side was heaped with boxes of pencils till both pans dangled at the same height. Anything is news these days. So why not an elderly couple marrying?

I wasn't a celebrity, but a reporter might recognize me. Last year I had received another national award. It had meant nothing to me. The time when I needed the assurance of awards and recognition was long past, but the newspapers had made much of the occasion. For a while you couldn't open a newspaper or a magazine without staring at my face, or reading what I preferred for breakfast, or a listing of my achievements, as they termed it.

So Maya and I married. The crowds stared. An elderly couple getting married was an anomaly.

'Must be sweethearts who were not allowed to marry when they were young,' I heard a voice say.

'Poor things, at least now they've been able to get married.'

'Maybe she is a widow.'

'Their children probably don't like the idea.'

I thought of the countless stories our marriage would spawn. The countless interpretations as to why two elderly people were exchanging garlands. Only the truth would remain unmentioned. That Maya was already married.

All they saw was a woman in a cream and gold sari and a man in a mundu with a narrow zari border and another mundu draped around like a shawl. They saw the laxity of our skin and the grey in our hair. They saw the smoothening of vicissitudes and the played out emotions.

We became man and wife in the eyes of God and a few strangers. 'Wife, are you happy?' I asked her.

'I am, husband. What about you?' she retorted.

We smiled at each other. A conspiratorial smile. One more secret added to the secret life we began to lead ten years ago.

Malini greets us with raucous shrieks. She glares at Maya and hops towards me. 'Any one would think I was the mistress and she the wife.' Maya laughs.

'She hates having to share me.' I scratch her head. 'What about you?' I drop my voice.

'You belong to me,' she says. 'Malini, he is mine. Do you hear me?'

We smile again at each other.

'Do you realize they've been here?' Maya asks. I nod. I saw it as soon as I walked in. How can Radha be so nonchalant about the risks she is taking?

'I get this feeling that she is trying to put herself into a corner so she is forced to make a decision,' Maya says, unpacking our bag. I agree, but I don't say anything.

Chris walks in then. He leans back in his chair and yawns. 'I wasn't sure if you would be back. I thought I would take a chance.'

'Do you know if Radha is coming?' he asks.

Weren't you together a little while ago, I want to ask. Instead, I say, 'So how have you been? Busy?'

I reach out to switch on the fan, but there is no power.

'Not too bad. A little bored. I keep thinking I should get out and do more touristy things.'

'Perhaps you should,' I say. I wish he would leave. I would like to be alone with Maya.

'I went to Shoranur to check my mail. The Internet connection is so damn slow. I wonder if they have even heard of broadband. And then the taxi driver wanted a hundred bucks to drop me back here. I would have walked, but it is so hot.'

Chris yawns again. The fan begins turning. 'Is the power situation always so bad here?' he asks. 'It keeps going off. I can't even do any writing. How do they imagine they can turn this into a real tourist destination if nothing works?'

'Do you want to play a game of chess?' I ask.

'Do you play?' His eyes are eager.

'I do,' I say. 'Besides, it will give you something to do.'

'I'll come by for a game tomorrow morning,' he says. 'Do you think Radha will be here then?'

I feel sorry for him. He is lonely, I think.

'I'll call and ask her to come,' I say. I pat his arm.

His smile is tinged with relief. And gratitude, too.

What is Radha thinking of, I wonder again. She has the boy all twisted up in knots.

'He is beginning to feel disenchanted with his Indian experience,' Maya says, when Chris has left.

'I thought so, too,' I say. 'Well, at least his reasons so far seem genuine, but I have seen this happen again and again. So many of my students come here with such great expectations. They imagine this to be a tropical paradise where they are going to have their life-changing experience. Then familiarity sets in and what was exotic becomes lurid; what was old-fashioned is dismissed as inefficient; and what is spiritual is termed bloody laziness. I have also seen how, when they go back to the comfort of their homes and lives, these negative images lose their edge and soon they can talk about their stay in India with such enthusiasm that they inspire a fresh lot to come, seeking the meaning of life here.'

'That is very bitter.' Maya's surprise at my vehemence halts me. 'You know enough people, foreigners, to know that it isn't true. And that you are generalizing. What about Philip? What about Anna? What about Susan? You can't say they are like that.'

'I know, Maya. I know it's an injustice to generalize. I know that there are people like Philip, Anna and Susan, but there are also the others, who do exactly as I am doing now—generalize. They make sweeping judgements about us and our country and anything that counters their views is not acceptable to them. Visitors from other countries come here, look around, see the lack of amenities, and are pleased. This is the India they were expecting. Cochin is too commercial, they tell me. Why do people in Madras and Bangalore ape the west so much, they ask me. What would they like us to do?

Spin thread with charkhas, read by lantern light and drink buttermilk instead of Coke? We can't remain in the dark ages merely because it adds to the atmosphere.

'I had a student who even brought geegaws as if we were still stuck in the times of Vasco da Gama. Someone must have told him that if you give the natives a few trinkets, they will be your slaves for life. He must have brought a thousand erasers and ballpoint pens, and he handed out a couple to everyone he met. The thing was, he actually thought he was buying favour by doing so. I had to finally ask him to stop; he was embarrassing himself. The other students and the locals called him the Rubber Sahiv.'

Maya is silent.

'I don't like it when you talk like that, Koman. It doesn't suit you. You are surly, you are arrogant, you don't tolerate stupidity. I know all this about you, and I always thought it was because you couldn't stand mediocrity. But you were never bitter...bitterness smacks of dissatisfaction. Are you dissatisfied with life, Koman?'

I listen to her speak. I know that my diatribe is born out of irritability with the Radha–Chris situation. And helplessness that our time together is drawing to an end. I would like to rant and rave at the fate that is taking my wife away from me.

I like the proprietary tone of her voice: I don't like it when you talk like that, Koman.

'We have been married for just a day and you are already finding fault with me.' I laugh.

Maya giggles. 'I am, aren't I?'

At night, I lie next to Maya, watching her sleep. Tomorrow, she will be gone. And I will retreat to my old life.

I feel fear then. This is a fear I have never known before. It isn't as though I have not been acquainted with fear. I have been swamped by fear, different kinds of fear. The fear of not belonging. The fear that accompanies a decision: am I doing right? The fear that every artist feels—will I be able to fulfil the expectations of my art? Will I be able to do it again and again?

But never this fear of being alone. I have never felt lonely before. I was always content to be alone. I never needed anyone or anything. My art was enough.

Now, as my art demands less and less of me, I fear being alone.

I think of Radha. Shyam is back. How is she coping? I worry that Chris's disenchantment will soon percolate into their relationship. What then? He will depart, leaving not even a trail of dust, and she will be the one to suffer. I have to engage his attention. I must start answering his original question. The artist and the man. Am I one or two people?

Some years ago, a film was made about a kathakali dancer. It had an international crew and a star cast. But it didn't do well at the box office. Too serious for the people who go into the movie theatres expecting entertainment, I heard.

One day, when I had gone to the institute, I met a journalist who often wrote on dance and dancers. Kaladharan's knowledge of kathakali was adequate enough for him to engage me in discussions about the merits and demerits of various performances.

'Did you see the film?' he asked me.

'No,' I said. 'Did you? I feel this strange reluctance. I heard it's way too serious for the public. I suppose that means the film has some depth?'

His eyes widened. His lips curled into a smile. 'It has no depth at all. It is merely an enactment of depth, if you know what I mean.'

I grinned. I understood perfectly. I had seen it done before. Complexities were introduced to make a work of art esoteric and exclusive. And yet, as we practitioners of art knew, such efforts merely skimmed the surface and worse, were pretentious…and try as an artist might, the calibre of that work of art would never rise above the peripheries of the ordinary.

It is this that worries me. Chris imagines my life to be exceptional. He has heard much about me as a dancer, and he thinks that only from an extraordinary beginning and existence can such artistry rise. Perhaps this is why I made the introduction to my life so full of lyric and vigour. My purappaad to the story, the beginnings of the story of my life, has had much to recommend it, but it is time now to tell him of my life as a veshakaaran and I fear that this veshakaaran's life will not compare with the characters he has been. How can I compete with gods and demons? Or even heroic mortals? My life has been singularly devoid of such exalted heights or infernal depths.

I turn to Maya. I take her arm and drape it around me. Tonight,

I have this. In the warmth of her embrace, I think I can even voice my fear.

Bear with me and hear me out, I will tell Chris. I am an ordinary man made extraordinary by my art. In this story of my life, perhaps you will discover, as I will in the telling, how my art ruled my thought and life, how it helped me escape the confines of my secret fears. In the end, that is what counts. That art imbues meaning to one's existence.

So this, then, is how it began.

1952–1960
Going Forth

The river had a name. So did I.

At the high school, Raman Menon peered over his glasses and said, 'Koman. That's a pet name, if I may use the phrase. Doesn't he have a proper name? And what about his surname?'

My father narrowed his eyes into slits. In the few days I had been with him, I knew the import of that look.

'His name is Koman, with no tails, tags or suffixes.' My father spoke softly.

The headmaster, who even in the heat of Shoranur wore a dark suit to work, blanched. I felt a chill blaze my back. He was the headmaster, but my father made him seem like a silly boy.

'Koman,' he wrote in a register. 'Age?'

So there I was. Koman with no tags, tails or suffixes, age twelve, enrolled in a school and a new life. With a ready-made family: father, mother, two younger brothers. And a river that cradled me.

I ought to have been happy. But I had this 'I' to battle with. When I had referred to myself as Koman, I knew who Koman was. I asked no questions of Koman. I accepted that Koman was a boy whose mother was dead and whose father lived elsewhere because he had a livelihood to earn. I ate, drank and slept, shat and peed, ran and swam, dreamt and prayed. I was Koman the boy, one among a million boys in the world.

Now Achan had decided that Koman had to be an 'I'.

And this 'I', I needed to know. So I gathered bits of myself. From stray comments and conversations, from my stepmother whom I called Amma, from her glances when she thought I wasn't looking and from my brothers' curious questions I shaped the 'I'.

When Achan and I drove to Kaikurussi where my mother and brothers were, my father asked me to wait in the car. He went up the steps of the house to where a plump lady with a sweet face stood. There was a red stone in her nose ring. Like a drop of blood, the dull red jewel was the only spot of colour on her pale face. 'Where is she?' he asked the lady.

She smiled. 'Resting. I will tell her that you are here.'

Another woman stepped out of the doorway. She was plump, and her mouth spliced into a smile when she saw Achan. He returned the smile hesitantly. 'I have something to tell you,' he said.

So then I knew that my father hadn't ever mentioned that I existed.

My stepmother was a good woman. Or perhaps she knew it was futile to protest and so accepted my presence without any recriminations. One day I was a near orphan. The next day I was a boy with a family.

Later I heard her tell Paru Kutty, the lady of the house whose face took its rosy hue from her nose ring, 'He used to be married. She died. I should have known that a man like him would have a past.'

'Better a past wife than a mistress in the present.' The lady's voice sounded as if she had bitten into a piece of raw bitter gourd.

I knew a certain relief then. My mother had been a wife. I wasn't a bastard.

My younger brothers were seven and five. They stared at me when my father called them to meet me. They said nothing at first. Then the elder one asked, 'Do you know how to play marbles?'

I nodded. I knew relief again. I played marbles. I could shy a mango from a tree. I could climb trees. I could swim and hold my breath under water to a count of sixty-nine. I could be a brother.

'See these,' the elder one, Mani, said. He pointed to a pair of wooden clogs. 'Velliyamma's,' he said. 'Let's play with them. She isn't really our mother's older sister—she's a cousin—but that's what we call her.'

'Whose are these?' I asked, stepping into a pair of clogs they placed on the floor for me to try on.

'Her husband's,' the younger one, Babu, said.

'Where is he?' I asked, trying to walk.

The two boys looked at each other. 'He has a new wife. They live there,' Mani whispered, pointing across the road.

I stopped. The wooden clogs were heavy, but I knew lightness. So this was something men did. Discard the past and step into a new future—even if the past held wives and children. The owner of the clogs had, and so had my father. It had nothing to do with my mother. It was what men did.

I looked at my brothers. Mani's face was a flock of birds. It never rested, lifting from one expression to another. His eyes enlarged and narrowed, his nostrils flared, his nose wrinkled, his mouth parted into a hoot of laugher or widened into a smile of singular sweetness. His teeth gleamed; his brow broke into a line of sweat beads, which he wiped away with the back of his hand. He was tall for his age and a little potbelly protruded from his middle. I am so hungry, he said all day, and later when he was an adult, that would still be his call to life. A hunger that was never satiated. A greed that demanded more and more.

In contrast, Babu was small and thin, with a pointed face that was fixed into one expression, and a wandering eye. When you looked at Babu's face, you felt a trickle of fear. It was as though one eye went with you wherever you went, constantly looking, leaving nothing unturned, while the other stared straight and steadfast, constantly assessing. He picked at his food and wept easily. If he didn't have his way, if he felt threatened, if he lost a game, he ran on his short, spindly legs with tears coursing down his cheeks and a tale to tell. His stories almost always ensured a whacking for Mani. Sometimes Mani didn't even know what he was being punished for. But he took it without complaint, sure that he deserved the beating, if not for this imaginary misdemeanour, then for a real one perpetrated some days ago for which he had gone unpunished. They were my brothers and when they called me etta, I felt a sense of pride and responsibility. My brothers, my little brothers, I thought. But already

I knew who would be my favourite.

We went back to my father's house in Shoranur. It was vacation time and we played all day. Sometimes I would catch my father's eyes on me and would feel a shyness come over me. What did he see, I wondered. In the evening, the tutor would arrive to teach me Malayalam and everything else that would make it easier for me to fit into Raman Menon's school.

One day, as the boys and I bathed, I felt them staring at my genitals. 'What is wrong?' I asked. 'It's not any different from yours!'

My brothers looked at each other. They did that a lot, swallowing words and exchanging thoughts with conspiratorial glances.

'Is it all there?' Babu asked. He spoke his mind more easily than Mani did.

'What do you mean?' I asked, holding up my penis.

The two of them bent forward to examine my penis. 'He is right,' Mani told Babu. 'It is all there. So what did Amma mean by asking us to find out if the tip was missing?'

I turned away. A great heaviness settled on me. Who was I? What manner of creature was I to have the tip of my penis missing?

Then Mani began to tickle me and giggling, I forgot all about missing penis tips.

School began. I was in the second form when I discovered that, while I would never be brilliant, I was better than average. Achan patted me on the head and said, 'Very good. But what about arithmetic?'

I smiled. 'It's simple enough,' I said, happy to be able to please this man who my brothers claimed was seldom pleased.

He patted my head again. 'Good. To be able to run a business, you need to conquer numbers.'

I turned thirteen in November. There was a big lunch to which everyone was invited. 'It is the first time I've celebrated his birthday,' I heard Achan tell Amma. 'I am thirteen years late, so we must try and compensate for the missing years. I owe that much to his mother and him.'

My father asked a jeweller to make me a gold chain, and the tailor brought me new clothes. My tongue was coated with the many flavours of the feast and my heart tripped with joy. My father loved me. My father had loved his wife, my mother.

The next day, a stone fell into this calm pool of my life. Hassan sat on the bench next to mine. 'Tomorrow is my brother's sunnath kalyanam,' he whispered.

My ears perked up at the word kalyanam. 'Isn't he rather young to be married?' I asked with a grin.

'Oh, it isn't a wedding. That is a nikaah! This is his circumcision. True believers of Islam have their foreskins slit. It's very painful, so they stuff his mouth with pori so he can't scream through the puffed rice, and then it is done. It hurts awfully, but after that there is to be a biriyani lunch. You must come if your father will let you,' Hassan said.

I said nothing. I thought of Mani and Babu peering at my penis. I thought of Amma asking them to examine it. I thought of the servant lady saying, 'It is a wonder that he picked up our prayers so easily.'

I had thought that she meant my intonation.

Everything I had used to shape my existence had suddenly no truth, no validity.

That night we went to a temple. I had never been to a temple before. At the entrance to the temple was a signboard that said: No Entry for Non-Hindus.

I felt a vice-like grip on the foot I had put forward. I saw that Amma noticed me hesitate. I felt Achan's hand at the small of my back, pushing me ahead.

I remembered suddenly what Mary Patti had once said. My father knew the Bible like no one else did, she said. I had assumed that my father was a Christian, like everyone else in Nazareth. Then I discovered that he wasn't.

No one ever spoke of my mother. Nobody seemed to want to. Mary Patti, the doctor, and now Achan. 'What is there to say?' they said, when I asked. 'She was a young girl who died in an accident.'

Now I know why they were so brief. They hadn't known what else to say. That my mother was a Muslim. That I had no religion to call my own. That I wasn't the 'I' I knew.

Which was why I had to be Koman with no tags, tails or suffixes.

My heart beat faster than the drumbeats that reverberated through the temple grounds.

I heard my father mutter, 'What have you been telling him?'

I saw him glare at Amma. She had an aggrieved expression. 'Nothing. Don't blame me! I didn't say anything.'

Achan's eyes narrowed. 'Quiet!' His hiss crackled through the air.

'Ever since he arrived, you've been different. What is it? Do you wish she was here? Look at me. I am Devayani. Not Saadiya, or whatever her name was. I am not her. I can't be her.'

I walked on. I didn't want to be sucked into the bones of their quarrel.

Mani and Babu came running. 'Come on,' they urged. 'The performance will begin any time now.'

On a raised platform, in the centre, was a huge lamp. The wicks glowed. Two men held a multi-coloured silk cloth. The beat of the drums ground all noise out. The pounding in my chest intensified.

The singing began. It was a chant. What did it mean?

'What is it?' I asked Mani.

'I don't know.' Mani shrugged.

I let the singing wash over me. What did it matter whether I understood or not?

The darkness of the night, the flickering wicks of the lamp, the shadows, the waiting. I wasn't sure what brought it on, but it swamped me, the sensation of something about to happen.

I heard the tinkle of bells approaching. What would the dancers look like, I wondered. Suddenly I caught a fleeting glimpse. Behind the curtain were two majestic creatures, their crowns elaborate and their costumes voluminous. As the drumming began, they held the curtain and peered over it. Their hands moved the cloth this way and that in a rhythmic motion.

I knew anticipation again.

When the curtain was finally taken away, I saw them, those magnificent beings in their costumes. Beneath the proudly perched crowns, their faces were painted green. Their red-tinted eyes were shaped with thick, black lines and their mouths were an exaggerated red. Along the jaw from one ear to another was a white frame. Every inch of their being resonated with a sheathed-in power. They looked ready to conquer worlds, vanquish enemies and bestow blessings. My heart turned on its axis. Who were they? Men or gods?

They dwarfed everything around them: the people waiting to see them perform, the singing, and even the deity within the temple.

'Etta, you are hurting me,' I heard Babu whimper.

In my excitement I had forgotten that his hand lay in mine and I was squeezing it.

Then Mani whispered, 'Etta, Achan says we must go.'

I turned to where my father stood. 'Please, a few minutes more,' I implored with my eyes.

That night, my mind flitted from one moment to the other. The day had been compounded of many: Hassan. My mother. Amma's anger. The temple. The drumming. Finally I arrived at the dancers, and there it settled.

Those glorious men who had pressed out my every uncertainty with the magnificence of their presence. Would I be as magnificent if I was one of them?

The next day was a Saturday and a school holiday. 'Let us try something,' I told Mani and Babu.

I gathered a turmeric root and charcoal from the kitchen. From the niche in the wall near the bathroom, where soap and other washing things were kept, I took some blue indigo used to whiten the clothes, and some vermilion from the puja room. 'Bring me a basket, an old white cloth, and that red towel hanging outside,' I told Mani, who could be trusted with the most complicated of errands. As for Babu, I sent him to find a piece of cardboard.

My father's house was new. Its attic held no remnants of the past. It lay vacant and quiet, trapping sun motes and dust. And it was here that I fashioned my destiny.

I made a paste of the turmeric and indigo to make a passable green. Trying to recreate the faces in my mind, I applied it to my face. I drew the charcoal around my eyes and mixed the vermilion with water to tint around my mouth. I cut a hole in the bottom of the flat basket and wedged it around my waist. I draped a cloth around myself and slung the red scarf around my neck. I cut the cardboard in the shape of the frame the dancers had worn around their jaw. I made two holes at either end of the fan-shaped piece, drew two pieces of thread through them and wound them around my ears. Then I peered at myself in the shard of mirror I had. I wasn't the man-god I had seen yesterday. But I wasn't the 'I' I knew.

I could be anybody. I could be god or demon. I, Koman, age thirteen, with no tags, tails or suffixes, had a face I could recognize.

'What is happening here?' Achan said, walking into the attic.

He stared at me. 'What are you doing?' he asked. His voice emerged low and hollow, as if the climb had robbed him of all air.

'I...' I said. The 'I' rolled off my tongue easily. 'I was seeing if I could be a kathakali dancer.'

'And?'

Achan looked at me. I had never seen him look as sad as he did just then. 'You are too young to know.'

I didn't offer an answer.

'You might change your mind when you are older,' he added, filling the attic with the extent of his doubt.

'I won't,' I said. I touched his elbow and murmured, 'When I am a veshakaaran, I will know who I am.'

'What is there to know? I can tell you who you are.' Achan's voice rose.

'It isn't that.' I paused. He knew what I meant, but it was his place to protest.

For two long years I clung to my dream and denied Achan his right to impose his will.

There were frequent arguments. One evening, I heard about a performance at a temple nearby. I sneaked out when everyone was asleep and stayed there all night till dawn broke and the performance was over.

My father was furious. 'I will not tolerate this. I will not let you grow into a vagabond.'

'But, Achan,' I protested, 'I wasn't doing anything wrong. I just wanted to see the performance.'

'You didn't think it was necessary to ask my permission?'

'I didn't think you would let me go,' I said.

'When you knew that I wouldn't approve, why did you do it?' Achan's fingers pressed into my shoulder.

'I can't help it,' I said. 'When I hear the drum beat, all I know is I want to be there.'

Another time, he found me practising expressions in the mirror. 'Why are you making faces?' he asked.

'I am not making faces,' I said. 'I am trying to practise expressions.'

'What do you need to practise expressions for? Are you going to be a clown?'

'No.' I shook my head. 'I will be a veshakaaran.'

My father struck the flat of his palm against his forehead. 'What am I to do with this boy? Why won't he see sense?'

He grabbed me by the shoulders and pushed me away from the mirror. 'Go, go to your room and work on your algebra. That is what you need, to do well in life. Not this facility to make faces. Get that idea out of your head. Do you hear me?'

Raman Menon sent for my father. 'I can't help him if he won't help us. He is clever and has a good mind, but he isn't interested. What is wrong? I have asked him, as have all his teachers, but all he will say is "My father knows!"

'What is it that he won't tell us? If we knew, we could do something to help him. You know the proverb: you can take a horse to water but twenty men can't make it drink. Koman is the horse.'

Achan looked at my face. He sighed and said, 'He wants to study kathakali.'

Raman Menon tried to check his features from contorting into a grimace.

He turned to me. 'Very well. Do your matriculation first.'

'It will be too late. I will need to study for at least ten years before I can even think of performing,' I said.

When the school year finished, Achan took me across the river and so began my tutelage as a wearer of guises.

My days followed a pattern. A programme of order in which every nerve and muscle in my body and every sinew of thought had only one purpose: to enable me to transform myself.

'You must withdraw into yourself. Shut your mind to questions and the need to know why. Later there will be time for all that. But for now, you mustn't let doubts prey on your mind. Do as I say and only as I say,' Aashaan said on my first morning there.

Aashaan. His face was all planes and shadows, with its broad forehead, high cheekbones and stern jaw. Aashaan had a face that said it would not tolerate insubordination of any sort. Yet, his eyes gave him away. They were the softest eyes I had ever seen. Luminescent, but soft. Mostly, he narrowed them in displeasure at what we were doing, and then they looked like black ants scuttling over our bodies, determined to seek faults. Aashaan, our teacher, whose voice belied the strength of his palms and the expanse of his chest. Aashaan, who stood six feet tall and whom everyone knew as a veshakaaran who couldn't be matched but for...

'But for what?' I asked Gopalan, a second-year student.

'You will find out one of these days,' he said cryptically.

What did he mean? I knew Aashaan had a temper that would make even a raging elephant seem like a gambolling lamb. Was it that?

One morning, during the preliminary exercises, my eyes wandered to a tree outside the kalari. The classroom was open on three sides and there were huge old trees around it. Trees that were home to many birds and squirrels. I thought I saw a streak of blue. Was it a kingfisher? I didn't realize that my rhythm had faltered.

I knew when I felt something strike my shins. The pain was excruciating and I yelped. It was Aashaan's stick, which he used to beat rhythm on a wood block. I paused. The rest of the class paused as well.

Aashaan rose from where he was sitting on the ground with a little leap. He came towards me, glowering and snarling. 'Where was your mind wandering, you fool? If you can't get your basic taalam right, what kind of a dancer will you be? Rhythm. Don't forget that, ever. You miss a step and you've ruined it all. Do you understand?'

As if Aashaan couldn't contain his anger, he reached out and slapped me. 'I've been watching you. Do you think I don't know what goes on in your mind? You think you love kathakali and that should suffice. No, it doesn't. You have to work hard at it, or you are just a dilettante playing at being an artist. A true artist is someone who knows that every step has art and craft sculpted into it. That is how you acquire your style. If you can't work as I expect you to, I don't want you here. Do you understand?'

I felt my eyes fill. I was fifteen years old and no one had ever humiliated me so. Aashaan looked at me for a moment and then his attention shifted to a boy in the line behind me.

'Ah, there you are. Sundaran. The handsome one, who thinks a handsome face is enough to become a handsome dancer. I suppose you really think that is true and so you needn't abide by the rules of practice,' he said, moving towards Sundaran. 'I saw you playing the fool this morning at the kannusadhakam. The eye-practice session is for you to strengthen your eye muscles. If you prefer to bat your eyelids like a sixteen-year-old girl, you might as well give up and join a drama troupe. Or study a woman's dance. This is kathakali. Kathakali is for men. It needs a man's strength and conviction. Even when you perform the coy Lalitha or the gentle Damayanti, your eyes will have to remember the rigours of all you have subjected them to and from that tutelage learn to be a woman's eyes. But first, your eyes have to be trained to do as your mind desires. A widening eye is abhinaya. You are depicting an emotion. A widened eye is merely a static expression. Kathakali has no place for static expressions.'

I never missed a step again. And despite the humiliation of that day, I didn't bear Aashaan a grudge or hate him. How could I? He was a veshakaaran who gave his interpretation of each character a dimension no one else could. And yet…The unspoken words emerged when he performed. Aashaan was almost always drunk when he performed.

He never missed a step. His mudras were masterly. His interpretations were the most erudite. His vigour was overwhelming. But he walked a tightrope of control. One more drop and he would be tottering, and each time he performed, his reputation was at stake. 'When he knows he can ruin everything, why does he do it?' I asked Gopalan.

Sundaran and I were watching him as he applied make-up to his face before a performances at the institute. Aashaan was sitting outside, smoking a beedi. He had been drinking all afternoon.

Gopalan shrugged. He was disinclined to talk. 'He should know better. That is all I can say.'

Aashaan knew better than anyone else the sanctity of the stage. That is why it baffled me, his tendency to risk everything.

Two days later, in class, Aashaan would pretend none of us had seen him in a drunken stupor in the green room after the performance. He would look us in the eye and he would say, 'On the stage, you are not you. That should be apparent in your rhythm and expression.

Don't think as you perform, or your performance will be a cerebral activity. Let your body speak who you are. You are the brahmin Kuchelan, now. You must be done with your thinking and imagining before you arrive on the stage.

'For now I will teach you how to become Kuchelan. Imagine that you are a pauper. That you have nothing, no hope of anything or anyone. Your sole hope is that Krishna will remember that you were once friends at school. And it is that tenuous link you hope to appeal to. It is with this on your mind that you visit Krishna. You have been told by your wife to ask him to help you. To give you something you may feed your hungry children. So you go to him, but when you see him, you realize that you cannot ask him for anything. All your expectations are in your mind, your eyes, but you dare not speak them. Now think of a similar experience in your life.'

I closed my eyes for a moment. I thought of the first time I stood on the railway bridge at Shoranur station. Clutching at a tenuous link and no more…

Slowly, over the next eight years, I discovered the different aspects of being a wearer of guises. To match gesture and expression, to perform intricate footwork, to be both nimble and vigorous, to enact emotion without words, to add layers of interpretation to a single phrase, to raise myself from a performer to a character.

I was grounded in the nine faces of being. Love, contempt, sorrow, fury, courage, fear, disgust, wonder, peace.

In that congress of body and mind, beat and word, I knew myself. Luring memories and possibilities, drawing on dreams and imagined happenings, I learnt to live the character I was to be. I learnt that beneath the guise, I was the character. For me that was the only way to be.

In the years I had been away from home, much had changed. Mani and Babu were almost men. Mani was a tall, strapping eighteen-year-old with a deep, gravelly voice that boomed out of his barrel-shaped chest and a thick moustache he devoted himself to. He worked scented oil into it and combed it so it adorned his mouth, black, bristly and gleaming, with its ends curving upward on either side. Mani thought he was a man twice over for possessing a moustache like that.

As for Babu, he wouldn't ever match up to Mani's physical magnificence. He remained the child he was. A weedy sixteen-year-old with a sunken chest and a voice that couldn't make up its mind whether it was a whisper or a shout. His eye still wandered, despite the correction glasses he had been prescribed—which he never wore. He didn't sneak any more to our parents. Instead, he used his tongue to shred even the most inviolable self-esteem to ribbons.

Amma still smiled the smile that spliced her face, but she no longer allowed Achan to walk all over her. When his opinion displeased her, she said so, and she had learnt to stare him down. Achan looked the same, except that his hair was streaked with grey and when he had walked some distance, he paused for breath. He complained of aches in his legs and was given to long silences as if he were wandering in a world where none of us had a place. More and more, his conversation was spiked with 'When I was your age…'

I went home when the institute closed for vacation three times a year. Two short breaks during Onam and Christmas, and a long one during the summer. But I felt myself an outsider more than ever. It wasn't that they didn't welcome my presence, or didn't include me in the mechanics of their lives. It was me. I found them and their interests limiting.

How could they be content to live like this? I repressed a shudder. Their thoughts seldom rose above the mundane: Father's business and the three meals they ate, titbits of gossip and the happenings in town.

Amma being so, I could comprehend. She was a woman, after all, and women's lives didn't need to go beyond the kitchen and pretty trinkets. It was my brothers and fathers who disappointed me. The presence of a new pomade in the market had Babu in raptures. Shrimps on the dining table or getting the screening rights for a new film in the talkies excited Mani. As for Achan, he spoke of a dent in his car as if he were Nala pondering how to go about wooing Damayanti, constantly asking himself, 'What am I going to do?'

How they frittered away emotion on the trivial and inane.

I tried to tell Aashaan of my discomfort at home. Aashaan looked at me for a long moment and sighed. 'You are determined to make it hard for yourself, I see. For now, do as I say. Every morning, when you shave, look into the mirror and say—I won't be supercilious. Kathakali is my life, but others have a right to live their lives as they see fit.

'If shrimps make your brother behave as if he were Narakasura describing the peacock's dance to his wife or whatever, so be it.

'You can't be immune to ordinary feelings. Until you know what it is to be human, you can't play a mortal. Do you hear me? Koman, there is life beyond kathakali. The sooner you accept that, the better it will be for you.'

Aashaan said what he had to, but he knew as I did that there wasn't a life beyond kathakali for us. This was to be both our blessing and curse. While we were epic heroes, we knew a magnificence, an exaltation of spirit, a leap into a world beyond the one we inhabited; as men, we were nothing. So we chose to remain aloof from mere mortals whose everyday was compounded of shrimps, films and dents in motorcars.

Yet, I loved my family, and they me. While my brothers and I had nothing in common—they perhaps found my world as limiting as I did theirs—we were bound to each other by affection. And in the knowledge that because our lives were so separate, we need never be rivals or enemies. That was the strength of our tie.

They travelled, Achan, Amma, Mani and Babu, to a small Shiva temple near Vellinezhi to see me perform. I was to be Dharmaputran in the second half of Kirmira Vadham. It wasn't the part I would have chosen for my debut, but it was the first invitation I received as an individual rather than as a member of the institute's troupe. It was a recognition of sorts, I told myself. I would like to have been Kirmira. A character partially evil and partially good. But Aashaan, who had suggested my name to the temple board said, 'To play a katthi vesham, you need to fill out more. It is the same when playing a thaadi vesham. I know that villains in real life don't have identification marks to help us recognize them as villains. Their vileness is badge enough. But in kathakali, the villainous nature has to be made explicit. The villains need to have ooku, noku, alarcha, pagarcha...do you understand? Your time will come.'

I nodded. Ooku—vigour. Noku—a piercing glance. Alarcha— roar. And pagarcha—imposing stature. At best, I could manage the piercing glance. As for the rest, I trusted Aashaan when he said time and experience would provide.

'You will all come, won't you?' I asked. I had gone home to tell them the news. It was lunchtime when I walked in and I joined them at the dining table. 'It is my first real vesham.'

'Who will you play?' Amma asked.

I flinched. The question ought to have been, Who will you be? Kathakali wasn't drama; it wasn't about playing. Kathakali was about being. But Amma wouldn't understand the difference.

I said, 'Dharmaputran.'

'Who is that?' Babu asked, heaping rice on to his plate. For someone his size, Babu ate more than the rest of us put together.

'Well, you see, this is a story from the Mahabharata. The Pandavas had lost their kingdom in a game of dice and were in exile. The story begins with Dharmaputran, the oldest of the Pandavas, looking at his wife Panchali and feeling sorry for her and guilty for having imposed penury on her.'

'Oh, don't start now. We'll fall asleep here,' Babu interrupted, laying fried sardines on a side plate. I stared at the rapidly emptying plate of fried fish and said nothing. After all this time, I still wasn't used to Babu's abrupt manner of speaking.

Mani laughed his rudeness off, but I felt a great urge to reach over and smack Babu's face.

'Etta, never mind Babu...tell us the story,' Mani said.

'Later,' I said. I was already wondering if I had made a mistake by inviting them to see my Dharmaputran.

'So yours is a very important role?' Achan asked.

I wondered if I should tell them the truth. Then I decided it would be wise to prepare them. 'Well, the role of Dharmaputran is so important and so strenuous that usually two dancers are needed. Aashaan will begin and I will finish.'

'So do you get to kill the demon?' Mani asked.

'No, the asura king is killed by Bheema.'

'What does Dharmaputran do then?'

'Since you didn't want to know the story when I began telling you, I suggest you come for the performance and find out,' I said. Babu could benefit from a taste of his medicine, I thought.

Mani laughed. Father smiled. Amma cleared the plates and Babu sneaked me a dirty look. Then Achan rose saying, 'Well, at least you are not playing a woman's role...I would find that very hard to stomach. My son dressed as a woman and preening like a woman in front of the whole world.'

Later Mani came to my room. 'Etta,' he said, 'do you need anything?'

'Like what?'

'Like toddy. It might help you get into the mood.'

'Oh no,' I protested, laughing. 'I will have enough trouble keeping Aashaan sober without having to worry about being sober enough to perform myself.'

Mani pulled a comb out of his pocket and gave his hair a cursory flick. Then he began grooming his moustache. Did he ever give it a rest, I wondered. 'Would you like me to take you there, then?'

He met my eyes in the mirror. Parthipura Kalyani's, he meant.

I felt my face flush. The last time I was home, Mani had decided that I had borne the weight of my virginity long enough.

'How can you be a romantic hero if you don't know what romance is?' he demanded.

'But this isn't love,' I had offered feebly.

'It is a part of love. Lust is its brother. Let me tell you something: when lust fills you up, it doesn't matter who she is. The woman in front of you is the one you love.'

'But a whore?'

'Who else is there?' Mani said. 'Besides, you don't have to worry about getting her pregnant. This isn't the old times when you can sleep with a servant and get away with it. Remember what your Aashaan said about using experience to make the emotions you portray that much more authentic? How do you expect to look like you have fucked when you have never fucked?'

I smiled. When Mani used foul language, he sounded like a little boy who relished the sordidness of the words only because it made him seem so grown up. I let myself be persuaded. In Parthipura Kalyani's folds and crevices, I mapped lust and knew the truth of Mani's observation. And I realized that Mani was more grown up than I in many ways. For lust did cloud the mind and when in lust, even an old whore like Parthipura Kalyani was the gracious Damayanti. Naïve and untouched, and the most perfect of all women.

But this moment, I knew, wasn't for lust or love. If anything, I needed to feel frustrated.

'No, not now,' I said.

'In which case, I will let you rest...will you be here when I come back ?' Mani asked, his voice already impatient to leave.

'I'll go to the institute at about six,' I said, knowing Mani would return much later. 'I'll look for you in the audience tomorrow,' I added.

I knew that he would be bored. And yet, I liked the thought of all of them being there.

The next morning, Aashaan and I went to Vellinezhi with the chairman of the temple board, in his car. Aashaan had a knack for asking for luxuries. He did it so deftly that it emerged as a reasonable demand.

'Is the temple near the bus stand?' I heard Aashan ask the chairman of the temple board when he came to finalize the arrangements.

'I think so,' the man said. 'It's only two furlongs or so.'

When Aashaan saw that he hadn't hooked the fish, he sighed. This was a sigh he had perfected. A sigh from the role Aashaan was to play. A sigh that spoke of exhaustion and thwarted desires. I hid my smile.

Then Aashaan said, 'I was just curious. I don't travel by bus. Oh, by the way, would you be able to provide a room for the taxi driver to sleep in? It is an all-night performance and he will need a place to rest.'

The chairman bit the bait as Aashaan had expected him to. 'Oh no, what is this talk of hiring a taxi? I'll send my car for you.'

'No, no,' Aashaan protested. 'That is asking too much of you.'

'Aaih!' The man stood up in his determination to have his way. 'It is nothing. No trouble at all. In fact, it is a great honour to have you travel by my car. And perhaps, if it isn't expecting too much of you, would you have lunch in my home?'

Aashaan waved a hand. It was a gesture that had no place in the vocabulary of over five hundred hand gestures we used. But it said just as much: If you insist; of course; I seldom do this, but as you are such a special person, I am willing.

So we drove to the Shiva temple. Usually, the temple committee chose Dakhayagam where Shiva was the central character. However, the chairman, who was a kathakali aficionado, had insisted that the committee choose something else.

'Are you nervous?' Aashaan asked in the car.

'No,' I lied. I quaked within, but I wouldn't let him know. Aashaan had no patience for novices or neuroses.

'Good,' he said, settling into silence.

Aáshan would slowly start retreating into himself. Sometime early in the evening he would begin to show signs of restlessness. Then he would have someone direct him to the nearest toddy shop.

I would have to ensure that he stopped with one bottle. That would be my guru-dakshina to him. A thanksgiving compounded of restraint, and perhaps indulgent censure.

The pettikaaran was waiting. He was more than green room assistant and make-up man. Gopi was part of the institute. He alone knew us as mere men and then as the beings we became. Gopi was part of that change.

Now Gopi arrived with a lamp. He placed it on the floor, gave the wicks a twirl and lit them. He straightened and turned to me. 'I think it is time to begin.'

I nodded.

Outside, the dusk had settled as shadows. The school was adjacent to the temple ground. One of the classrooms was to be our aniyara, the green room where all the actors would prepare their faces and minds, don their costumes and characters.

Just then, the chairman arrived. His face was set in an expression I couldn't fathom. 'There is no need for any of this,' he said in a cold voice.

I stared at him. 'I don't understand,' I said.

'I have a reputation, a standing in society. I would rather cancel the performance tonight and have a group of school children perform a childish folk dance rather than let a drunk make an ass of himself and a mockery of me in front of the entire village and the neighbouring ones as well. This is a divine art. Does he even realize that? I took a chance by having Kirmira Vadham performed instead of the usual Dakshayagam. I took a chance by inviting your aashaan to be the main artist. And what does the man do? He is lying outside a shop, so drunk he doesn't know his elbows from his hands. I have made my decision. I suggest you pack up and leave. I will have my car drop you off at the junction,' he snapped.

I felt fear seize me with taloned hands. It wasn't Aashaan I thought of, and the humiliation this meant to him. I thought of myself. I thought of my parents and brother arriving to discover the performance had been cancelled. I thought of the few friends I had invited to see me perform. I thought of the stories that would percolate to the institute. I was a failure even before I had begun.

I felt tears rise in my eyes. And I did what even to this day makes me cringe. I prostrated myself at his feet. 'Please don't do this. Please. You will ruin my career and my reputation.'

He looked at me. 'I cannot change my mind,' he said.

'Please show me some mercy. This is my debut. My life as a dancer will end if anyone hears about this…please, please…' I wept.

Why did I beg and plead? Why couldn't I have left? In retrospect, it wouldn't have diminished my career in any way. But I was young and vulnerable. I was also unsure of myself. In that moment, all my insecurities came back to haunt me and it was the fear of being a failure in my own eyes that made me swallow all my pride and grab his feet.

'Aashan will be able to perform. He drinks. Everyone knows that. Perhaps he has had a little too much this evening, but I promise I will have him sober and ready. Please don't cancel the performance. Please think of me, if not him,' I pleaded, hoping to reach the man.

He wiped his face and looked away. 'I am not sure why I am doing this, but I will let you go ahead. But if I see that drunk fumble even once, I won't think anything of halting the performance right then. Do you hear me?'

I nodded. When he left, I sat there holding my head. I felt humiliation over me in waves. I felt shame. I felt tainted. What was so precious to me had become a curse. Is this how it would always be? Would my art always be a burden, making me humble myself merely so that I could keep it alive?

Gopi cleared his throat. 'Where is Aashaan?'

I looked around wildly. I had stayed by his side all evening. It was only when I went for my bath that I had left him alone. He had been asleep then.

'I am here.' A voice emerged from the shadows.

I hurried towards him. He reeked of toddy. 'How much have you had to drink? Do you know that the chairman was here and he wanted to cancel the performance?'

'Don't worry,' he said. I wondered if his words were slurring.

'How much?' I asked. I felt rage gather in my mouth. This was my debut. How could he ruin it so? His drunkenness would overshadow everything else.

'I will be all right. I always am,' he said.

The rage was suddenly replaced by a thought: if he was too drunk to perform, then I would have to be him. My mouth filled with bile. I was ashamed of the rogue thought.

'Aashaan, shall I get someone to bring you black coffee? It will clear your head,' I said.

He looked at me for a moment. Then he said, 'Come here.'

I went up to him. He pressed his hand down on my head. I felt the strength of the hand as a benediction. 'You will do well. But no matter how successful you become, you must remember that you are an artist first and only then a performer.'

I met his eyes. It wasn't often that I had the courage, but I did then. 'Is there a difference?'

He kept the flat of his palm on my head. 'An artist is a slave to his art. It rules him. It determines his life. It won't let him compromise. It won't let him accept mediocrity. It is his conscience. A performer? There are so many performers. People who go through the motions of exercising what they think is art. They are not artists. When you are older, you will understand this yourself.

'Go now. Be Dharmaputran. Not Koman who is playing Dharmaputran.'

He took his hand away. The imprint of his palm felt heavier than the crown I would wear as part of my costume.

'One more thing…' he said.

I turned.

'I know you expect to come in during the third act. I want you to come in the middle of the second act itself. You will play the furious Dharmaputran. You will confront Shri Krishna.'

I swallowed. The third act was tame. It involved very little of having to be anything. I had prepared as well as I could. I would have been the humble king in exile, greeting the sage Durvasa, offering hospitality and prayers.

But this scene called for much more. One minute of being on the stage necessitated hundred hours of practice. Would I cope? Would I be able to be Yudhishtira, the king who feels cheated? Would I know how to be fearful, having summoned divine forces with my rage?

I stood in front of the lamp with folded hands. Please, all you gods, whoever you may be, that rule my destiny, let me be Dharmaputran to the best of my ability.

I sat in front of the lamp. Gopi had the box open. I took a deep breath. The classroom exhaled a combination of smells—the stale smell of sweat, the starch in uniforms, cheap soap and coconut oil, boredom and exertion; the odour of countless school children filled my nostrils. I watched Gopi turn Aashaan into Dharmaputran. Soon it would be my turn.

I finished outlining the markings that would be my visage. Then I lay at Gopi's feet as he worked on my face. I thought about the evening. My family would be there. Would they stay as long as it took for me to appear on the stage? I doubted it. Neither Mani nor Babu had the patience or inclination. Amma tired easily and Achan would go with her. It was possible they would never see my Dharmaputran.

Did it matter? Should it matter? I thought of Aashaan. I was an artist, not a performer. Only performers worried about acceptance. And yet...

I felt Gopi fit the chutti. The whiteness would frame the face of the character I would become.

The colours waited. The yellow mannola, ground with coconut oil and zinc white. When indigo was added to it, it would turn green and that would be the colour of my face. I filled in the colours and Gopi helped me with my costume. When I was done, I felt the sixty-four knots that bound my costume to me.

The sound of the melappaadam had long ceased. The first part of the evening had begun.

I took out the canister of chundapoo seeds. I had plucked the purple flowers myself. The grounds of the institute were covered with the plants. The stamen had tiny dark seeds. I had rubbed several of the seeds in the palm of my hand till they tuned black, and dried them in the sun. I had stored them in a small container of ghee. Now I offered the seeds to Aashaan. His eyes were bloodshot already, but he took two seeds. It was a ritual that none of us dared deviate from. I left him and went to a quiet corner of the room. There was a cobweb in the corner. Beneath it was a stool. I sat on it and watched the spider. I felt myself escape the skeins of my everyday, and wander away from my skin.

Then I took one seed and inserted it into the cradle of my lower eyelid. There it lay, an uneasy baby wailing red screams, flailing its anger that would turn the whiteness of my eye into a furious red. All the better for the pupil in the eye to show its prowess. All the better for the man to turn into the character.

It stung. It always did. But it didn't swim in my eyes as it used to. I closed my eyes and rotated my eyeballs. When I opened them, the colouring had begun.

It was time to don my crown. When I did that, I would cease to be Koman. I would be Dharmaputran. The king who lost his kingdom gambling and caused his brothers and their lovely wife to live in exile. The husband who dragged his much-cherished wife Panchali into summer winds and blazing sunshine, robbing her of youth, comfort and happiness. The man whose fate it was to endure remorse again and again.

I could hear the singing of that first padam: *Baale, kel ne…*Maiden, listen to me.

Aashaan was Dharmaputan showing his grief and remorse; giving vent to a conflicting mixture of emotions.

When I became Dharmaputran, I would be the one who awakened Krishna's ire, but when Krishna decided to cut down my enemies, I would be remorseful. My enemies were not his. My destiny was not his. So how could I allow this to happen?

I placed the crown on my head. I felt it burden me with the weight of Dharmaputran's soul. As the son of duty, I could not let evil prevail, even if it was for my own welfare. I slipped the silver talons on to the fingers of my left hand. Steel rings gripped the first phalange of each finger. Every gesture I made would be emphasized…

Soon it was time for me to go forth.

BOOK 3

Neethanne venam thava gunagaatane

For the rest, you are the architect of your own fate

—Nalacharitam [Third Day]
Unnayi Warrier

Beebhalsam

The very word causes your face to wrinkle in disgust. Beebhalsam: the expression that contorts your face when you stumble across the grotesque. All you have to do is exaggerate it. Crinkle your eyes, flare your nostrils, screw up your facial muscles. But remember that this is the expression that balances itself on your ability to draw breath from the muladharam. From the base of the spine, let the breath rise, and then eject it forcefully through the nostrils. You exhale as if you do not wish to taint your insides with even the tiniest bit of breath that bears the stench of the grotesque. You exhale as though you are disgusted.

Beebhalsam is disgust. But what is disgust?

Is it the mild dislike you feel when the relentless rains cause a musty odour in the rooms and cupboards of your house?

Is it the revulsion, the detached revulsion you feel when you see a thoti kazhukan, its bald dome-like head and scabby visage, wrinkled neck and potbelly? Who among you does not feel that tinge of revulsion when you see a vulture?

Or is it the loathing, the all-consuming repugnance that swamps you when the air carries up your nostrils the stench of a dead and decaying rat? You wander in search of the stench. You exhale till you've released all the air in your system, then you hold your breath, but the stench is still so powerful that you know the only way to get rid of it is to seek out the source and destroy it...You walk on through the wooded parts of your garden and there you see the plant. At first you think it is the common yam, then you see the white markings on the stem and the flower, and you realize why you almost threw up. When the elephant yam blossoms, it smells of death. Do not confuse it with the yam you see in your kitchen. This is *Amorphophallus paeoniifolius*. Until pollination, the flowers send out a scent of putrid flesh to attract midges and carrion flies. Once the flower is pollinated, the stench dies, but who can wait that long? Loathing has no place for reason and so you grab the scythe from your waist and cut it down and throw it to the farthest corner so the stench dies with the plant. But wait. There is more to disgust. Beebhalsam is not just about disgust that you experience on account of the external world. Beebhalsam is not just about encountering the grotesque.

Beneath the plant lies a tuber. The elephant yam, which is smaller than the chena you eat at home. The yam you cook is bigger, but sometimes there is a rogue elephant yam that grows large. If you are an amateur gardener who doesn't know better, you will think it is the edible one. So you take it home and cook it. After the first morsel, you will know the worst agony of all. Hundreds of small needles will begin to pierce your mouth, tongue and throat...that is what the elephant yam can do to you.

This is the other dimension of disgust. An abhorrence you feel for yourself and for an action of yours. Revulsion and agony.

Radha

I touch his arm. He looks up. I smile. 'Uncle just called,' I say.

I see the familiar fences go up in his eyes. I sit by his side and trail a finger up his arm. 'He would like us to go there,' I say, and continue with my one-finger caress.

'You, or us?' he asks.

I make a little face, and marvel at myself. How easily they come to me, these little gestures and throw-away caresses. How well I play the role of a mistress!

I must have observed Rani Oppol more often than I thought. I am mimicking her, I realize. The little girl voice, the bated breath, the widening of eyes, the pouting of lips, the touching and stroking as I talk. I am being Rani Oppol at her coquettish best. All I need to do to complete the act is scream and turn pale when I see a cockroach. Shyam would love it. He would love me to be the helpless shrieking female while he squashed the cockroach under his slipper. Me Tarzan, you Jane, etc. Instead, I am given to thrashing scorpions and snakes mercilessly and carrying frogs in my bare hands.

I let my finger pause. It is meant to suggest hurt. 'Us, of course. You see, ever since Uncle began talking about himself—not the story of his parents, but his own life—he seems to be in a hurry to get it over with.'

His smile is twisted. 'I agree with that part of it,' he says. 'I wish Uncle would sum his life up in a few sentences and finish with it. What is there to say, after all? He is a dancer, not a diplomat, for heaven's sake. And he's not even in the league of say, Kalamandalam Gopi or Krishnan Nair. Those men are icons. But Uncle! How many people know Uncle or even consider him a success? Look at Pundit Sundar Varma. Weren't they contemporaries? That man is world famous while Uncle, he is just another dancer. What does he have to show for having spent all his life dancing? I mean, if your grandfather hadn't bought him that house, he wouldn't even have one of his own. Sometimes I think all this talk about artistic success being a personal milestone is his way of evading the real issue, namely his lack of success!'

For a moment I want to reach out and slap his face. How can he be so flippant? How can he reduce everything to how much money it might fetch? Doesn't he realize that Uncle chose to live his life this way?

I feel that sense of disquiet again. I have always suspected that Shyam resents Uncle for his place in my life. I know that he thinks Uncle is a fool for not having made more of himself. For the first time, it occurs to me that perhaps Shyam has been pretending all along. What he feels for Uncle is not affection, but contempt. I see it in his eyes and in the snarl his mouth curls into.

But I don't say anything. Instead, I let my fingers glide between his. He gazes down at our hands and his face softens.

'You go,' he says, trapping my fingers in his palm. 'I have some things to attend to. I'll come by later, at about lunch time. We can return together.'

Shyam leans back in his chair and takes up his newspaper. I sit there humming under my breath, pretending to read the supplement. Don't hurry. Don't leap up and rush to dress. Pretend this is a chore rather than a pleasure, I caution myself.

I yawn. I sigh. Then I rise with exaggerated reluctance. 'I must get going,' I say.

From behind the newspaper, I get a grunt for an answer. But I am not fooled. I know he is watching every move.

I walk languorously to our room. I have managed to escape for now, I think.

I dress quickly. When I pause at the dressing table to put some lip-gloss on, I discover that I can't meet my own eyes.

I feel disgust for what I am doing. Can anything be worth this repugnance? How much longer can I do this? This cheating, lying and pretence?

'Where were you?' he growls in my ear.

'I...I...' I am not sure what to say. How much do I dare tell him of what I am trying to do to deflect Shyam's suspicions?

But he doesn't let me finish. 'It's been almost two days since I saw you. If you hadn't come this morning, I would have come to your home.'

He doesn't even wait for me to step inside. He pulls me in and shuts the door and pushes me against it. I have never seen him like this. This is a new and masterful Chris. I am not sure how much I like it. He is talking and nuzzling at the same time. I feel my heart stop at his words. 'No, no, you mustn't ever do that. He...Shyam is already suspicious.'

Chris raises his head. 'Does that mean you will never invite me to your home?'

I shake my head. 'No, I didn't say that. I will have you over one of these days. I want you to see where I grew up, or at least spent part of my childhood. But you must promise to behave.'

His eyes glint. 'When I look at you, I don't want to behave.'

'We have to go,' I whisper. 'Unni will be timing me.'

'In that case...' I hear his laugh explode against my skin.

Fifteen minutes later, we walk to Uncle's house. I see Unni watching us as we walk past the reception area. What does he see? Two people, casual acquaintances, chatting as they walk. We're separated by at least three feet and an expression of disinterest I am careful to wear on my face.

I think of the hasty jumbling of clothes, the embrace, the shuddering, the reckless coupling against a wall because to move to the bed would have been to rob ourselves of a precious few minutes.

Outside the cottage I could hear the swish of brooms as the women swept the leaves off the pathway. I could hear the snip-snip of secateurs pruning a bush. I could hear a crow cawing and parakeets calling. And the footsteps of the electrician as he checked the garden lights.

When I felt the tidal wave drag him and me into an abyss and a moan emerged from my mouth, it was he who shut it off by gathering it into his mouth.

What is this passion that carries all sense of propriety away?

I glance at him. His pupils seem dilated. Can sex do that? What about me then? Do I too show the branding of an injudicious moment, of adulterous desires that have swept aside all that is decent and moral about me? Would Unni see and know? And would he think: Look at her, like a bitch in heat, careless of who is around or what they may see.

I am not listening to Chris. All I can hear is the beating of my own heart and an inner voice that berates me. How can you let lust rule you? There is nothing more stupid than careless lust. There is nothing more disgusting than your inability to control your wantonness. Do you want to undo all that you have been trying to build? Chris might want you like this, reeking of abandonment and sex, but in his heart he probably thinks you are a slut! Disgusting, disgusting, disgusting, it snickers.

I try to pull myself out of my despair. I try to concentrate on what Chris is saying. 'Have you been watching the Saddam trial?' he asks.

'Some of it,' I say. 'I keep thinking of the picture they ran of him when he was captured, and the footage of him in the courtroom. He was in total control, not like the decrepit, dazed old man in the picture. They ran a transcript of the trial in the newspapers. Did you see it? He kept insisting, "I am Saddam Hussein, President of the Republic of Iraq". I must confess he had a great deal of dignity sitting there.'

'Dignity! He's evil. Think of the carnage he was responsible for. If he hadn't been stopped, he would have continued with it,' Chris snorts.

I stop. Chris halts by me. 'He said he shouldn't be penalized for what he did to protect the Iraqi people's interests,' I say.

'You mean his interests?'

'What about Bush then?' I retort.

'I don't believe you are saying this.'

'Why not? Everyone knows that it's all about oil. There was no horde of weapons of mass destruction. There was nothing to warrant Bush and his bunch of buddies invading Iraq. Chris, I never thought you were a Bush supporter.'

'I am not a Bush supporter, do you hear me? But do you realize what you are saying? Forget all about oil or WMD, Saddam was a threat to peace in the region.' His nostrils flare.

It strikes me then that we have never argued before. In our insular world of flesh tones and soft caresses, neither of us has ever spoken a harsh word to the other. We've never sounded each other out on our beliefs or ideals, on our politics or principles. For the first time, I see that he dislikes his opinion being questioned.

In his first week here, Chris had been quick to condemn Bush, Blair and the other boy scouts as he had called them. '"Be prepared", they must have whispered around to gather support,' he had gibed.

And Shyam had spoken up, 'I was a scout. Nothing wrong in being prepared. I mean, I wouldn't have known how to make four different knots or light a fire if I hadn't been one.'

Chris turned to me then, rallying my support. 'You know what I mean, don't you? That smug, beatific, do-gooder attitude,' he had said.

Something urges me to press my point now. 'I understand that he was a threat. But that is for the UN to decide and do something about. Not Bush.'

'Look, no one can remain neutral about the justification of war on Saddam. And that is what you are doing. You are saying you know that he is evil, but it is not our business to intervene. And that was your country's stand too, if I remember right. How can you let evil perpetuate? That is almost as evil. Tolerance is just another word for laziness. To have an opinion and to stand by it necessitates making an effort, and you don't want to make that bloody effort.'

'Forget it, Chris,' I say. 'You will never understand what tolerance is about. It is beyond you westerners.'

'Jesus, that is a racial comment if I ever heard one.'

'What do you want me to say? That Bush and Blair and the coalition are right and we are wrong? Please understand. I am not justifying what Saddam did. All I am saying is, one country does not have the right to take away the sovereignty of another. That is all.'

Chris's eyes are piercing. 'What are we talking about? Why do I get the feeling that you have moved away from Saddam and the Gulf to something more personal? Is this about us?'

Yes, I want to tell him. Our opinions, even when they are about a world that has no direct bearing on our lives, are us. And yes, I do think that you have taken away something that is mine. You invaded my mind, my body, and while I had to suppress my desires and dreams and even forfeit my freedom to live the way I wanted to, under the previous regime, at least that existence had a pattern, a method. What do I have now? How am I to function without your support? I am a country that has to rebuild itself from nothing. I am a country that has to face recriminations and challenges and I don't know where to begin. Worst of all, I don't even know if you will be there to hold my hand through the rebuilding process. So wouldn't it have been best to leave me alone?

We are outside Uncle's house and Uncle is frowning. 'What is wrong? Have you two been quarrelling?'

Chris runs a hand through his hair. 'We were arguing about politics and war, except that Radha seems to have gone off in a direction that I can't follow...' His eyebrows rise.

I smile. I try to erase the belligerence from my face and the thought that our worlds can never be the same.

'How is Maya?' Chris asks.

I try to catch his eye. He looks away. He is still furious, I can see.

'She is fine,' Uncle says. 'We spoke last evening and she said she wished she could come back here right away.'

'So what's stopping her?' Chris asks.

'Well, there is her husband for one,' Uncle says, and turns to Malini's cage. The parakeet is nipping at a piece of jackfruit. When he faces us again, I see him trying to erase the sorrow in his eyes. What is the nature of his relationship with Maya, I wonder.

'Would you like some jackfruit?' Uncle asks. 'It's come rather late this year, and some of what I have eaten so far has tasted watered down because of the rains, but one of my old students brought me one this morning. It's delicious. He had his wife prepare them, so I didn't even have to get my hands messy.'

'How messy can a fruit get?' Chris asks.

Uncle and I look at each other and laugh. 'You should try cutting one open and prising the pods out,' Uncle says.

'It's like sticking your hand into a huge gob of much-chewed chewing gum,' I giggle.

Chris grimaces.

'It's quite disgusting and the process is very tedious, but the fruit…' I say.

Chris looks at the delight on my face. 'Do you think I could try one? Eating one, I mean…' he adds hastily.

Uncle brings out a platter of jackfruit. Picked and cleaned, the pods lie on their side, plump and inviting. Sweetness that glistens.

Chris surveys the plate, unable to decide. He picks one gingerly. 'Its smell is rather strong, like the durian,' he says, looking at it suspiciously.

'Never mind the smell, bite into it,' Uncle urges. 'And take care, there is a huge seed inside. You don't eat that. Not raw, at least. One of these days Radha will make you a curry with it.'

We watch his face as he nibbles at a golden yellow pod.

'It's nectar…It's sweet, smooth, with a little bite. It glides down your throat.' He spits the seed out into his hand and when he looks up, he is rapturous. 'It is quite unlike anything I have ever eaten before; it is incredible.'

I am pleased. It gratifies me to know that he finds the jackfruit, fruit of my country, delicious. Nevertheless, I cannot resist the temptation to say, 'Thank God, there is something about this country that you like.'

Chris eyes narrow speculatively. 'Oh, I like everything about your country, even…' He stops abruptly.

'Even what?' I ask.

'I'll tell you if you promise not to be furious.'

'I promise.'

'"Even its cussedness,' he says, proffering a jackfruit pod.

Buying my silence with a sop and sweet nothings, I think rather wryly.

Uncle tears a pod into long strips and chews one. 'What was your quarrel about?' His eyes are speculative.

We don't speak.

'Well, it doesn't matter, now that you seem to have resolved it,' he says and pulls out an envelope from a stack of letters. 'Here, I wanted to show you this.'

He draws out a sheet of important looking stationery from the envelope. 'This letter says that I have been given yet another award by the government, this time by the state government.'

'Congratulations. But you don't seem pleased at all.' Chris and I speak simultaneously.

'Well, if I had got the award twenty or thirty years ago, it would have pleased me, but now...' He makes a face.

It is a grotesque face. One I recognize from the navarasas. Beebhlasam. Disgust. Disdain. Repugnance.

'I find it utterly pointless. There was a time when an award, or even a felicitation, would have helped prop my self-esteem. Those days I was working relentlessly at my art, giving it all I had. During the nights, when I was on stage, I was a stranger to self-doubt. But every kathakali artist has to face life during the day, when there isn't a character to submerge himself in, and then a question pops into his head: Why am I doing this? At those times, appreciation for what I was doing, for the homage I paid to my art, would have lifted me out of the intense bouts of melancholy I fell into. Now, when I seldom perform, when age and time have made me more secure as an artist, I don't need public recognition or these stupid expressions of appreciation. In fact, I see it like a sarcophagus closing in on me. In the hallways of the state assembly, or wherever they decide these awards, they are probably saying: Oh, let's give that old man an award. What if he pops off one of these days? The whole world will start talking about how wonderful he was. We'll look like boors who didn't recognize his worth while he was still breathing.'

'Don't say that.' I take his hand in mine. I am unable to understand the expression in his eyes, but it distresses me. 'Uncle, the award is not about now. It is to felicitate you for the artist you were and are, and is a tribute to your talent.' I use words that I hope will please him.

He shakes his head. 'Such big, hollow words. Don't you dare talk to me using such words, Radha. You sound like one of those reporters who is sure to hound me when the award is announced. 'Sir, when did you first know you wanted to be a dancer? Sir, what was your inspiration? Sir, do you think art can change society?' He mimics a shrill voice.

'No, Aashaan,' Chris joins in. 'She is right.'

I look at him. Chris has learnt to enunciate 'aashaan' almost perfectly. My heart leaps at how effortlessly the word comes to him.

'This award will inspire so many others. Think of it as a recognition of who you are. Both dancer and man.' He wraps his hands around ours.

Uncle smiles. It is a watery smile.

Chris and I look at each other. I see relief in his eyes and he in mine. For now, we have a commonality of purpose.

And so we stay there, our hands clasped in a temple tower of affirmation, of the hope we have in each other. I raise my eyes and see Shyam standing at the gate. I think of the picture we must make. I see on his face another version of beebhalsam. Hatred. Pure hatred.

Then he sees me and the look disappears. I wonder if I imagined it. I hear him say, 'Hello, what is going on here? An oath of allegiance...'

Shyam

They fall apart. A house of straw that trembles when the shadow of the big, bad wolf falls upon it. I didn't even have to huff and puff to blow their tower of hands down. Just the sight of me was enough.

I wipe the anguish from my eyes and put on my most hearty voice. 'Hello, what is going on here? An oath of allegiance...'

Uncle is the first to speak. 'They are trying to comfort me.'

Chris looks up and says, 'Hello, Sham. How are you?'

Not Sham, you bastard. Can't you get it right? It is S-H-Y-A-M. More and more, when I think of him, I have a recurrent image in my head: Of Chris huddled in a corner while I kick him with booted feet. I can see the boots in my mind's eye, the leather gleaming and the undersoles studded with vicious spikes. I would kick him again and again till there was nothing left of him but ribbons and the echo of his torment.

Radha touches my elbow. 'Shyam, are you listening? I asked, how did you get here so early?'

I shrug. 'I finished work quickly.' I had, of course, planned to arrive early, to see if she was with Uncle or if the two of them were ensconced in some cosy corner.

She is not happy I am here, I know. But I pretend that I don't. I am getting good at this: pretending to not know what is going on, pretending that I don't see through Radha's caring wife act of the last few days, pretending that I don't know that Uncle is their ally, aiding and abetting their intimacy.

All this while, I had thought that Uncle had some measure of love for me. Esteem, too. Now I see there is nothing. He doesn't care what any of this will do to me as long as it pleases his precious Radha. I think I would like to kick him as well, draw blood from that smug face. I suppose all of them think they have managed to fool me completely. Perhaps they even laugh together about it.

I draw a veil over my thoughts and smile. I don't want any of them to realize that I am aware of what is going on.

I have thought hard about what I can do to resolve the situation. The simplest thing to do would be to get rid of Chris. The situation would then cease to be a situation. I have contacts who would do the needful. There would be a bloated corpse in the river one morning and no fuss thereafter. But if I do that, I will lose Radha forever. She will enshrine their lust and turn it into a temple. She will appoint herself its high priestess, shave her head, wear white, and sever our ties and my life with it.

I thought half-heartedly of stashing some drugs in his cottage. My friend the SP would do the rest. There would be no harm done to Chris, but he would have to leave. Except that I fear Radha would suspect me of having set him up and she would never forgive me. There is also the worry that the name of the resort would be dragged through mud. I cannot let that happen.

Radha is mine and I will not let Chris take her away. I will have to think of something else. Meanwhile, I will continue to pretend and plot my revenge.

'Shyam, Uncle's been given a state award and he's treating it like it's a burden,' Radha says.

I offer my hand to Uncle. 'Congratulations! But why don't you like it?'

'These things don't matter,' the old man says.

No wonder you have nothing to show for all the years you have spent capering on the stage, I think. It is not enough being good, you need what my mother considered an essential virtue: saamarthyam. Efficiency of thought. Skill in spotting an opportunity and capitalizing on it. Dexterity in managing your affairs.

I switch on my widest smile and say, 'But this is such good news. I am delighted. Can I see the letter?'

Uncle gives it to me. I can see from his face that he is unable to decide if he should be pleased by my reaction or vexed. 'This is fabulous,' I say, holding up the letter. 'Radha, did you read this? It's is so exciting. I tell you, the press is going to camp here once they know about it.'

'That's exactly what I fear,' the old man says.

'We must celebrate; make a song and dance about the award. I think we should host a reception at the resort,' I say, folding the letter. Then I look at it and say, 'May I photocopy this and give it back to you? I could use something from it for a press release.'

'Shyam, Shyam.' Uncle holds up his hand. 'I don't want any fuss.'

'It's a celebration. Not fussing.'

'Thank you. I am really touched by your wanting to do all this, but no. Do you hear me? No.'

I give him back the letter. I pretend a reluctance I don't feel. I pretend to be aggrieved. But within, I laugh. Listen, you old man, you don't think I mean it, do you? I have absolutely no intention of wasting my time or money on something I will not profit from. Especially not for you, who have been an accomplice in this crime that the two of them, your niece and her lover, have committed against me.

'Radha, tell him,' I insist.

Radha sighs. 'If he is not willing, how can we force him?'

I raise my hands in an expansive demonstration of helplessness.

Then I see the smudge on her shoulder. It's a love bite, one my mouth did not cause.

I reach over and touch the spot. 'What is this?' I ask.

She starts. She turns pale. She touches it. Unknowingly, her eyes dart to Chris. Then she pulls together the collar of her shirt to hide the bruise and gropes for an explanation. 'I think I must have hit the door jamb. The one in the dining room that sticks out. You know how clumsy I am.'

She seeks Chris's eyes to check if the explanation is satisfactory, but he, practised seducer that he is, looks elsewhere. I know then that they fucked this morning.

I feel it again, that gathering of loathing from the ends of my limbs, the pit of my stomach, the base of my spine, through my veins and nerves. I know that if I contain it within me, I will explode, or strangle the two of them. I exhale my hatred.

I look at Uncle. He looks embarrassed.

He shifts in his chair and taps the birdcage. A shaft of light falls on him. It catches the gold of his button. Is it real gold after all, I wonder.

Uncle wears a blouse-like shirt. It is the kind you pull over your head, its collarless ends held together by a gold stud. Hardly anyone wears such old-fashioned clothes any more. Even old men have switched to bush shirts. But Uncle, of course, has to be different. So the particular cotton material has to be procured and the tailor has to stitch it according to the pattern he provides. Radha does all this willingly. But when I ask her to go with me to choose a shirt, a note of weariness enters her voice: 'Do you really want me to? I am not good at selecting shirts. You should do it yourself. You are the one wearing it. What does it matter whether I like it or not? It's enough if you do.'

I wonder if it is on the old man's bed that they fuck. Does he stand outside, here on this veranda, keeping watch, ready to warn them, while within they squeal and grunt?

I mop my face. I am sweating and I do not like to be seen as a man who has lost control. My methods and means are subtle.

For now I think I will content myself with a petty act of revenge.

'Uncle,' I say. 'I have been meaning to ask you a favour.' I look around, gathering all of them into the discussion. The old man pauses in the process of folding a betel leaf. 'What is it?' he asks.

'When I was in Kochi, a tour operator took me to a few resorts. You know that, unlike them, we have very little to offer by way of landscape—apart from the river, that is. What we do have here is kathakali. At a few of those resorts, they take the tourists for a performance and they tell me that the tourists love it. I was thinking, why don't we do the same? Except that we host the performance at the resort during the season.'

'Shyam!' I hear the horror in Radha's voice.

I hold up my hand to silence her. 'Please, let me finish. Not a full performance, mind you. My guests would fall asleep. Just enough to interest a western audience. We could choose something from Duryodhana Vadham or Prahaladacharitam or one of the battle scenes. Something vigorous and colourful...and gory.'

'Shyam,' Radha says in the voice she puts on when she is trying to convince me to change my mind. It is a voice that suggests 'I-know-you-are-stupid-but-I-will-still-try-and-make-you-see-some-sense'.

'This isn't like tethering an elephant to a tree in the resort.'

'Exactly,' I say. 'Padmanabhan is a great success. My guests love him. All of them tip the mahout and actually give him an extra fifty-rupee note to buy Padmanabhan bananas. I tell you, kathakali will be a great draw!'

'Just because kathakali is colourful and...and...energetic, you can't turn it into a before-dinner act to amuse your guests.' Radha doesn't even bother to hide her annoyance any more.

'But Sham, this is preposterous,' Chris says. 'Surely you can't ask that of Uncle...'

'Did I mention Uncle's name?' I ask the two of them. 'You jumped to that conclusion. I didn't. Uncle is too old. I am sure he doesn't have the strength to perform such energetic scenes. Besides, no one wants to see an elderly Krishna or Bheema.'

I see Uncle wince. Somewhere within me, the injury he has done me begins to hurt less.

'Shyam, how dare you?' Radha is furious, as I knew she would be.

'Why? What have I done? I was only asking Uncle if he knew someone who could come here once a week. One or two dancers...young performers. We won't have to pay them as much.'

My tone is querulous, veering towards injured. I am beginning to enjoy the discomfort I am causing.

'I think it is ridiculous. Other resorts might do it, but you can't turn an art form into a circus act.' Chris is just as furious as Radha.

Uncle stands up. 'May I interrupt?'

There is silence.

'You will need more than a veshakaaran or two,' he says.

I nod. 'Yes, of course.'

'You will need two singers. You will need the percussionists—the chenda, maddhalam and idekka.'

'Can't we use a recording?'

'It won't be the same. Live music adds to the atmosphere.'

I agree, but don't say anything. Uncle waits for me to speak. When I don't, he continues, 'You will need a pettikaaran and you will have to either rent the costumes and the crown, or invest in a set. In the long run, it might be cheaper to invest. Also, you might not be able to rent a crown when you need one. Kathakali may have turned into a commercial business, but the crown is still considered sacred. So the first preference would be a temple performance rather than one at a resort.'

'How expensive would it be?' I ask.

Uncle frowns. 'I don't know for certain. About sixteen thousand rupees maybe, for just the crown. Give me a day or two and I will let you know.'

'Uncle.' Radha's face is a study in disgust. 'You are not going to agree to this, are you? Shyam doesn't even understand that he is trivializing what is sacred to you.'

'It is a desecration. How can you even consider it?' Chris demands.

The old man looks at them. He shakes his head. His tone is mild, but his eyes are tinged with anger. 'I have a student who is a full-time employee in a film studio. After eight years of intense training, do you know what he is reduced to doing? Every morning he dons a full costume, including the crown, and waits. He waits, hoping that one of the sets in the film city will require his presence. On a good day he will be asked to show a few mudras, perhaps even do a kalasham. Some days he is merely a prop. Some days he just waits. That is desecration. I am not blaming my student. My heart goes out to him. I can imagine what he must endure, the revulsion he perhaps feels for himself. But he has to eat, he has to live, and kathakali equips him to do nothing except perform. I blame the society that makes a mockery of this art. Haven't you seen that commercial for liquid blue that uses a kathakali dancer in full costume? What does a veshakaaran have to do with the whitening of clothes? Haven't you seen film sequences where the hero and heroine hold hands with a line of kathakali dancers and all of them perform high kicks like they are chorus girls in a Broadway show? That is desecration. I would never blame the dancers. A scene like that would keep the kitchen fires burning for a week in a veshakaaran's home and when you are hungry, you can't cling to your principles. We are an anachronism in today's world. Our art demands effort from us and the audience. But who has the time for all that? A kathakali dancer has no place in the modern world. He is an endangered species.

'So here are Shyam and his foreign guests, eager for a glimpse of a Kerala art form. At least once a week, a veshakaaran can be a character he has trained to be. So what if it is abridged, so what if he is asked to play only the spectacular scenes, so what if his scope to interpret is limited? Amidst all the selling of his soul he has to do, he is allowed respite. He is given his dignity back.

'Why, Shyam is a patron. In his own way, he is keeping kathakali alive. You need to appreciate that and not condemn him and his proposal.'

I flush. I look away. In matters of revenge, I think, it is best to be savage rather than subtle.

Loathing surfaces again. This time, though, it is for myself. For the malice I had intended. For wanting to hurt the old man. I realize that no matter what, I can't really hate him. Just as I can't hate Radha.

Uncle

Radha is furious. Her eyes blaze. She turns to me. 'Uncle, I don't understand you at all. On the one hand, you dismiss this award as of no consequence, and on the other, you think what Shyam is proposing is almost laudable.'

For the first time, I am beginning to see what Shyam is up against in his marriage. Perhaps the bravado he shows, the Mr Fix-it exuberance, the know-all air he wears, is merely to hide this constant corrosion of self-esteem he must have to endure. And yet, I cannot help being touched by Radha's concern. For some time now she has appointed herself my keeper and like a mother hen she will rush to defend me at the slightest hint of danger. In many ways our roles have reversed. She looks out for me like I used to for her. I pat her head soothingly.

'You must try and understand that Shyam's idea has a lot of merit attached to it. I do see in it a ray of hope for the art itself. The award, now, is personal. I don't need any awards to tell me the calibre of my artistry. In fact, the only award that means anything to me is this,' I say, touching my button.

'The gold button?' I hear the amazement in Chris's inflection.

'I always thought the gold button must be a memento. I didn't realize you got it as an award,' Radha says.

And Shyam—only Shyam would ask, 'Is it 18 or 22 karat gold?'

I touch the gold button. 'Does it matter? It is the most precious thing I have ever been given in my life.'

My performance at the little Shiva temple, I had thought, would elicit some comment from the world. As time went by, it occurred to me that my Dharmaputran had gone unnoticed. Every day I got angrier and angrier. I shouldn't have let Aashaan talk me into it, I thought. I should have waited for a more prestigious occasion, a more important venue. Who had even heard of this Shiva temple? If I hadn't gone there myself, I wouldn't have known it existed.

The resentment that consumed me began as a sense of doubt. Had I made a mistake by accepting the invitation to be the lesser version of Dharmaputran? At that time, it was enough that I had been asked. The doubt transformed into displeasure and when it became bitterness, I felt as if my whole being was changed. I couldn't meet Aashaan's eyes. I felt my gestures become clumsy and my expression harden into wood. It was only when he asked me to be a villainous creature that my feelings surfaced.

And so it was that one morning, while Aashaan was watching me, he said, 'Good! I think your resentment is ready to be made use of now.'

I stopped. It was unheard of for anyone to pause in the middle of a class unless Aashaan asked them to. But I couldn't help it.

Aashaan drew his chellapetti closer. He waved his hand to dismiss the class. Then he opened the chellapetti and drew out two betel leaves. Slowly he prepared them. I felt anger uncoil within me. I knew he was doing it deliberately. Once the betel leaves were in his mouth, it would be a full five minutes before he spat out the juice, rinsed his mouth, drank water and was ready to talk.

'Aashaan,' I said, not bothering to hide my impatience.

He raised his eyebrows: wait.

I stared at my fingernails. I swallowed. Words. Anger. Bile. Two can play at this game, I decided.

Then Aashaan cleared his throat. 'Here, look at yourself.'

I raised my eyes. Aashaan held a small mirror in his hands. 'Look at your face. Do you see the righteous indignation? This is the Balabhadran I wish to see.'

I turned towards the older man. I felt my heart do a kalasham.

Tai nta. Ti. Nta. Ta. Ti. Ti. Tai. A series of steps in the ten beats of the champa tala to match the rhythm of my unruly emotions. Is he–angry with me–or does he mean something else–could it be?

'What do you mean?' The words merged with the tempo of my thoughts.

Aashaan looked at me. There was indulgence in his eyes, and a trace of sorrow. 'After your Dharamaputran at the Shiva temple, I received many invitations on your behalf. They chose to write to me instead of you, perhaps because I was and…' he paused, 'am your guru. They asked you to be this and that. All second-grade characters. I decided to not even let you know, because I was waiting for something like this.'

'Waiting for what, Aashaan?' I knew joy then. My Dharmaputran had made an impact. I was an artist, an artist of calibre. Unable to hide my excitement, I drew closer to him. 'Who do they want me to be?'

'Patience, patience.' Aashaan moved a step back. Then he said, 'Balabhadran in Subhadraharanam.'

I closed my eyes. Balabhadran. Balarama. Brother of the more famous Krishna. Hero. Noble being with the mustard yellow colouring of the pazhuppu character.

'Do you realize now why I had to let you stew? Dharmaputran was perfect for a debut. But to make an impact, for your artistry to be recognized, you need a vesham that is full of energy. Where your abhinaya and natya capabilities receive equal attention. Your interpretation of the character and your dexterity with your hands and feet need to be demonstrated. And Balabhadran is that platform.'

I felt shame creep over me. I had thought that Aashaan's silence had been prompted by a sense of insecurity. I had told myself that my vesham had made Aashaan feel inadequate and so he was trying to put me down.

'Aashaan,' I began, wondering how to phrase my apology.

He raised his hand to stall the words. 'I know you wanted praise. I know you craved for words of appreciation. I know that you wished me to say I was happy with your Dharmaputran.

'I was happy. I was happy that the boy who stood before me eight years ago and said, I know that when I am a veshakaaran, I will know who I am, had lived up to the promise of his words.

'Here, this is all I have to offer you.'

Aashaan undid the gold button from his shirt. Then he opened my palm and pressed it into it. I felt the pressure of the button. An indelible print of recognition.

'Koman, you must understand this. I knew if I were to tell you what I thought of your vesham, you would think that there was no need for improvement. You, like the other men of your age, are arrogant. That arrogance is what I wished to tame. Then the offers began to come and I thought you would, in your eagerness to perform, accept them. And those roles, Koman, would have ruined you. When I heard that they wanted you for Balabhadran, I was happy. My Koman would be Balabhadran.

'But first you had to be prepared. So I decided to keep quiet for some more time. I did want to talk to you about your vesham that night. Of how you stepped into my place and were Dharmaputran like no other, perhaps.'

I flushed. My palm tightened around the gold button.

'But how could you be Balabhadran till you knew a fury such as this? Have you ever known righteous indignation? That is Balabhadran's presiding emotion.

'Imagine this: you have chosen a groom for your sister Subhadra. He is none other than Duryodhana, your favourite student. That he is a vile man, you choose to ignore. You only know him as an exemplary student and a good person in your interactions with him. Then your brother Krishna invites an ascetic to the palace. He insists that your sister be his handmaiden. The ascetic is Arjuna in disguise. The handsome, valiant Arjuna. Your sister and he fall in love and, when you are away, they elope with Krishna's blessing.

'You hear of the elopement on your way home. You hear of it as gossip. And you realize that your brother and Arjuna have betrayed you. And it is not just anger you feel, it is righteous anger.

'When the padam begins with *kutravada kutravada, vrithariputrane…*, you need to be almost shivering with rage. For you are asking: where is he, where is he, that Indra's son Arjuna and my enemy, whom I shall destroy the moment I see…

'What do you know of such righteous anger, Koman?

'*Manam-anghum mizhiyi-inghum*,' Aashaan hummed the padam from Nalacharitam.

I stared at my feet. I knew what he was implying. The words of the padam said it plainly enough: What good is it if your eyes are here and your mind elsewhere? Aashaan was right. What did I know of righteous anger?

Aashaan took a deep breath. 'I knew that with every day I kept mute, your anger would grow. I saw displeasure. I saw resentment. I saw doubt. I saw hate. I saw these grow in you, one by one: the components of what makes a man feel betrayed. When your sense of betrayal was complete, I knew that you would be Balabhadran incarnate.'

The kalari was silent. I felt tears in my eyes. I stepped towards Aashaan and touched his feet. '*Samastha paapam porukkanam*; forgive my trespasses.'

'There is no need for you to use such words as forgiveness,' Aashaan said. Then, as if he couldn't help himself, he said, 'Eight years ago, I thought you were too young to mean what you said. How could a child speak with such conviction?

'I thought, does he know what he is saying? Does he know what it is to be the mistress of kala? We are kept men, Koman, you and I. Ruled and presided over by our art's whims and desires and in return kathakali alone makes us feel as if we are exalted beings.

'But a true artist is also someone who is able to sustain his belief in his art, and knows that what the world thinks of his art is irrelevant. Why did my words of praise or lack of them make such a difference to you? Didn't you know for yourself? Can't you be objective and know when you've done your best and when you were merely mediocre? Wasn't that good enough for you?'

I watched Aashaan leave. I sat on the steps of the kalari, looking at the gold button in my palm. Was it enough for me to know, I wondered. Was I even old enough to know? A few years from now, perhaps, I would be content with my own objective analysis of my artistry. I would feel a sense of accomplishment. But for now, I needed gold buttons and words of praise. I wanted adulation and applause. I wanted the world to pause at my feet.

'You must be satisfied that your dream came true; your talent was recognized and is still being celebrated...' It is Shyam who breaks the silence that follows my reminiscence.

Malini cackles. I smile. The bird has an uncanny ability to interject the right emotion at times when I am hesitant to say what I really think.

'Am I satisfied, Shyam? I don't know. You see, there was a time when everything in me ached for recognition. Perhaps recognition is the wrong word. For the truth is, all I sought was a true evaluation of my talent, except I didn't know the difference then. Do you know there is a game to be played in this whole business of being an artist? Contacts to cultivate, people to flatter, the need to be seen in the right circles, to attach oneself to a clique, whoring your integrity, these are all pre-requisites for an artist's career graph to shoot upwards.'

'So, did you play the game?' Chris asks.

'No, I didn't. Perhaps only because I didn't know there was a game to be played. What scares me is the thought that I might have played the game if I knew how to.'

'Uncle, you are too hard on yourself.' It is Radha who again seeks to soften the edge of my memories.

'No, my dear. I wasn't always so sure about my artistry. There was a time when I let someone else's opinion affect me. For a while, it made me hate my art. It wasn't even a true or formed opinion. A few ugly words, and I was ready to give it all up. Which meant that all my training, my dedication, my artistic soul as I called it then, was a surface act. I wasn't an artist who knew a oneness with the universe when I was at my best. How shall I describe it? On a day when I have caught the essence of the role, I know a serenity, a sense of completion that is like no other. In those days, however, I was a performer hungry for applause.

'I should have known, shouldn't I, if I was true to my abilities or not? Perhaps that is why Aashaan gave me this gold button. To remind me of what I was capable of. But I allowed myself to be distracted and clamoured for something else. Even after all these years, when I think about that episode, I feel my insides shrivel in self-loathing.'

I decide to tell them about it. 'Do you have the tape recorder?' I ask.

1961–1970
The Altar of Burnt Offering

It seemed in those first few years he was destined to cast a shadow longer than any of his peers. The invitations came from small temples and prestigious sabhas. Everyone wanted him. Koman was Balabhadran. Koman was Bheema. Koman was Dharmaputran. Koman was Krishna. Koman was a hero many times over. Koman was a veshakaaran like no other.

In the nights, when Koman didn't have a stage to set himself upon, or an audience to capture, he lay in bed hugging a thought: I did it. I did it. I am making a name for myself.

Some days, it would come to him that despite all the offers, he was yet to receive public acknowledgement of his artistry. 'Aashaan, I wish a critic would come to one of my performances.'

They were sitting in his room. Aashaan poured himself more toddy. Koman by now was used to the reek of alcohol and, as long as Aashaan wasn't performing, he seldom objected.

Aashaan put his glass down. 'I hope you don't mean that,' he said quietly.

Koman's eyes widened. 'I do. I would like an evaluation of myself.'

Aashaan shook his head, bemused. 'Don't you know how good you are?'

Koman laced his fingers and looked down at his clasped hands. I know you think that I ought to. But you don't understand that I am not you. I need to know. But Koman didn't voice his thoughts. Instead he said, 'A critic would point out the good and bad...'

'Don't I do that? Or don't you trust my judgement any more?' Aashaan's voice was soft but dripping with acid.

He started to explain, to apologize. 'No, no, I didn't mean it like that.'

'One of these days your wish will be granted and you might not be so pleased. I always think you must be careful what you wish for.'

The trees shivered.

It was a month later that Koman received the invitation to play Keechakan in Keechaka Vadham. He read the letter a few times. The organizers were the Fine Arts Club at Thrissur. They would be visiting him soon to discuss the performance and terms.

Koman walked to his room. His hands shook with excitement as much as nervousness.

For the first time he would play a katthi vesham. He would be an arrogant and evil man redeemed only by the noble blood in his veins. With red and white markings on his face, he would represent all those who disdained refinement and heroism. He would bear as the emblem of evil two white bulbs, one on his nose and the other on his forehead. Koman touched the tip of his nose. Suddenly he wasn't sure. He stared at himself in the mirror. How could he be Keechakan?

Keechakan was arrogant. Keechakan burnt with lust. Keechakan desired to make love to a married woman. Keechakan thought it was his right to do so. Keechakan was vile and base. When he didn't have his way, he threatened and became violent. Keechakan was unlike all the heroes Koman had been. How could he be a convincing Keechakan then?

In the mirror, a face stared back at him. A broad-browed, brown-eyed face with high cheekbones, shaggy eyebrows and a straight nose that curved into a slight hook, bearing testimony to his Arab lineage. As if to offset the brutal strength of the upper half of his face were his lips, fleshy and pink, finely defined, the curve deep and inviting. His mouth suggested softness. It was a mouth that would only know how to kiss and perhaps nibble. The chin was studded with a dimple. I can be either, the face suggested. Don't you see that? The heroic pachcha, or the brutal katthi.

His body was a mirror. He was a reflection, not an imprint, Koman heard Aashaan's voice whisper in his ear.

Koman ran a finger over his face. I am both pachcha and katthi. Man and beast. Why then do I doubt myself? I can be anybody I choose to be.

At the performance venue, the pettikaaran sidled up to him with mounting animation. 'You won't believe who I spotted in the audience.'

Koman was seated on a stool in full costume, his eyeballs acquiring a patina of red. With every passing moment, Koman was transforming into Keechakan—vile, arrogant, lustful. When the crown was placed on his head, the metamorphosis would be complete.

The pettikaaran was whispering in his ear, but the voice emerged as if from a great distance.

He felt a crack splinter the process of his transformation. He turned with a barely reined-in impatience.

'What is it?' It was Keechakan who snapped—or was it Koman?

The pettikaaran's eyes gleamed. He didn't even register Koman's rudeness in his excitement.

'He is here. Nanu Menon, the art critic, is here. You are blessed, truly blessed. Now everyone will read about this performance. Your Keechakan will be world famous.'

Koman felt air rise from his toes to his chest. He knew his breath as a thread connecting his heart to his head. His eyes widened. The wonder of the moment. It was Koman who spoke now. 'Where? Which one is he?'

'You can't miss him. He is a thin man with a beaked nose like a parrot's, sunken cheeks and a receding hairline. He is sitting in the third row, in the middle.'

Koman felt a curious trembling. It was his favourite place, as well. Being too close to the stage foreshortened the dancers and robbed the gestures of their ability to stoke the imagination. Too much distance from the stage distanced the magnificence. Nanu Menon choosing that particular place was an omen, he thought. A good omen.

Nanu Menon. They said one word of praise from him could change a veshakaaran's destiny. He seldom went to see young dancers perform. Tonight he was here.

The pounding began in his temples. He could hear the rhythm of the wrestling scene: Mallan matching his prowess against Vallan. It was a tremendous scene to open with. For the first time, Koman wondered if he should have demanded to be Vallan. For Vallan was, after all, a synonym for Bheema, the hero of the story. In the wrestling scene, he could have displayed his sense of rhythm by dancing the sequence where he had to move seamlessly from one timing to another, without missing a step. Later in the evening, as Bheema, he would have emerged as Raudrabheeman, the epitome of fury.

No, no, he shook his head to dispel the thought. 'A veshakaaran should never let doubt cloud his mind. There are no heroes or villains, only characters. It is not who you are, but how you are that makes a veshakaaran,' Koman thought he heard Aashaan say.

'You are Keechakan. You have to be him. You have to forget Vallan, or that Nanu Menon is here,' Aashaan's voice continued to murmur. 'All you must think of is Keechakan and how you are to be him.'

Koman felt his disquiet settle. He touched the white balls at the tip of his nose and the centre of his forehead. With their presence, they told him he was Keechakan.

It was Keechakan who looked at the pettikaaran and said, 'Bring me my crown.'

Keechakan. The noble being who stood holding the middle of the tirasheela that separated him from the world. Above it, his face alone emerged. Here is Keechakan, it said. Bearing the mark of the knife. By itself the knife is not evil. But as a blade, it draws blood, causes pain and instigates terror. It is this irony that Keechakan is cursed with.

Keechakan went to sit on a stool placed for him in the centre of the stage. The lamp lit his face. Beware, the markings on his face said. This is no ordinary being to be toyed with.

The two men holding up the curtain moved away and so Keechakan was revealed to the world. Sitting, holding the end of the two red sashes slung around his neck, his face grave. As the rhythm changed, his eyes suddenly spotted Malini. His gaze fixed on her; his eyebrows rose. Beautiful, he said, with a movement of his neck. His eyes widened with interest. Who was this woman? This beautiful woman?

For a moment Keechakan's eyes glazed. It was Koman who searched the third row of the audience seated before him. Are you there, Nanu Menon? Is that you I see sitting there craning your neck? Are you looking at me? Do you see how well I can be Keechakan?

Then Keechakan thrust aside Koman and took over.

So who are you, pretty woman, Malini? Where are you from? I don't know how it happened, but just looking at you makes me want to touch you, caress you, romp through the valleys and shadows of your curves. Are you Lakshmi whom Vishnu cradles to his chest? Or are you Parvati whom Shiva cuddles on his lap? Or perhaps you are Saraswati whom Brahma with his four faces and four sets of lips kissed again and again? Who are you, pretty woman? Earthly creature, or heavenly nymph? You heat my blood, you fill my senses, you, you, you…

What use is it being a man, and a man as valorous as I, if I can't fulfil my desire to feel your body against mine? To make love to you. To have you pleasure me. If I can't have you, I might as well be dead.

Why do I get the feeling that I have seen you before?

Yes, of course. I know now. This is the woman Sairandhari, my sister Queen Sudeshna's handmaiden.

You, my lovely, I shall call Malini.

Malini, you who seem to be blessed with beauty, listen to me. You will never know what it is to want again, you will know no sorrow. Your hair, dark and dense as thunderclouds, has turned me into a dithering fool. Lust makes me tremble. Just looking at your curved eyebrows, Kama's jasmine bow, makes me weak with desire.

You have to let me love you.

Malini-ruchira-gunashalini. Keechakan began his first amorous move. The night deepened. The story began.

When the Pandavas were exiled for the second time, one of the conditions laid down by the Kauravas was that they should pass the thirteenth and final year incognito. If they were discovered before the year came to an end, they would be exiled again.

In the thirteenth year of their exile, the Pandavas disguised themselves and entered the service of the king of Virata. Yudhishtira, as a brahmin, became a gamester in the court; Bheema became a cook; Arjuna as a eunuch taught singing and dancing; Nakula became a horse trainer; and Sahadeva a herdsman.

Draupadi, who pretended that she was in no way related to the five new servants, became an attendant and needlewoman in the service of Queen Sudeshna. She took on the name of Sairandhari and told the queen, 'Did I ever tell you about my husbands? They are Gandharvas and, even though I live here under your protection, they guard me all the time. They are so possessive that they are jealous of any man who dares to look at me even twice.'

The queen smiled, content with this new maid of hers. For a while Draupadi and the Pandavas led a quiet life, immersed in their new roles. Then Queen Sudeshna's brother, Keechakan, a wicked and powerful man who was the chief commander of the army, saw Draupadi and was bewitched by her beauty. He began to waylay her at every opportunity and make improper advances. Draupadi complained to the queen, but the queen ignored her. So Draupadi appealed to Yudhishtira. Instead of reassuring her, Yudhishtira scolded her for behaving like a child. 'You shouldn't take offence so easily. Besides, you can't keep running to us every time he mocks or insults you. Don't you realize that if we interfere, our true identities will be revealed?'

Draupadi went away quietly, but she decided to appeal to Bheema who she knew would listen to her demand and fulfil it as well. So later that night, she went into the royal kitchens where Bheema resided. Bheema looked at her tear-stained face and asked, 'What is it, Draupadi? Why are you crying, darling?'

Draupadi wiped her face and said, 'It is the queen's brother, Keechakan.'

She told Bheema about how troublesome Keechakan was.

Bheema bristled with anger. 'How dare he? Don't you worry. I'll get rid of him.'

Draupadi smiled, relieved. But she remembered Yudhishtira's words of caution and said, 'You have to be careful. We don't want anyone discovering who we really are.'

Bheema nodded. He scratched his chin and said, 'This will have to be done secretly. Tomorrow you must set up a meeting with Keechakan in a quiet place. Ask him to come to the dance hall after midnight and I will take it from there.'

The next day, Draupadi as Sairandhari did not move away when she saw Keechakan. Instead, she smiled coyly and whispered, 'Come to the dance hall after midnight. I will be there waiting for you. Come alone or my Gandharva husbands will know.'

Keechakan was so besotted by her that he didn't suspect a thing. That night, he went to the dance hall. He saw a veiled woman seated at the far end of the room and his heart beat faster. 'My lovely woman, why are you hiding from me?' he whispered. 'Come here, let me show you how I feel about you.'

The woman didn't budge. So Keechakan shut the door and went towards her. Could it be a ruse? But no, Malini wouldn't cheat him. I will lie down beside her and then I will know what it means to be truly alive, he thought.

When the final scene began, the curtain was held up by the two men again. They moved it ever so slightly, allowing only a fleeting glimpse of Keechakan as he lay suddenly paralysed, the object of his desire beside him. All he had to do was turn and take her in his arms.

But what was this? A muscular arm had reached over and grabbed him. The vice-like grip dragged a howl of pain out of him.

The curtain was drawn away. Vallan, now bearing the countenance of the almost demonic Raudrabheeman, had forced Keechakan to the ground.

Keechakan tried to shake the furious Bheema off. This couldn't be happening to him. How could Malini have tricked him?

But the blows fell, each like a sledgehammer. Keechakan's face seemed to descend into his body. His voice, his breath, began to lose life, his eyes popped as the weight of the blows smashed and mutilated his flesh, yet his eyes were fixed on a point above, even as he gasped for air. He could not die.

He sought Malini, she who still reined his life to his body, Malini, his precious Malini. One final gasp and Keechakan lay, a mangled ball of flesh, pulverized beyond all recognition.

It took some time for Koman to realize that the performance was over. The music had paused. The tirasheela once again shielded him from the audience. The flame of the lamp flickered. All was quiet except for the hammering of his heart.

He rose and went backstage. As if in a daze, he went to the pettikaaran. He took the crown off and sat by himself. I have to be me. I have to be the man Koman, he repeated to himself. I was Keechakan. Now I am me.

Then they began to arrive. Members of the audience and the committee members, each one bearing praise as if on a platter. Koman searched their faces. Would Nanu Menon come?

When they had left, he wiped his make-up off quietly. There was no need to be perturbed. Nanu Menon may not have come backstage, but he wouldn't be able to ignore him in print. Koman knew that. His Keechakan warranted it.

The following Sunday, Koman glanced through the newspaper eagerly. Would there be anything about him and his vesham? Koman stared at the newsprint. The words swam in front of his eyes. It couldn't be...that was the thought that ran through his brain, again and again. A furtive rat seeking an escape from the sewer pipe it had been thrust into. Eyes beady, moustache twitching, it ran. It couldn't be. It couldn't be.

'Contrived': the word spat at him. The letters blurred. '...predictable performance. Swamped in technique veering towards the theatrical...'

Koman felt the air in his tracheae leave in a rush. A fist slammed his throat. He gasped. Trying to suck in air, reprieve, his eyes scanned the print. 'Still we sit watching Keechakan as he first woos and then abuses his Malini...yet, even that is not the tragedy of this veshakaaran. It is his wanting to be more than who Keechakan the mythical character is. Interpretation is fundamental to kathakali, but an interpretation that has been perfected over the years by the masters. This veshakaaran seems to imagine that there is a Keechakan beyond the poet's characterization. With that he does his obvious talent an injustice. As for that final moment of Keechakan's death, what was it, kathakali or drama?'

Koman sat huddled on a chair. He felt his body tremble, suddenly cold. He wrapped his arms around his legs and wedged his face between his knees. He would have to seek a place within himself to shake off the repugnance of Nanu Menon's words and gather courage. What was worse? Total decimation, or the devastating faint words of praise? What hurt more?

When the day spent itself out, Koman went out. Shadows hung in street corners and stillness wrapped the hour. Koman heard the crunch of gravel beneath his feet and tried not to weigh down his steps with the heaviness of his grief. He didn't want to be seen or heard. He didn't want any attention. He wanted to be alone, to lick his wounds and summon back some vestige of self-worth. Enough to let him meet the eyes of all those who had read the review, with nonchalance if not a wry smile. But above all, he needed to forget.

The man wrapped the bottle in a sheet of newsprint. Koman searched the sheet to see if by some strange and macabre coincidence it was the one with his review. No one had seen him walk to the toddy shop. He searched the man's face. Had he read what Nanu Menon had written about him? He dismissed the thought. The man was not interested in kathakali. But was it pity he saw in his eyes?

The man counted out change. 'Will this be enough?' he asked with half a laugh.

Koman felt his lips twist into a smile. The man thought he was buying the toddy for Aashaan. For a moment, he considered saying, no, no, it is for me.

Then he let it be. Aashaan didn't care that the world thought he was a drunk.

In his room Koman took the bottle out of the fold in his mundu. Then he took a glass and poured a measure of toddy. He gulped it down. Sour, rancid and vile, the stench of its fermentation rode his nostrils. His stomach heaved. But for the first time that day Koman felt his nerve ends settle. The second drink wrapped him in a layer of cotton wool. The third sent the annoying gnat-like fears out of his mind. Now there was only one thought: the next drink. The next drink. The next drink...

When the vomit came up his throat, Koman just leaned forward and let it spew. It felt as if every ugly thought he carried within was finding its way out. When there was nothing left to vomit, he retched. Great, loud sounds that seemed to drag themselves from the bottom of his soul. His throat hurt. His tongue felt like wood. Words slurred out of him: a line from a kathakali padam. Even as he drifted into a senseless state, he knew this physical degradation was nothing compared to the humiliation he had felt.

In the morning, the light penetrated his brain with the edge of a blade. He sat up, dragging his limbs and senses from the ground. Around him were remnants of his dissipation. A bottle lay on its side. The glass stood on its head. Pools of dried vomit patterned the floor. His clothes were strewn about on the floor and the stench of vomit and festered pain swamped the air.

He held his head. It felt heavier than the crown he was used to wearing. And just as weighed down.

His mouth tasted foul. Even the back of his eyes hurt when he peered cautiously at the morning light. Koman wanted to lie down and die. To drift away to some place from where he would never have to return.

But Aashaan would be back this morning and it wouldn't do to let him see him thus.

They came, each one of them, bearing solace as they knew how to shape it.

Mani hammered the door, his rage tempering every word and gesture. 'Open the door, Etta,' he thundered. 'I know you are in there.'

Koman flinched. The sound made his head hurt. He looked around him. The room was clean enough. He touched his cheeks. They were smooth. He had carefully shaved his stubble away. No one must know that last night I was an animal, wallowing in my own pain and vomit. No one must know that I wept all day. No one must know how much I grieved, he had told himself sternly. So he forced a smile and opened the door. 'What is the matter?'

Mani stared at him. He pushed a lock of hair from his hot forehead. 'You ask me what is the matter? Didn't you see it? Didn't you read yesterday's paper? That nasty little man. I'll tell you what. When Babu is back this evening, he and I are going to round up a few friends and we'll pay him a visit. I'll personally break every bone in his right hand.'

'Ssshhh…' Koman laid his hand on Mani's mouth. 'It doesn't matter.'

'What do you mean it doesn't matter? This morning, when one of the men at the gymnasium pointed it out to me, I bloodied his nose. You know what upsets me? When someone writes nice things about you, not one bastard says a word. But just one bad notice and they take pleasure in pointing it out. Do you know what that son of a cunt said? "I thought you said your brother is a top-class performer. Did you see this?" I gathered his collar, shook him and then sunk my fist in his nose and came here straight.'

Koman gazed at his brother. He felt a great cloud of love for this ungainly, loutish brother of his. 'These things happen,' he said. He tried not to let the doubt show on his face.

'All that is very well. But Nanu Menon needs to be taught a lesson…'

'Let it be, Mani,' Koman said. 'Go home now. I'll come by later. We will talk then. I have a class now.'

'Are you sure?' Mani asked, pushing his fists into his pockets. 'Do you want something? A bottle?'

Koman shivered. 'Go home, Mani,' he said, giving him an affectionate push.

Koman sat on the bed. His legs didn't have the strength to hold him. Within him the trembling began again. He had to go to the institute. He'd had a day's reprieve yesterday, but there was no escaping today. He had a class and he would have to see his students and colleagues. What would their response be?

Anger on his behalf. Indignation, too. Or would it be smirks and mockery? Or perhaps it would be embarrassment? He swallowed.

There was a gentle knock on the door. Koman stared at it. Who could it be? Mani had left a while ago. Babu was away. Aashaan was expected to return from his trip only by midday. He had no friends. Over the years, his association with Aashaan had isolated him from his peers. Inevitably, it had fractured all his friendships. He didn't need anyone. His art, his master and his family had sufficed.

He went to the door and peered through a crack in the wood. It was his father.

In all the time Koman had been away from home, his father had not once come to see him. When he was a student at the institute and later when he took this room in the lodge, his father had wanted to disassociate himself from his life. Yet, he was here.

'Achan,' his voice started, unable to hide his astonishment. He opened the door.

'I came as soon as Mani told me,' Sethu said. He stared at the young man in front of him. His firstborn was a handsome man, but now his nostrils were pinched and his eyes wore black shadows. About him was the scent of a hunted animal.

'Come in,' Koman said, trying to still the tremor in his voice.

Sethu hesitated, then stepped in. He looked around, trying to gauge his son's life in one swift glance.

'Sit down,' Koman said, clearing a few books off his bed. He wished he could hide his face in his father's lap and weep.

Sethu sat on the bed. 'I don't know what to say,' he said, trying to conceal his awkwardness.

Koman said nothing.

'Listen,' Sethu said suddenly, 'I have some friends who know the editor of a rival newspaper very well. They could ask him to organize a feature about you. Won't that undo the damage? At least to some extent?'

Koman smiled. He knew an incomparable joy seep into him. I have this. Whatever happens, no one can take this away from me. My family's implicit faith in me, their total love for me.

'It is all right,' he said. 'It doesn't matter. There will always be people who hate my vesham. I can't let it affect me. So don't let it upset you, either.'

Sethu stood up. He felt uneasy in this room with his son who wore disgrace so effortlessly. Either he was totally inviolable or he was a superb actor.

In my home, I can hold him, comfort him, but here, I can't seem to even reach him. He isn't my son. He is Koman, the veshakaaran.

'If there is anything you need, let me know. Or if you change your mind about the newspaper feature,' Sethu said. He put his hand on his son's shoulder. Koman nuzzled it with his cheek. Sethu felt his eyes fill. His son had never let his defences down before him. He must be deeply hurt.

'I will come by,' Koman said, as Sethu left.

When he was alone again, Koman felt paralysed by nerves. It had been easy to play the valorous hero in front of Mani and his father. All he had to do was invoke a vesham. But alone, he had no disguise to hide behind. He felt bereft.

If his family who knew nothing about kathakali and understood nothing about the appropriateness of a vesham were offended by Nanu Menon's words, what would they say at the institute? How could he face them?

He lay on the bed and stared at the ceiling. A splotch on the plaster resembled Nanu Menon's profile. As he looked at it, he thought he saw the profile turn full face and gaze down at him. The baleful eye of criticism.

He shut his eyes. What am I going to do?

He slunk into the kalari quietly. The students filed into the classroom, chattering. There was abrupt silence when they saw him already there. In that dense silence, a voice cut through. It was a student who had failed to see him. 'Did you see that piece on Koman Aashaan?'

Koman flinched, but what the voice thought he would never know. Its owner spotted him and hid himself in a back row, fearing Koman's wrath.

Koman pretended that nothing was the matter. For the rest of the morning, he pretended a serenity he didn't feel. He led the boys through a scene from Lavanasura Vadham. The boys, taking their cue, responded with their best. When the class was over, he walked to Aashaan's room. He would find respite there.

Aashaan was waiting. There was a furrow on his brow as he prepared his betel leaves. Koman sat on a chair heavily.

'How was your class?' Aashaan asked.

Koman shrugged. 'What am I going to do?'

Aashaan folded the leaves into a triangle and popped it into his mouth.

'What you will do,' Aashaan said through a mouthful of betel leaves, 'is ignore whatever you read and go on as if nothing ever happened.'

Koman stared at him in astonishment. How can I pretend nothing happened? My career as a veshakaaran has as much worth as the red-stained earth.

'How can I?' he snapped. He could rein in his impatience with Mani or his father. But Aashaan? Aashaan ought to know better than to mouth such platitudes.

'How can I pretend that Nanu Menon's criticism means nothing? Everyone who has anything to do with kathakali would have seen it.'

Aashaan leaned forward and touched the skin beneath Koman's left eye. 'What is this?' He felt the puffy skin. 'Is this meant to be your face of mortification? Didn't you sleep last night? Why are your eyes bloodshot?'

Koman moved away. How could Aashaan be so indifferent to what Nanu Menon had written?

Aashaan looked at him and smiled. 'Anyone who has anything worthwhile to do with kathakali knows the exact worth of Nanu Menon's criticism.'

Koman sat up straight. 'How can you say that? Even the pettikaaran, I think his name was Shankaran, seemed to be in awe of him.'

'That's my point. Shankaran may be lord of the green room, but he is not a veshakaaran or a musician. And he is not even a very skilful pettikaaran. Shankaran is impressed by Nanu Menon. He might even take him seriously. But speak to our Gopi. He will tell you what he knows about Nanu. Do you know that Nanu was a veshakaaran once? They said he was destined for great things, but I thought he was a mediocre artist. In fact, his most convincing role to date has been that of a great artist who had to give it all up because of illness. I am sure his illness is a myth. He probably realized that one day he would be discovered for what he was. A poser. Now he is the self-appointed guardian of the performing arts.

'You know me well enough to know that I don't gossip or spread vicious stories about other artists, or even critics. But Nanu…

'Do you know what they call him in kathakali circles? Neerkoli. It's not just that he resembles the water snake, thin and slimy creature though he is, with his pointed face, seeking faults everywhere he goes. It is that his words carry no venom. He is a failed veshakaaran, now a failed critic. He ought, with his background, to be able to review kathakali from the performance point of view rather than a literary point of view. Yet, any deviation from the attakatha, from the composition, is viewed by him as sacrilege. You are expected to be Keechakan as he understands it, don't you see? He will not tolerate an interpretation that is beyond his comprehension—which is what a true kathakali critic would ideally seek.

'More importantly, though, if you had prostrated before him and appealed to his ego, he would have written of you as the future face of kathakali. You ignored him. That, my boy, was your crime. It had nothing to do with the Keechakan you were.

'The average man reads him. But by evening, he has already forgotten what he read. How does it matter to him who you played— Keechakan or Bheema? And kathakali connoisseurs don't let anyone else decide for them. Neither does a self-respecting veshakaaran. Do you understand?'

Aashaan stopped abruptly. A spasm of coughing contorted his face.

Koman thumped his back. 'Are you all right?'

Aashaan sipped some water. 'This will pass, but what worries me is you.'

Koman stared at the floor. 'Nanu Menon may be a neerkoli, a harmless snake without venom. But even a neerkoli's bite hurts. I feel like I never want to be on stage again. I know I should listen to you, but I feel that I have lost my nerve. I have to find my courage again.'

The afternoon heat lay between and around them, muffling all thoughts except Koman's admission of cowardice.

Aashaan sighed. 'You will know when you are ready to wear the colours of kathakali again. Only you can decide that.'

In the twilight, all his uncertainties returned. What was he without his colours and crown? Who was he? Koman felt diminished, stripped of his own self and worth. Tears welled again. What nature of being was he? How could a grown man weep? But he didn't know what else to do. Then a little voice whimpered in his ear: you could end it all.

Koman huddled in his bed. He had played heroes and villains. He had made love and murdered. He had vanquished and been vanquished. He would give it all up. End it all. He would turn his back on this world which was unable to recognize his devotion to his art, or his worth.

And so Koman wiped away the colours of a veshakaaran and slipped into the role his father had hoped to cast him in. Dutiful son. Rambunctious young man. Ordinary being without any artistic pretensions.

He was tired and drained of all emotion. For the first time, he saw the value of being with people whose minds were contained by the practical needs of everyday. He let it comfort him.

Koman did everything his father wanted him to. He accompanied him to the rice mill and timber yard. He went with Mani to the talkies. He went with Babu to the rubber estate. 'Tell me which one of these would suit you best and I'll help you start a business of your own,' Sethu offered. His pleasure at having retrieved his son from the morass of art was transparent.

'Give me time,' Koman pleaded. He had turned his back on the stage, but he couldn't forsake what had consumed more than half his life.

'There is no hurry. Take your time,' Sethu said, afraid that any pressure would cause his firstborn to escape again.

So Koman took time. Stolen time that allowed him to quell the memory of failure which stared at him pointedly and whispered about him in hushed tones.

Stolen time that he shared with his brothers, seeking respite in what seemed to fill their lives. But there was no escaping what had seeped into his blood.

When he went with them on a hunting trip, Mani whispered, 'You will have to tread very quietly.'

It was like the footwork of a padingiya padam: quiet, gentle steps that essayed the slowness of the song's rhythm.

He saw Babu gesture to Mani with his chin. He watched Mani raise the gun. The shot rang through the air. They heard the sound of hooves drumming the ground. Mani threw down the gun in disgust. 'I missed the boar. What next?'

Babu was the scout. He knew the forest better than Mani did. 'We have to wait till dawn. There is a meadow by a stream. If we start walking now, we'll get there in an hour's time. A herd of deer grazes there every day, at dawn.'

As they walked, cutting down vines that swung into their faces and bushes that brambled their skins, Koman knew again a sense of familiarity. I am Bheema in Kalyanasougandhikam, cutting a passage through the dense forest. He stopped abruptly. Why am I thinking of the world I have left behind?

Mani got his deer. As they turned to go, Koman stopped his brother. 'May I try shooting?'

The brothers looked at each other in amusement. 'This isn't kathakali,' Mani grinned. 'You can't pretend to shoot. You really have to pull the trigger.'

Koman smiled. 'Believe me, I want to.'

Koman's shot didn't fetch them any game. But it filled him with a sense of power. First, there was the weight of the barrel as it pressed against his shoulder, the pointing of the muzzle, cocking the safety catch, pulling the trigger, the recoil of the shot...the explosion of the dawn. In the silence thereafter, fragmented only by the flapping wings of birds, Koman felt his insides swell. I am not just a veshakaaran. In me is the power to maim, kill and destroy. This is me.

Mani grinned. 'Achan will be pleased that you actually wanted to hold a gun. I think he is scared that all this dancing has turned you into a woman.'

Babu smirked. 'I think he would be even more pleased if you got a woman pregnant. All he does when you are not around is whine about kathakali stealing your masculinity away.'

Koman ran his palm along the side of the rifle. He looked up and said, 'I don't know about getting a woman pregnant, but I would like to fuck a woman all night long.'

The brothers stared. Then Mani chuckled. 'If only Achan could hear you.'

Babu sat on a tree stump and scratched his chin. 'I'll tell you what. Let's go to the plantation. I'll get some toddy and have the venison cooked. Mani, you get the girls, and we'll eat and drink and fuck. What do you say?'

His brothers gave him a gift that night. A virgin. He had said he didn't want a tired old whore. When he saw one, he was reminded of a demoness parading as a pretty young thing. Kathakali was full of them. But this girl was truly a beauty and a virgin.

'Listen, I am not sure. Why add this to my burden of sins?' Koman asked.

'If you don't, someone else will,' Babu said. 'At least with you she will know kindness.'

'I am not in the mood for kindness. I told you I want to fuck. I'll probably end up telling little stories to amuse her.'

'Etta, you can do whatever you want. The girl will not complain. Fuck her or tell her stories. By the way, she is not a virgin in the real sense. I think she had a lover. The son of the family she worked for. They sent her away when they found out.'

Koman blinked. 'So she isn't a virgin after all.'

'Ah.' Mani stretched his legs. 'She is a virgin whore.'

Babu burst into laughter. 'I like the phrase. What next? Married whore, grandma whore.'

Mani smiled, pleased at his little joke. 'Well, you can have those as well, but our virgin whore is special. Enjoy her, Etta, you'll never find another like her!'

She waited for him in a room, her hair adorned with flowers and her eyes lined with kohl. She raised her eyes and met his gaze.

Koman didn't know what to say. She smiled and said, 'I saw you perform once. You were so gentle as Dharmaputran. When the man said you were here, I asked to meet you.'

Koman stared. What did the girl think she was here for?

'Do you know why you are here?' he asked abruptly.

She turned her head away. Then she said, 'I do.'

She met his gaze again. Her eyes were large and fearless.

He pulled her towards him and began fondling her breasts. 'What is your name?' he asked.

His fingers pinched her flesh. 'No, don't tell me. I'll call you Lalitha. That is who you will be for me. Lalitha.'

He bit her lower lip. 'Lalitha, when I send for you, will you come without fail? Tell me you will,' he said, transferring his attentions to the curve of her waist.

She gasped.

Once again he was Bheema, beating a trail through her nerve ends, nudging open lips and limbs. Koman razed Lalitha's body till he was too tired to think.

When she rose and he heard the tinkle of her anklets, he felt a pang. It was a sound that had echoed his every step.

'Don't wear your anklets the next time,' he said.

'Will there be a next time?' she asked.

He watched her plait her hair. 'Where are you going?' he asked, reaching for her wrist.

Thunder growled. Lightning tore the sky. She gasped. He liked that. He liked to hear her indrawn breath. She did it easily enough, and naturally. When his mouth sucked on her breast, when his toes caressed the back of her knees, when he drew her to him by her hair, when he entered her with a forceful thrust, she gasped as if she had never known anything like it before. He liked that. Lalitha, my Lalitha, he thought.

Koman was to discover that the past is never left behind. One night, when he lit a match, the whiff of sulphur rode up his nostrils. For a moment, the familiar stench of the mannola, the colours he had worn, filled his senses.

Another time, a peacock feather reminded him of the crown he wore as Krishna.

Is there no escaping, he asked himself.

One day he knew.

For twelve years his life had been lived according to a regimen laid down by the institute. There was no room for excess or time to laze. Now there was no clock to dictate his movements or his day.

He ate, slept, drank and fucked when he felt like it. His bowels rebelled. He felt his faeces harden and crouch in his rectal passage. He squatted for hours over the toilet, willing it to emerge and reduce his misery. He clenched his jaw and, holding his breath, pushed. As the stool emerged, he knew a sense of shame.

The life force that had once given meaning to the navarasas, the breath that had helped him summon the nine aspects of being, was this what he had reduced it to? Eight years of training, four years of studying and performing, only so he could move his bowels. Twelve years of work just so he could shit, he thought.

The next morning Koman went back.

Aashaan was in his room. 'Are you visiting or have you returned?'

Koman took a deep breath. 'I am back,' he said.

'In which case, I would like you to go to Madras. A dance school there has asked for a senior aashaan. The exposure will do you good,' Aashaan said.

Koman stared. 'But they probably meant you.'

'They did, but I am too old to uproot myself. They will be happy with you. And more importantly, you with them.'

Koman allowed himself to breathe again. In Madras he would find his courage. It would take him a while to venture on stage again, but he would one day.

'There is one more thing,' Aashaan said. 'For the past twelve years you have led an insular life. Your world has been this institute and little else. I want you to start reading. Read not just kathakali texts, but anything you can lay your hands on; reading will broaden your horizon. Observe, for that too is important. See, hear, taste, feel and absorb everything around you. Art cannot feed off itself. It needs life to sustain it. So go and live life.'

Sethu was unhappy about his going away. So were Mani and Babu. But Koman wouldn't let it hold him back.

As for Lalitha, she stood with her back to him, the buttons of her back-open blouse undone, stilled by grief.

He kissed her between the shoulder blades, dropping a kiss for every button he pressed into place. 'I am not going away forever. I will be back every now and then,' he said, repeating what he had told his family.

Six years later, Koman opened the latched gate and walked towards the house. He had been annoyed by his father's decision to buy him a house. Letters had flown between them. I don't want to put down roots. How can a tree fly, Koman had written.

I am not young any more. I have to do things at the right time. You are my son. You have to inherit at least some of my wealth.

That apart, you will love this little house by the river, Sethu had written.

The house stood right at the edge of the Nila. Countless floods had eaten away the land around it, so it perched, a grain of rice on a tongue of earth stretching into the river. On one side were steps that descended into the river and here the stones had stilled the erosion. On the other side, the dip was sudden and abrupt. I will have to shore this side, Koman thought. Build a wall so that the river won't encroach any further and take away what's mine. That last notion took him by surprise: he had a house of his own.

Koman walked around the house. It wasn't very big and the land around was studded with old trees and dense bushes. It was once the palace administrator's cottage. The local raja had had a summer palace built on the edge of the river. Palace was too grandiose a word for the building, but the people around called it kottaaram. Alongside was the cottage for the administrator.

Koman climbed the steps to the veranda. A waist-high wall crested with a wooden plank ran its length. He sat on it and leaned against the wooden railing.

What are we to do, Sethu had written. Mani is only twenty-seven, but I have had to arrange this marriage in a hurry. Circumstances demand it be so. But it is improper that he should consider marriage while you are unmarried. It is time you thought about a family. Shall I start looking for a bride?

Koman had read the letter with a smile. Mani had got a girl pregnant after all. Koman's tenure at the dance school was drawing to an end. He was ready to return home, but not willing to be married.

Marriage was not for him. In fact, he often wondered if marriage was for anybody. When Amma had asked him if he knew of anyone suitable for Meenakshi, a girl in her family, he had introduced Balan to them. Balan was his batch-mate and an accomplished dancer. The horoscopes matched and the families liked each other. But Balan the veshakaaran had overwhelmed Balan the husband. Meenakshi, Amma had told him, was an abandoned wife and mother of a child. 'He doesn't even send her money for the child. What kind of a man is he?' Koman heard Amma complain. He had felt guilty and written to Balan, but there was no response.

I am not ready for marriage, Koman wrote back. But perhaps

you could help me locate a little house to rent near the institute. I would prefer it to be by the river. I will have to return soon and Aashaan has already fixed for me to start teaching from the next academic year. Besides, now that Mani is to be married, it would be best for me to move out.

Sethu had read the letter with a mounting sense of desperation. All along, he had hoped that one day Koman would find his way back home. That he would have cause to rejoice. These days, more and more he knew a flaring of the past. As if his mind needed to remember to find solace.

It had been a long time, but his memory threw up a line from the Bible. 'For this my son was dead, and is alive again; he was lost, and is found.' Where was it from? Yes, Luke 15.11-32.

But it was not to be. Sethu looked at himself. My time will come soon, he told himself. And I still wouldn't have done right by my firstborn.

One day it occurred to him that there was a way to keep his son by his side. He would buy him a house. A house by the river. When he has a house, he will want a companion. And they will fill the house with their hopes and children, he told himself. Sethu had a vision: a little house in which children came and went. Why, he thought, this could be Jacob's ladder, and he smiled again. If only the good doctor knew how the good book rules me.

Koman walked to the side of the house. The river was almost dry; the steps ended in a deep, still pool. The water was cold. A breeze lifted off it and blew into his face. He had walked from the station to his house instead of going home. There would be time for that later. First, he would sit here and gaze at what he had fled from.

How could he have been such a coward? In retrospect, everything seemed so simple. At the time, he had thought it was the end.

Tomorrow he would have to go to the institute and resume his life. But for this day he would be his father's son and a brother to his brothers. He would eat, drink, make jokes, tell stories and, when night fell, he would send for Lalitha. Once again he would mount her as if she were a stage and on her body perform. Slow and gentle, furious and vigorous, erotic and grotesque...He would be himself again.

The institute seemed the same, Koman thought when he walked through the gates. Nothing had changed. Nothing ever will, he thought, with trepidation. This couldn't be real. Everything everywhere—people, weather, plants, animals, fashions—change. There is disease and despair, hope and happiness, that is the nature of life; it demands that nothing be constant.

But here time was held captive in the beating of rhythm, stilled in the colours painted on faces. Change was nullified by the souls of the characters they wrapped themselves in. How could he move on in life if the life he had chosen did not recognize the passage of time?

Koman heard a voice hail him. It was Sundaran, batch-mate, once friend and now an instructor at the institute.

'What are you standing and gaping for?' Sundaran demanded. 'You probably think this is a hole in the ground after where you were. Why did you come back? I can't understand that. I wouldn't have.'

Koman thought he heard a flicker of envy in Sundaran's voice. Why would anyone envy him? He shrugged. 'This is my home,' he said. He saw the disbelief in Sundaran's eyes and felt compelled to explain, 'You see, in Madras, they focussed on bharatanatyam. Kathakali was an oddity in some ways. How could I stay in a place where kathakali isn't supreme? Here there is no such confusion.'

Sundaran's smile grew into a smirk. 'Still the same, aren't you? Earnest. Earnest Koman. Have you seen Aashaan yet?'

Koman stared at Sundaran in surprise. Why, he doesn't like me, he thought. Then reining in that thought, he said, 'No, I just walked in. Is he here already? Isn't it too early for him?'

'He's here. He is here all day, drinking. He seldom goes home. If you stand one mile away, you can smell the stench of toddy. It is in his breath, his sweat, why, I think he pees the stuff. The man is an embarrassment and a nuisance, if you ask me. The students bring back stories of all the places they have found him lying in a drunken stupor. By the side of the road. On the railway platform. Outside a shop. The other day he fell into a field and had to be pulled out before he drowned in six inches of water. I don't know why they keep him around. And he hardly has any performances. No one seems to want to take the risk of having him.

'But why am I telling you this?' Sundaran said, turning to go. 'You probably know it already. You were like this, weren't you?' he said, portraying companion or was it mentor or was it kinsman, with his hands.

Koman stood there for a while. There was no word to describe his relationship with Aashaan. Even Sundaran could see that. And yet, he hadn't known. Why was Aashaan doing this?

Aashaan sat in his room, reading. Koman glanced at the title. Bhaagavatam. Koman knew disquiet then. Why was Aashaan reading the Bhagavad Gita?

Aashaan raised his eyes from the page. 'Listen to this,' he said in greeting. 'There is no work that affects me, nor do I aspire for the fruits of action. One who understands this truth about me does not become entangled in the fruits of the work.'

Koman chewed on his lip. 'Aashaan,' he said, 'how are you?'

Aashaan has aged, he thought. When I saw him nine months ago, he was an elderly but able-bodied man. Now he looks decrepit and old. He has given up. But why?

'Aashaan, how are you?' Koman insisted. Then he couldn't bear it any longer and demanded, 'What is wrong?'

Aashaan removed his glasses and put the book down. 'What could be wrong? Don't you see I am reading the Bhaagavatam? What could be better than that?'

Koman walked towards Aashaan. A long time ago, Aashaan had said, when I am ready to die I shall read the Bhaagavatam. That is the last thing I will do in life. Not before. If I still the demons in me, I might as well be dead. How can I be a veshakaaran unless I have demons jostling within me?

'You don't look very well,' Koman said. Without mincing words, he added, 'I hear you drink all day now.'

'Do I look or behave like a drunk?' Aashaan's voice bore a petulance that made Koman want to lay his head in his arms and weep. What are you doing to yourself, he wanted to shout.

'Who's been feeding you stories about me?' Aashaan demanded.

Koman began stacking the books on the table. 'Does it matter? You look terrible. You look what you are—an old drunk,' he said, hoping the brutality of his words would injure Aashaan's pride, prompt him into action.

'It won't work.' Aashaan's voice was low but sure. 'I am an old drunk, I know that. If you think you can make me angry by pointing that out to me, you are mistaken. I really don't care. There is a line in the Bhaagavatam that says, "The humble sage sees with equal vision a learned and gentle brahmana, a cow, an elephant, a dog and a dog-eater." I draw strength from that. I know who I am and what I am. I place the burden on you, on how you wish to see me. I don't care how you see me: as a cow or a dog, a dancer or a drunk. What is that Greek's name? Epicurus. Do you know what he said? The wise man lives hidden and only deals with his similars. All the others are merely acquaintances. So you see, anyone who knows me, really understands me, will not care that I was found lying drunk by the side of the road. As for the others, they are only acquaintances. What does it matter what they say or think?'

Aashaan rubbed the stubble on his chin and murmured, 'If you really want to help me, you can give me a shave. My hand shakes and I cut myself in too many places.'

Koman looked at his teacher for a long moment. The Bhagavad Gita owed its existence to a man who put down his weapons in the middle of a battlefield and said: Now I have lost all my composure and am confused. How do I go on? Actually, I would rather not go on. What is the point?

Was this how Aashaan felt? Was this why he sought refuge in drink and the Bhaagavatam?

Koman let his breath dribble out slowly. He had come to Aashaan expecting to resume his stewardship as student. But Aashaan wanted more of him. Or was it less?

'Aashaan,' Koman said. 'I'll fetch some hot water from the boys' hostel. Would you like me to bring you a cup of tea?'

Aashaan blinked. 'Tea?' He considered for a moment. 'Tea would be good.'

Koman slid the razor from ear to chin. Gently, every stroke deliberate and careful, he shaved away soap, stubble and what he thought was Aashaan's disdain towards life. He dipped the razor in a mug of cold water and put it down.

'Aashaan,' he asked suddenly. 'Why?'

The old man peered at the shaving mirror. He puffed out his cheeks. Lather padded under his chin. The curve of his jaw was a neat brown line defining his face. For a moment, the lather made Koman think of the chutti and its white curve defining the painted face of a veshakaaran.

'I seem to have left bits of stubble here and there. You must excuse me for not doing it properly the first time,' Koman said as he daubed the brush on the shaving soap, trying to make it lather. He painted soap again on Aashaan's cheeks. 'Is this a vesham? Are you playing somebody?'

Aashaan puffed his left cheek out for Koman.

Koman raised the razor again. Aashaan was pretending he hadn't heard him. But he would persist till Aashaan told him the reason for his dissipation.

The door opened suddenly and Sundaran stood framed by the doorway. The razor slipped and a drop of red broke through the foam on Aashaan's cheek. Koman blanched. Aashaan hissed. Sundaran broke into a guffaw. 'What is this? Are you a barber or a dancer? I thought you were teaching kathakali in Madras, not training as a barber's apprentice.'

Aashaan cocked an eyebrow and growled, 'Don't you knock before you enter a room?'

'I came to tell you that there is a meeting at eleven. The principal wanted me to tell you,' Sundaran said, ignoring Aashaan's displeasure at the intrusion.

'Isn't that the peon's job?' Koman asked drily.

Sundaran shrugged. 'I offered to inform him.'

He sauntered into the room and picked up the shaving mirror. He looked into it and tugged an errant curl into place, licked the tip of a finger and ran it over his eyebrow.

Koman felt a curl of distaste. What a peacock of a man. He said nothing, though. Aashaan had always held his students at arm's length. What had changed while he was away? Sundaran affected a familiarity that even Koman didn't dare presume. He glanced at Aashaan's face.

'Are you done?' The old man's voice was stiff with anger.

Sundaran looked up from the mirror. 'Oh, what?'

He put the mirror face down. 'Don't get upset. I am on my way. Now that your boy wonder is here, I suppose you don't need any of us any more. But who is to say when he will go off in a sulk next? He's done it once before.'

He turned to Koman. 'You are expected to attend as well.'

'He will be there,' Aashaan said. 'Now please leave. The soap is drying on my face.'

When Sundaran left, whistling under his breath, Koman exploded, 'Why do you let him be so...so...' he groped for a word.

'Familiar?' the old man offered.

'Yes, so familiar. He's familiar to the point of being disrespectful.'

'I know,' Aashaan said. 'He has always tried to stake a claim on my affection. He resents you. That you probably know. The two of you are the best students I have had. But he knows that I have always preferred you to him. I respect your dedication to your art, and the fact that you are totally unconscious of your talent. All this is beyond his comprehension. He always has to be number one, whether on stage or in my affections, and hence his rivalry with you.

'Last year he found me face down in a pool of vomit. He thinks he saved my life. And that gives him a claim on me. We are both drunks, Koman, he and I. I am drunk on toddy and he on the notion of his importance to me. I merely show him the tolerance one shows a drunk. He doesn't know what he is doing.'

Koman rubbed the bridge of his nose. Things had certainly changed here.

Koman finished shaving Aashaan. As he put away the shaving things, he turned abruptly and said, 'Aashaan, I won't ever ask you this again, but I have to know. Why are you doing this to yourself? You always drank too much, but now that's all you do.'

The man who stood buttoning a fresh shirt was the Aashaan he knew, though a little worn. The drunken slouch and the glaze in his eyes had been replaced by an arrogant tilt to his chin and the all-pervasive look.

'In a few months' time, I'll retire. What will I do after that? There are fewer and fewer roles coming my way. I am a drunk. Unreliable, they say. I cannot blame them. But how I wish they would understand that I used to drink to wake the demons inside me. Only when they sprang to life did my vesham come alive.

'My demons are dead now. They do not even respond to drink any more. And when I leave this institute, my life will be over. I can't imagine a time when my skin will not know the fragrance of the mannola. Yes, now that I know that I may never wear the mannola, even its reek has become a fragrance. I can't imagine that my head will never wear the crown. All that is left is for me to finish the process of life.'

Koman shook his head impatiently. 'So many dancers continue even into their seventies, and you are still so youthful. Don't you see, retirement isn't death. Instead of repairing the situation, you are ruining it even further.'

'I am an actor, a veshakaaran. I will die a veshakaaran,' Aashaan said. 'And we have to go now.'

In the sunlight, Aashaan's eyes narrowed into slits. He paused for a moment, with his hand on Koman's shoulder. 'I have many regrets in life. But there is one thing I will never regret. Kathakali. It is my life. It is my salvation. It is all I ever wanted. It is not the fame or the money or even the appreciation of a connoisseur, but the single-minded joy of creation, of putting life into a character and a story, of going beyond the expectations of this puny, mortal existence. Look around you, Koman. Don't you feel the singing in your veins? How can you escape it? How can you abandon it?'

Koman heard it. With the quietness of a sringaarapadam, the beat began, the rhythm of a love song. The tempo began to change…faster…louder, with the vigour of a yudhdha padam, the battle song that urged him forward. There was no looking back now.

Adbhutam

ringaaram. Haasyam. Karunam. Raudram. Veeram. Bhayaanakam. Beebhalsam. You have learnt to identify the thought that leads to each one of these emotions and to school your features accordingly. You have seen how first the thought, then your breath, then your face resolves the process from knowing to experiencing to expressing. There is a build-up, so to say. Not so with adbhutam. For this emotion alone does not offer you a time frame within which you may work on the feeling.

For adbhutam is wonder. And wonder is immediate. It cannot be premeditated or calculated. If you do that, it isn't wonder. It is someone pretending to be wonderstruck and you must understand that while we live in the world of make-believe, we do not pretend emotions. Widen your eyes. Widen them without a trace of fury or valour. Your eyebrows emphasize the wonder and so do the muscles of your face. Your nostrils flare as if drawing in the very essence of what fills you with wonder and your mouth widens in an involuntary half smile.

Let me make this easier for you to comprehend. Think of all that may cause wonder to strike our souls. There is the rainbow, but we do not have the child's innocence to be struck by a rainbow. Our minds know it as a mere phenomenon of nature. Think instead of a cold December night and the stars emerging, clear and luminous. In our part of Malabar, we see in these clear cold months the Milky Way. Train your eyes and you will see a star shining brighter than all the others. That is Sirius, the Dog Star. Open your eyes wide and look at it, and you will feel wonder. What is it? A star or a heavenly chariot? Can anything be as luminous?

Take the jackfruit now. Lumpy, green, enormous prickly things that cling to the trunks of the jackfruit tree like babies hanging from a mother's neck. Splice one and the two halves fall apart with the golden yellow pods gleaming within. I see the surprise in your eyes.

But we all know the jackfruit, you are thinking. What is so wondrous about it? This is true. But when you bite into a pod and nectar fills your mouth, don't you think: I have never eaten anything so wondrous before? I have never known such sweetness, such goldenness, such ripeness.

Even the familiar can cause wonder. That is what I would like you to remember.

Often, though, what causes wonder is what we seldom see. Between the months of September and May, in our gardens there comes a visitor. Nearly a foot long, with a black crest and face and a white body from which two feathers like satin ribbons flutter. This is the nakumohan. Some people call it the rocket bird and others the ribbon bird, but its real name is the paradise flycatcher. When you see it, you realize why there couldn't have been a more appropriate name. This is a bird whose true perch could only be the gem-encrusted trees of paradise. Such is its beauty, its elegance and its unusual looks. And you ask yourself: What is this bird that is so beautiful? Where does it live? What does it eat? A million questions race through your mind as you look at it. That is the hallmark of wonder. A curiosity to know, a yearning to possess. And when you do, the wonder ceases. That is the nature of adbhutam. To be transient. For you will never know it again in exactly the same degree.

Radha

I stare at my nails. I begin filing them again.

I raise my eyes and see Shyam's gaze fixed on me. 'You shouldn't be filing your nails at twilight,' he says.

I stare at him, baffled. 'Why not?'

'I don't know. That's what my grandmother always said. It probably has a very sound and scientific reason.' His eyes shift back to the TV.

Shyam is a strange mixture of superstition and rational thinking. On the one hand he believes in most of these silly superstitions and on the other hand he is the first to adopt and use technology, be it gadgets or practices. Despite having known him all my life and intimately for eight years, I am unable to comprehend how his mind works.

There is *Baywatch*, for instance.

How can a man of his intelligence watch such inane stuff, I wonder. But he smiles and says, 'It doesn't require an effort. I just sit here and watch. You must try it some time. You don't need to turn everything you do into an intellectual exercise, you know.'

I sense a barb there. These veiled barbs have been coming my way with greater frequency in the past few days. I realize that he doesn't aim to hurt, but he doesn't care if I am. I know fear then. This is a Shyam I do not recognize.

He zips from one channel to the other. There are six Malayalam channels to choose from. He will switch a fight sequence for a song, an advertising commercial for a piece of dialogue. All evening it goes on, and it makes my head spin to try and catch up with him.

'Why do you do this?' I ask. 'Why don't you just watch one channel at a time?'

He doesn't say anything. I go back to filing my nails.

I wonder if he knows. What is the point, I think. They are all dead now. My mother and the two brothers, one of whom was my father and the other an uncle. The only thing is, I am not sure who is who. Even if they were alive, would it matter?

'Shyam,' I say.

'Hmm...' His eyes remain fixed on the TV screen.

'Shyam,' I say his name again.

He turns the volume down and looks at me.

'Did you ever hear anything strange about my parents' wedding? You must have been about seven years old then, weren't you?'

I see the expression on his face change. When Shyam is engrossed in a movie, it is easy to gauge the emotional content of what he is watching by the expression on his face. He will smile with the hero and suffer with him. The navarasas and a whole ancillary of sub-rasas come and go. But when he looks at me now, his face is wiped clean of all expression. More and more, Shyam wears a mask of impassivity when he is with me. A dutiful, but deadpan and disinterested face.

I do not like this wooden Shyam. He worries me.

'What did you hear, Shyam?' I ask, dropping my file on the table.

Shyam sighs. 'I was seven years and four months old then,' he says and rises to take away the newspaper I had spread on my lap to catch the nail dust. He puts the file away in its case.

'Your mother, my aunt, was to have married the elder brother, your uncle Mani, but he disappeared three nights before the wedding. So your father married her. Didn't you know?'

'No,' I say, shaking my head. Was that all?

'Well, it was common knowledge. I assumed you knew,' he says, raising the volume again.

I sit there, oblivious to the voices from the TV. What I hear is: 'She is mine, isn't she? Tell me...I can see it...She looks nothing like you or that runt brother of mine.'

I leave the room. I go upstairs to my parents' bedroom. I have left it untouched. No one sleeps here. But the bed is made and sachets of sandalwood dust perfume the wardrobe. There are too many rooms in this house, I think. And too many secrets.

My grandfather buried his past in its walls and my parents interred their past here as well. This house welcomes and encourages secrets.

I go downstairs and take my manicure case with me. There is a bag of toiletries hanging on the bathroom door. Shyam must have left it there, I think. He probably intends to put it away later. I decide to surprise him. Then I notice a packet of sanitary napkins. I feel that familiar swell of rage. Why does he have to buy even sanitary napkins for me? Why can't he let me breathe and bleed on my own?

I pause suddenly. I can see last month's packet in the bathroom cabinet, lying untouched. I feel a little bolt of shock. I rush into the bedroom. I have a little calendar there. I flip through the pages. I look at the dates, counting and calculating. I am ten days late.

I sit down. My legs are shaking. I may be pregnant, I think. I touch my abdomen. Can it be possible? After all this time, and when I least want the responsibility?

What am I to do now? It must have happened the night when Shyam raped me. Shyam will never let me go if he knows I am carrying his child. What would Chris say if he knew? How can we even think of life together with me carrying another man's child? Are you entirely sure it is Shyam's, a voice asks me. Don't forget you made love again, two nights after the rape. It was the last day of your safe period. Accidents are known to happen.

Don't panic, I tell myself. I will wait another week and then, only then will I think about it.

'Are you going out?' I ask Shyam.

'I may. Why?' He frowns. He hates being disturbed, particularly during the last few scenes of the film. The hero, a brawny man, six-feet tall, is mouthing expletives that are meant to pack as much punch as his fists. The villains stand quaking in their sandals as his voice thunders.

'Can you drop me off at Uncle's? I need to speak to him,' I say. 'It is important.'

'Why don't you call him?'

'His phone isn't working,' I lie.

'Can't it wait till tomorrow?' he says.

'No, it can't,' I snap. 'It's ridiculous that you won't let me drive. Why do I have to beg and plead when I can easily drive myself there?'

'Enough. I'll drop you. You can't drive. I have seen you drive. You have no traffic sense and you use the wrong gears all the time.'

I glare at him. I drove all over Bangalore when I lived there, yet he talks as if I don't know my clutch from my brake. I will have to resume driving again. That will show him that I am not to be pushed around, I tell myself.

'Get ready,' he says. 'This will be over in a few minutes.'

'For what? I am only going to Uncle's. What I am wearing is good enough.'

'Won't you see Chris?' he asks in a silky voice.

'I think Chris is away,' I lie. I can't see Chris yet, I think. I can't till I know for certain.

Suddenly I long to see him again. It is an excruciating urge. Just to feel his arms around me and tell myself that nothing had changed.

The night sky is overcast. Thunder rumbles. Shyam walks with me to Uncle's house. He takes my elbow as we walk through a dark patch of ground. I ache to shrug him off, but I don't. I dare not offend this new Shyam.

'Your phone isn't working,' he tells Uncle.

Uncle frowns. 'No, it is…'

'It wasn't when I tried a while ago,' I say quickly.

Uncle lifts the receiver and holds it to his ear. 'Ah yes, I have had this problem for a few days now. There's no saying when it works and when it doesn't.'

I wonder if Shyam knows that Uncle is covering for me.

Shyam doesn't say anything. He looks down at the books spread on Uncle's table. I can see that he would like to tidy up. He says, 'Don't you get bored? What do you do here by yourself?'

Uncle smiles. 'I read, I write, I doze off, and then there is Malini. It is a very full life.'

When Shyam leaves, Uncle looks at me for a long moment. 'What is it, Radha? Is there something on your mind? Is it Chris?'

'I think I may be pregnant,' I tell Uncle.

I see the shock in his eyes. 'Are you sure?'

'I am quite sure, but I'll wait another week and then see a doctor,' I say.

I see the question in his eyes.

'I don't know,' I say, thinking that for now I prefer the uncertainty of its paternity rather than the thought that this child could tie me to Shyam for life.

He doesn't say anything for a while. Is he thinking what I am? That history is repeating itself? Like mother, like daughter. Does wantonness, like diabetes and multiple sclerosis, pass from one generation to the next?

'What will you do?' he asks.

'I don't know,' I say. I cover my face with my hands. 'Perhaps it is just a mistake. Perhaps I am not pregnant at all,' I say through my fingers.

'Who was my father? Which one of the two brothers?' I ask him. I don't try and couch the implications. I don't even try and phrase it better.

Uncle removes his spectacles. His eyes are tired. Will he tell me the truth, I wonder. Uncle rubs the bridge of his nose. 'You know who your father is.'

'No, I don't. Do you remember the time Uncle Mani came? I heard him quarrel with my mother. He was claiming me as his daughter.'

'And what did your mother say?'

'She didn't say anything. But you must know. You know the truth,' I tell him.

Uncle's face wears a faraway look. I don't want to interrupt or hurry him. I can see that he is choosing his memories.

'Mani. My brother Mani. The brother who, when I stood unsure and uncertain, not daring to intrude, took me by the hand and pulled me into the family. I loved him more than I did anyone else.

'Forever hungry. Forever demanding…he treated life as if it were a chicken leg to be gnawed on till the last shred of flesh was in his mouth and then he would crack the bones with a loud crunch and let the marrow coat his tongue.

'Mani seldom wasted time thinking about how the world perceived him. It was a kind of raw courage. When he was in the third form, what you would call class eight, he set his heart on winning the all-rounder's prize at the school festival. His marks were good and he had a long line of sports trophies, but he needed to win a prize in a cultural activity. He saw that most events had a long list of contestants except for the classical music competition which had only three. Mani decided to enroll as the fourth contestant. Mani, who had never had a single singing lesson, can you imagine? All he knew was a varnam that was part of a Singing Lesson programme on the radio. He sang that and won the third prize. But it required courage, a foolhardy reckless courage, to pull it off. That was the kind of person Mani was.' Uncle smiles.

'When we were boys, your grandmother often set rat traps around the house. There was a room in which paddy was stored.' He turns to me suddenly. 'What do you fill it with these days?'

'It's empty,' I say. 'Like most of that huge house.'

He nods.

'The paddy was an open invitation for rats to come and set up home. My mother was tired of them. They didn't just steal the paddy, they made holes in clothes left to dry, gnawed huge chunks out of vegetables, left droppings, and were a great nuisance. So the rat traps were brought out. But she was much too squeamish to kill the rats once they were trapped. And my father couldn't be bothered with such trifles, she thought. I had left home by then.

'Mani was the official rat killer. He didn't thrash them to death with a broom like anyone else would have done. He would open the rat trap into a sack and then tie the mouth of the sack and take it to the washing stone.

'When he was sure he had an audience—the servant maids, our mother and perhaps even a few children from the neighbourhood— he would say, "Look at this gunny bag. How did it get so dusty? I suppose I have to clean this as well..." And he would beat the sack on the stone till the rat was pulverized, while everyone else giggled. Mani knew how to make even death seem comic.

'Everything to him was calculated in terms of a laugh or the ability to provide pleasure. He loved life so much. That was what I loved about him. His capacity for happiness.

I think my father had no capacity for happiness at all. Everything was constructed around social standing and honour. If something was acceptable to society, he liked it. If it bore even the slightest taint of the illicit, he refused to have anything to do with it. Was he always this way? Or did he become so rigid in order to ward off any gossip or speculation about his family? I can only theorize...

'When we were young men,' Uncle begins again, 'Mani was the same. Instead of squashing rats, he took to seducing women. That was all it was for him: a sport. An unconventional sport, but no more than that. He was handsome and exuded charm. The women loved him. He was Prem Nazir, Gemini Ganeshan, Shammi Kapoor and Gregory Peck rolled into one. Do you see what I mean? There was a particular pose he affected when talking to women. He would cross his arms so that they squared his shoulders, and lean forward. He was tall, so he loomed over the women, and he would affect a look that merged intensity with a faint glimmer of lust. It worked, each time.

'Babu would shake his head in amazement. "Look at him," he would say. "How does he do it? Don't these women know any better? He should have been an actor. That woman probably thinks he is swearing undying devotion to her...what a bloody performer!"

'Mani got away with his romantic escapades. But with Gowri, he made a mistake. She wasn't a poor cousin or a servant maid whose silence could be bought. She was from a respectable family and, before the whole town could find out what had happened, their marriage was fixed. Gowri was pregnant and it couldn't be delayed.'

'Me,' I yelp.

'No, not you. Gowri miscarried a few weeks after the wedding. I am not surprised she did. Imagine this: the man she ought to have married disappeared three nights before the wedding and what could she do but agree to his brother marrying her? Family honour and her future were at stake. The pregnancy was a secret, but if the marriage was called off, her life would be ruined.

'Mani came to see me that night. "What am I getting into, Etta?" he asked me repeatedly. He was beginning to realize that it wasn't a prank he could put behind him.

'I dismissed it as nerves. "Don't worry. Everything will work out," I assured him. "It is time you settled down and had a family." I was repeating my father's words to me.

'"I don't know. I really don't know." He was in a strange mood that night and we sat there together, talking late into the night.

'He brought forth reminiscences, of escapades he had managed to survive and get away with, of women he had slept with. Of hunts he had been on, of drinking parties and revelry. He seemed to need to reassure himself that he wasn't trapped and was still a creature free to prowl.

'"But what I really want to do is see the world. How can I, with a wife and child? I'll be tied to this place for life," he said.

'"Now you are exaggerating," I said. "Why can't you travel when you are a married man? I never heard such nonsense. The baby will grow up and you can always leave him with your parents," I said.

'"But it won't be the same."

He walked into the night and I heard his motorbike start. No one saw him after that till he returned seven years later.

He went to Calcutta, where someone he knew found him a job on a ship. He was determined to put as much distance as he could between himself and what my father expected of him.

'There was pandemonium. One of us was expected to step in. But I couldn't, Radha. I couldn't. I wasn't ready for marriage. And something in me balked at the thought of marrying the woman Mani was to have. It felt too much like incest to me. So your father did the honourable and unselfish thing. He offered to marry Gowri.

'No one liked Babu very much. He was caustic and abrasive. And his wandering eye unnerved most people. When Mani was around, no one had eyes for anyone but him. Mani shone. His wit, his charm, his presence robbed Babu of any stature he might have had. Did Babu resent him? I am not sure. Mani wore his emotions on his face, but Babu didn't. He hid behind his face. You never knew what he was thinking. But that night I began to respect him. He seemed to fill Mani's absence and impose himself on all that was around him. He was willing to offer himself to salvage the situation. What must have gone through his mind?

'That day, when Babu laid down a condition, none of us dared say anything against it. He said we were not to refer to Mani ever again in that house. "I don't want the baby to know that I am not its father," he said. "I don't want Gowri ever wondering, what if I had married him."

'Overnight, Mani ceased to exist. A month later, Gowri miscarried. Mani was well and truly exorcized from our lives then.

'Six months later, Gowri was pregnant again. You. That baby was you. And how your father loved you! Even before you were born, he worried about your prospects.' Uncle smiles.

'Have I answered your question?' he asks.

'How do I know that you are telling the truth?' I ask doggedly.

'You have to believe what you choose to. Would you prefer it if Mani was your father? Would it suit your fantasy better? To have a daring, romantic hero for a father? Don't forget, he was also the selfish and unreliable one. The man who abandoned a pregnant girl three nights before they were to marry. Your father was an ordinary man, dull and reeking of respectability, but he was an honourable man. A man of dignity. Don't ever make the mistake of dismissing dignity in favour of flamboyance.'

I feel sorrow envelop me. I wish I had made an attempt to understand my father better. And loved him for what he was, rather than finding him wanting for what he wasn't.

'This doesn't absolve my mother,' I tell him.

'Don't judge your mother, Radha. She led her life the way she thought it best. Shouldn't you allow her the freedom of choice?' he says quietly.

I think of my parents. I remember their wedding photo. My parents, too, had once been young and impetuous, with reckless dreams. Groping to make sense of adulthood and responsibility. And I realize that it is the nature of children to never allow parents their youth, their mistakes or their fears. In the end, this unspoken tyranny children exercise over their parents is just as oppressive as the rules parents lay out for children.

What will my child think of me when he or she is old enough to know right from wrong? Will he sit in judgement over me as I do now over my parents? Will my child allow me my mistakes and errors in judgement? Will my child love me despite everything?

I feel a cold hand grip my shoulder. All I want to do, I think, is to be with Chris. To see him. To hold him. To reassure myself that nothing has changed between us and nothing will.

Chris is in his cottage. I know that he is there. I see him through the window.

'Chris,' I whisper.

He looks up. He stares at me, but I know he can't see me. I am in the shadows. He comes to the window.

'I know you are there,' he says.

I emerge into the light.

'How?' I am curious.

'I know your fragrance.'

I feel my insides flower. Can it be that the child is his? I hug the thought to myself. And even if it isn't, will he hold it against me? Will he ask me to get rid of it? I feel the flower within me wilt.

Chris takes me in his arms. 'I missed you.'

'I missed you, too,' I murmur. 'I can't stay. Shyam will be here any time now.'

'Here?'

'No, I mean, he will be at the gate once he discovers that I have left Uncle's house.'

'Then there is time enough,' he says.

I lie there, willing and submissive. Shadowed by his flesh, I feel my terror subside. He will never forsake me, I think. History will not repeat itself. I will not be bound to a man simply because the man I love has abandoned me. Chris isn't like my uncle Mani. Chris is not a child playing at being a man.

'Slowly, slowly,' I say.

'Why slowly?' he murmurs against my mouth. I arch my neck in reply.

A phone rings. It rings and rings. Then I realize the sound is from my bag. I grab it. 'Where are you?' Shyam demands.

'I am on my way,' I say, keeping the panic out of my voice.

I push Chris away. 'I have to go; he is here.'

I splash water on my cheeks and push my hair behind my ears. 'I am sorry,' I say.

'Do you realize that we never seem to have any time together any more?' he asks.

Something in me rebels at the tone of his voice. 'What can I do?' I ask.

'This is so frustrating,' he says, raking his fingers through his hair. His face wears a frown.

'Is this all our relationship is about, Chris?' I ask. 'Sex?'

We never seem to talk any more, I say silently in my head. All we do is pounce on each other.

'Oh, come on,' he says.

'I have to go now,' I say and rush through the door. I feel his eyes on my back. He is furious. So am I. Why doesn't he understand what I am going through? I rush through the trees, trying to compose myself.

Shyam is in the car. 'I thought you said the Sahiv was away,' he says.

'He came back this evening. Uncle wanted me to drop off a few papers. Something that came yesterday, which he knew Chris was waiting for.' I know I am talking too much and too fast.

He doesn't say anything. I huddle by the door. I feel a sense of shame wash over me. Something in me moves. Is it my conscience? Or is it the child, no more than a zygote, demanding of me—Do you know what you are doing to my father?

Is this how my mother felt? Torn between two men, feeling like a slut whether she was with one man or the other?

The wonder of this love is beginning to show its slimy, seamy underbelly to me.

As I look at Shyam, and see that his face reveals nothing, neither anger nor pain or even a hint of suspicion, I see my love as sordid, the wonder diminished. I begin to see it as no more than a slaking of lust, a mere shrugging away of ennui.

Shyam

It begins to rain as I wait in my car. I look at the clock on the dashboard. I have been sitting here for the past ten minutes. Where is she?

Uncle was waiting for me on the veranda. 'Didn't you see Radha on the way here? You must have missed her by a few minutes.'

He was fidgety and nervous. Something was on his mind. I could see it, but I didn't ask him. 'What did Radha want to see you about? She said it couldn't wait till tomorrow,' I said. 'Was it about her parents?'

He sighed. 'Her parents. Yes, yes, she wanted to ask me about her parents.'

'I thought as much! Earlier this evening she wanted to know about them, the circumstances of their marriage. But why couldn't she have waited to ask you tomorrow?' I demanded. I knew he wasn't telling me the whole truth. Perhaps she only needed an excuse to get here.

'You know how she is…impulsive!' he said.

I nodded. I knew that well enough. Then I decided to ask him about something that had been worrying me.

'When you were talking about the buying of this house, you said your father bought it around the time of your brother Mani's wedding. I suppose you meant the marriage he ran away from. Or did he get married after that?'

Radha is the sole beneficiary of her grandfather's estate. She was her father's only child and Uncle has no heirs. I worried that in the future there would be new contenders for a share in the inheritance.

'Mani died. He had no wife or children, legitimate or illegitimate,' the old man said.

'He died in rather suspicious circumstances, didn't he?' I asked.

'He died in an accident. It was a stupid accident, but there wasn't anything suspicious about it,' he said.

'The car he was driving rammed into a parked petrol carrier and exploded. The police weren't wholly convinced it was an accident, I hear.'

I saw the frown on his face.

'I had my friend the SP dig out the records. I thought it would make sense to find out everything about him. We need to be prepared if someone ever comes claiming to be his progeny. That was when I heard that they thought someone might have arranged the whole thing,' I explained.

'But who would want him dead?'

'Radha's father, for one,' I muttered.

'He was an honourable man. He would never do anything like that,' Uncle said. But I saw that he sat down, unable to trust his legs.

'Think about it,' I said. 'The brother who was cast away comes back claiming his right. The property is one thing, but what if he claimed the woman and child as his? It's precisely to preserve your honour that you might do something like that,' I said.

Uncle didn't say anything. He looked at me after a moment. 'You must leave the dead alone,' he said.

I sit in the car and watch the windshield wipers. I am beginning to understand what Radha's father must have felt when his brother arrived suddenly, back into their lives. I see threats everywhere. I see forces coming alive that will usurp all that is rightfully mine.

Where is she?

What is she doing, I wonder. I dial her number. The phone rings. It rings at least eight times before she picks up. I feel my patience snap. 'Where are you?'

I hear her voice. It is unnaturally calm. 'I am on my way,' she says.

I realize then that I have interrupted them.

A howl of outrage bursts from my mouth. The night swallows my anguish.

I rest my head on the steering wheel. What is the husband of an adulteress allowed to do? Am I permitted to vent my fury at being betrayed? Will I be able to defend my honour? Will any court of law, human or divine, hold it against me?

When I was still a child, I heard a story about a neighbour who had chopped his wife's head off. He had discovered that she had a lover. He went to the police station with his axe in one hand and the woman's head held up by her hair in another. The policemen offered him a chair, it was said. Even they, those men in uniform, understood that adulteresses deserved to be killed. It was a matter of honour.

But this is Radha. My Radha. What am I to do?

Then I see her. She emerges into the light from the headlamps. She holds a hand over her head to protect herself from the rain. Only Radha would think that her tiny hand can offer protection from the hard drizzle. Just as she thinks that I will not find out about her affair.

The rain patterns her face. Raindrops cling to her.

She opens the car door and gets in. I smell his fragrance on her.

I want to coil her hair around my fist and hold her down. I want to trap her neck between my fingers and squeeze the air out of her treacherous body. I want to see her flail her arms and struggle for breath. I want her to see how deeply she has hurt me and I want her to suffer for my suffering.

Instead I control my anger and my voice. 'I thought you said the Sahiv was away.'

She rattles out an explanation. Her words gush and tumble, roll over and turn cartwheels. Clowns filling intervals in a circus. She smells of secrets and guilt.

I say nothing. I am afraid to speak. If I do, it will be an accusation. It will be venom and hate. Then all will be lost.

She goes to bed early. I sit in the living room. I am unable to sleep.

It is almost midnight when I go to our room. She is asleep. Her clothes are scattered on a chair. I hang them up and thrust her undies into the basket in the bathroom. The wall cabinet is not shut properly. I open it and start arranging the toiletries. There are two packets of sanitary napkins. Why does she hoard them? They take up so much space. Then suddenly I know what is wrong, what it is I have missed.

Radha hasn't had her period. I calculate in my head. It was due ten days ago. For a moment I hear a wild singing in my head. Can it be? Can it be that she is pregnant? Have I finally fathered a child?

Then I stop.

What am I thinking? I know that I cannot father a child. What is growing in her isn't mine. It is a mass of sin. Living evidence of her betrayal.

A wrenching pain tears through me. I bite on my hand to muffle the sound of my agony.

All that is mine will soon forsake me. My love. My life. My dreams, my honour. All that I will be left with is humiliation. How do I go on?

Something wet courses down my cheeks. I am crying, I realize.

I weep because all I have is my grief to cling to.

Uncle

I have always chosen the memories I want to dwell upon. When the ones that I do not want to think about rise to the surface, I thrust them away. But tonight I am being forced to remember. It is their fault. Radha's and Shyam's. I believe that they have been raising the dead.

I think of when Mani returned. The brother who had no place in our lives any more was a presence no one could dislodge. I tried to persuade him to stay with me. 'Why should they feel awkward about my arrival?' Mani asked.

'You know that your presence worries Babu. So why do you do it?' I asked.

He shrugged. 'Babu doesn't mind. All that was in the past. Besides, there is the little girl. Isn't she adorable? And to think she could have been mine.'

'She isn't yours,' I said quietly.

'Don't lie, Etta,' he said. 'I can see she is mine. She looks nothing like him or her.'

Mani wouldn't listen. He saw Babu as the usurper. He saw that he had no place in the family any more and didn't like it. Mani wouldn't have done any real harm. He wasn't an evil man. He was merely a child in a man's body. Everything was a game. If Gowri had agreed to go away with him, Mani would have fled again. But Babu couldn't take any chances.

The images refused to dislodge themselves from my mind. Mani in the car. Mani trapped within. Mani, his skin rolling off him, his flesh melting. Mani screaming and screaming, and trying to escape. Mani exploding. A fraction of a second—that was all he would have had to know that there was no escaping now. It was almost instantaneous, we were told, when they brought his remains home. Some shards of bone and teeth were all that was left of him. Master of the disappearing act, Mani.

With my father's death, Mani ceased to exist forever. There was no one now to keep his memory alive.

Yet, tonight I heard him knock at a door within. Open your memory vault, Etta, and let me out. All that is left of me are your memories. You must let me live through those at least.

I hear the gates open. It is raining. Who can it be at this hour? Then I see it is Chris.

'I am sorry to walk in like this,' he says. 'But I couldn't sit in there any more. I felt so cooped up. What do you do when it rains all day?'

'The monsoon has that effect,' I say. 'This year the monsoon has stretched longer than it ought to. Some months ago we were all talking about rain-water harvesting. Now everyone is talking about soil erosion and the devastation caused by the rain. Your trip must have been awful. Did you get to see and do all that you wanted to?'

'No, not really.' He runs his fingers through his hair and leans forward in his chair. The tips of his fingers meet in a tower on which he rests his chin. I know that gesture, I realize.

'How is the writing coming along?' I ask.

'I haven't written a word since I arrived. I thought I would get so much work done while I was here, but I only seem to have procrastinated.' His face wears a wry expression.

'You will write when you are ready,' I say. On an impulse, I ask, 'What will you do when you go back?'

'I have to write this book. And take on some journalistic work, which means travel a bit. I may go to Africa.' His expression is contemplative. 'I have to ask Unni to speak to the travel agent and re-schedule my flight. I may have to go back earlier than I planned to.'

What about Radha, I want to ask. Do any of your plans include her? What will she do when you go away?

'Does Radha…' I begin.

He yawns and stands up. The light is behind him. I see him in silhouette and I know a sense of wonder.

Of the nine bhavas, it is only adbhutam or astonishment that is sudden. All the others have a process, a certain time that stretches from experience to reaction. Love or anger, fear or disgust…we experience, we realize, and then we move into that state of being. But wonder can only be experienced. Adbhutam raises a question in your heart even as it fills you: 'Can it be possible?'

Why didn't I see it, I think. I know him. I know who he is. I feel my heart beat faster. But how can I ask him? What words do I use?

I feel weary. 'Chris, you must go now,' I say. 'I am tired. I need to rest.'

His eyes narrow in speculation. 'There is something else. I meant to ask you this days ago. Did you know an Englishwoman called Helen Pullman?'

I feel my eyes widen. Adbhutam again. 'Helen Pullman? She is a painter, isn't she?'

'She is my godmother,' he says. 'My mother's name is Angela,' he says, searching my face.

The wonder turns into certainty now. 'Why didn't you tell me this before?' I ask him.

'I thought you would be reluctant to talk about yourself.'

'Why did you think that?' I ask. What does he know about me? 'Did Angela say anything?'

He searches my face again. 'You didn't exactly part as friends,

did you? I tried asking my mother about you, but she was evasive.
She left too many blanks in her story.'

I rub the bridge of my nose. I feel a pounding in my head again.
'Come back tomorrow. We'll talk then,' I say. 'I really must rest
now.'

The rain is pelting down. The sound of it fills my house and head.
I realize then that he is here to do more than just write about me. In
fact, I wonder if the book exists at all or if it is a mere pretext. He is
here to seek the missing skeins. What has Angela told him? Or what
hasn't she told him?

I make a quick calculation. Suddenly all of it falls into place. He
thinks I am his father. For a moment, I know a deep sense of regret.
I would like to have had a son like Chris. But Chris isn't my son. I do
not know his father. I do know, however, that there is nothing of me
in him.

He will not believe me if I deny it. So I decide I will tell him all
about his mother. And this time I will not choose my memories. I
will tell him what happened the way it did.

1970–1971
The Crucible

Koman

Within a few days of my return from Madras, my life acquired a
pattern. Three months later, it felt as if I had never been away. The
newly-weds lived with my parents. I lived in my little house by the
river. An occasional airmail arrived from some distant land, testifying
to Mani's well-being, at which time I would go home to see my
family. I would choose a moment to call my father aside and give
him the letter. He would read it quietly, weep mutely, and dry his
eyes before joining the rest of the family. I would leave a little later.
I couldn't bear to be in that house where Mani was never mentioned.

Aashaan was drinking less. The bond between us seemed stronger than ever. Then one day Aashaan looked up from a letter he was reading and said, 'She is coming back.'

I looked up from my book, at the airmail form in his hand. 'Who is coming back?' I asked.

'Angela. She was my student for two years.' Aashaan's eyes were thoughtful.

'Your student?' My eyes widened. 'When did the institute start letting women study kathakali?'

'She is the first. I suppose they think there is no harm done if the woman is a foreigner. Also, she is admitted as a short-term student, not for a full course. I don't understand it all, but she's doing some research as part of her dissertation. She's been here twice already.'

'What is she like?' I was curious. What did a Madaama make of kathakali?

'Not bad at all.' Aashaan smiled. 'Her sense of rhythm is exquisite. She works very hard and her Malayalam is adequate. But she tires me with her questions. She is hard work.'

I smiled. Aashaan's tone was wry with amusement.

The old man folded the letter carefully. 'She is going to be disappointed when she knows I am up for retirement.'

'What will she do then?' I stood up. In a little while, the afternoon classes would begin.

'I am going to suggest that you teach her. She is ready for the third-year class.'

'Me!' I was horrified. 'I can't teach a woman kathakali.'

Aashaan frowned. 'Don't say that! She is good, and very dedicated. That's all you need to consider. Besides, you speak some English, don't you? So she can tire you with her queries.'

'Sundaran does, too,' I said.

'Ah, Sundaran.' Aashaan's smile carried a hint of irony. 'Sundaran. Our Mr Handsome. To send her to him would be like leading a lamb to the slaughter. He won't see her as a student but as an opportunity. That I can't allow.'

I looked away. I had two male foreign students in Madras. They had been interesting to teach. This woman would be the same. I just had to remember to see her as a genderless being.

She arrived the day the rains did. The day before, all morning the cuckoo's song had filled the air, piercing the stillness. Sweat ran down my body in rivulets and I thought that if the weather didn't break, I would suffocate from the stillness. Even the deep pond by the house was a sheet of green glass. I drank water and fanned myself. I took countless baths and at night I slept with a wet towel draped on my chest. The heat was relentless and both day and night were stricken with torpidity.

Dear departed wind, please come home, all is forgiven, I whispered, standing on the riverbank. Please come back and I will never ever complain about how you make the tiles on the roof rattle or the coconut palms writhe in a manic dance. Release me from this rigor mortis of thought and limb. I can't think. I can't breathe. What use am I as a wearer of guises if my mind can't infuse my movements?

Then it began.

The listless air moved. Clouds gathered and moved up the coast. Hope scuttled out of the river bed. Leaves rustled and the skies darkened. Lightning and thunder. The bars of heat loosened and with its first drops the rain snapped apart the inert month.

The earth fed on the rain like a greedy baby devouring the colostrum of fecundity. More, more, more, the earth craved for the thin, watery rain. Then, sated for the moment, it belched. A deep, dank fragrance. Moist earth laden with the memories of sun-baked days and crumbling surfaces. The wetness of rain. The wetness of release.

On my skin it felt like a thousand arrows shot by a god. A tingling, ringing, singing that punctured my pores and jingling my senses. Or perhaps it wasn't the rain at all. It was that first glimpse of her.

She was for me the beginning of the monsoon. Her fragrance was the fragrance of the dark, wet earth.

'Have you seen her?' Sundaran asked.

'Who?' I pretended not to understand.

A student crouched at his feet. A frog. So was I at one time, I thought. With the advent of monsoon and the month of karkitakam, the official massage sessions, the uzhichil, had begun. Ninety days of massage to prepare the body for the rigours of dance.

I remembered how feet had trampled and squashed my breath and hurt my body despite the film of oil that coated it. It was only with Aashaan I discovered that pressure needn't always be brutal.

'Who?' Sundaran echoed mockingly. 'The Madaama. Aashaan's new student. Have you seen her?'

I let my foot move across the back of the student. Up and down, then on the small of the back. 'If you mean see, I did see her. She was waiting for Aashaan outside the office room. If you mean meet, no, I haven't. Why would I anyway?' I said, not raising my eyes from the boy's back. 'I don't know all of Aashaan's students.'

Sundaran snorted. He was disinclined to believe me. He knew that one of these days Aashaan would have to ask either of us to take her on. He darted a venomous look at me. I saw a vein throb at his temple. I saw him look at the student lying at his foot.

The boy lay on his back. Sundaran prised his legs apart brutally. He pressed his foot down on the boy's thigh. The boy yelped in pain.

I looked up. 'Careful,' I murmured. 'You'll maim him.'

Sundaran snorted again. 'You and I had to endure worse and neither of us is maimed. Anyway, he's my student and I'll give him the massage as I see fit.'

As if to emphasize his lordship over the boy and his muscles, Sundaran's feet trampled on him viciously. I turned my eyes away. To intervene would be to make the child suffer even more.

Later in the day I went to the tea shop outside the institute. I saw Sundaran there. I went to sit beside him. 'What is wrong?' I asked. 'Why are you angry? Have you noticed that the boy is limping?'

'Perhaps I was too harsh this morning. But I had to vent my anger. I couldn't keep it bottled inside me. I had a letter from home demanding money. No matter how much I send, it's never enough. And as long as I am stuck here, nothing will change. If only I could find a way of getting out!' Sundaran twisted a piece of paper as he spoke. Suddenly he raised his eyes and said, 'Not all of us are fortunate to have rich fathers like you or a godfather like Aashaan. But let's not talk about it. I am to be Damayanti, the first day of Nalacharitam, two weeks from now.' He began talking about a vesham.

I didn't pursue the conversation; I could see that Sundaran was making an attempt to camouflage his bitterness. I nodded and listened. I would talk to Aashaan about Sundaran. Perhaps it would be best for the Madaama to study with Sundaran. And yet, I felt again the piercing rain, the fragrance of the wet earth, the cool breeze, and knew a strange reluctance to thwart Aashaan's plans.

The invitation came the same evening. 'We've been trying to reach you for the past few days,' the organizers said. Would I play Nala?

I agreed. Sundaran and I paired each other well. Sundaran's finely chiselled features and large eyes had steered him towards female roles and in our student days we had always been cast as lovers. There was a chemistry between us which enhanced the storyline. Besides, it would please Sundaran. The first day of the play was well balanced between Damayanti and Nala.

Nala. Monarch of Nishada who fell in love with Princess Damayanti on mere hearsay of her beauty. In her kingdom, Damayanti too pined for Nala; neither had even seen each other, but their souls had already communed. Then Nala sent an emissary—a handsome golden swan—to Damayanti. All I need to know is if I dare hope, he beseeched the swan to find out. The swan carried a message of love and yearning to Damayanti.

She blushed and admitted her feelings. How can I say more? It doesn't befit a woman of good breeding to flaunt her feelings, she said. And yet, my dear brother swan, I declare my love for Nala without shame or fear.

She had the swan paint her a picture of Nala and this she pressed to her bosom, imprinting his face forever on her heart.

Then Damayanti's father announced her swayamvara. The gods Indra, Agni, Yama and Varuna, too, decided to attend, along with other royal invitees. Kings, emperors, princes: Damayanti would choose her husband from amongst them. Nala also set forth, confident of Damayanti's love for him.

On the way, Nala was delighted to meet the four gods and as a mark of homage, he bowed before them and said, 'Your wish is my command.'

The gods smiled at each other and said, 'In that case, we would like you to go to Damayanti and ask her to choose from amongst us.'

Nala, having given his word, had no way of extricating himself from this mess. He pleaded, 'How can I see her? She will be in her chambers.'

The gods smiled. 'That doesn't matter. We will teach you to be invisible and you can then enter her chambers and tell her our heart's desire. But remember, the mantra will work just once.'

Nala did as they asked him to. However, Damayanti, who didn't know it was Nala who had come as the gods' messenger, sent him away saying her mind was made up. So he came back saying she was in love with someone else. 'Perhaps you should send another messenger whose persuasion skills are better,' he advised.

The gods smiled, having understood with their divine powers that it was Nala whom Damayanti loved. 'Is that so?' they asked.

Nala nodded.

'We'll find a way,' they said. Then they added, 'Tomorrow we will go to the great hall and each one of us will look just like you. But you are not to let her know by word or gesture which of us is really you.'

So the four gods and Nala entered the great hall where the swayamvara was being held and they were announced as Nala, the king of Nishadha. Everyone looked up in surprise when they saw five men, exact replicas of each other. Damayanti's eyes widened, too. She smiled without saying anything.

Soon Damayanti walked into the hall carrying a garland. She walked past all the kings and headed straight towards the five Nalas. Everyone held their breath. Who was the real Nala? And would Damayanti recognize him?

Damayanti looked at the five men and without any hesitation she garlanded the real Nala. The gods assumed their real forms and Yama asked, 'How did you know the real Nala?'

Damayanti smiled and said, 'My love for Nala is strong and true and I would know him even if there were a hundred lookalikes in the room. Besides, Nala is a man and I knew that the other four were gods. I saw how Nala's feet touched the ground and that his body threw a shadow and that his eyes blinked. And I knew for sure that my heart had guided me to the man of my dreams.'

The four gods smiled and blessed the couple and left. And so Nala and Damayanti were united.

This then is the first day of Nalacharitam and that was the Nala I was to be.

I smiled again at the thought.

Later, Aashaan said he would be there and he would bring Angela with him. 'Let her watch both you and Sundaran perform and she can choose who she wants to study with.'

I felt my mouth go dry. She would see me in a vesham, as the romantic Nala. As Nala who was honour bound to not speak, even though it was his love at stake. As Nala who had to leave everything to chance. What would she think of me? 'Does she know the story?' I asked.

Aashaan smiled. 'She knows it very well indeed!'

Angela

'This is Angela.' Aashaan smiled.

I raised my eyes and said, 'An-ga-la. That is how my father calls me. He is German.'

I saw a mixture of emotions in Koman's eyes. Surprise, curiosity, excitement.

Our eyes met.

Angela, he repeated. In the German way. It sounded like a name he knew and didn't.

'Are you German?' he asked and I saw that he almost bit his tongue. I had just said my father was German.

I smiled. I didn't want to cause him any embarrassment. Already I felt something akin to awe when I was in his presence. 'My father was. But my mother was Spanish. And I grew up in England. So what do you think I am?'

He flushed.

I felt contrite. To make amends, I said, 'He has talked to me about you. Do you know how proud Aashaan is of you?'

Again I felt a timbre of something else creep into my voice. It would come to me later what that inexplicable timbre was, I thought. For now I smiled again.

'And I am glad that you are to be my Aashaan,' I added.

He looked at the old man with a question in his eyes. Aashaan nodded. 'My time here is up; I retire in two weeks' time. Why do you look so surprised? I told you, didn't I?'

'But Sundaran,' Koman said.

'She chose to be taught by you,' Aashaan said. 'Teach her well. She is good.'

Our eyes met. Mine blue and his a pale brown. Sea and sand. A frisson of excitement flowed between us.

Koman broke the gaze.

Koman

The rain fell. Sheets of rain that separated us from the rest of the world. A haze of water that dispersed people and sound, trapping colour and light and refracting forbidden desires.

When the rain stopped and there was a lull splattered only by the trickle of water down the eaves, the drip from the leaves, I knew with a start that I had sinned again. That despite being separate, each in a designated space, I the teacher, she the pupil, the distance had dwindled and we had enmeshed, limbs and souls touching fleetingly and yet with the impact of two heavenly bodies colliding. A teacher and student in harmony. I knew, however, that there was more to it than harmony. I feared that she knew it as well. I could smell it in her sweat. Did she in mine? Our bodies longed to leap the distance. This is lust, I admonished my vagrant senses. An aashaan cannot lust for his student. An aashaan must not.

In the afternoon Angela came back for the theory classes. Her eyes were blue and her hair a deep brown. There was a mole above her lip, on her left cheek. Freshly bathed, with her wet hair falling to her waist, she sat before me cross-legged. Her skirt swirled around her like the petals of a lotus. The familiar stranger, I thought.

'The Madaama is turning into a Malayali girl,' Sundaran remarked.

I looked at her with Sundaran's eyes. He was right. Angela was adopting the dress and mannerisms of her new world. She wore her hair like Malayali women do, with two strands drawn from behind her ears and braided into a narrow plait. It held the hair away from her face, exposed the curve of her ears and the line of her throat. Between her brows was a tiny red dot. Her eyes were lined with kohl and anklets dressed her feet. When she walked to the kalari, her long-legged gait abruptly became the nimble steps of the Indian woman. When she sat with the boys, she remembered to lower her eyes. I am besotted, I thought. This softening of my heart when I see her, what is it?

I tried to stop myself from doing so, but my eyes followed her as she danced the man's dance. I saw how it enhanced the tilt of her breasts and the arch of her buttocks. Again, the softening within. How could it be?

Now I watched her perform the navarasas, is part of the preliminary routine of the theory session. She is my student and I must remember that, but how can I not feast on the energy she radiates? She loves what she is doing. How can I not love that love?

'Koman Aashaan,' Angela's voice broke through my crazy spiralling thoughts. 'I know this will sound silly, but I didn't dare ask Aashaan.' She spoke in English.

The other boys, her batch-mates for now, paused. Their faces reflected their perplexity. They had understood just one word. Aashaan. Even they realized that the Aashaan she was referring to was not me. The long-drawn vowel of "aa" bore the awe of reverence.

I smiled. 'Entha?' I asked in Malayalam. What?

One of the boys couldn't hold back his curiosity. 'Aashaan, what is the Madaama asking?' He spoke in Malayalam.

'Do your work,' I snapped.

'It is one more of the Madaama's questions. Don't you remember how she tired out Aashaan last year?' In the silence the whisper was amplified.

I groaned. Didn't the boy know she understood Malayalam?

Angela hid her smile. She drew her lips in. I felt the beginning of a smile stretch my lips. Our eyes met and we burst into laughter.

The boys stared. They had never seen me laugh before.

'What is it?' I asked, wiping the amusement from my face. This would not do, I rebuked myself sternly.

Angela placed her palms sideways on the ground. 'Why are the sides of the feet used? Like this? Rather than the flat of the feet?'

'What she wants to know...' I translated her question into Malayalam, turning her query into a lesson. 'Anyone?'

The boys stared at a point behind my ear. I sighed. Could standards really have dropped so much since my time? Or were the boys not interested enough?

'If we placed our feet flat on the ground like in bharatanatyam, for instance, the impact would be brutal.' I stood up and performed a step. Then I turned my feet sideways. 'The steps in kathakali are vigorous. This is a masculine dance. Even the slowest of compositions has an underlying vigour. Think of the damage it would cause the eyes and spine, the vital organs. With your feet placed sideways, the impact is gentle and it gives the steps a lightness.'

Angela nodded and turned to her book.

Rain fell. The questions didn't cease. She was like I used to be. A vulture, I thought, picking between the bones of kathakali. How? Why? When?

'Sometimes you have to forget all the questions and let your mind slip away. Ignore your doubts and become the character. If you let your mind dominate, then you will be Angela playing a character and not the character,' I said. I was repeating the words with which Aashaan had once chided me. I looked at her bent head. I was once like her. Is that what drew me to her? When I saw her, I saw a reflection of myself. Was this love? To seek in someone a mirror image of one's own hopes and dreams, one's own soul?

My head ached. I knew I was unhappy, but I couldn't understand the desperation I felt.

Rain fell, ushering shadows into the late afternoon. Angela rose and put on the light. The naked bulb glowed. It caught the glint of her gold stud. I felt my breath catch. She lights up my world, I thought.

Karkitakam passed. So did kanni. Two months of knowing Angela, and yet I know nothing of her, I thought. She is the crown I wear as part of a vesham, precious and sacred, inviolable and, despite its beauty, a burden. The weight of this crown will snap my neck. The sanctity of our relationship demands that I keep her at a distance, but how much longer can I restrain myself?

Why did Aashaan do this to me, I asked myself every now and then. And if he knew, he would be furious. I sighed.

Then I sat up with a start. Where was Aashaan? It was almost two months since I had seen him. Every now and then I told myself that I ought to go and visit him at home. But the pace of my routine left me with little time.

This weekend I would go to his house. He was probably lonely…and drunk. I felt guilt coat my tongue. Bitter, acrid guilt.

For the first time I began to understand Aashaan's anguish. Without a vesham, a kathakali dancer had no place.

Later, and for as long as I lived, I would never forgive myself for abandoning him. 'It isn't your fault,' she told me again and again. 'It isn't neglect that did it. He knew. Don't you see that? He knew that he would never dance again.'

'But if I had been there, I would have been able to talk him out of it,' I said.

'Could you have got him a performance? Even if there was someone willing to listen to you and take the risk of having him play a vesham, do you think his pride would have allowed it? Don't do this, Koman. Don't blame yourself. Let him go. It is sad, but you must respect his decision.' Angela laid her hand on my arm.

I realized that for the first time she had called me by name and not Aashaan.

I covered her hand with mine. I felt the need to cling to someone. I wanted to lay my cheek against her breast and weep. Each time I shut my eyes, on that darkened screen, the image appeared—Aashaan hanging from a beam.

I was in the middle of a class when Gopi, the pettikaaran, came looking for me. 'There is a man here from Aashaan's village. He died early this morning,' Gopi said.

His eyes filled. The pettikaaran and Aashaan had known each other a long time. Gopi had transformed Aashaan into so many characters. He probably knew every wart and wrinkle on Aashaan's face.

I felt a leaden weight settle on my brow. 'What happened?'

The boys and Angela paused in the middle of a kalasham. I turned on them furiously. 'Who asked you to stop? Go on, finish the sequence and then scene three from Uttaraswayamvaram—*Gowri, Gowri*…I have to go now. I expect you to continue as if I were here. Do you understand?'

Gopi and I walked towards the office room. 'I am going to see him,' I said. 'Will anyone else come?'

Gopi nodded. 'The principal has called for a taxi. Some others are coming as well. The man said the panchayat president is trying to hush up the whole thing. He was a drunk, but every one respected him. When he was sober, there was no one like him and never will be...'

I stopped mid-stride. 'What do you mean, hush up?'

Gopi looked away. 'They found him hanging from a beam in his house. The maid found him, in fact, this morning.'

'But how? Wasn't anyone else in his family there?'

'What family? His wife died some years ago and they had no children,' Gopi said. 'Didn't you know?'

I felt guilt rail its fists against me. I had burdened Aashaan with my worries, real and imaginary. My relations with my family, my dreams, my speculations about characters and interpretations, but I had never once asked Aashaan if he had demons of his own, burdens I could have helped lighten if not alleviate. I had been so wrapped up in myself. If I had known, I would have brought him to my house and looked after him. But Aashaan hadn't wanted charity. He hadn't wanted to lose his dignity. It is better to be dead than a veshakaaran without a vesham, he had said again and again. And Aashaan had no vesham left. On stage, or in life.

I watched a distant nephew light the pyre. The flames leapt and burnt. Are you at peace now, Aashaan, I asked.

The flames cackled, hissed and spat in reply. It could have been Aashaan answering me.

In my home by the river, I knew a remorse that tore my soul. No matter how much I tried to rationalize Aashaan's death, it was hard to not grieve. I sat on the steps leading down to the river and wept.

Angela

I found him there. I looked down at him. He wasn't even aware of my presence, his isolation was so complete. I wanted to reach out and take him in my arms, comfort him, hold him to my breasts and stroke his brow. I laid my hand on his shoulder.

He turned abruptly at my touch. His eyes sought mine, imploring me to understand. 'If I had known…' he said, trying to explain his anguish.

'Don't blame yourself,' I said.

I sat beside him on the step.

'There is a poem called "Final Act", by a poet named Rilke.'

The words, in an unfamiliar tongue, seemed to sooth him.

He leaned towards me. 'What does it mean?'

'Death is large.

We are the beings

With laughing mouths.

When we think we are in the middle of life

Death dares to cry out

in the middle of us.'

He smiled in the darkness.

He looked at my face. 'How did you know where I live?'

'I know everything about you,' I said. How could I tell him that I had been collecting bits of information about him? 'Aashaan told me.'

'He was planning this. He gave you to me.'

'No one could give me to you. I am not a parcel. I chose you, remember?'

'I know. But he knew that when he was gone, I would need a diversion.'

'I don't like to think I am a mere diversion. But it is true. Aashaan was a wise man.' I steeled my voice to bear the finality of a goodbye. 'Was,' I said.

Tears sprang into his eyes. 'If I had been less wrapped up in myself,' he said.

I took his hands in mine. 'You can't live another man's life. It was his decision to die. You must respect that.'

Koman

A few weeks later came another invitation. The second day of

Nalacharitam. Would I play Nala? I agreed. It would take my mind off Aashaan and Angela, I told myself.

Two days before the performance, Angela said that she would come to see me play Nala. 'It will be interesting to see how you transform from the heroic and romantic Nala to an ineffectual and crazed man.'

I flushed. I felt self-conscious. Why couldn't it be a vesham where I was a truly heroic being instead of this mortal creature pulled and twisted by destiny's doings, I asked myself wryly. I would be Nala who was a slave to his senses, doing their bidding, all good sense distanced.

It was only in the first scene that I would be allowed to be Nala, the noble and sensitive man. Suddenly I knew. With that one scene, I would tell her what I was feeling.

After Nala went back to his kingdom with his bride, he discovered yet another impediment to their happiness: Damayanti's shyness.

'*Kuvalayavilochane bale, bhaimi*...My lotus-eyed beauty, my precious girl, my wife, having got this far, don't you think we are wasting our youth and time? Think of all that we had to go through. Think of the various impediments that came our way. Now it is your shyness that stands between us; it is your bashfulness that is my greatest enemy. Don't you think it is time you shrugged that away and let me fulfil my desires?'

I thought of the scene as I lay on my back. Gopi was working on my face. He knew better than to intrude on my thoughts. Yet, as he drew the rice-paste patterns, he murmured in a hushed voice, 'Why do I get the feeling that this is you lying here and not Nala? What is wrong?'

I felt a great wave of mortification. What was I thinking? I had no place here. My dreams and desires did not belong here; mine was merely a body for Nala to be. I was Nala. And my love was Damayanti, not a blue-eyed Madaama.

And yet, when the music began and the singers poured forth the longing in Nala's heart, *Kuvalayavilochane bale, bhaimi*, I knew that I was incapable of retreating. That it would be I, not Nala, who stood there and wooed her. With this slowest sringaara padam amongst all kathakali padams, I would make my intentions clear.

For once, I would use the power of the veshakaaran to beguile the audience into thinking I was Nala. Only she would know better.

Angela

I wasn't shy, or bashful. Neither was I easily overwhelmed by pretty words or a handsome face. Otherwise, I would have chosen Sundaran to be the object of my desire.

I worried that I would end up a cliché. It had happened before. A blue-eyed foreigner falling for a dark-eyed Indian. I loved India, but I wasn't here to discover myself or curb my restless spirit. I was here to research and finish my dissertation. I didn't want a relationship of any sort. Yet, with Koman, I felt the edge of attraction getting sharper and sharper.

I could see that he too felt the pull, but he worked hard at resisting it. I could see that he thought it was wrong to admit his attraction for me. I was his student.

I don't know when I stopped seeing him as my master and saw the male in him.

Perhaps it was at the exhibition performance of Kuchelavrittam they held at the institute once. I had decided to document every step of the performance. So, as his face was being made up, I sat by his side watching him change. Later I sat in the front row of the audience, waiting for the performance to begin and suddenly, there he was. Krishna.

In him I saw the shaping of my desire. A man who was playful and mischievous, affectionate and teasing, generous and romantic.

My heart stilled. The redness of his eyes drew my gaze. Suddenly his eyes met mine. I let him see the desire in my eyes.

When Krishna threw a handful of thechi flowers at Kuchelan's feet to welcome the poor brahmin and to show him respect, a flower fell into my lap. It occurred to me that he had intended it to happen. I felt a secret smile tug at my lips. I held the dainty flower between my fingers and slipped it between the leaves of a book. An imprint of his desire, I thought.

The next day in class, I said, 'I'm going to attend all your performances while I am here.'

He looked up in surprise.

'It helps me in my research to see as many veshams as possible,' I said. 'I know my understanding of kathakali is negligible but when I see a vesham, I come a little closer to understanding it.'

Koman smiled. For a moment, he searched my eyes. I knew he was asking: Is that all you've come for?

I could see that some instinct told him there was more.

I met his gaze for an instant and felt my eyes drop in a wave of confusion.

I sat in the front row. The rest of them made way for me. My obvious foreignness invited comment. Everywhere I heard, 'Madaama is Koman Aashaan's student.'

And I would smile secretly to myself. I am not just his student, I am more than that. He wants it to be more than that. I felt a flush of power then. This magnificent being was mine. He would like it to be so.

Could this be termed an obsession? I didn't know. But every role he played, I saw myself as the woman who stood alongside. It didn't matter who she was, I was her. So I was Urvashi the heavenly nymph, wanton slut, beseeching Arjuna to let her taste the nectar that resided in his lower lip. When she cried, the arch of your brow fills me with a desire that is as painful as a whiplash, I wanted him to cast away the demands of the libretto and pleasure me.

When he was Arjuna disguised as an ascetic, I was Subhadra, the princess, now his handmaiden. I was prepared to forget my loyalty to my brother's wishes, set aside my modesty and elope with him.

It was pointless and fraught with danger and yet I couldn't stop myself.

On the second day of Nalacharitam, I watched him carefully. Was this Nala or Koman, I wondered. What did it matter? They were one and the same.

I watched his face, the dancer's face. He seemed to be addressing me rather than Damayanti. Then he turned and looked at me from the corner of his eyes. I saw a repertoire of glances. Lust. Shyness. Sorrow. Affection. Valour. Respect. Suspicion. With each of these he told me: It is your hesitation, your shyness that is my enemy now. *Kalayallo veruthe kaalam ni.* Aren't you wasting time, my precious?

· 369 ·

I met his eyes. The desire in his gaze kindled a certainty in me. He is, I thought, a man who knows how to love. A man who knows no mortal limits to love.

Later we quarrelled even about that, hurling accusations, each seeking to blame the other: you seduced me.

But when we resonated with that first wild yearning for each other, who could tell who made the first move? Was it him or me?

A widening of the eye. A touch. An embrace. A love affair begins with all these and more. Who could tell who leaned into whom? When we finally sought each other, it was in a frenzy to satiate suppressed desires. An ashtakalasham of lust and want. The dance of all dances. A complex sequence of steps that was the natural culmination of all those months when we had done nothing but watch each other.

Our days and nights became one. A matrimony of limbs, thoughts and oddments. My suitcase found a place alongside his in the attic and my mirror-work cushions lay scattered on the mattress on his floor. My body lotion stood beside his hair oil and his comb nestled amidst the bristles of my hair brush.

We read poetry together. I read Neruda aloud to him and he fashioned my words into mudras, each gesture pulsing and alive.

I lit incense sticks and let the coil of smoke bind us together. A wedding ring of smoke and fragrance.

He braided my hair and adorned it with flowers. A jasmine star into every twist. He held a mirror for me to admire my hair in. 'Do you see this?' he asked.

'I do, I do,' I said in amazement that he, godly being, was doing this for me.

He brought leaves of the mailanji plant from a house nearby and ground them into a fine paste. Then he daubed my fingertips with it and forbade me to move or use my hands for the next hour. He pressed down my eyelids and then flicked the dried paste off my fingertips and showed me the colours of the sunset that tinted them. 'Do you see this?' he whispered.

'I do, I do,' I murmured in wonder.

He laid me on the bed and peeled my clothes away. He dripped oil into the well of my navel and with his fingertips he drew the oil into my skin, anointing me his woman. I lay on my back, a willing supplicant to his administrations.

I do, I do, I cried. What could be more perfect than this? You and me, and our life.

Koman

In the little house by the river, we found a home for our passion.

A few days later my father came calling. In one glance he took in the changes that affected my home and me. His eyes said it all. That he had heard rumours of his son and the Madaama.

'You are old enough to know what you are doing,' he said. 'Why don't you marry her? All your life has been wasted on kathakali. Will your art fetch you a glass of water when you are thirsty? Will it lay a wet cloth on your brow when you are burning with fever? Will it hold you up when your legs tremble, or hold your hand when you are lonely? That is why you need a family and a home.'

'I have a home and a family,' I said. 'I don't think Angela wants to be married now.'

'Then when?'

'Maybe later. Maybe never. Angela is my wife. Sometimes relationships don't need rituals to sanctify them.' Have you forgotten about you and Saadiya? How can you talk about rituals, I left unsaid. But he understood and didn't dare say anything more.

When my father left, I went to sit on the steps by the river. Angela and I had been living together for only three months, but already things were not the same. What could have gone wrong, I asked myself again and again. What had begun as the most perfect time of my life had dwindled into a greyness I couldn't even understand.

I wondered what she would say when I told her about my father's visit.

We had never discussed marriage, Angela and I. Would she want to? It would be very hard to live here unless we were married. I couldn't even take her home until then. I knew she felt hurt that, though we lived so close to my family, I hadn't even introduced her to them. But what could I say? 'Achan, Babu, meet Angela, my lover!'

I was worried about her. And I worried that she was the way she was because of me.

After she and I began to live together, I had to draw very clear lines between our personal and professional lives. 'I can't be your teacher by day and lover by night,' I had said. 'I suggest that we ask Sundaran or one of the others to take you into their class.'

But she refused. 'It won't be the same.'

She had given up kathakali for me. What more could I ask of her?

Angela

I wasn't happy. I couldn't understand it. I had a headache some days and on other days my neck hurt, or my back. Or it was my digestion. Until now, I had never known a day's illness. But now I felt ill all day.

'I feel so tired,' I complained.

'Do you want to go to a doctor?' he asked gently. The concern in his voice made me angry. I didn't like feeling ill or listless.

'I feel so bloated and full,' I said.

'It is because you are idle all day,' he said and went to the kitchen to find me a piece of ginger and pound it with salt.

'Here, eat this, you will feel better.'

I nibbled at it and he asked me again, 'Why don't you practise at home?'

'How can I practise without the accompaniments?'

'I could get you a recording. Or we could even make one during a class,' Koman offered.

'Oh no, it isn't the same,' I said, turning away.

'I wish we could go away,' I said. 'I feel suffocated here. What am I doing here, Koman?' I asked suddenly. 'I can't fritter my life away as I am doing now.'

'But what will I do elsewhere?' he asked. 'No, you have to give up that thought. I cannot leave this place. If you find it so hard to live here, then you must return,' he said.

Was that an ultimatum?

I cried then. 'But I can't. How can you even suggest it?'

'Then try and understand me better,' he said.

For a few days I made an effort and then I felt that familiar desperation settle back over me.

Koman

It occurred to me that she seemed to have no further use for kathakali. She no longer even came to see me perform. When I asked her to, she said she didn't feel up to it. It isn't envy, I told myself. It is melancholy. So I let it be.

I felt as if I was crippling her soul, sucking all the happiness out of her.

In desperation I took her to a doctor. 'It is the change in environment,' the doctor said. 'Otherwise, she is perfectly all right. I am going to start her on some mild anti-anxiety treatment and she should respond to it soon.'

I bought the medication and said it was for her poor digestion.

The old Angela would have wanted to know everything about it, including its pharmaceutical composition. This Angela, with slack jaw and dull eyes, swallowed her pills dutifully without any questions.

At night, we lay side by side. She slept deeply, entombed in the arms of the all-comforting pill. Her loneliness ate into me. Then there was the guilt. What use was my art if it made her so unhappy? Was I a monster to put her through such agony? How could it be that what had brought us together could also distance us?

One morning I woke up with a start. I'd had a strange dream. Of my beautiful Angela in a white anti-septic ward of a hospital. Her face had lost all traces of knowing. Her hair was scraped into a knot on top of her head. Her smile was vacant. Her melancholy had taken her where I and kathakali no longer existed.

The picture stung my soul. I felt a heaviness in my heart. What next, I wondered.

Should I let her go? Or should I go with her? Her love, I saw, was tinged with an unconscious envy, and unhappiness at her inability to do something with her life. How could such a love thrive?

Then Babu came to see me. 'This is a small town, Etta,' he said.

'People talk. You know that Achan and I will stand by you. Why don't you marry her? There will be no room for gossip then. You should hear what they say about the two of you in the marketplace.'

'Does it bother you that much, Babu?' I asked gently.

'It does. I cannot let our family name be disgraced. You know that. You know how far I have gone to preserve our social standing. Now I also have my child to think of. This is a small town, like I said. I don't want any slander spoiling my child's prospects.'

'The child is not even born,' I said.

'So what? These things return to haunt you. Do you know what my life is like? Every day I fear that he will come back and stake a claim. That all I have worked to put together will fall apart. I don't need this. I can't handle this.'

I nodded. 'I will sort it out,' I promised. 'But I will not give her up.'

'Who asked you to? Marry her. Make her your wife. That is all we ask of you.'

Angela

I listened to Koman vent his fury on small towns and people with even smaller minds.

'Let us go away,' I said. 'You can't let them dictate to you how you should live. You are an artist, not a bank clerk. Artists have to be left alone. But people in small towns don't understand this. They lead such rigid lives and are so worried about what their neighbours will think. If you live here, your art will die, I can tell you that. They will turn you into a respectable man and a boring artist.'

I felt guilt sting me. I knew I was saying this only because I was unhappy with the town and my life here. If only I could persuade Koman to leave.

'But where? Where can we go?' he asked.

'We will go to London first and then move on to the rest of Europe. We will make a life there,' I said. I felt my face lighting up at the prospect of escaping this world, and introducing him to mine.

'What will I do there? I am a kathakali dancer and I know nothing else.'

'You will dance, Koman. What else? You are a dancer and I would think it sacrilege for you to do anything else. You will be feted and applauded. Everyone there will love you. Look at Ravi Shankar, the sitar player.'

Koman shook his head. 'He is a musician. And music isn't bound by cultural boundaries. Kathakali isn't like that. Even people here are unable to comprehend it. How will anyone there understand it? It won't work.'

'No, listen to me. Haven't you heard of Ram Gopal? He is a kathakali dancer who trained here, under Kunju Kurup. He is much admired and respected. Even Njinsky went to see him dance.'

Koman frowned. 'But he doesn't perform kathakali any more. Are you asking me to forsake kathakali? I can't do that, Angela!'

I took his hand in mine. 'Koman, how could I ask you to give up kathakali? I am not. All I am saying is, you will find your place there. Some years ago Ram Gopal and Alicia Markova, the prima ballerina, performed together their Radha Krishna duet at Prince's Theatre in London. He choreographed the duet and taught her the steps and to see them together you would think they had danced together all their lives. That was when I fell in love with Indian dance and, more specifically, kathakali. I was only a teenager then, but I knew. Like I know that there is so much you can do. Think about it. To start with, we must try and meet Ram Gopal. He lives in London. When he knows you are from here, and sees you perform, he will want you to be part of his company. He can spot talent, and nurture it.

'Think of it, Koman. You will be famous all over the world. Your talent deserves a worldwide audience. You do realize, don't you, that you are being wasted here.'

Koman

The rapture in her voice excited me. Her eyes sparkled and there was a lightness to her movements that I hadn't seen in a long time.

I thought of the fear that had haunted me for some time now. I saw her withdrawing into her shell. I saw her brittleness. I saw the demons that dragged her thoughts this way and that and I worried that she would do something drastic.

I knew I was being silly, but when I went to the institute, it was with fear pawing my throat. I would rush home in the break to check on her. Was she all right? When I went away for a performance, I came back the moment it was over. There was no more lingering, no discussing or analysing the evening. The truth was, I was afraid to leave her alone. I didn't think she was suicidal, but I feared the fragility of her mind. I thought of my mother and what she had done. I knew an even greater fear then.

As she planned our life ahead, Angela was almost her old self. The woman I had fallen in love with. It was as if she was gathering the unravelling threads of her mind and braiding them all together again. It was as if she was regaining control over herself. Would our going away really make her happy?

And yet, how could I take such a chance?

Angela

I saw that he was still unsure, so I said slowly, 'I know Aashaan always said that you only need to satisfy your own standards and everything else is extraneous. I always thought that was a form of denial. Denying reality to make yourself feel better. But surely you are not in denial, Koman?'

Koman

I listened. I could see what she was saying. I had once dreamt of it. Then I had learnt to repress my ambitions and sought solace in Aashaan's dictum that it was enough to know that I was true to my art and could meet my own exacting standards. Angela was right. I was burying my head in sand and pretending that none of the trappings of success—fame, money, acceptance, recognition—mattered. They did matter. So much so that to think of it caused me pain. I was an ostrich that called cowardice courage.

I felt the stirrings of ambition. I would find new worlds to conquer.

New stages to set myself upon and display my artistry. All that I had once hoped for would be mine.

I would dare to ask the world again what it thought of my art.

And so I became Bahukan. An ugly dwarf of a man, uncouth and lubberly, with a thousand uncertainties.

I, Bahukan, Black Nala, shorn of all that I was and all I had, crouched under a mound of blankets.

I stared at the floor, the red and yellow lino with triangles and squares. When I was tired of looking at the geometric patterns, I stared at the electric fire. It waited, like I did, for Angela.

The electric fire was a hungry god, Agni of the seven tongues, demanding and devouring shillings as obeisance before it would condescend to bless us with heat. Angela was the high priestess, the only one who could satiate its hunger. So I waited. I looked at the clock. Another half hour to go before Angela returned.

In twenty-five minutes, I would switch on the electric fire. I would go into the kitchenette and fill the kettle with water and slice the bread for toast. I would make the bed and stack the cushions the way Angela liked them to be. I would lay out a stack of records and switch on the radio. When all was neat and tidy and there were no signs of my lonely and cold vigil, I would put the kettle on and the toast. When Angela got back, toast and tea would be ready and waiting in a room that would finally be warm and crackling with sound from the radio.

But I still had another twenty-five minutes to go. Where am I, I asked myself again.

I am in London, I told myself. I am living on a street that I can't even remember the name of. All I know is that the Earl's Court tube station is around the corner. The bed-sit faced the street on one side and a wall to the right. There was a sash window which, even in milder weather, I wouldn't open. It looked on to a brick wall. More than anything, I hungered for a glimpse of green.

I pulled the blankets closer around me and huddled in the armchair. At home, I would have gone to the kitchen, gathered a handful of dried coconut fronds, lit a fire and warmed a huge cauldron of water. While the water heated, I would rub oil into my skin and then bathe in that water scented with smoke and wood fire. After that, I would serve myself a plate of rice. Not these bleached white grains, but reddish-brown rice still tasting of the earth and sunshine. There would be a curry of green papaya cooked in buttermilk and a piece of fried fish. Dried sole, or chunks of dried shark. Pappadum on the side and mango pickle. My mouth watered. Where in this city could I find what I hungered for?

It began to rain. I saw the drops of water splash against the window. In my home even the sound of the rain was different. Here, the rain was feeble and the smell of it was a musty, dank odour of unwashed bodies and rationed heat. Grey skies, the stale, sour smell of damp, and a perpetual hunger. What had I exiled myself to?

Nineteen minutes to go. It was Bahukan's lot to wait, all the time asking, why?

Angela left some weeks before I did. 'I would so love for us to travel together, but I can organize things better if I go first.'

That was when the implications of the move occurred to me. A house to live in. A job to find. How would we manage? Where would we find the money? 'Are you sure, Angela?' I asked again. 'We could perhaps go to Madras or New Delhi. There are dance schools there. I don't have much money; won't London be expensive?'

'There you go again, shying away from life. You need to be where the world will see you and not tucked away in a little dance school. Don't worry, we will manage. I will have everything ready by the time you get there,' she said. I saw the resolution in her eyes and felt less troubled.

Achan and Babu were not pleased at the thought of my going away. 'Isn't this rather drastic?' Babu asked.

'Are you sure?' my father asked.

'It is time I thought about my career. Angela says I am wasted here.'

'But do you have to go that far?' my father asked.

'Angela says that once I am accepted in London, the whole world will want to see me dance.'

Achan frowned. Babu smirked. He said, 'It is strange to hear you say Angela this, Angela that. I wonder what magic potion she has fed you to enchant you so completely.'

I glared at him. Babu looked away and said with a sweep of his hands, 'Well, if it doesn't work out, you can always come back. You have a house here.'

'In fact, Angela was saying that we should perhaps sell the house. The money will come in useful. London is expensive.'

My father's face turned grim. 'I don't care what your Angela says, but I will not let you sell the house. If in a year's time, you find that all is well there, you can rent it out. But there is to be no talk of selling it till I am dead. You can tell your Angela that.'

'Achan is right,' Babu said. 'Real estate prices are very low and this is a bad time to sell.'

I let it be. Deep inside, I hadn't wanted to part with the house, either. But Angela had been so persuasive. It was good to have the right to decide taken away from me.

I felt something within me wrench as I pulled the door shut. I went to take a last look at the river. During the monsoon, it had turned into a raging beast, sweeping all that came its way into its waters, flooding the banks and knocking down trees and homes. But now the Nila was a timid river flowing quietly. A cloud of dragonflies floated by. The breeze bore the scent of flowers. For a moment, I knew anguish. In the new land I had chosen to live in, what would the flowers be like? Would the stars look the same? Would the earth beneath my feet hold me up as it did now?

I heard the car horn and knew it was time to leave. I locked the house and left the key with Babu. 'I'll have it cleaned regularly,' he said. And again, 'Your house will always be here.'

In the plane, I had an aisle seat. Angela had said—ask for an aisle seat. You won't have to leap over people's knees when you need to go to the bathroom. It is a long flight.

I sat in my seat, numb with excitement and anxiety. To my left was a couple. Foreigners. They held hands. I wished Angela was with me.

The plane soared into the skies, wading through oceans of clouds. Would some wandering god pass my way, I wondered.

The hours passed. I arrived in Heathrow. Where was Angela?

An hour passed. I announced my presence over the paging system. I was frightened now. I heard my father's voice: 'Are you sure?'

Then I spotted a familiar face. 'Angela.'

Angela

'It is not much, but it's all I could find,' I said, opening the door of the bed-sit.

I saw Koman's face pale. He didn't look pleased and, though I hadn't meant to, I found myself blurting, 'And this is all we can afford.'

I saw Koman look around him. I hoped the familiar things would make him feel at home. My mirror-work cushions and a cotton rug I had bought in India were thrown on the floor. There was his little bronze Nataraja figurine and my incense-stick holder in the shape of a frog. There were spider plants on the window ledge and a brass dish I had brought from his house. It held the pebbles we had picked from the riverbank. Shawls draped the back of the two armchairs.

'It is strange to see these things here,' he said.

I touched the Nataraja. Shiva frozen in the cosmic dance. All dancers worshipped him. The god had lived on a ledge in his house while I was there and suddenly, I felt a pang of uncertainty shoot through me. What had I done?

'Strange nice or strange bad?' I asked. I felt my mouth droop.

'Just strange. I have to constantly remind myself that I am in London and then, when I see these things that were in my house just a few days ago, I wonder if I have travelled at all. Give me time. I'll get used to it,' he said quietly.

I saw him look at the stack of LPs. He flipped through them and held up a record sleeve. Ravi Shankar. 'I see you have your favourite here,' he said.

'I don't know why you dislike him. He is so good. I listen to him almost every day,' I said.

I saw him try to hide his grimace. I don't know why, but it bothered me. He made me feel as if my preferences were suspect.

Then he spotted the TV. 'How does this work?' he asked.

I hadn't known that he hadn't seen one before. There was so much I didn't know about him.

I saw his face clear as I leaned forward to turn it on and showed him how to work it.

In those first few days, everything was edged with the wonder of newness. The black-and-white TV and the shiny linoleum; the Baby

Belling electric oven and the two-bar electric fire; the bri-nylon sheets and the sash window; the tube station and the escalators. The sun shone, the leaves rustled and the air was cool enough for Koman to feel that he was in a faraway country. It wasn't cold or damp enough for him to miss the sun. In those first few days, he and I walked a great deal and I saw London through his eyes.

St James Park and Westminster Abbey. Hampstead Heath and Camden town. Streets and places. Lights and sounds. There were people the like of whom he had never seen before. Tall black men and women with frizzy hair and a swing to their hips; dainty yellow-skinned men and women with narrow eyes and jet black hair; men and women with bleached hair and eyes. Hair colours he had never seen: russet and gold, grey and yellow, red and silvery white; eyes that were green and brown, grey and black, shades of blue.

The flavours of this new life, this new world, filled his senses. I took him to meet my friends. I took him to my favourite restaurants. We ate Chinese food in a little restaurant hung with red paper lanterns, and fish and chips wrapped in a newspaper. We went to pubs where a head of foam parted to an amber fluid. Bitter, lager, ale, stout, the words rolled off his tongue with the ease of the beer flowing from the tap. Again and again, I would whisper: Don't stare. But how could he not? He had never seen anything like this before. Pubs you sat in and drank, men and women together…

Even the downs were ups. We timed our baths so we could stretch the hot water. We kept a log so we knew when the occupants of the two other bed-sits used the bathroom and we could race in before they did. We took turns to be electrocuted, our word for the moment when we slipped into bed and the sheets came alive with static and caught our skin with a little hiss. The toast burnt on one side. The sash window jammed. But we laughed it all off and sought each other again and again.

We were still Damayanti and Nala, trying to make a new life. Our future was uncertain but our love was insatiable. Our life was the first scene of the second day's play.

Then I went to work and the serpent sank its fangs into him.

Koman

For twelve years, Nala and Damayanti lived in perfect happiness. Their love knew no impediments. Meanwhile, for twelve years the spirit of Kali, the evil one, waited in a tree, looking for a chance to wreak havoc in Nala's life. Finally Kali found his moment. He instigated Nala's brother to invite Nala to a game of dice. The wager was the kingdom.

That day Nala forgot to wash the heel of his feet as he performed his evening ablutions and Kali found an entry into Nala's system. There Kali crouched and waited.

Nala played and lost his kingdom. It was Kali who controlled the fall of the dice. So Nala was exiled and the people of the kingdom were forbidden to help him. 'Go home to your parents,' Nala pleaded with Damayanti.

She refused. 'My place is with you. Where you go, I will.'

So Nala and Damayanti went to the forest. They had nowhere else to go. In the forest, when hunger dragged their feet, Nala decided to try and snare a few birds using his clothes as a net. But the birds flew away with his clothes. Damayanti had to tear off a piece of her sari to help him hide his nakedness. Nala insisted again that Damayanti return to her father's kingdom. But she refused. So, in the middle of the night, Nala stole away. He hoped that Damayanti would have no recourse but to go to her father's kingdom. Nala settled into a life of wandering.

One day he saw a forest fire sweep through the trees. He saw clouds of black smoke and the carcasses of birds and animals burnt in the fire. He saw trees singed and ash flying in the air. He saw a serpent, trapped in a ring of fire, screaming for help in a human voice.

Nala rushed to rescue the serpent and the serpent sank its fangs into his heel. 'You have behaved true to your type, haven't you?' Nala hollered. 'Is this how you repay me for rescuing you? By biting me?'

The serpent said, 'I did you a favour. You might not think so now, but trust me, you will see for yourself soon.'

And Nala saw that instead of dying of the snake's venom, he had turned into an ugly dwarf with a muddy complexion and a limp. 'Look at me. Do you call this a favour?'

The serpent replied, 'First of all, the evil Kali who lived within you is writhing and dying of the venom. He will not be able to addle your brains any more. The way you are, no one will recognize you. Retrieve all that you lost. Start all over again. From now on, you will be the architect of your own fate.'

In my little house by the river, I was content. I did not desire anything from life, or art. So who planted the thought in my mind that I wanted more? When did Kali creep into me?

It had to be Kali, or would I have gambled the way I did? I had hoped that I would emerge from this snarl. The gods would help me. My destiny wouldn't fail me. Our love, like Nala and Damayanti's, would sustain us.

But I forgot that Nala was transformed into Bahukan. He had to lose all he had and be diminished. Nala as Bahukan would never know a night's sleep. What he would know was humiliation and heartbreak, countless recriminations and a complete corrosion of self-worth. All along, there hovered in the air the serpent's rider: you are the architect of your own fate.

I looked at the clock. Ten minutes to go. Outside, the light had almost faded. It was twilight and I had to clean up before Angela returned. I took my shirt off and went to the kitchen sink. I splashed water on my face and underarms. I sat on the counter and washed my feet at the kitchen sink. The first time Angela saw me do this, she was horrified. 'What are you doing?' she asked.

'My evening ablutions,' I said, washing the heel of my foot carefully.

'You can't do it in the kitchen sink. It isn't hygienic…This isn't Shoranur, Koman. This is London. You can't do such things here.'

I stared at her. How dare she use that tone of voice, I thought.

'I can't not do my ablutions,' I said.

'Then go to the bathroom.'

She knew as well as I did that there was no telling if the bathroom would be free when I wanted it. But I didn't want to start another argument, so I simply did what I had to before she reached home.

What she didn't know wouldn't bother her, I told myself.

I heard Angela's step on the stairs. I switched on a smile and waited for the key to turn. She came in, taking her outdoor things off even as she stepped in. 'Hello, darling,' she said. 'It's foul outside. It's so snug and warm in here. Mmm, I smell toast.'

I mouthed the words as she spoke them. I had heard them repeated so often. I kissed her as she had taught me to. Then I let the familiarity of the routine lead us along.

'Did you go out?' she asked me a little later.

I nodded.

'Is that a yes or a no?' She frowned.

I looked at her. Once she comprehended every move of my body. Now she couldn't read a nod from a shake. How could I blame her? I didn't understand all that she said, either. The words sounded different, the sibilants seemed to hiss all the time. I thought of my students who tried to imitate her speech, making garbled noises; sometimes these days, I felt that way. All I heard were garbled sounds.

'Koman, you are drifting off. I asked, where did you go?'

'I went out to fetch some bread and milk,' I said. I knew she would be upset.

'That's it! You only went as far as the Patels' shop near the tube station? What's wrong, Koman? Why don't you walk around, explore the neighbourhood? You have the A to Z and I showed you how to use it. You can't stay in here all day. What do you do all day?' Angela's voice was shrill with exasperation.

I didn't say anything. What could I tell her? That I went to the Patels' shop for the occasional whiff of familiar smells from the kitchen? Because their faces looked like the faces I knew? That I understood what they said and they understood when I spoke? As I hovered around there, watching Mr Patel count on his fingers and his wife in a sari, with a cardigan over it, murmur to her husband, I felt more in touch with reality than I did anywhere else.

'Did you manage to get through to Ram Gopal?' I asked.

'I left a message on the answering machine. He is out of the country and should be back soon,' she said. Her eyes didn't meet mine. For the past five weeks, Angela had offered me the same lie in various forms. I knew her well enough to know she was lying.

'How long can we go on like this?' I asked her. 'I feel so bloody useless. It is not right that you work and I sit at home doing nothing.'

'It isn't for long. He will be back one of these days. Do you need any money?' she asked.

I shook my head. Then, afraid that she would read it as yes, I said, 'No.'

'Is there anything good on TV?' she asked.

'I don't know,' I said.

'Don't you even watch TV while I am gone?'

I was silent. In those first few days, I watched TV all day. I didn't have to understand what I was watching; it was enough to see life unfolding before me. One evening, she came back vexed. I didn't know what the reason was: crowds in the tube, a shoe heel that had snapped, or perhaps a frustrating day at work. She said, 'Aren't you lucky to stay at home and watch TV all day while I...?' And then, realizing the import of what she had said, she tried to brush it off with a laugh. 'Don't you tire of watching that thing?'

I didn't blame Angela for how she felt or what she said. I could see that she was trying very hard to make things work. She had every right to feel imposed upon. I felt like a parasite more than ever. I stopped watching TV.

There was a long silence that stretched between the time she got home and bedtime. She lit her incense sticks and put her LP of Ravi Shankar on. I knew every scratch and hiss on the record by now. From some recess of memory, I heard Aashaan say : 'Every morning, look into the mirror and say—I won't be supercilious. Kathakali is my life, but others have a right to live their lives as they see fit. You can't be immune to ordinary feelings. Do you hear me? Koman, there is life beyond kathakali. The sooner you accept that, the better it will be for you.'

I would have liked for us to talk. For her to tell me about her day. But all she wanted to do was close her eyes and sway to the music. It occurred to me that we hardly conversed any more. We had nothing left to say to each other.

I wanted to talk to her about the dance performance we had been to at the Queen Elizabeth Hall last week with a group of her friends. I had never seen a performance by this particular Indian dancer, and was eager to. Perhaps after the performance, I could go backstage and chat with her, I thought. It would be nice to make a contact in the dancing world here.

I sat there appalled. I had never seen anything as bad as this. My first-year students had a better sense of rhythm and more dexterity in fashioning their mudras. I watched her make a mess of all the rules of natya shastra. And I wondered what it was about this mediocre performer that made it possible for her to get so far, while I still hadn't been able to find a way to resume dancing again.

For the first time in many years, I knew self-doubt. Was it that I had no talent? Was it that my artistry didn't rise above the ordinary? Or, was there something that I lacked? In this great big city, wasn't there one person who would understand my work and invest their faith in it?

I'd like to have told Angela all this.

We went to bed. She was tired and fell asleep quickly. I waited for her breathing to settle. Then I rose and went to sit on the armchair. The room was warm, but I couldn't sleep. What am I doing, I asked myself over and over again. There was a time when I knew who I was. Everyone in the world of kathakali knew of me and my artistry. And now what did I have? In this place where I knew no one and had nothing to do, I waited all day and night for something to happen. All those years of studying and practising, all those years of honing my art, none of it had any meaning now. Moved by an impulse, spurred by greed, I had chosen to give up all I had, to chase a shadow. What had I done?

Angela was asleep. I looked at her. The love I had for her was tinged with resentment and something else. She had brought me to this; she had isolated me from all that I was familiar with. My family, my home, my art. It occurred to me that this was perhaps how she had felt in my little house by the river. But there was more to it. I felt beholden to her. I depended on her for everything and I did not like to feel beholden. I was a kept man who had been robbed of everything, including my dignity.

I wished she would be angry. I wished she would say something. Instead, she chose to be kind. She settled all the bills without my even seeing one. She left money around so I could buy cigarettes without asking her for a handout. She brought airmail forms and put them on the table so I could write home to my family. She bought Bolts curry paste and condiments so I could cook food that was familiar to my palate. She bought books and magazines so I had something to read. She took our clothes to the laundromat and folded them in neat piles. She took good care of me, as if I were an invalid. As if I were an old and incapacitated man. I felt stripped of everything, my pride, my maleness and virility. I was Bahukan now. Shrunken, useless and impotent.

I went back to bed. She nestled into me. She wanted to make love. I felt removed from all such feelings. Love. Lust. Passion. All I could feel was a sense of loss. But I had to husband her in bed if not in life. That was the least I could do for her.

I remembered how, in the little house by the river, she once said to me, 'Koman, what is the rush? Haven't you heard of foreplay?'

'Foreplay?' I had teased her then. 'We'll save it for the time when I can't get it up.'

For a moment, I wondered if I would ever have an erection again. I pleasured her as perhaps a eunuch might—with fingers and tongue. Later, when she lay curled on her side and I felt more ineffectual than ever, I asked the night: How long can this go on?

In the morning Angela said, 'Darling, you must get out. You can't stay cooped in here all day. Why don't you go to Leicester Square? Or the National Gallery? It's free.'

I didn't say anything. She laid her hand on my shoulder. 'Surely you are not still upset by what happened at James's house? That was horrible and completely unusual. Things like that don't happen here. This isn't the American south.'

I tried to smile and reassure her that I had put it out of my mind, but my lips refused to stretch. All I could come up with was a grim parody of a smile.

Ten days after my arrival, Angela went back to work. I went out during the day; I wandered through the streets, sitting on a bench when my legs ached, pausing to stare at buildings. When it rained, if a department store was nearby, I would walk through countless aisles, marvelling at the merchandise. I didn't feel the need to buy any. Just looking glutted me. And punctuating my day was the call I made to Ram Gopal. I still hadn't given up hope.

Every day I heard a woman's voice say, 'He is unavailable. Can I take a message?'

The first few days I left a message. 'Would you tell him that Koman called? I am a kathakali dancer from Shoranur. I would very much like to meet him. I can be reached at…' And I would give Angela's telephone number and her name.

Once she said, 'Please hold on, I think he is here.' A few minutes later, she came back on the line saying, 'He is in a practice session and can't be disturbed. Would you please call back later?'

When I did try again, I got the stock answer. 'He is unavailable.'

I was undeterred. He was a famous man and it was natural for him to be busy. I would reach him one of these days. That weekend, we were going to James's house in the country. James was Angela's godfather. He was a stockbroker who had retired to the country.

'You will see the real English countryside,' Angela said happily. 'You will love it, Koman.'

In the train, I saw the landscape change and felt a swelling of joy. The bleakness that was settling on my soul seemed to lift.

James and his wife Anne were kind. They asked me countless questions. They had both been to India. But never to the south, they said. 'We went to Rajasthan and Delhi. Then we drove to Agra to see the Taj Mahal and we went up to Kashmir, too. It was very beautiful; we have such fond memories of India.'

Later that evening, Angela and I strolled through their rather extensive garden. In the distance I could hear a sound. A hollow, cupping sound. 'What is it?' I asked Angela.

'Someone is playing tennis,' she said.

She went back inside and I walked around, looking at the trees. It was getting cold but I was reluctant to go back in. I felt as if I was back in a world I could understand. I examined the trees and plants; felt the leaves between my fingers and dug my fingers in the soil. Eventually the chilly night sent me in and I walked in to hear James on the phone. 'Oh no, he is a friend. A friend of my god-daughter's. They are visiting. They are here for the weekend. Thank you for calling. Thank you very much indeed. Of course, I do understand.

One must look out for one's neighbours. No, no, not at all. Thank you. Good night.'

'What is wrong?' I asked.

'Nothing at all.' James wouldn't meet my gaze. He was embarrassed. 'A neighbour called. They were a little concerned. They said there was a stranger in the garden. That is all.'

That night I asked Angela, 'Do neighbours here do that sort of thing all the time?'

She flushed. 'Well, this isn't London and they are not used to Indians, so they tend to be suspicious.'

'So it is because I am not white...' Perhaps it was then that I felt Bahukan's hues settle on me. I held her hand alongside mine. Hers was creamy. Mine, in contrast, was muddy. Coffee with a cloud of milk. 'Angela, tell me, does it make a difference to you? My colour?'

It became colder and colder and I knew a reluctance to step outside. I would rather stay indoors huddled under the blankets, living off tea and toast, than go out. What was there to see anyway, or do, I thought. Like a refrain, a voice in my mind asked: What are you doing here?

Without Angela I felt naked and unprotected. I was prepared to do whatever she wanted, as long as she went with me. It made her furious. 'I am not your mother, Koman,' she said. 'You can't cling to me. You were never like this. I thought you were the most self-sufficient person I knew. What has happened to you?'

I would look at her and say, 'I hate it here. What am I doing here? I am just living off you.'

'Oh, don't say that. Something will work out soon, you will see. I am trying to arrange an appointment with an agent. Though, with kathakali, I can't decide if I should speak to an agent who works with dancers or actors. If an agent would take you on, you would at least have your foot in the door. You can't give up in just a few weeks' time,' Angela would say and that evening we would go out together 'to take you out of this gloom you have sunk into' as she put it.

Now I looked at Angela and the concern in her eyes. 'I will leave in a little while,' I told her. 'I will go out. I promise.'

I went to Trafalgar Square. The pigeons descended. I saw their red-rimmed eyes and felt enraged at their ability to swoop and fly and do as they pleased. I looked around. There wasn't anyone on the side where I was. I raised my leg and kicked at a pigeon. My shoe made fleeting contact but it was enough. I felt alive. Around me the pigeons rose, flailing their wings.

I felt my desperation lessen. Slowly I felt a new sense of purpose gather in me.

I went back to the bed-sit and searched for the address my father had given me. 'He is not a dancer or even remotely connected with the arts. But his father tells me that he has a good job there. He works in a hotel and if you ever need anything, he will help. His father has already written to him about you.'

I called the number. 'Damu, this is Koman,' I began. The next day I went to see him. Damu worked at Kandaswamy's, the most famous Indian restaurant in London. 'I can find you a job in the kitchen. It will be temporary, but maybe later we can see what can be done. Will you want to do something like that? It is a menial job...not what you are used to...'

I smiled. How appropriate, I thought. Bahukan, after he left the forest, became a menial in King Rituparna's service. He was his cook and charioteer. It was befitting that I become a menial.

'Right now, I will take anything. All I ask is that you don't tell your father. It would break my father's heart to know I am working as a porter in a restaurant,' I said quietly.

Damu sighed. 'You don't have to tell me. I understand. This is the conspiracy that we have to keep alive so that in our homes back in India, they don't bemoan what we have been reduced to doing. You don't have to work as a menial washing dirty dishes and sweeping the floor, my father and yours would say. Come back home and I'll ensure that your belly is full three times a day. It is hard to explain to our families. There is no dignity of labour there, that is the truth.'

I worried what Angela would say. But she didn't seem to mind. 'It is not for long anyway,' she said, closing the wardrobe door with a movement of her hip. It won't be for long was a myth that Angela liked to perpetuate.

Our lives began to unravel. My hours were different from hers and we seldom saw each other. I left money on the table, now that I had some, for her to pay some of the bills with and she left me notes to find. We were merely room-mates sharing a bed. Strangely enough, I found fulfilment at Kandaswamy's. I was busy all day and had very little time to spare, but I knew the satisfaction of being seriously occupied.

One evening, the chef joined me for a smoke in the backyard. We talked about food and dishes from Tamil Nadu. He was from Madurai. I told him about growing up in Nazareth. His eyes mellowed with nostalgia. 'I need an assistant. Do you want to work for me?' he asked.

'Why?' I asked. 'You know nothing of me. Not even if I can cook.'

'It is enough for me to know how a man views food. You see it as I do. The rest you will learn as you go along.'

Bahukan wrought miracles in the kitchen. There was none to match his culinary skills. I learnt to cook and in time I was even able to contribute three new dishes to the Kandaswamy menu. They were called K's Enna Kathrikai, K's Ulli Theeyal and K's Fish in Buttermilk Stew. The K stood for Koman but it was usually interpreted as Kandaswamy's. I didn't mind. I was happy enough to be doing something even if it wasn't kathakali.

It was almost three months since I had arrived in London. I was yet to make any contact with the world of dance or performing arts. Angela still continued to cling to the hope that I would resume dancing some day. I didn't. I had stopped thinking about it. I thought about going back, but the humiliation of admitting that I hadn't been able to achieve what I had set out to do stopped me. More than ever I feared the mockery waiting for me at the institute.

It was the first week of December and my day off. Angela arrived early saying, 'We are going to a party tonight. Helen is back in town and someone she and I know is having a little party for her. And guess what, Helen knows someone who knows Ram Gopal. So maybe now you will finally get to meet him.'

I didn't say anything. I didn't have much hope left. But it would be nice to go out with Angela.

It was the first house I was going to, in London. An old red-brick house with a little walled garden. Angela's friend, a writer, picked us up in his car. Angela sat in the front passenger seat and talked to him. I sat at the back, trying to keep track of where we were going. Her voice was the kind she used when talking to people like her. The regime of the garbled sounds, I thought.

'He is a dancer,' she told everyone.

I whispered in her ear, 'I haven't danced in the last three months.'

'That doesn't matter,' she snapped.

'Why don't you say I work in a restaurant? Are you ashamed of what I do?'

She glared at me and switched on a smile for someone she recognized.

I turned away, with the beginnings of a headache. The room was warm and filled with too many people and scents. There was incense burning and Ravi Shankar's sitar in the background.

I walked away and went into the kitchen for a glass of water. There was a woman sitting at a table. 'Hello,' she murmured.

I poured myself a glass of water. 'Don't you want to join the party?' I asked. Then I realized that she was the hostess. 'You have a nice house,' I said, trying to dispel the awkwardness. 'Nice party, too.'

She smiled. 'You don't have to be polite. My husband is the artist. They are all his friends. I really don't know any of them. I am a nurse, you see. And my feet are killing me; I stand all day at work and I didn't want to stand again all evening. I am giving my feet some rest. The party will go on without me.'

I took a sip of the water and sat opposite her. 'I work in a restaurant and stand all day, too. I think I will give my feet some rest as well.'

'I heard someone say that you are a dancer. Do you have ballet in your country?' she said.

I ran my fingers through my hair. It felt coarse and dry. A few days after I arrived, Angela had asked that I stop using hair oil. 'The smell is rather strong and you know it puts people off,' she had said.

'But you didn't mind it there?' I said. What else didn't she like about me, I thought and threw my hair oil away. All I wanted to do was please her.

'No, I don't dance the ballet,' I said. 'It is something else. It is called kathakali.' I looked away and said, 'I used to be a dancer. I haven't danced in three months.' Her eyes were sympathetic and I found myself telling her everything.

'It is a pity that you are wasting your talent,' she said. 'It is rather sad, too. You should go back. People make mistakes. There is nothing wrong in admitting you made one. But to continue making a mistake when you know it is one, now that is wrong.'

I saw Angela through the doorway. She was laughing with her head thrown back. I couldn't remember when I had last seen her laugh. And I realized that our life as a couple had destroyed all that had once drawn us together.

She was looking into the man's eyes. It was the writer who had brought us here. Her face was rosy and flushed. He touched her cheek with the tip of his finger. Her eyes gathered his gaze. I thought, if they aren't lovers yet, they will be soon. I went back into the room and walked towards Angela. Helen stopped me and pushed a glass into my hand. 'Hang in there, everything will be all right,' she said. She was already drunk. 'Didn't Angela tell you? My friend is going to speak to Ram Gopal.'

I glared at her. I realized I was tired of all the pretence. Angela pretending that I would dance. I pretending that all was well between us.

'Helen, don't bother,' I said. 'I don't think I will ever dance here in London. All we are doing is play-acting that nothing is wrong. Angela knows it and so do I. Do you know that I work in a restaurant these days? I don't mind. I even enjoy it. But I am a dancer and there is no place in this life I lead here for dance. My kind of dance,' I snarled. 'No matter how hard Angela and I may pretend to each other, I made a mistake coming here and I just wish she would accept that.'

I heard the silence in the room. Helen tried to fill it up with a laugh and banalities. 'Don't we all make mistakes? Life is a mistake.'

I put down my glass in disgust and touched Angela's elbow. 'I am leaving. Do you want to go with me?'

Angela

We did not talk in the tube. When we reached the bed-sit, I flung open the door and turned on him furiously. 'You humiliated me in front of my friends.'

'Friends! You call that pretentious lot your friends? They are disgusting. I am sick and tired of people like them. Pseudo artists and no more. How can you even bear to be with them?' he said.

'You think you are such a great artist, don't you? What you are is a bloody liability and an embarrassment,' I said. I stopped abruptly, covering my mouth. What had I done?

Koman

I steeled my face to show no emotion. There was no room for me to walk away into. There was no place for me to retreat to. All I had was my face to hide behind.

That night I couldn't sleep. I thought of Nala in the forest.

Nala who lies awake while Damayanti sleeps. Nala who eases her head off his feet and slips away into the night. She doesn't deserve to suffer for my sins, he tells himself as he creeps away. In her father's kingdom, she will be cherished again. She will have food to eat and clothes to wear, gardens to walk in and the softest of beds to sleep in. She will know happiness again.

Nala wasn't thinking straight. He was crazed with unhappiness and guilt. All he wanted was to be left alone. Even Damayanti, the love of his life, was a burden, a reminder of his worthlessness. So Nala wandered through the forest, railing against the gods, 'Who will ever worship you again if this is what you do to people like me who have invoked your name diligently, observed fasts and penances, made offerings and performed sacrifices?'

As time passed, it occurred to Nala that perhaps even gods are not above the machinations of destiny. And he felt a calm descend upon him. All that was left for him to do was seek their help again: Please help my wife find her way home. Please do not let me go insane with grief. Please do not let anyone know of my acts of cowardice. Please, oh gods, please.

I thought, there in that cramped room, I will never escape the roles I am condemned to play. I will be both the ineffectual Nala and the twisted Bahukan. I am a liability and an embarrasment. If I go back to my little house by the river, however, I will break free of this curse. I will be who I was, once again.

Shaantam

So we arrive at the ultimate expression in the navarasas. Shaantam. How do we depict peace? What do we school our features into? Shaantam is not a face devoid of expression. Shaantam is not the absence of muscle movement. Shaantam is not turning yourself into a catatonic being.

To understand what we need to do, we must first decipher what Shaantam is.

Is it the stillness of the hour before dawn in a summer month, when a thin line of light appears on the horizon? The sky is devoid of all movement and so is the earth. The birds are still asleep and even the breeze is reined in by the heat that waits. There is a stillness to that hour that you can learn from. Rein in all thoughts. Calm your mind. Feel the stillness within your being.

It is not the stillness of sleep. Which is why I suggest you watch the charamundi. Do you know it? The grey heron that lives by the river, with its thin, scrawny legs, grey back, slender snake-like neck and dagger-sharp, straight beak. It is the king of water birds because, unlike other water birds, it does not stalk its prey. Instead, it waits knee-deep in water without a flicker of movement or emotion. The grey heron is stillness personified while it waits.

So you see, there can be stillness that is alive. The mind works but the thoughts must be like the palmyra fruit.

Why the palmyra fruit, you ask?

Shaantam is a discipline. Think of the purplish black cannonball-like shell of the palmyra. It does not let anything permeate it. And even if something does manage to, it has to be filtered through the fibre. That is how your mind must be. As for your thoughts, look at those little sheathed sacs nestling in the fibre. You peel them with your fingernails and then you see it: soft and tender, the fruit glistens, devoid of almost all odour or taste. Translucent as ice, the fruit is the epitome of shaantam. Alive, there and yet not there.

That is Shaantam. Detachment. Freedom. An absence of desire. A coming to terms with life. When all is done, that is what we all aspire to. Shaantam.

Radha

I feel a core of calm reside within me. All the passion I burnt with, the contempt I felt for my life, all the sorrow I knew for chances wasted, the anger I felt at being trapped in an existence so stifling, the fear of what lay ahead, the disgust I felt for myself, the yearning, the deceiving, the worrying, the aching…the whirling, twisting chaos has settled into this quietness that floods me.

I think of Shyam. I see him sitting on the toilet seat, his head in his arms and tears in his eyes. I knew then that he knew about Chris and me. All along, when I lied and deceived and lay in Chris's arms and he in mine, I hadn't ever felt that I was committing a crime. When we made love, wanton abandoned love, there was no shadow of betrayal. But I cannot erase from my mind the sight of Shyam as I saw him that night. Everything that I think he has put me through is outweighed by what I have turned him into. A broken man, hurt and humiliated, and I know that it is I who have caused him such anguish. The extent of my callousness frightens me.

I have no love left for Shyam. That I cannot love him, I can live with. But I have robbed him of his pride. How could I have done that to him? It was cruel. Far worse than the fact that I had never loved him.

I must spare him his pride, I think. I must leave him at least his dignity.

I am racked by guilt but I am also racked by the thought that this love affair of mine is no more than an act of defiance.

Do I really think I can make a life with Chris? What do I know of him except that our bodies respond to each other and that at first, when we were together, the rest of the world ceased to exist? Once this was enough. Not any more.

Now when I am with Chris, I look at him and wonder if I know him at all. And I ask myself, what am I doing here with him? The passion is spent and there is little else.

Adultery, I assumed, dragged itself into murky places. Hotel rooms and box beds, bathrooms with dripping faucets and bed linen that wore bleached spots of previous assignations. Stolen kisses and clandestine couplings. Cars with tinted, rolled-up windows and dingy movie theatres.

In my mind adultery's beast was lust. A creature that stretched its claws, ran a pointed rosy tongue over its lips and draped itself on a vantage spot. When lust pounced on you, it tore away every inhibition, every ligament of restraint away. The fuck was filled with the unholy C of cocks and cunts; defying, daring, draining all that was decent and illuminated, allowed and unsullied. All of it stank of stealth and the forbidden. All of it was accompanied by a beating heart and countless whisks of a lying tongue.

My love was none of this, I had thought. My love was neither murky nor rank. My love rose above the sludge of conventional adultery. My love was born in a perfumed garden where fireflies and stars stood vigil. My love lived in a room where curtains billowed and the breeze blew. My love grew amidst music and words, and a thousand buds. How could such a love be dismissed as squalid or vile, I told myself.

Yet, when I think of Chris, what I see is the shadow of Shyam. And when I think of Shyam, what I see is the possibility of escape with Chris.

I know for certain that I cannot live with one or the other.

I go to see Chris one last time, to reassure myself that I know what I am doing. Is it possible that someone who impelled me to take such wild risks and shed my fears and inhibitions, can leave me cold now? How can it be that all the passion, the dreams, suddenly mean nothing?

He is talking, but I hear nothing of what he is saying. I see his lips move and the expression change in his eyes. I see the smile that once caught at my throat. When I look at him, my heart stays in its place. There is no answering chord. There is no leap, no flash in the dark.

He is trying to tell me what I already know. 'I know. Uncle told me,' I tell him. 'Why weren't you honest with me?' I ask.

He flushes. 'How could I ask him if he was my father?'

'Is he?'

'I don't know yet. My mother and he were lovers. That much I know.'

I rise to leave. I realize that there's nothing left to say.

'How does it make a difference to our relationship?' he asks. I think it would be kinder to let him think that his revelation has changed things between us.

'It does,' I say. 'You deceived me. I thought we had no secrets. I thought I knew everything about you. What else have you kept from me? Is there a wife, perhaps? A child?'

I mouth clichés. This is the grand denunciation act.

He is appalled. 'You can't be serious,' he says.

'Believe me, I am,' I say. 'I never want to see you again.' One more cliché.

It works. I think of what Shyam once told me: Clichés are clichés because they are true. They are guaranteed to work, no matter how often they have been used before.

'This is ridiculous,' he says.

I leave the room. I dare not look back.

One time when were together, Chris took out a metronome. 'It's old. I need to wind it like a clock,' he said and showed me how it worked.

Then he set it again and said, 'This is the slowest this metronome can go. Forty oscillations to a minute. We have about eight minutes before it will wind itself down and so that is all we have...three hundred and twenty oscillations. Ready?' His eyes had glinted and his mouth swooped.

When the metronome stopped, our rhythm had too, and there was an odd silence. An absence of all movement and time. Everything stopped—the heaving and panting, the moans and sounds that emerged from his throat and mine, the beads of sweat, bodily fluids, skin against skin. It is this silence that resounds in my head. Our need for each other had wound itself out.

An act of defiance for me; an interesting encounter for him. Loneliness and a funnelling need that had exploded into unbridled passion. That was all it was. And as is the nature of such things, it died as it was born. Abruptly.

I walk into the reception area. Shyam is in the office. We left home together. When I said I was going with him, he didn't comment. I was prepared for his anger. His silence terrifies me.

I go into his office. He looks up from his files. 'You were with Chris,' he says. It is a statement, not a question.

'Yes,' I say.

He continues to look at me. His face doesn't reveal what he is thinking.

'Shyam,' I say. 'I am leaving.'

'Shashi is outside. Send him back,' he says, turning back to his files.

'Shyam, you don't understand.' I shake my head. 'I am leaving you, Shyam.'

The pen in his hand falls on the page with a soft plop. 'I suppose I must be thankful that you had the decency to tell me instead of running away with Chris.'

'No,' I say. 'I am not going with Chris.'

He fiddles with a paperweight. 'But you are pregnant.'

I stare at him. How does he know? I suppose I shouldn't be surprised. Shyam feels compelled to monitor my entire life, including my menstrual periods.

'Yes,' I say. 'But it makes no difference.'

'A child needs both its father and its mother.' His voice is quiet.

'I will never deny you your parental rights. You can see the child, spend as much time as you want, but I cannot live with you any more, not even for the child's sake.'

'The child isn't mine,' he says. 'I can't father a child. Not unless it is assisted. I am not your child's father.'

His words boom inside my head.

I sit down on the chair. I feel a churning within. What have I done, I think. Why hadn't it ever occured to me that Shyam could be sterile?

'What can I say?' I hear myself tell him. 'I am sorry. I didn't mean to hurt you. I didn't mean to put you through any of this.'

'Listen,' I add, 'I don't need anything. The house, the business, my property, you can keep all of it.'

His face is grim. 'Don't insult me, Radha.'

'Shyam,' I say. I reach across to touch his hand.

He shakes me off. 'I don't need anything. I can't be bought. Your father was the same. He thought he could buy me and now you are doing the same. I am not to be bought. Do you hear me? All I ever wanted was for you to love me.'

'But the house,' I try again. I know how much he loves the house. I think of what it must have cost him to confess his sterility. I think of the hurt I have caused. I think of him waiting for me to start loving him. I wish to absolve myself of the guilt I feel.

'Yes, the house,' he cuts in. 'I'll send someone to your house to fetch my things.'

He looks at me. There is sorrow in his eyes. 'Will this make you happy? To free yourself from my clutches? It suits you to think of me as the uncouth, tyrant husband. Perhaps it is best then that we separate. All I wanted was a chance. I loved you. I loved you more than anything in this world. That was all I hoped for from you. Your love. If I showed you how much I loved you, I thought you would…it doesn't matter,' he says, stopping mid-sentence.

Love me as I need to be loved. He doesn't say it. But I read it in his voice. In the resignation that is beginning to dawn in his eyes.

'I have left Shyam,' I say.

Uncle's expression is hard to read. 'So you have decided to go with Chris,' he says.

I shake my head. 'No, Chris and I…' I am unable to speak the words. Have nothing in common? Have drifted apart? Have severed ties?

'It is over,' I say.

Uncle shakes his head. 'What have you done, Radha? What have you done?'

I don't say anything.

'Have you told Chris about the child?' he asks suddenly. 'You must.'

'No,' I say. 'I don't want him to know.'

'Why not? He might want to take responsibility for the child if it is his. There are tests to prove paternity, I read somewhere,' Uncle murmurs.

'No.' I shake my head. 'I know who the father of the child is. Chris. Shyam just told me he is sterile.'

'You are being irresponsible. You have left your husband. You don't want Chris. What do you want?' Uncle is angry. I have never seen him angry before.

'I don't know. I really don't. All my life I have stumbled from one thing to another, persuading myself that this is how it should be. I have never behaved as if I have a mind of my own. I have never made a decision. I have let myself be swept along. Isn't it time I assumed some responsibility for my life?'

'What will you do?'

'I don't know. But I will, one of these days.'

Shyam

I let her go because that is what she wants.

I let her go, knowing that if I didn't she would leave me anyway.

I let her go because at that moment I hated her with a savageness that scared me.

Uncle looks at me. She has been to see him, I realize. He greets me as one would a bereaved man. His silence is weighed with pity.

'What do I do now?' I ask him.

'Give her time,' he says.

I stare at him. Is that the best he can come up with?

'No, Shyam,' he says. 'I am not offering you a platitude because I don't know what else to say. She has to sort herself out. She will. Trust me. She is an intelligent woman and a sensitive one. When she has, she will listen to what you have to say.'

'I thought she would go with him,' I say. 'It is his child.'

Uncle looks at his hands. 'She hasn't told him,' he says. 'She doesn't want to.'

'I loved her. I loved her more than I did anything or anyone,' I tell him.

'I know,' he says. 'And now?'

'I don't know.' I am not sure any more how I feel. All I can think of is the hurt that courses through me. And the anger. The humiliation, the betrayal, the despair.

'The Sahiv will be leaving tomorrow,' Unni tells me. 'His tickets have been confirmed.'

I nod.

The night sky is clear. The stars hang low and bright.

I think of what Rani Oppol would say: 'You are well rid of her. At least now you can find a girl who is more suited to you, to us…someone who will be a good wife and bear your children.'

I think of what my employees would say among themselves. "He is well rid of her. She never valued him enough.'

And I think that I know it is true, but I can't bear to be parted from Radha.

I will give Radha the time she wants. I will not force her or ask her for more than she is prepared to give.

I walk towards the wall that banks the river. A breeze rustles through the leaves. The night is bathed in a bluish haze. I look around and feel a swell of pride again. All this is mine, I think.

Peace washes over me. All that is lost, I will regain.

I dial a number on my phone. Padmanabhan's owner comes on the line. 'Will you sell Padmanabhan to me?' I ask.

I hear him suck in his breath. He doesn't speak. Then he says, 'I have a younger elephant. Vasudevan. He is just as handsome.'

'No, I want Padmanabhan,' I say.

'He is expensive.'

'It doesn't matter. I want him.'

We agree to meet next week to discuss the sale. It is an omen, I tell myself. When I have Padmanabhan, my life will be mine again.

Uncle

My fingers tremble as I dial the number. I get a busy signal. I try again. Who are you talking to, Maya?

I feel an overwhelming urge to talk to her. I want her here beside me. I want her to wrap her arms around me and still my thoughts.

'Radha and Shyam. And Chris,' I will say. Only Maya will understand how I feel.

But I get a busy signal again.

I think of my father in the days after Mani's death. I had never seen him so distraught. It seemed to me that my father's will to live had left him. He began to spend more and more time in my house. He would come after I left for the institute and stay there all day. Some days Babu came looking for him. 'Why don't you tell us where you are going, Achan?' he would say angrily. 'We were worried about you.'

My father would hang his head like an errant child, guilty and remorseful. 'I meant to, but I forgot,' he would say.

We noticed the change in him. He couldn't remember what he had eaten for his last meal but he recited whole chunks of the Bible at us as explanation for what he had done or how he felt.

'What is my trespass? What is my sin, that thou hast so hotly pursued after me?' he asked Babu, reverting for a moment to the thundering old patriarch he had always been.

Babu shook his head in dismay. 'What is wrong with Achan?' he asked.

A few days later he would be at my doorstep again. The little house by the river exerted a strange fascination for him. 'It is so peaceful here,' he would say.

'It is,' I would agree. The Nila was in full spate and everything was green and soothing.

'You don't understand,' he said. 'This house has no memories for me.

'"When the unclean spirit is gone out of a man, he walketh through dry places, seeking rest; and finding none, he saith, I will return unto my house whence I came out. And when he cometh, he findeth it swept and garnished. Then goeth he and taketh to him seven other spirits more wicked than himself; and they enter in, and dwell there and the last state of that man is worse than the first." It's from the gospel according to Luke. That is how I feel in that house. Tormented by seven evil spirits.'

'What have I done, Koman?' He turned to me. 'What did I do wrong to see my son die? What could be worse than to know that one son of mine slew the other? Who do I grieve for? The dead son, or the living one who must be racked with guilt? It is better for me to die than to live.'

'You surely don't believe that,' I said. 'Babu might have come to hate Mani, but he wouldn't kill him.'

'I don't know what to believe any more, Koman. All I know is that my sins must be visiting upon my children. Look at you, look at Babu. None of you seem to have coped with the business of life well. I gave you all that you wanted. I stood by everything you did and let you go your way. And yet, none of you have known what it is to be happy.'

'Why do you say that, Achan?' I asked. I wasn't angry at his words but I was perturbed to know he felt such a failure. 'What we do with our lives is no reflection on you. You can't live through us. I do not know about Mani or Babu, but I am happy, Achan. I am truly happy. I am not saying that I haven't known despair or anguish. But I am where I want to be. My art keeps me happy.'

'There is darkness in that house. Too many secrets. I am glad they sent Radha away to boarding school. If she lived here, she too would be tainted by it. I miss my Devayani more than ever now. She alone knew how to calm the restlessness in me. If I were younger, I would go away somewhere. But I am too old to do anything by myself.'

'Where do you want to go?' I asked him.

'I would like to go to Mannapad again,' he said.

So we went to Nazareth. I did not know what it was my father sought there, but we hired a taxi and we traced his life there. The new superintendent had heard about my father but didn't know any of the scandal attached to his name. I began to feel a new respect for my father then. To go back to where he had known both happiness and unhappiness must take a great deal of courage. Where did one source this fortitude to confront one's past?

My father was seeking familiar things, traces of the life he had once lived here. He gazed at the cork tree and said, 'It is still here. Look at it, a foreigner like I was when I first came here.'

James Raj was dead but his family still owned the house by the sea at Mannapad. One of the sons came with us to the house. 'We were so happy here at first, Saadiya and I. It was my fault, of course. She was so young and I left her alone far too long. She was lonely. "She is empty, and void and waste: and the heart melteth, and the knees smite together, and much pain in all loins, and the faces of them all gather blackness. Nahum 2.10."'

I didn't know what to say. I didn't understand what he was saying. Later that night he told me about my mother. The next day we drove past Arabipatnam. 'There lives your mother's family,' he said. I looked at the gates with interest, but I felt nothing more than curiosity. My mother was Devayani. I had no desire to go looking for a phantom mother.

A few days after we returned home, my father died. He had said his goodbyes.

I hear Malini's squawk, then a low voice.

I step out. It is Chris. His face is drawn and his eyes are listless. 'My tickets are confirmed,' he says.

'When do you go?' I ask.

'Tomorrow.'

I wait for him to ask me the question I know he wants to. He doesn't.

I sigh. 'Do you still think that I may be your father?' I ask him.

'I don't know,' he says. He raises his gaze to mine and demands, 'Are you?'

'No,' I tell him. 'Would you have liked that? For me to be your father?'

He smiles. It is a wry smile.

I reach across and take his hand in mine. 'I loved your mother once. I loved Angela as a young man loves a woman. With passion. With an intensity I have never been able to match again. I believe it was the same for her. But that love died. In those last few weeks with her, we barely even touched each other.'

I see the doubt in his eyes. I think of what I told Radha earlier. 'If you still don't believe me, I can do one of those tests they do to establish paternity.'

He doesn't say anything.

He stands up. 'So this is goodbye then,' he says.

'Yes,' I say. I feel a sense of loss. I wonder if I should ask him about the book he is supposed to be writing. 'Tell me,' I would ask, 'is there really such a book or was it an excuse to make me talk?'

I decide against it. I do not want to embarrass him. In these few weeks I have come to feel great affection for him.

'You must send me a copy of the book when it is published. I would like to know how you have portrayed me.'

He smiles. It is that sweet lopsided smile of his.

And I think that is how I would like to remember him. Chris from across the seas. Chris with the cello. Chris with the smile that caressed my soul. Chris who might have been my son.

'Do you have your tape recorder?' I ask.

He pulls it out.

'Leave it here. There is little left to say, but I don't like leaving stories unfinished. I will have it sent across.'

I realize then that I will be relieved to see him gone. The sooner he does, the sooner all our lives will fall into place.

1971 to Now
The Manner of the Resurrection

In the play Kalyanasougandhikam, when Bheema realizes that the old monkey lying across his path is none other Hanuman, his brother, he implores Hanuman to reveal to him the form he took when he flew across the ocean, holding a mountain aloft on his palm.

Hanuman tells him, 'I am not so sure I should. It isn't a form that is pleasing to the eye or acceptable to the mind. It will not be what you think it will be. You may even be terrified!'

Chris, that is how I felt as I revealed my past to you. Is this what you expected? Is this what you wanted to hear? I cannot tell you untruths and couch my life with half lies and shadows to make it more agreeable to you. Like Hanuman, I am honour bound to reveal who I was and who I am, so listen:

I borrowed money from Damu. I would arrange to pay back his father, I said. I left Angela a note. I didn't know what else to do. There was nothing left to say. We had made a mistake and I was doing what I thought was the only decent thing: severing ties so she could go on with her life. She was handcuffed to my side because she thought she had a moral obligation to be with me.

As long as I was here, I would be Bahukan. Never her equal, and smouldering with bitterness. Unlike Bahukan, I didn't have a magic cloth that would retrieve my old self and give me back my pride.

In the airport, on a whim, I tried Ram Gopal's number once again. The great man finally came on the phone. 'Why didn't you call earlier?' he said when I said I was on my way home. 'I am always looking for new talent for my company.'

I wondered if I should tell him about all the abortive attempts I had made. I wondered if I should tell him how I had staked all I had on a slender chance. How I had sold my soul to appease my ego. But none of that mattered now. For the first time, I knew the ordeal was over. I would never again expect my art to propitiate my ego. It was enough that I be allowed to give expression to what I understood of a vesham. All else was immaterial.

When I was a student, there was a story that made the rounds about a kathakali dancer. A famous veshakaaran who turned into a lunatic. Madness ran in his family and his illness was his destiny, his relatives and neighbours said. He was so violent that he had to be chained all day. The physician advocated that they pour a thousand pots of water on his head to cool him down and reduce the intensity of his insanity.

One evening, there was a performance at a temple nearby. All evening the man heard the drumbeats announcing the performance at the temple. He broke his chains and fled to the temple. Behind the temple, in a little makeshift shed, the dancers were getting ready. When he appeared, they didn't know what to do or say.

'What is the katha?' he asked.

'Duryodhana Vadham,' someone said.

'I will be Duryodhana,' he said.

The men looked at each other. What were they to do? The actor who was to have been Duryodhana murmured, 'Humour him and dress him up.'

The pettikaaran said, 'Send for his family to take him home.'

When the time came, the lunatic veshakaaran wrenched apart the hands that held him back, went on to the stage and was Duryodhana. No one knew that this was a lunatic dancing. No one knew that this was a man who was chained all day and who grunted and growled and rolled in his own filth when his madness was at its worst. When the performance was over, he went to sit in a corner. Someone helped him undress. Someone else took him home. But those who saw him that night would never forget his Duryodhana. It was the performance of a man in total control.

It wasn't easy for me to go back to being who I was. I was still shadowed by the memory of what it was like to be Bahukan.

At the institute, the students accepted me back. They were more curious about my life in England than why I had come back. The other instructors, including Sundaran, and my family pretended that I had gone away on a holiday.

I retreated into a place in my head and hid there. All I wanted to do was dance. It was enough. I had no desire to participate in reality. I would think of the story of the lunatic. If within insanity, art could be his sole means of sanity, so it would be for me. Henceforth, my life would be led through my art. It was the only way I would be able to retrieve some of my self-worth.

Most days, in the evening, I sat on the topmost step of the veranda. The dog would lie on the ground, its eyes fixed on my face to catch even a flicker of emotion, its snout edging my foot, content to nuzzle and merely be there.

One evening a breeze rose from the dry river bed, turning sand, raising dust and leaves in its path. Over the deep pool the breeze acquired a beading of dampness so that when it blew into my face, I felt a pleasing coolness. It eroded the density of my thoughts and prodded me to move. I sat up straight and yawned, my body stretching and flexing, the yawn emerging from the concave of my belly and expanding to form a whole set of syllables: aa-ooo-uu. The dog raised its head and watched intently this unfolding of movement, of life. It stood up, tail wagging in salutation and joy.

I saw the dog's tail wag. I patted its head. 'Lie down,' I said. 'I am not going anywhere.'

The dog put its head on its forepaws. Drawing courage from the rare caress, it rose and settled once again on the ground, but with its snout now resting on my foot. I looked at the dog. My eyes met its imploring gaze. Don't push me away, it begged.

For so long now I had felt drained of all emotion. The weight of the dog's snout on my foot, its eyes, stirred in me a tiny squiggle of…what could it be? I dared not ask myself.

I bent and stroked the dog's head. The softness of its fur and the slow mechanical movement of my fingertips caused a trickle of images to wander into my mind. Time spelt in a series of vignettes. Life held within the palm of the hand. Chances that trickled between the gaps of my fingers because I willed it so. Memories and now life experiences. The dog closed its eyes in pleasure. I felt the weight within me rise and slowly dissipate.

The dog raised its head, ears cocked, eyes searching. Someone was coming up the alley. I straightened. Who could it be? I was not inclined to make conversation. I wanted to be alone with my thoughts.

The dog, as if pursuing my line of thought, rose and raced to the gate. It stood there, its feet firmly planted, its hackles raised, barking. A series of powerful barks that rumbled and filled the air with threat: go away, we don't want you, go away, leave us alone.

I stood up. I would go into the house and wait there. Whoever it was would leave after a while. Then I saw her. Lalitha. What did she want?

She stood on the other side of the gate, her hands clasping the latch. 'Call the dog away,' she said.

I whistled. 'Come here; it's all right,' I said softly.

The dog's hackles went down; its tail began wagging. She looked at it with a smile. 'You have trained him well.'

I went to sit on a chair on the veranda. She stood on the bottom step, waiting for me to invite her in. When I didn't, she said, 'I heard you were back. I thought I would see for myself.'

I drew my chellapetti closer. She climbed the three steps and sat on the low wall near me. 'How have you been? When did you get back?'

'Some months ago,' I said. 'Do you want this?' I pushed the betel-nut box towards her. She looked at it for a moment. 'This is a new habit. When did you start?' she asked.

I shrugged.

She opened the chellapetti and took out a few betel leaves.

For a while we both sat there, our mouths full, our minds wandering, chewing on betel leaves and slivers of areca nut, letting common memories stream down our throats.

Then she cleared her throat and stood up.

'Are you leaving?' I asked, suddenly stricken by the thought of being left alone.

'Do you want me to stay?'

I looked at her as if I was seeing her for the first time. Lalitha. That was my name for her. I had forgotten what her real name was.

Lalitha, who in reality could be Nakrathundi, the demoness who fed on lust. No, that was unfair of me. I was no Jayanthan, the guiless youth deceived by her. I had known all along who she was. Which was why I had chosen to call her Lalitha.

'Will you?' I asked, unable to meet her eyes.

She laid her hand on my arm. Conflicting images tussled before me. I tried not to flinch. Nakrathundi or Lalitha: who was she?

And then I thought, does it matter? She was there for me, once. Isn't that enough?

'I am here. All you have to do is ask. You have to ask me to stay,' she said. I could hear the measure of power in her voice.

I had hurt her and she was exacting revenge. Is this what living is all about? This perennial scoring off each other; this seeking of retribution. I sighed. I would have liked to lie in bed and feel her cool, adept fingers slide over my skin, her body pressed against mine. Someone to make slow and practised love to me, so all I had to do was surrender myself.

She would do that. She would hold me against her and let me feed off her. She would do all that and more because that was her trade. To fulfil needs of iniquity. But she had also saved me a place in her being, ever since that first time. That had been my measure of power. No matter how I treated her, she always forgave me.

When I had cast her away and said she shouldn't ever come to my house again because Angela would be horrified if she knew, I had hurt her and now she wanted me to know how precarious my perch was within her.

I would allow her that. I was weary of everything. All I wanted for now was someone to hold me and heal me. 'Stay, please stay,' I said.

I lay on my stomach, my head cradled in my arms. She sat by my side, trailing a finger down my spine. Up and down. Up and down. Again and again. 'It happens,' she said softly.

Outside I could hear the dog snuffling. I heard it sniff around the doorstep, then the soft plop of its body as it collapsed into a heap on the coir mat.

I felt my body sink. It had never happened before. There had been times when I couldn't have an erection but once I did, I always ejaculated. This evening though, I heaved and panted and laboured over my need to find release. It felt as though I was running down a road, a long, endless road, without hope of getting to the end. In disgust, I drew myself out and turned on my side.

I heard her rearrange her limbs. The bed creaked. I turned over and lay on my stomach. Misery. A twisted gut. A muscle pulled. Wanting to feel that blessed release and not being able to. Misery wrapped me in her arms.

I felt her press her fingertips into the dip above my buttocks. 'I love this curve. Only kathakali dancers have it…I love the way the buttocks rise high and taut. Must be all the exercise you people do.' Her fingers slid over the curve and crested the cheek of the left buttock.

I felt a frisson. Angela had said the same thing. I spoke from the corner of my mouth, 'In all these years, you never said that.'

Her fingers paused. 'I haven't said much, have I? Like the fact that…'

'What?' I was curious enough to raise my head.

'Like the fact that you can't fuck with your mind. It is the body's function and you have to let your body fuck. I don't know what's on your mind but you have to let it be.'

I groaned. I didn't want to listen to a lecture on the kinetics of lust.

'You don't agree with what I am saying?'

'Never mind. Go on,' I said.

She bent and kissed the nape of my neck. I felt the beginning of desire again. I slowly turned and lay on my back. Her eyes met mine. She knew what I expected of her. Our bodies had known each other a long time.

She held my gaze and allowed herself the trace of a smile. I read triumph in the gentle elongation of her lips. I was the fly, she the lizard. The thought rolled off my mind. I watched her, curious, detached at first as her tongue darted and snapped, slithered and bounced, cupped and fondled. Then I felt her mouth gather me, drawing away scar tissue I had retreated behind, breaking down my resistance. How simple it is when we know what we want of each other, I thought as she lit the first trails of pleasure.

Lalitha rose to go. Dawn smeared the skies. She opened the door. The dog stood outside, wagging its tail. She patted it on its head.

She looked at me. I was lying on my side, pretending to be asleep. I felt untroubled and serene in my pretence.

'He is lonely,' she told the dog. 'He has no one but you and me. We must look after him, make him whole again, you and I. Will you, dog?'

The dog wagged its tail and moved closer to her. She bent down and scratched its nape. 'Do you have a name at all? Or is that what he calls you? Dog? Like I am Lalitha. Whores and dogs don't need names, I suppose. Our names don't matter. But we do. Dog, do you see that?'

'Lalitha,' I called. 'Who are you talking to?'

'The dog. Don't you have a name for him?' She smiled.

'The dog. That is adequate enough. Dogs don't need names. They will respond to anything you call them.'

'But I can't call him dog. In my neighbourhood there are Kaisers and Jimmies, Brunos and even a few Paandans. I like Kaiser. Why don't you call him that?'

'My students call him Ekalavyan. You can call him that if you insist on a name.' I yawned.

'Is there anything in your life besides kathakali?' Lalitha laughed.

'No,' I said abruptly. 'Once I thought there was. Without kathakali, I am nothing.'

'What about me?' Her eyes were serious.

'You and the dog are the only two living creatures who I can relate to these days,' I said. 'You will have to be content with that.'

She smiled. 'I am.'

There is nothing that time cannot heal. I learnt that as the days passed. I learnt that from my house by the river. And from Ekalavyan and Lalitha. A dog and a whore. Together they broke down the walls I had surrounded myself with. I stopped being a catatonic being who sprang to life only when I wore my colours. I learnt to laugh and suffer; I learnt to delight and complain. I learnt to accept love when I found it. I learnt to be human again.

Two years later, the institute troupe was invited to Europe and we travelled from country to country, dancing our stories of gods and demons. It was ironic that all I had once sought came to me now that I had stopped seeking it.

I was offered a teaching fellowship by a university in Germany. I declined.

'How come you don't want it?' Sundaran asked.

'It won't work,' I said, deciding to be honest.

'How can you throw away chances? How can you be so disdainful of the opportunity you have been given?' he demanded. 'If it had been me...'

'Sundaran, for three months there I will do nothing. Do you call that a great opportunity?'

'But think of after that. You will have become part of the circuit.'

I thought for a moment about 'after that' and shuddered.

'Sundaran,' I tried to explain. 'London was nothing. It came to nothing. I tossed away my life here, thinking I would find a place there, and nothing came of it. Kathakali has no place there. Do you know how long it took me to recoup my losses? Do you know how beaten I was when I returned? Aashaan was right. We need to feel right, here,' I said, touching my chest. 'Only then will we know what it is to be fulfilled. Everything else is just an illusion.'

'You talk such utter nonsense only because you have had everything offered to you on a platter. That is why you have such disregard for it,' Sundaran said. 'I have to make my own destiny, and what can I do or be when I am trapped here in this life? Where is my escape route? You tell me. Now, if I had been the one to go to London, I would have made my way.' Sundaran's bitterness shocked and saddened me.

He was all twisted and tangled inside. I turned my face away. I felt as if I had intruded into a very private and intimate moment. It embarrassed and confused me.

A few minutes later, I knew remorse. Sundaran had once been my friend. 'Aren't you happy that you are dancing so well?'

'What is the point?' Sundaran snapped. He stared at the plate of food before him. 'I am sick and tired of this. I want more. I want fine food and clothes, money in my purse and people to recognize me on the streets. I want all this and more.'

'But kathakali?'

'Oh, don't be so bloody naïve. Kathakali is a means to an end. You don't get it, do you? Aashaan was the same. Which is why there was never any use talking to him. If only I could spend some time here in Europe.' He stopped abruptly.

I saw how much he longed for it and recommended they offer the scholarship to Sundaran. They did, and Sundaran finally had his chance.

He never returned.

I was happy. I was dancing. And I was dancing better than I had ever done. For the rest, I had my little house by the river. I had Lalitha and I had the dog. My little world was complete.

I proposed marriage to Lalitha. 'Why?' she asked.

'I thought you might want to,' I said.

'Do you think I sleep with other men?' she asked.

I didn't say anything.

'I don't. I haven't in a long time. I work in a tailoring shop. I make enough to look after myself. It is best we remain this way,' she said. 'You in your house and I in mine. Besides, this way there is no room for gossip. Can you imagine what would happen if you married me? The scandal! Your family would sever all ties with you.'

I nodded. Babu would never accept Lalitha. 'That doesn't matter,' I said.

'No, Koman. I prefer it this way. I also know that this way you will never tire of me,' she said.

I smiled.

Over the years I went on several trips with the institute troupe. We even acquired a following of sorts.

Some years ago I was in Paris and, on a whim, I took the Metro. As I went down the steps into the station, I saw posters on the wall. I paused and looked at the face. It was Sundaran. He was performing that week in Paris. I asked my host in Paris to go with me for the performance. 'We were together as students and he taught at the institute for several years,' I told Stefan.

I saw Sundaran dance again. He was still handsome, still the elegant dancer. His gestures were graceful, his presence complete. But it wasn't kathakali. It wasn't dance at all. I looked at the programme. It was in French. Stefan translated it for me. 'Dancer Extraordinary. Pundit Sundar Varma. Hailing from a royal family in Kerala, Sundar ran away from his noble ancestry and palatial life when he was twelve, seeking to express himself in a language of gestures and expressions.'

I smiled. Sundaran had reinvented himself. The Sundaran I knew came from a poor Warrier family who thought that by having him enrol at the institute they wouldn't have to worry about feeding him three meals a day. The institute took care of all that. I supposed that when he was giving himself a whole new history, he had thought royal ancestry would lend greater charisma to his reputation. It needed some skill to carry it off. I could see that Sundaran had it. He was a performer extraordinaire.

Stefan read on: Soul of Fear—an exploration of all that is dark and distorted, narrow and incongruous in man…using traditional kathakali techniques…I stopped listening.

I couldn't comprehend the performance. It was pretentious and false. It made a mockery of what we had given most of our lives to. It trivialized it and I felt shame and anger, then relief. If I had stayed on in London, would this have happened to me as well? Would I have compromised in order to survive? Would I have changed the tenor of all that I respected and loved, to make it accessible and popular?

When the performance was over, Stefan wanted us to go backstage and meet Sundaran.

'I have nothing to say to him,' I said.

'You don't approve of him,' Stefan said.

'No, I don't,' I admitted.

Later, Stefan and I went to a café. While we waited for the drinks to arrive, Stefan asked, 'Why? You don't like what he is doing?'

I took a deep breath. Perhaps Stefan thought I was envious of what Sundaran had. That it was resentment that made me reluctant to see him. 'I do not like what Sundaran has turned kathakali into,' I said.

'But it is simpler now. You think that is wrong?'

'Let me tell you something. In India, the most popular form of dance these days is something called cinematic dance. It is a combination of folk and classical, salsa and the twist, aerobics and jive...of perhaps every imaginable dance form, but the boys and girls who dance it don't make it out to be anything but cinematic dance. It is wonderful in its own way, but best of all, it doesn't pretend to be anything but a light form of entertainment.'

I saw the disbelief on Stefan's face. I smiled. 'I know you are surprised. I don't think there is anything wrong with popular art. It demands very little of an audience. Anyone can enjoy it.

'Classical art requires an effort from the audience. You don't become a connoisseur overnight. You need to imbibe it. You need to educate yourself, and it takes time to reach a level where you can understand the artist's interpretation. Naturally, this means the audience is limited and the rewards even more so. So, when I see someone like Sundaran butchering kathakali to ensure greater popularity, to the extent that all that is noble and brilliant and complex about it is removed, I find it repugnant. He is playing to the gallery, providing light entertainment disguised as classical art. It is devious and deceitful, to say the least.'

Stefan sipped his drink slowly. 'You are very hard to please,' he said. 'It is only art after all. Not a matter of life and death. There are no ethics involved. It isn't like cloning or the manufacturing of chemical weapons or even vivisection.'

I smiled. 'You are right,' I said. 'I shouldn't be so hard on him. It is art after all, as you say.'

He peered at me carefully to see if I was being sarcastic.

'No,' I said. 'I wasn't mocking you. I agree. If he can live with himself, who am I to condemn what he is doing?'

Artistic success is a strange thing. In the end, who is the judge? A handful of critics? Since the episode with Nanu Menon, I have moved on and indictments, precise or otherwise, seldom affect me. I see critics as a group of deluded beings who live within a tiny galaxy; anything that doesn't fit within its boundaries and the limits of their knowledge puzzles them. What they do not understand, they either intellectualize or dismiss. Are they the ones I ought to hitch my artistic destiny to?

Then there are the art lovers, capricious people who will go with you if a review does, and cast you aside if a reviewer rejects you. Lovers who make no promises to love or honour you forever. It is a world that chooses to recognize your talent by the trappings of success—fame, money, awards.

Finally, there is the artist, who has to contend with his own standards again and again, despite all that the critics or the world might tell him. Have I been able to rise above all that I have done so far, or have I been merely mediocre?

In the years thereafter, I was to pose this question to myself again and again. How successful was I as a veshakaaran?

Art doesn't make anything happen except for the artist. In fact, art is useless. It has no bearing on real life. I know that as well as all other practising artists do. Art occupies a bare fraction of time in most people's lives. It is a piece of music you listen to as you drive or a book read at the airport, a painting on a wall in a hotel lobby or a flower arrangement at the dentist's clinic. A filler of time and space, a point of diversion and no more. If it is to satiate this meagre need that we slave and reach into ourselves, what chance is there of ever knowing fulfilment? We seek strange pleasures and subversive modes, we thrust away what is there before us and look beyond and there is no knowing whether this quest will mean anything to anyone but us. So, when at times, the ghoul that rides on every artist's shoulder comes to perch on mine and whispers in my ear, 'But no one understands what you are doing', I pat its head and tell it, 'Does it matter? I do.'

After many years of being ignored, I was given my first national award. For years, I was overlooked in favour of lesser, but decidedly more visble and flamboyant artists. It hurt me. I wouldn't be human otherwise. I was still a young man then. An award at that point in my life would have meant a validation of what I had set out to do. But that was not to be.

In my fifty-third year, when I no longer sought or even wanted these tokens of recognition, someone decided that I was to be given a Padma Shri. Suddenly my art, no, I must correct myself, I as an artist, had an audience. An eager and demanding audience. The world seemed to assume that they owned me. More awards followed. I realized with amusement that awards, like invitations to international dance festivals, have a snowball effect. All you need is one to start the ball rolling. I thought of Sundaran. He was right, after all. It was all about being part of a circuit.

All my life was held up for scrutiny. My student years, my relationships, even the memory of my dog and later Malini were dwelled upon. Thankfully, Lalitha was dead by then. Or she would have occupied column space as the harlot muse. All that was good and kind about her, all her nobility and understanding would have been ignored and instead, she would have been given an insidious place in the rooms of my life. She had died of cancer, however, and all they could write was: 'His long-time companion succumbed to cancer even as his star ascended.' I was cast as the solitary and exceptional being whose lover, wife and mistress was dance.

I hugged to myself my secret. For I had Maya. Twelve years ago I stopped at Delhi on my way back from Europe. I had been invited to France for a lecture-dance tour. It had been a hectic three weeks and on my way home I paused for breath. I had a few things to attend to, a few friends to meet. At an art show opening I was taken to, I was introduced to Maya.

I stood there holding a glass in my hand, watching. What am I doing here, I wondered. My friend introduced me to many people, but I barely registered names or faces. I let the alcohol wrap me in a little haze that cut out this world I really had no connection with.

Who are these people, I asked myself.

Everyone there had something to do with the artistic world. Their eyes darted furiously as they looked around to see who was worth cultivating. Smiles came on as if a switch had been pressed, and didn't even reach the eye. Everyone seemed to know everyone else and all of them were either writing a book, or making a short film on peace or terrorism, putting together a one-man show or researching cave paintings, or championing a cause, or just about to leave for some foreign destination as part of a cultural contingent.

I felt a wave of panic. Had I become one of them? Had I become more of a performing animal than an artist, and turned my art into a circus?

I felt disgust and revulsion. All I wanted to do was escape to my little house by the river. So, in the first few minutes of meeting Maya, I dismissed her as yet another of the performing seals and was rude to her. 'So what is it you do? Write? Paint? Dance? Sing? Make films? Save the whales?'

She smiled. 'I wish I did one or all of those. I feel as if I am here on false pretences. Nandini,' she said, pointing to a woman who could only be a dancer, with her jewellery and eye make-up, 'insisted I come with her. I don't live in Delhi. I am just visiting. I am an accountant.'

She had never known a male dancer before. What was it like, she wanted to know.

'I have never known a female accountant before,' I retorted. 'What is it like?'

We laughed. Her laugh made me look at her again. It was a low throaty laugh, suggestive of overcast skies and wet earth. I looked at her carefully. Maya was a voluptuous woman then. Her mind, I discovered, was just as fecund as her body. She was also lonely. Her husband and her family kept her busy, but despite them she was starved for companionship.

We met once more before I left Delhi and talked into the wee hours of the night. 'Will I see you again?' I asked.

'I hope you will. I don't know when I last felt so comfortable with another person.'

I frowned. I did not like the allusion to comfort. Was I an old, familiar pillow?

'Comfortable?'

'That is a compliment, by the way. It means I can tell you what I am thinking. That I don't have to be guarded,' she said.

'I thought compliments ran on the lines of handsome, charming, etc.,' I teased.

'Too many women have been telling you that. I wanted to be different.'

'You are different,' I said, and took her hand in mine. She let it stay there. And I was smitten.

A month later I went to Madras, where she lived. I called her; we met. Inevitably, we became lovers. There was a certain complicity that drew us to each other. In the curves of her body, in the undulations of her mind, I sought a partner who was my equal and she revelled in the love affair. That was all she would allow it to be. An affair of the heart and the body and no more.

Now when I am with her, I understand what she meant so many years ago. I am comfortable with Maya and she with me. I know Shaantam when I am with Maya.

In these last few years, each time I've performed, the auditorium has been packed. And I've asked myself: Have they come here to see my vesham? Or have they come to watch Koman, winner of a national award, perform? Do they wish to see the artist or the celebrity?

Worse, there are those who want me to repeat myself. There is always someone who says, 'Koman Aashaan, I cannot forget the vesham you played at Tripunithara in 1995. Dharamaputran in Kirmira Vadham. I hope we will see you do the same tonight.'

I smile and don't say anything. What does it matter, I tell myself. I will be the character I want to be. I am not going to succumb to pressure of any sort, no matter how flattering. Nothing will change that.

A well-known film-maker has made a short film about me. A journalist attempted what he called a fly-on-the-wall biography. I am invited to perform at every prestigious venue and participate in workshops and seminars. My opinion is solicited and my presence required. There have been many interpretations of my technique and style.

I feel removed from it all. It is of no consequence to me how I am perceived or what the world thinks of me, as a man or a dancer.

What more do I say, except that it is enough that I don my colours. It is enough that I am allowed to slip into the skin of a character.

When I dance, I know who I am.

Epilogue

IT IS HIS LAST EVENING at Near-the-Nila. Chris looks around him to see if he has forgotten anything. His bags are all packed. He hears a knock at his door. For a moment he imagines that it is Radha. His Min-min who has come to say goodbye. His Min-min is here, his heart leaps.

He had called her that morning. Radha came on the line. A Radha he did not recognize. Her voice was measured, her words careful. What went wrong, he asked himself when he put the phone down.

He went to see Uncle then. They had already said their farewells the night before, but Chris thought he had to see the old man again.

'I didn't expect to see you,' Uncle said.

'I had some time to spare,' Chris began. Then unable to pretend any more, he cried, 'Radha. You know about Radha and me, don't you? I don't understand what went wrong. I really don't. I can't accept that she walked out on me because I didn't tell her that my mother and you…'

Chris felt his face crumple. He covered his face with his hands.

He felt the old man's palm caress his hair. 'You must think your family and mine were enemies in our past birth. First I hurt your mother. Now my niece breaks your heart. What can I say, Chris? What can I say to make you feel better? Perhaps it is best that I don't make you feel better. If you are angry, you will hurt less.'

Chris looked up in surprise.

Uncle stood up and went to stand by Malini's cage. 'Philosophers say that love is not to be owned, that you can't possess it, that the moment you try to do that, love will forsake you. For a long time I believed that. Then I met Maya. One part of me said that what we had was sufficient. The other part of me began to feel dissatisfied with the situation. As I grew older, it was this part of me that began to dominate. I wanted Maya to give up her marriage and make her life with me. But the silly part of me which believes that love can't be owned, stilled my tongue. I never asked her to. I expected her to do it on her own. I wanted her to make that decision without my prompting her. When she didn't, I was hurt and even angry with her. It is only now that I realize how foolish I was. How arrogant and cowardly. I wanted to be absolved of all blame.

'When Maya was here, at some point she talked about a life with me. I told her she could live with me. That she was always welcome. But I never told her how much I needed her. It seemed like admitting to a weakness that I might need another person in my life to make it complete. So I hid behind my face. This face that can wear so many emotions except that of a needy man.

'Do you know what I did last night? I called Maya and asked her to come to me. I said—I need you. I want you here with me. I let Maya know how much I need her.

'I don't know what Radha wanted from you. Did you ever ask her? For that matter, did you know yourself what you wanted from the relationship?'

Perhaps it was for the best, Chris thought when he was back in his cottage. In the beginning, he hadn't meant to get so involved. But their relationship had galloped into something he had no control over. Her intensity had been flattering to start with, but it was tiring to have to match it constantly. Their relationship wouldn't have lasted anyway.

Do you really believe that, Chris, a voice in his head asked. A voice that bore the timbre of Uncle's voice. Aren't you running away because she expected more from you than you were prepared to offer?

The muted knock on the door again. It is Shyam.

Chris opens the door.

'There are no taxis available. I will drop you at the railway station,' Shyam says.

Chris cannot meet Shyam's eyes. I haven't done right by you, he wants to tell Shyam. I didn't seduce Radha. I didn't mean any of this to happen. All I came here for was to find the truth, to know if Koman Aashaan is my father. I didn't want to break up your marriage or cause you any harm. I would be lying if I said I wasn't attracted to her. I was. But she could have thrust me away. Instead, she said that your marriage was dead. And sometimes there is little one can do to stop oneself when a woman shows you she is willing. Radha was lonely. Anybody could see that. And Radha was willing. I am only human, Shyam.

He presses down his impulse to confess and seek redemption. Shyam probably doesn't suspect a thing. Would he be here otherwise?

'That's it,' he says, slinging his cello case on his back and picking his bag up.

Shyam watches. 'I never heard you play it,' he says.

Chris looks up, suspecting sarcasm. But Shyam's face is bland.

Shyam waits for the train to arrive. When it does, he waits until Chris has arranged his bags and instrument on the lower berth.

Chris goes to the door. He doesn't know whether he ought to apologize or thank Shyam. In the end, he does neither.

'Goodbye,' Shyam says.

'Goodbye,' Chris replies.

As the train moves, his eyes search the crowd. It feels wrong to go away like this. He thinks of his arrival. The grace of the moment. He feels a wrench. Radha. If he could, he would do it differently. Start all over again so they might have a better chance of keeping their love alive.

But does he really want that chance? The truth is, he doesn't know what he wants.

Chris looks at the landscape for a while. Through the tinted glass, everything is a muddy brown. He can't concentrate on the book he is reading. In the end he takes out the tape and plugs his earphones on.

For now, there is this to look forward to. The story of being Koman.

Shyam climbs up the stairs and pauses at the railway bridge. He stands there gazing at the river.

A thought hurls itself. Shyam feels his feet grow wings as he races down the stairs. Radha, I will say to her, he thinks, this child, your child, will be mine.

Perhaps then she will learn to love him.

Radha sits on her rocking chair, staring at a row of anthuriums. I sent him away, she tells herself again and again. I sent him away. I sent him away. What else could I have done?

She knows a great pang of hunger. She thinks of Chris's unshaven chin nuzzling the line of her throat. She thinks of his smile. How the curve of his lips tugged at her. She thinks of his slow, lazy voice and the inflection he chose to bequeath her name with. And she thinks of how she has already cast him as a memory. Something to look back upon with a curious bitter-sweet sense of loss. This happened to me, once...

A bar of sunlight falls across her lap. In the July noon, the rains pause and the sun sucks in all the mustiness. Tranquillity surrounds her.

She feels a great yearning to lean back against a shoulder and feel comforted. It is Shyam she thinks of now. She closes her eyes and smells the freshly showered, squeaky clean Pears fragrance that Shyam emanates.

It is fear that makes me seek him, not regard for him. What am I going to do? I have forgotten what it is to step out and fight the world. I have forgotten all the skills needed for survival. How do I cope?

I cannot continue to play wife merely because it frees me of worries. I have not done right by Shyam. I have played wife all this while, despising him. For this I know remorse. I went to him broken, and expected him to heal me. When he couldn't, I began to despise him and I knew sorrow.

The hurt she has caused him eats into her. And she wonders, does God punish us for our sins or does he leave it to us to punish ourselves?

The house is quiet. So is her heart.

The child in Radha grows. A child who fills every step and hour of hers with wonder. She loves it already, and it is this love she wears as a talisman.

She leans back in the rocking chair. She has time enough to think of what she wants to do with her life. She has time to count her joys and blessings. She has time.

She rests her hands in her lap. And she rocks herself ever so gently.

The Kathakali Lexicon

Sringaaram	Love
Haasyam	Contempt
Karunam	Sorrow
Raudram	Fury
Veeram	Valour
Bhayaanakam	Fear
Beebhalsam	Disgust
Adbhutam	Wonder
Shaantam	Detachment
Abharam	Mica dust
Alarcha	Roar
Attakalasham	A complex dance sequence in kathakali
Chundapoo	*Solanum pubesscuce*
Chutti	Built-up facial frame attached to the performer's face
Chuvanna thaadi	Red Beard; an indication that the character is evil
Kalari	Place of training; gymnasium
Kannu-saadhakam	Eye exercises
Katthi	Knife; an indication that the character is both arrogant and evil and yet has some redeeming qualities, usually a streak of nobility
Mallan	Wrestler
Mannola	Yellow pigment applied to the performer's face
Minukkuvesham	Radiant or shining; an indication that the character is gentle and has spiritual qualities. Included are female heroines, brahmins, sages, etc.
Noku	Piercing glance

Ooku	Vigour
Pachcha	Green; an indication that the character is a hero, refined and with high morals. Divine beings, kings and epic heroes wear this make-up.
Padingiya padam	Slow song
Pagarcha	Imposing stature
Pazhuppu	Ripeness or yellow; a special make-up used for specific divine characters
Pettikaaran	Greenroom assistant. Literal translation: box-carrier. The box refers to the costume and make-up box.
Sringaara padam	Love song
Tirasheela	Curtain
Vallan	Synonym for Bheema
Veshakaaran	Actor
Vesham	Role
Yuddha padam	Battle song

Bibliography

The Kathakali Complex, Philip Zarrilli; Abhinav Publications, New Delhi, 1984.

Cholliyattam, Volume 1 & 2, Kalamandalam Padmanabhan Nair; Kerala Kalamandalam, Vallathol Nagar, 2000.

Nalacharitam Attaprakaram, Kalamandalam Krishnan Nair; Kerala Sangeet Natak Akademi, Thrissur, 1984.

Keralatthile Pakshikal, Induchoodan; Kerala Sahitya Akademi, Thrissur, 1958.

A Classic Dictionary of Hindu Mythology and Religion, John Dowson; Rupa & Co, New Delhi, 1982.